THE CURSE OF THE JADE MIRROR

By the same author

The Jade Mirror Chronicles:
The Curse Of The Jade Mirror
Daughter Of The Mirror
The Wheel Of Glass

The Shadow Over Myeong-dong
Wither, Blister, Burn And Peel
The Black Path
The Pallification™ Parallax
Möbius Strip

The Book Of Neferusobek series:
Standing On The Edge Of Forever
God Killer
The World-Encircler

The House Of Altimsah series:
Altimsah
We Are All Stardust
Song Of The Universe

Project Shambhala series:
Divergence

MARTIN DENCH

THE CURSE OF THE JADE MIRROR

This is a work of fiction. Names, characters, businesses, places, events, locales, and incidents are either the products of the author's imagination or used in a fictitious manner. Any resemblance to actual persons, living or dead, or actual events is purely coincidental.

A CIP catalogue record for this title is available from the British Library.

ISBN (Hardback) 978-1-917972-60-4
ISBN (Paperback) 978-1-917972-61-1
ISBN (Ebook) 978-1-917972-62-8

www.martindench.com jademirrorchronicles.com

To Anran

感谢你一直以来都是我伟大的朋友、不断给予我灵感的源泉，以及一颗美丽的灵魂

"Speak of Cao Cao, and Cao Cao appears."
Traditional Chinese proverb

"I have a dream that one day brilliant sunlight will illuminate the dark forest."
Liu Cixin, *The Dark Forest*

Dramatis Personae

It should be noted that naming conventions in China dictate that family names come first. Thus, Xiang An-ren. However, when an English name is taken, naming follows western conventions, thus Victor Lam.

Iron Palm Zhang is sometimes referred to by his friends as "Old Zhang". This is a term of respect for an elder.

Xiang An-ren – [pronounced 'shyahng ahn-ruhn'] a model for *MeiXiu*.
William Reed/Zhu Wei – [pronounced 'jhoo way'] owner of The Golden Lantern, and general "fixer" for *MeiXiu*.
Lin Ye – [pronounced 'lin yeh'] the Mirror Courtesan; Grand Axis-Marshal of the Sepulchral Mandala; Blade of the Meridian Wheel; General of the Glass Phalanx.
Luo Ban/Meng Yao – [pronounced 'lwo bahn'/'mung yow'] Imperial Preceptor of the Sepulchral Mandala/Tomb Wheel Dynasty.
Zhang Qiang/Iron Palm – [pronounced 'jahng chy-ahng'] a retired policeman.
Fiona Murphy – a paranormal detective.

Xu Bo – [pronounced 'shyoo bwaw'] a *MeiXiu* employee.
Ying Yue – [pronounced 'eeng yweh'] a retired model, now working for Lin Ye.
Madame Jiang – [pronounced 'jya-hng'] owner of the Eternal Seal salon.
Victor Lam – [pronounced 'lahm'] a realtor and also a dealer in ancient relics.
Li Tong – [pronounced 'lee toong'] a smuggler of ancient relics.
Su Xiaoyu/Xiao Yu – [pronounced 'soo shyao-yoo'/'shyao yoo'] a model for *XiuShi.*
Qi Mei – [pronounced 'chee may'] a *MeiXiu* employee.
Wang Wei – [pronounced 'wahng way'] a patron of The Golden Lantern.
An Lian – [pronounced 'ahn lee-en'] the long dead wife of Luo Ban/Meng Yao.
Zhang Zhenwu – [pronounced 'jahng juhn-woo'] the long dead Daoist monk who fought against Luo Ban and Lin Ye.

CHAPTER ONE

Her phone pinged. She pulled it out of her bag, irritated. She knew exactly who had messaged her. She was only five minutes late, yet she was already being harassed about where she was. She was the star of the show, nothing could start without her, but she seriously wondered if any of them had given a single thought to how busy the traffic was in Shanghai at this time of night.

She swiped her finger across the screen and read the message. She'd been right. It was from Xu Bo.

"We're here! Where are you?"

She put the phone back in her bag. She'd be at the hotel in about two minutes, and then he'd be able to see for himself exactly where she was.

She peered out of the taxi's windows. The lights of the former French Concession were no longer visible in the distance, a clear indication that they were about to arrive.

The car turned a corner, and there it was, straight ahead of them. The Lumen House, Xuhui's premier boutique hotel. It was lit up like a Christmas tree, lights bleeding out into the surrounding night sky from every floor.

The cab pulled to a halt by the entrance, and she jumped out, grabbing her kitbag and pulling her coat tighter, keen to hold onto the warmth she'd acquired on the journey.

As the car drove off, she suddenly felt something. She couldn't say what it was, but it felt almost as if an icy hand had suddenly fastened itself around her heart.

She turned towards the hotel, saw two people coming towards her. The closest was a man in a very fancy uniform, a doorman, no doubt. His face wore a curious mixture of disapproval and desire. She was used to that.

The second person, running all the way from the entrance, was Mr Xu Bo himself, keen to get to her before the doorman could.

He ran past the uniform, almost brushing against him as he did so, and stumbled to a halt, directly in front of her.

'An-ren!' he screeched. 'Where have you been? Everyone's waiting!'

By everyone, she presumed he meant himself, the photographer and the stylist. Not exactly the Chinese State Opera.

'It's 7.37 pm,' she responded. 'I'm seven minutes late. This is Shanghai, or had you forgotten?'

'It doesn't matter,' he glared at her. 'Come on!'

He rushed back towards the hotel, trying to grab her elbow to hurry her up as he did so, but she guessed he would, and simply eased it out of his reach. She followed after him, at a comfortable pace, glancing impassively at the disappointed doorman on her way.

She knew the man now recognised her, and, therefore, knew why she was there. He might even have seen her there before, but she suspected it was more likely that he subscribed to *MeiXiu*. Either way, he no longer looked disapproving. He probably wanted to ask her for a selfie, something he could then send whirling around his limited circle of internet friends, and maybe impress his drinking buddies. Assuming he had any.

Maybe she'd indulge him later, after the shoot, if he was still around, when she would be dressed in the sort of outfit that she didn't mind having splashed across the world's social media.

Xu scurried through the large revolving door that formed the primary interface between the Lumen House and surrounding Xuhui. An-ren followed him at a discreet distance, not wanting to be seen to hurry, especially after a worm like him, but also not wanting to lose sight of him and be forced to phone him to find out the room number. He'd probably enjoy that, spiteful wretch that he was.

Xu was an exception, though. Most of the people she worked with, on the other side of the lens, weren't petty and backstabbing. There were always going to be people who were difficult to work with, but she viewed herself as lucky. *MeiXiu* was a relatively enlightened publication, unlike some of their competitors. Or so she'd heard. She'd worked solely for *MeiXiu* for the past five years, so she could only base her opinion on what others had told her.

Her only real anxiety at the moment was her lack of a manager. She'd recently been forced to part company with hers, due to some serious financial irregularities on his side of the relationship. As a result, she was feeling more than a little vulnerable. There were plenty of people eager to take his place, of course, but she was worried that whoever she chose might just turn out to be another apple that had fallen from the same tree.

The entrance foyer was so bright that she found herself blinking slightly, briefly blinded after the relative darkness of outside. She stopped for a moment, to orient herself, and glanced around, trying to see where Xu had gone.

He wasn't hard to spot. He was standing by a lift, gesturing wildly in her direction, looking even more irritated than he had before.

She didn't bother to acknowledge him, merely made her way to where he was holding the cabin doors open. As she cruised past him into the glass-lined interior, she stood as straight as she could, reaching all five feet seven inches of her flat-shoed height. She was taller than him, even without heels, and she knew how much he hated that. In a few minutes she'd be towering over him. She found that thought highly satisfying.

Xu hurried into the lift after her and stabbed the button for the tenth floor.

'We are going up. Our destination is the tenth floor,' the lift calmly, but forcefully, declared, as the doors shut.

An-ren noticed an almost indiscernible vibration in the floor, before the numbers on the control panel next to Xu started to move rapidly upwards. The lift was smooth and fast, and it reached the tenth floor in a matter of seconds.

'This is the tenth floor!' the same female voice vigorously announced, as the cabin doors opened.

Xu stomped out, not even having the good grace to let An-ren go first. He did, at least, know where they were going, she thought, so his rudeness was, at least in some small way, practical.

He pulled out a key card and swiped it on the handle of room 1024, pushing the door open and scurrying inside. She had to hurry to stop it from slamming and locking her outside. She knew that was probably what he'd wanted to do, and she didn't want to give him the satisfaction of having to bang on the door and ask to be let in.

She was, once again, blinded as she let the door swing shut behind her. The room was bathed in the brightest light imaginable, all coming from the vast array of bulbs that had already been set up at key points around the suite.

'She's here!' she heard Xu report in his whining voice.

As her eyes adjusted to the light levels, she studied the two other people in the large room. The first she knew very well. Qi Mei, the stylist. She didn't recognise the other person, though. She was quite certain she'd never met him before. She'd done many photo shoots over the past seven years, and had met many people only once or twice, but she tended to remember the sometimes provocative faces of the ones who poked cameras at every possible part of her body.

'Who's he?' she demanded, turning to Mei, preferring not to address herself to the petulant Xu.

'The photographer.'

'Wasn't Chen Rui booked for tonight?'

'He was,' Xu interrupted, 'but he had a bit of an existential crisis. He's had to babysit.'

'I'm Liu Haoran,' the photographer introduced himself, bowing self-consciously and clumsily arching his hands together in greeting.

'Have you done any photo shoots before?' she asked him, his nervous manner fuelling her scepticism.

'Plenty,' he nodded, avoiding her eyes.

'Any for *MeiXiu*? Or any of the others?'

He was silent for a moment, glancing at Xu, before replying.

'No,' he admitted.

She rolled her eyes dramatically, and scowled. Why did it have to fall to her to initiate a newbie into their world? It really annoyed her when this happened. These guys should learn and hone their skills with the junior models, not people like her.

'I've done lots of tourists and weddings. Photography's photography,' he smiled, weakly. 'A good photo's a good photo, regardless.'

'Is that so?' An-ren muttered, turning to Mei. 'What have you got?' she demanded, finally realising that the stylist's hands were full.

Mei handed her a large shopping bag and a pair of white high-heeled stilettos. An-ren took them without saying a word and crossed to the door that she already knew would lead to the bedroom.

Stepping inside, she slammed it shut behind her and put her bags down on the bedside table.

This was going to be painful, she knew it. In fact, she'd sensed it earlier in the day. A strange sense of doom had attached itself to her at some point in the morning, and had refused to relinquish its grip, no matter how hard she'd tried to shake it off. She'd spent some time focusing on skincare and false nail maintenance, as well as indulging in a *gua sha* massage with chilled jade. None of that had helped, though. She'd tried to read, but had found herself curiously distracted. In the end, she'd simply turned on the TV and lost herself in a bunch of mindless soaps, as well as drinking far too much cold jasmine tea.

She thought about her experience outside the hotel. It wasn't the first time she'd experienced something like that, but it hadn't happened for a while. She opened her kitbag, pulled out her makeup bag and retrieved her "wishing thread", a narrow six-inch-long ribbon faded to the colour of muted cinnabar, with a small shard of jade tied to one end.

Her *waipo*, her mother's mother, had given it to her when she'd been little more than a baby. She was long dead now, and this little piece of silk was the only tangible connection An-ren still had to her. She wasn't a particularly spiritual or religious person in any shape, manner or form, but, if nothing else, it was comforting, reminded her of the old that still sat, no matter how uncomfortably, amongst the new.

She tied it to the zip of her makeup bag and stroked it gently once, twice. Nothing happened, of course, although she was aware that the black cloud that had been following her so closely all day had now been replaced by a storm of annoyance. So, maybe the ribbon had worked, after all.

She turned her attention to the bag that Mei had given her, emptying out the contents onto the bed. A short-sleeved, short-bodied, pure white fur coat. A piece of pale pink lingerie, with a halterneck and some beading, and which, she could already tell, was unlikely to cover very much at all. And, as usual, a pair of sheer, body-hugging, flesh coloured *siwa*. What the Americans liked to call "pantyhose".

She'd developed a strong reputation as an "office style lover" over the past five years, focusing primarily on recognisably everyday outfits that were both sensual and sexually charged. However, every now and then, the marketing gurus of *MeiXiu* liked to treat their readership to something that was either radically leftfield or left almost nothing to the imagination. And often both at the same time. Tonight, clearly, was one of those shoots. Still, maybe it would be worth it just to see the expression on the face of the callow photographer when she left the bedroom.

Resigning herself to the inevitable, she emptied her kitbag onto the bed, taking the clothes and shoes she'd brought for later, and stowing them in the wardrobe. She then got undressed, carefully folded everything up, and secreted them in the now empty kitbag.

She pulled the *siwa* on first, sitting down to work her feet and toes into them, before standing up to pull them all the way up to her waist and smooth them out. It wouldn't do to have any wrinkles, at least not until she was taking them of.

She stepped into the lingerie, and pulled it most of the way up her body, but stopped before her breasts were covered. Reaching into her makeup bag, she pulled out a pack of silicone nipple covers and dark fabric pasties, opened them, and put them in place, before continuing to pull up and fasten the halterneck.

She crossed to the full-length mirror and studied herself from every possible angle. The guidelines were clear. Nipples were not to be seen. Of course, the combination of silicone and fabric was slightly darker than her flesh, providing a tantalising suggestion of what was being concealed, but that was all part of the game. Treat them mean, keep them keen, as the Americans liked to say.

She put on the small jacket, which, she had to admit, was actually very chic. She let it slope down over her shoulders, studying the fine marble contours of her upper body from the same angles as before. It looked good. She looked good. That was all that mattered.

She moved her head to one side, watching as her long, straight black hair cascaded in waves around her back and shoulders. She quickly ran a brush through it again, finally satisfied that it looked as soft and silky as it actually was.

Reaching into her makeup bag again, she pulled out her perfume. She was never really sure why she used perfume on photo shoots, but some habits died hard. And, of course, the better she felt about herself, the better her performance.

She'd used Ye Xiang by Luyan Atelier for as long as she could remember now. Her good friend Xinyi had introduced her to its subtle tones of honeyed osmanthus wrapped up in gentle smoke, and she'd fallen in love with it, had used nothing else ever since.

She sprayed a little on, enjoyed the sharp hit that always came with the first application, and then put the expensive looking bottle back in her bag.

She pulled on the white high heels, instantly enjoying her elevation to somewhere just short of six feet, and crossed to the door.

'Mei!' she called out, before making her way back to the dressing table.

The door opened behind her and she heard the scurrying feet of the stylist running to finish preparations.

'Wow!' the woman exclaimed, studying An-ren as she threw her back of tricks down onto the bed. 'You look amazing!'

'Do I?' An-ren asked, disinterested.

She hated being poked around by others, wished that *MeiXiu* would let her do her own hair and makeup. After all, who knew it better than her? No one did it for her when she wasn't on a shoot, and absolutely no one other than her was responsible for the heads that turned, as if on cue, everywhere she went. But, rules, it seemed, were rules.

Mei then began to fuss over her, reinventing the wheel, it seemed, working hard to create perfection out of something that had already been close to perfect before she even got near it.

As Mei fumbled around, searching for something, An-ren handed her a lipstick.

'You're still using this?' Mei asked, studying it as if she'd never seen it before.

'It suits me,' An-ren told her.

Both women knew, of course that Siyan Atelier's Ember Brick was also a stylistic complement for her perfume, providing a faint whisper of osmanthus to match its warm brick-red satin finish.

'You might as well put it on, then,' Mei shrugged, handing it back.

The stylist gathered her gear up from the dressing table, and hurried back out of the room.

An-ren applied the lipstick, then gently pressed a tissue to her lips, removing just enough to make sure her mouth looked perfect. She stood up, studying herself once again from all possible angles, before reluctantly striding less then purposefully across the room and out into the main space.

The silence that greeted her arrival made it all worthwhile, though. Xu and Liu looked stunned, especially the latter, who clearly hadn't been properly prepared for the transformation that had been taking place while he'd been checking light meters and SD cards. Just to turn the screw a little tighter, she paused as she entered, lifting her left leg slightly, bending it at the knee, and pretending to do something with her shoe.

She nonchalantly studied the two men's faces as she briefly hovered on one leg, her left arm arched back towards her raised ankle. She was pleased with what she saw. She knew the science behind this small but powerful gesture very well. On a physical level, it flexed her calf muscle, subtly highlighting the tone and contour of her leg, while, at the same time, lengthening the line, creating a graceful S-curve. More significantly, though, she was very well aware that this subtly small act identified her as both empowered and vulnerable, a contradictory tension that many men found irresistible. It was also a little flirtatious, but entirely on her terms.

'I'm ready,' she declared, to no one in particular, as she returned her foot to the carpet.

She was greeted with yet more silence. She looked at the three of them in turn. Mei was now looking a little disdainful, no doubt unimpressed by An-ren's small display of control. Xu was still running his eyes all over her barely clad body, while Liu was looking like the proverbial rabbit in the headlights.

'Where shall we start?' An-ren asked, looking directly at him.

'Um? Fuck!' was all he could manage to bluster.

She sighed and glared at Xu. She blamed him specifically for this mess, although she realised he had no real responsibility for anything beyond his own uptight and very unpleasant anxiety.

She crossed to the photographer and bowed respectfully in front of him, drawing the fur jacket across her cleavage as she did so.

'Mr Liu. Haoran. I know this seems very intimidating, but it really isn't. I'm the same woman you saw walk in wearing leggings and a t-shirt. Just think of this as another one of your tourist photo shoots and let's get it done.'

She studied the look in his eyes, recognised a little bit of it from her very first photo shoot, which had taken place in a far less salubrious establishment than The Lumen House. So much so, that there had been two photo shoots going on at the same time, and the other one had involved two people having sex. Now, that had been a learning curve.

However, she'd been photographed enough in the intervening years to know exactly what was required. In fact, if the owners of *MeiXiu* gave her a selfie stick and a tripod, she could probably do a reasonable job all by herself.

She turned to Xu.

'Go and get us some coffees. You can pay. You owe us all, anyway.'

'What the fuck do I owe you for? You're the one who was late?'

'But you're you. Isn't that enough?' She gave him her best saccharine smile. 'Go on, do something useful.'

He scowled at her, but moved towards the door. However, halfway there, he stopped.

'I almost forgot,' he said. 'I brought a little prop for you.'

He pulled an ancient looking wooden hand-held mirror out of his jacket pocket and offered it to her.

She took it, reluctantly, and studied it, turning it around and around in her hands. She noticed something embedded in the edge, next to the mirror itself, something light green. But it was wedged in too deeply, and there was no chance of her getting it out even with her ultra-long nails.

'What am I supposed to do with this?' she asked.

'Just use it in some of the shots,' Xu said. 'It'll add some class.'

She was tempted to hit him around the head with it, but, instead, she put it down on the coffee table next to her.

'Go and get some drinks!' she ordered.

As Xu scurried off, and Mei became lost in social media on her phone, An-ren began to lead Liu through the intricacies of a *MeiXiu* photoshoot.

It was almost like role reversal. Rather than him telling her where to stand, which light to look towards, which button or strap to undo first, which order to slip her legs out of the pantyhose, she was the one telling him where to stand, what angles and lighting to make best use of.

He was a quick learner, though. Not, she thought, that he even needed to learn. What he needed was to get used to having a very beautiful and sexy woman slowly undressing in front of him in the impersonal setting of a rented hotel room in downtown Shanghai.

He was actually considerate and thoughtful, apologetic and embarrassed, as more and more of her body became exposed. She knew she was highly skilled, had all the ability of an artist. She could easily blend smoulderingly disdainful expressions with slow reveals of very desirable and delicately contoured flesh, while, in fact, revealing nothing that would seriously compromise anyone.

As she worked the room, and Liu, Xu returned with the coffees. And even he was soon entranced, drawn in by the show she was putting on for all their benefit. By the time her lingerie, *siwa* and shoes were all off, and her modesty covered only by the carefully draped jacket, all three were avidly watching, their phones and other distractions put to one side.

An-ren smiled to herself. She felt a warm glow of triumph. She, and only she, had snatched victory from the jaws of defeat. And she knew, as only she could, that her devoted coterie of fans, both locally, and internationally, were going to love this photoset.

In fact, she felt so positive and so in control, that, when she noticed the mirror Xu had handed her lying on the coffee table, she picked it up and began to work it into the last few shots. That was a challenge in itself, holding the mirror in one hand, while still carefully shielding her nipples and the small mound of hair between her legs from the intrusive lens. But, she was a consummate professional, no challenge too great, especially when she was in the zone.

She moved the mirror to her right hand, raised it up next to her face, and turned her most sultry glare on Liu's lens. As she did so, a blood-curdling scream crashed through the air, destroying the appreciative and admiring silence.

CHAPTER TWO

All eyes turned to Mei, who looked as if she'd just seen a ghost, and was backing away towards the bedroom.

An-ren pulled the jacket around herself as best she could, glancing at Liu to make sure he'd stopped snapping, before crossing to the stylist.

'What's wrong?' she demanded, perplexed and confused.

She'd witnessed many strange and bizarre things over the course of her seven years of photoshoots, but had never experienced someone screaming.

'Keep that thing away from me!' Mei cried out, her eyes locked onto the mirror.

An-ren glanced at it, even more bemused.

'The mirror? What about it?'

'Didn't you see it?' Mei almost shrieked. 'Didn't any of you see it?'

Xu and Liu exchanged puzzled glances and shrugged their shoulders in answer.

'What did you see?' An-ren asked, putting the mirror down on the arm of a settee.

She suddenly felt a little self-conscious, having found herself trying to comfort a hysterical woman while naked, with two typically detached and disinterested men lurking in the background, probably doing little more than ogling her body. She draped the fur jacket over her shoulders, and pulled it down as far as she could without exposing her nipples. She hoped that it covered at least some of her bottom.

'It was a ghost!' Mei wailed.

'A ghost?' Xu laughed. 'You're fucking crazy, Mei!'

'How do you know it was a ghost?' An-ren asked, glaring balefully at Xu. 'Are you sure it wasn't just a trick of the light?'

'I've done this job long enough to know what a trick of the light looks like! It was there, behind you!'

'Behind me? Was it a figure? A man, a woman?'

'It was like a double exposure, a sort of secondary reflection that seemed to blink against the frame!'

'Did you see it?' An-ren asked Liu.

'All I could see was you,' he responded, looking sheepish.

An-ren picked up the mirror and studied it closely. Apart from the small shard that was wedged into it, the thing appeared completely unremarkable, in every way. In fact, it was so unremarkable that she couldn't help but wonder why Xu had picked it out. She always looked glamorous and sexy, so surely he could have found a more suitable object for her to pose with.

'There's nothing there now,' she said. 'Do you want a look?'

'Keep it away from me!' Mei whimpered, as An-ren held it out to her. 'I'm going to call *MeiXiu*!'

Knock yourself out, An-ren thought. As if they'd care. Their only interest would be in the successful completion of the shoot. And, as far as she was concerned, that was already history.

'Do what you think's best,' she said, 'I'm going to get showered and dressed.'

She walked past where Mei had already pulled out her phone and was frantically dialling, and into the bedroom, shutting and locking the door behind her. She threw the fur jacket onto the bed and entered the en-suite bathroom.

She showered quickly, years of practice having created a thorough and effective rapid cleansing programme. As she exited, towelling herself down, she felt reasonably refreshed, please to have wiped the stylist's unsubtle makeup off her face.

Once dry, she opened the wardrobe and pulled out her clothes. Black lingerie. A short thigh-length strapless and sleeveless black dress, designed to show off the shapely smooth contours of her shoulders and much of her chest. A diaphanous black bolero jacket, with a ring of fur around the cuffs. A thin silver necklace, and a pair of six-inch platform heels with peep toes and ankle straps.

Her experience was that, while no one may have been prepared for her arrival at The Lumen House, word would have already spread, and, by the time she left, there would be some admirers loitering outside, all desperate for some sort of acknowledgement of their existence. It was important to give them something to remember her by. She certainly didn't want photos of her in her baggy coat, trainers and leggings doing the rounds overnight.

She quickly got dressed, taking care of her hair, perfume, makeup and lipstick, before strapping herself into her shoes. She was going to dwarf the two men, and Mei, even more than she had before. She knew that a lot of men found tall women intimidating, which made the whole exercise highly worthwhile.

Getting to her feet, she knew that she now measured around six feet and one inch tall. There was a time in her life, a decade or so ago, when she'd been very conscious of her height, had worked hard to make herself seem smaller than her five-seven. But, her experiences with *MeiXiu* had changed that, had, effectively, empowered her. Although the majority of Chinese women, like men, weren't tall, height was considered sexy and desirable. As a result, tall models were highly popular and sought after. She certainly wasn't the tallest, but her belief in herself had been dramatically affirmed by the public response to her arrival on the visual modelling scene. She had been widely feted, and, the powerful combination of an S shaped figure, taller than average height, and devastatingly aloof facial beauty, had ensured an almost meteoric rise to the highest levels of *MeiXiu* aristocracy, along with her fellow queens of the glamour photoshoots, Xīnyí and Zi Han.

Not for the first time that evening, she studied herself in the bedroom's full-length mirror. She felt far more pleased this time, though. Before, her outfit had been purely functional, chosen for her as a vehicle for her conceptual muse skills. But, now she was dressed in her own clothes, and that felt infinitely more satisfying.

She checked that she'd packed everything into her kitbag, and made her way back into the suite's main space, fervently hoping that the furore that had started earlier had now died down. It was, surely, just a storm in a teacup. How could there really have been any sort of double image in the mirror? That was insane.

As she stepped through the bedroom door, she was genuinely shocked to find that she wasn't the tallest person in the room anymore. Liu, Xu and Mei, all significantly shorter than her now, were all still there, but they'd been joined by someone else. A man who was, to her surprise, slightly taller than her.

Just as she had earlier, she paused on the threshold, lifting her left leg, ostensibly to do something to the ankle strap on her shoe, but mainly to give her an opportunity to take the scene in fully while appearing to be otherwise occupied.

The newcomer had his back to her, but she strongly suspected he wasn't Chinese. Apart from his six feet plus height, his hair was a rich brown colour. It might have been dyed, but his whole bearing seemed to indicate foreign origins.

'Who's he?' she whispered to Mei.

'Zhu Wei,' she answered. '*MeiXiu* sent him. He's one of their fixers.'

'That's Zhu Wei?' she responded, even more shocked.

She'd heard his name bandied about on various shoots and on social media, but had never had the opportunity to meet him. She realised that, in fact, his name was all she did know.

He whirled around at the sound of his name being uttered, and, despite her own bemusement, she was pleased to see the look that crossed his face when he saw her. If it wasn't quite worship or adulation, then it was something very close.

She'd been right. He was a westerner. White skinned. Pale, in fact. Far paler than she was, too. Shortish brown hair, clean shaven. Dressed in dark blue jeans, ankle boots and a heavy chore coat. Buttoned up.

He crossed to where An-ren was standing next to Mei, and bowed graciously.

'William Reed,' he said. 'And I'm going to guess that you're Xiang An-ren.'

She was impressed. His Mandarin appeared almost flawless, coloured with hints of a Shanghainese accent that would have flattered a native, and all framed in a deep and resonant tone.

'I am,' she said, returning his bow. 'But are you really Zhu Wei?'

'Two people in one!' he laughed. 'It's easier to be Zhu Wei in China than William Reed. It opens more doors.'

He stepped back slightly, never once taking his eyes off her. He'd seen her before, of course, although never in person. And there was absolutely no substitute for seeing someone like An-ren in the flesh.

There were women in this world, he thought, a very few, in fact, who were so intoxicating that it was possible to drown in their presence. Xīnyí was one, and, he now realised, An-ren was another.

He forced his eyes away, out of respect and good manners, if not from choice. Her body, he thought, curved like a calligrapher's brushstroke, soft at the top, cinched at the waist, and flowed into the fullness of her hips. She had an S-figure born, not of vanity, but of quiet power. At least, that was how it seemed to him.

She was easily the most beautiful woman he'd seen for a long time, and also the tallest. His eyes lingered on her shoes for a moment. Six inch platform heels. She was bold, too. And only an inch or so shorter than him with them on.

'Mei was telling me about the mirror,' Reed said. 'There was some sort of double image.'

'No one else saw it,' Xu interjected.

'It was there!' Mei insisted, and her tone made it clear that she hadn't retreated too far from her encounter with hysteria.

'Is this the offending object?' Reed asked, picking up the mirror from where An-ren had discarded it earlier.

'Yes!' Mei said. 'Keep it away from me!'

Xu crossed to Reed's side and grabbed the mirror.

'I'll take it,' he said. 'It's just a useless prop.'

Reed, however, didn't let go.

'I know a little about mirrors,' he smiled. 'I'll check it out.'

'There's nothing to check out,' Xu argued. 'I'll stick it with our other props.'

'Mr Xu,' Reed smiled. 'Your boss personally asked me to investigate this matter. Surely the mirror belongs to him? I'll return it to you when I've studied it.'

Xu glared at Reed for a long moment, before finally letting go and walking sulkily back to where Liu was standing.

'Thank you,' Reed smiled. 'I know we're all a little on edge, but we just need to stay calm. I'm sure there's a perfectly reasonable explanation.'

'There is. It's haunted!' Mei exclaimed.

Reed turned the mirror over in his hands, pausing as he noticed the small shard embedded in it.

'I noticed that when I first picked it up,' An-ren volunteered. 'I couldn't get it out, though.'

Reed glanced at her long and ornate fingernails, and nodded his head in understanding. He seriously wondered how she'd even managed to get dressed with nails like that. Although, she struck him as the sort of woman who would probably find a way to be able to do most things. Or, at least, would be able to find someone who'd do it for her.

He held the mirror up to the light, moving it around slightly to get a better look at the shard.

'It looks like jade. There's some sort of mark on it, maybe a brand, or something. I'll be able to get it out back at the bar,' he said, although it seemed he was talking more for his own benefit, rather than for anyone else's.

'Can we go?' Xu demanded.

'Yes, of course you can,' Reed nodded, putting the mirror into a jacket pocket.

Liu grabbed his cases and opened them one by one, beginning the task of dismantling his lights and stowing all his equipment. Mei picked up her valise and almost ran to the door, disappearing without even saying goodbye.

An-ren reached into her bag and pulled out her phone.

'Do you need a lift somewhere?' Reed asked, just as she was about to book a taxi.

'A lift? With you?'

'I'm not offering to find someone to drive you. I'll be going soon and I thought I could save you the cost of a cab.'

'I don't want you to have to go out of your way,' An-ren demurred, although her fingers remained still.

'If you live in Beijing, it's out of my way. Anywhere in Shanghai is good.'

'I live in Shanghai.'

'Then it's no trouble. Where in Shanghai?'

'You don't need to. Not on my account.'

'Miss An-ren!' he laughed. 'Do you want a lift or not?'

'Just An-ren will do,' she said, scowling slightly at his mocking tone, but graciously offering him a small shred of informality. 'Thank you,' she finally agreed, against her better judgement. 'What sort of car have you got?'

'Does that make a difference?' he asked.

'It might. I don't want to be seen getting into something small and tacky.'

He laughed.

'It's definitely not small and tacky!'

CHAPTER THREE

As they exited Room 1024, Reed reached out and took her kitbag from her.

'I can carry that,' she complained, reaching out to take it back.

'I'm sure you can,' he replied. 'But if we walk out of this hotel with me at your side and you carrying that bag, then people are only going to draw one conclusion.'

She pursed her lips, but said nothing. He was, of course, right. Better for him to be seen as her driver than her boyfriend. And Xiang An-ren being so brazenly out and about with a boyfriend, and a western one at that, would not be good business.

'I should get a taxi,' she concluded, as they entered the lift cabin.

'Just think of me as an unpaid taxi driver,' he said, pressing the button for the ground floor.

As the lift sped downwards, he tried hard not to stare at her, although, given the fact that the cabin was lined with mirrors, that was no easy task. He moved his eyes onto her kitbag, and noticed a little ribbon poking out, a shard of green tied to it.

'What's this?' he asked, holding the bag up to get a better look.

'It's nothing,' she said, moving quickly to poke the ribbon back into the bag and fully fasten the zip.

'It looked like a piece of jade,' Reed said, frowning slightly.

'It is jade,' An-ren agreed, 'but it also isn't important.'

'It is a coincidence, though.'

'A coincidence?' she asked, confused. 'In what way?'

Before he could answer, the lift doors opened, and she instantly marched out, striding purposefully towards the revolving door on the far side of the entrance foyer. She braced herself. It had been cold when she'd arrived, and she'd had her coat on then. There wasn't much protecting her from the elements now.

As he watched her walking ahead of him, it occurred to him that although her body was delicate, with her soft curves wrapped in skin that resembled gossamer silk, there was no denying the fire that lay beneath.

He hurried after her.

'It's going to be cold outside,' he said. 'Do you want to borrow my jacket?'

She stopped and turned to face him, looking almost scandalised.

'Are you referring to that jacket?' she demanded. 'The one you're wearing?'

'Of course.'

'Why would I dress like this and then hide it all underneath that drab, humdrum thing?'

'Because it's cold outside.'

'I appreciate your kind and thoughtful offer, but no thank you,' she declared, turning her back on him and marching out into the night air.

He laughed a little as he followed her outside. She really was quite arrogant, but also very self-aware and clearly an expert in self-marketing. He understood exactly why she was dressed the way she was. It was what most of the models did after a shoot. He would have been a little shocked, not to mention disappointed, if she'd actually accepted his offer.

As An-ren had anticipated, a small crowd of about a dozen people had gathered outside The Lumen House, and it wasn't too hard to guess who had started the ball rolling. Standing at the front of the hotel, marshalling the exclusive gathering, was the same doorman who she'd spurned on her way in.

'An-ren!' the group called out.

She feigned surprise, turning in their direction and walking towards them. Reed watched as she milked the moment for all it was worth, which wasn't really very much, he thought. He didn't blame her, though. Being a *MeiXiu* model was a reasonably unique occupation. Neither mainstream nor underground, trapped in an almost spectral middle ground.

Selfies were shared, although An-ren had to bend down for most of them. What impressed Reed was that although An-ren gave them what they wanted, she never once smiled. She maintained her sultry aloofness even in the selfies.

He did notice one or two fingers pointed in his direction, but could see the ease with which An-ren instantly shut down any suggestion that he might possibly be anything more significant than a baggage handler and driver.

Eventually, the small group finished bowing and offering their undying love, and slowly moved away.

'You're a real professional,' Reed told her, as she finally arrived back at his side. 'You gave them what they wanted without having to give them anything much at all.'

'Where's your car?' she demanded, ignoring what she thought may have been more mockery.

'It's just over here,' he said, walking towards a Candyapple Red 69 Mustang.

He popped the trunk and carefully put her kitbag inside, before walking around to the passenger side to open the door for her.

'Be careful,' he warned her. 'It's a long way down.'

'This is your car?' she demanded, simply staring at it, and him, in turn.

He studied her expression carefully, trying to work out whether she was disappointed, impressed, or simply bemused.

'It's very dramatic,' she finally said, lowering herself in.

'I'd never thought of it like that,' he said, shutting her door and making his way round to the driver's side.

'Did you bring this with you?' she asked, as he gunned the engine into life.

The car roared as he pumped the throttle, something she hadn't quite expected. She'd never been in a car like this before, had never heard an engine growl like that. She was shocked at just how loud it was.

'What do you mean?' he responded, strapping himself in.

'When you arrived in China.'

'No, I had it imported from Japan a couple of years ago. It's an automatic. I love that.'

He put the Mustang into drive, and they roared their way out of the hotel's car park, inevitably drawing every watching eye.

'Where are we going?' he asked, as the car joined the main road.

'French Concession. Wukang Road,' she muttered, avoiding his eyes as she spoke.

He glanced at her, his eyes widening in mild surprise. He said nothing, but he was impressed. Wukang Road was known for its lines of sycamores, European-style villas and historic architecture. It was also quiet, atmospheric and steeped in the kind of faded glamour that seemed so popular in the modern world.

As he drove, he was very conscious of her presence so close to him. Her dress was tight, and had risen up as she sat down, her black-clad and very shapely thighs seeming to torment him simply by their very proximity. Her perfume was also powerful. He was no expert, but he could pick out bergamot lying underneath the osmanthus. It was, he thought, rather like her. Highly intoxicating.

He knew he was beginning to feel a little awestruck by the woman sitting next to him, so he did the only thing he could. He turned on his iPod Classic, which was already plugged into the car's Aux socket.

Career of Evil by Blue Öyster Cult instantly blared out, filling the car with a 70's hard rock guitar groove that instantly made him feel more relaxed.

However, after no more than ten seconds of the song, he realised she was staring at him, her face both uncomprehending and pained.

'What is this?' she demanded, making no attempt to hide her distaste.

'It's great driving music!' he laughed. 'Blue Öyster Cult.'

'What is a Blue Öyster Cult?'

'Not what, but who. A 70's American rock band.'

'It's horrible,' she declared. 'Can we listen to something else please?'

'It is my car,' he observed.

'And I am your guest,' she noted.

'Okay,' he sighed, flicking through playlists until finding what he wanted.

Crop Circle by Monster Magnet instantly burst out of the Mustang's speakers.

She turned to glare at him.

'This is horrible, too!' she declared.

'It's art,' he muttered, in English.

'It's something, but it certainly isn't art,' she responded.

'I didn't know you could speak English,' he said, although, when he thought about it, he wasn't at all sure why he should feel surprised.

An-ren struck him as the sort of person who had a whole raft of hidden skills that she would call on only at such time as she absolutely needed to. And, of course, even more significantly, many of her fans and admirers came from countries who didn't speak Chinese.

'There are a great many things you don't know about me,' she told him, reaching into her bag and pulling out her phone.

'Okay,' he said, his pride now dented. 'We could listen to G.E.M., or Sa Dingding, if you prefer?'

She muttered something about unreconstructed dinosaurs and, at the same time, pulled the lead out of the iPod and jammed it into the headphone socket of her phone.

'Hey!' Reed exclaimed. 'This is my car, you know.'

'This is art,' she said.

As she turned to face him, a look that he couldn't quite read briefly crossed her face, just as a thin, high voice emerged from the sound system. A voice that instantly sent a cold chill racing down his spine.

It was, without any doubt, the most disturbing thing he'd ever heard. Even more disturbing than listening to Einsturzende Neubaten making music with power tools.

It was some sort of opera, sung in Chinese, but the voice was shrill and far too high pitched, almost as if it was meant to be a parody of a female voice.

'Please!' he begged. 'Play whatever you want, but turn that off!'

She simply sat staring at him, her face impassive and as cold as the chill that had disappeared down his spine. And then she burst into laughter, and the terrible, fiendish noise suddenly stopped.

'Your face!' she continued to laugh.

He wasn't impressed, but he did like the relaxed smile that had spread across her face. Yes, it was essentially an expression of cruelty and inhuman torture, but it was nice to see something other than carefully crafted aloofness and impassivity. She was even more beautiful when she smiled. Maybe it was worth being mocked just for that moment.

'That was real art,' she said.

'Real art,' he echoed. 'I think I'll stick to the unreal, then.'

'Haven't you ever heard that before?'

'I can assure you I would have remembered hearing something like that. I'll probably need some sort of therapy now.'

'It's traditional Chinese opera, William. How can you have lived here and not heard it?'

'Maybe all the people I've met aren't as cruel as you.'

'It's the *Qing Ye Lament* from Zhang Licheng's classic *Silk Night* opera. Do you really not know about *Nandan*?'

'I've obviously been spared that joy.'

'I won't bore you with the details, but, until relatively recently, women weren't allowed to perform on stage in any capacity, so men played and sang their parts in plays and operas.'

'So that was a man pretending to be a woman.'

'Essentially. This version was sung by Man Ye. He's an expert in sounding thin at the top of phrases, getting those jarring and uncanny effects that you obviously enjoyed so much.'

Jarring and uncanny, Reed thought. That summed it up perfectly. He hoped that he'd never have the misfortune to hear another *Nandan* as long as he lived.

'And this is what you listen to when you're sitting by yourself in Wukang Road sipping a cup of tea?'

'Of course not,' she replied, turning back to face the road ahead. 'I can't stand it.'

He glared at her, although what he really wanted to do was to laugh. But he wasn't about to give her that pleasure.

There was no question that not only was An-ren overpoweringly beautiful, but she was also quite overwhelming in other ways, too.

'Play whatever you want,' he said. 'I'm sorry that I put on something you didn't like. That was very insensitive.'

'As you so rightly said, William, it's your car. I was just teasing you.'

'You got me good,' he nodded, keeping his eyes on the road, desperately trying to avoid glancing at her very distracting black-clad thighs.

'So how long have you lived here?' she asked him.

He was impressed. She was finally showing some interest in him. Possibly, though, she simply felt guilty for winding him up and subjecting him to the torture of Chinese opera, and was trying to make up for it. However, she didn't strike him as the sort of person who would ever feel much guilt over anything. It occurred to him that maybe she was simply being polite. Maybe, he thought, she was simply making polite conversation.

'In Shanghai? Or China?'

'Both.'

'I've been in China for six years, Shanghai for five.'

'What brought you here? It's an exotic destination for a westerner.'

'Is it? There seem to be more and more of my fellow countrymen living here.'

'And which country's that? I'm sorry, I'm useless with accents.'

'England.'

'Oh, you're English? Now that's exotic.'

He laughed, unable to stop himself.

'An-ren, there's nothing even vaguely exotic about England, or any part of the United Kingdom!'

'Really?'

'Really. How about you? How long have you lived in Shanghai?'

'How do you know I'm not a native?'

'You've got a hint of something else in your accent. You've been here a while, I reckon. But, it's in there.'

'You're quite the detective, aren't you? I was born in Chongqing, moved here when I was five.'

Reed nodded, but wasn't quite sure how to follow that up. He didn't want the conversation to die, especially since they were now almost at her home, but he also didn't want to sound like he was talking for the sake of it. If he'd learned one thing about An-ren tonight, it was that she didn't suffer fools gladly.

'I heard that Zhu Wei had a bar in the Bund. Is that right?' she asked, much to his relief.

'Yeah. The Golden Lantern. I sunk my savings into it, and now it's my golden nest egg. You should come along some time. I get some proper singers in from time to time.'

'Proper like Blue Öyster Cult?'

'No. Proper like jazz and blues.'

'Why do you call yourself Zhu Wei?'

'It's like I said earlier. Having a Chinese name often makes my life easier. Certainly, when I first bought the bar it helped.'

'I know why you took a Chinese name,' she said, dismissively. 'I just wondered why you chose that one?'

'It's just a name.'

'Is it? "Red Power".'

'I tend to think of it more as "Heroic Vermilion".'

She shook her head slightly, although he wasn't sure if she was amused, irritated or simply disapproving.

'We're here,' he told her, slowing down as they entered a very wide tree-lined avenue. He pulled into the kerb and put the car into park.

He suddenly felt a little anxious. Although she'd been a complete stranger to him less than two hours earlier, he felt despair at the thought of her just walking out of his life. And it wasn't just because she possessed goddess-level beauty. There was something about her that had grabbed him by the throat and was refusing to let go. It was quite apparent that she was obstinate, stubborn and very strong-willed, but it was also very clear that she had many other interesting and equally dynamic qualities hidden inside her.

He peered out of the window at the house she'd indicated was hers.

'No one waiting for you?' he asked, although he instantly cursed himself for saying it.

It was the worst sort of fishing, and she'd have to be some sort of idiot not to pick up on it. After all, she'd already made it abundantly clear that the only idiot in the car was him.

'I live alone,' she responded, opening the Mustang's passenger door and gracefully getting out and to her feet.

He threw open his door and jumped out. He ran around to the rear of the car and retrieved her kitbag from the trunk.

She threw him a look that clearly asked what he thought he was doing.

'It's dark and it's late,' he blustered. 'I'll walk you to your door.'

'This is Shanghai, William,' she reminded him, 'not the Bronx.'

'I'm just protecting one of the company's major assets,' he told her.

He was glad it was dark and that she couldn't see the nervous look in his eyes.

She simply sighed and marched up the driveway. He hurried after her, digging his phone out of his pocket as he did so.

'Goodnight, William,' she said, opening her front door. 'Thank you for the lift and the entertaining conversation.'

It was pathetic conversation, he thought, even more embarrassed by her gracious lie.

'Can I have your number?' he asked, realising that he was now sounding like a lovelorn teenager.

'Why?' she asked, staring straight at him, her gaze intense and unnerving.

Why, he thought? That was such a good question. Why did he want her number? As if she didn't know.

'The mirror!' he exclaimed. 'I need to check out that shard that's stuck in the mirror. I should let you know what I find out.'

'The mirror?' she responded, briefly seeming confused.

And then she obviously remembered.

'I don't care about that,' she said. 'Tell it to Mei. She's the one who was hysterical.'

'There's also that bit of jade you've got,' he persisted.

'That's nothing,' she insisted. 'Just a family heirloom. Not even much of an heirloom, either.'

'All the same, I'd still like to let you know. If you don't mind.'

She was silent for a moment, simply staring unwaveringly at him. For a horrible long moment, he thought she was simply going to turn, go inside and shut the door, without even a "no".

A look of resignation passed across her face, and she reached into her bag, pulling out her phone. She swiped it open, and moved across a few screens, before finding the one she wanted.

'Quick,' she said. 'Before I change my mind.'

He rapidly entered the number into his contacts, memorising it at the same time, just in case something terrible happened to his phone on the way home.

'Thank you,' he said. 'Is there anything else I can do?'

'No, thank you, you've done more than enough,' she retorted, bowing slightly and going into the dark interior of the house, shutting the door after her.

Reed stood staring at the door, hoping against hope that it might suddenly open again and that An-ren would invite him inside for a cup of tea, or coffee. He felt as if someone had just turned off a blindingly bright light.

Eventually, when it became painfully apparent that the door was staying shut, he pocketed his phone and turned back to the Mustang.

However, as he did so, he caught a hint of something on the breeze. Almost a whispering, or a sense of something that shouldn't really have been there. It definitely wasn't a voice, probably wasn't anything more than his tired mind playing tricks on him. And, yet, he thought he'd heard a single word, somehow not spoken, not even muttered or murmured. He would have disregarded it, would have instantly dismissed what was, essentially, an absurd sensation. But that one word was as jarring as the sound of that horrible singing voice earlier.

"An-ren!"

CHAPTER FOUR

Reed had driven back to the Golden Lantern trying to focus on the issue of the mirror, but had found it difficult to concentrate on such a mundane issue. An-ren's heady, sensual perfume still filled the car, and he struggled to think about anything other than her.

But his thoughts weren't purely focused on the obvious. He'd sensed something when she'd gone indoors, a presence that seemed both nameless and timeless. It meant nothing to him, but he felt it had been reaching out to her in some way. Could the same thing have happened with the mirror? He didn't see how that was even vaguely possible, and, if it hadn't been for what had happened on her doorstep, he wouldn't have even bothered to do any work on the mirror.

He'd met Qi Mei before, had already formed the opinion that she was, at best, flaky. He hadn't believed her at all, had merely turned up to keep everyone happy and to ensure that everything continued as it should, business as usual. As it was, An-ren had already drawn the shoot to a successful conclusion. So, everyone could go home happy. Even Mei.

He thought about the tiny shard of jade poking out of An-ren's bag. He was fairly certain that the object jammed into the hand-held mirror was also jade. Coincidence? Probably. Jade was everywhere in China. At least, it was if you knew where to look.

When he'd returned to the bar, he'd spent a little bit of time chatting with some of the regulars, before going upstairs to his apartment. Living over his place of work had its disadvantages, but there was no substitute for not having to commute to work.

He turned the living room lights on and pulled the mirror out of his pocket. He turned it over, once more, studying it from every possible angle. It really was as dull as ditch water, merely a plain wooden mirror. It wasn't even that old. Possibly ten, fifteen years, at the most. It was an odd choice as a prop for such a glamorous photoshoot.

He went into the kitchen and rummaged around in the drawers until he found what he wanted. Strong tweezers. Holding the mirror in his left hand, he took the tweezers in his right and fastened onto the object stuck into the frame. It was tightly wedged in, and didn't seem to have any interest in being retrieved.

Reed was a patient man. He'd made hundreds of plastic models as a boy. Ships, planes, tanks, just about everything he could get his hands on. As a result, he understood the need to be painstakingly thorough and, above all else, patient. So, he simply moved the tweezers slowly from side to side, working the object loose. He knew that the wood it was embedded in was reasonably soft and that whatever it was would eventually come out.

Finally, it came loose and he pulled it out. He put the mirror down and held it up to the light. He'd been right. It was jade. A jade shard. He couldn't help but wonder just what it had been doing there, jammed into that crappy old frame.

There was something carved into the shard. It was only a fragment, so whatever was there wasn't much of anything. But he felt certain it wasn't an imperfection or a chip. It looked like a part of some sort of maker's mark, or branding. Although it was incomplete, it seemed to resemble some sort of wheel. He also realised that it wasn't actually carved, but had been inlaid, and shimmered when held up to the light.

He put the shard down on the kitchen table, pulled out his phone, and took a close-up photo, ensuring that the remains of the marking were as clear as possible. He then sent it as an attachment, with a brief message, to one of his irregular patrons, a man called Wang Wei.

This was one of the many advantages of owning a bar. Almost everyone passed through at some point, and, if they were provided with good beer and a decent service, they all felt they owed you a favour. Or, put another way, they were more amenable to requests for assistance.

He waited for a few minutes, but there was no response. He wasn't worried. He knew Wang would come back to him with an answer. So, he put his shoes back on and returned downstairs. It was time to roll out the charm and make a few more friends, as well as to make the old ones feel like they were the most important people in his life.

By the time the bar closed, and the last patron had finally been cajoled into going home, he'd gone back upstairs and taken himself straight to bed. After so much casual and mostly inane chatter, and quite a few drinks, he'd forgotten all about the shard. It was only when he was drifting off that the memory of it came back to him. But, by that time, he was too cosy and comfortable to even consider moving again. It could wait. It wasn't as if there would have been a response so late at night, anyway.

He woke to something of a shitstorm. His phone, usually the recipient of few messages and even fewer calls, was almost throbbing with content. For a brief moment, he wondered whether World War Three might have started, but he soon realised that most of the notifications were from social media. Ignoring them for the time being, he opened the email that had arrived at 08.04 am, from Wang Wei.

The message he received was stilted, unlike Wang's usual friendly tone. It suggested that the shard wasn't just any shard, and the partial maker's mark that he'd photographed almost certainly originated with someone or something called Luo Ban. The only other bit of information appended was that it was almost certainly a modern replica.

Reed pondered the name Luo Ban. He knew that it meant compass in Mandarin. But he'd never heard of a person, or a company with the name. Still, he could research that.

He moved onto the social media messages. His jaw almost dropped when he saw the hundreds of notifications, all related to a single photo. It seemed that the very diligent Liu Haoran had very dutifully surrendered the SD card from last night to the management at *MeiXiu*. They were never going to miss out on an opportunity to get some publicity, and so they'd posted some of the images of An-ren holding the mirror up next to her face.

What had happened next had taken social media by storm. Someone, somewhere, had turned the images into a looping slideshow. In it, the unidentified reflection behind An-ren could clearly be seen to be moving independently of her. It was unbelievable, and quite possibly a fake, but when he looked through all of the ten originals it was obvious that something behind her was indeed moving, and it wasn't just a reflection

The clip had gone viral, literally. Reed had no doubt that the guys at *MeiXiu* would be rubbing their hands with glee, anticipating the best-selling edition of the publication yet. He wondered, though, if they'd given any thought to what it might actually mean.

It was, of course, possible that the whole thing was a fraud. But he doubted it. Mei had been truly shaken and upset, still scared of the mirror by the time he'd arrived. She might have imagined it, possibly, but it was too much of a coincidence, and he felt certain that neither Haoran nor *MeiXiu* had the imagination to create such a convincing fake.

Reed thought about it all, trying to decide what to do for the best. It might still mean nothing, but he'd started to develop a nagging feeling that there'd been some sort of sudden change in his life, a subtle shift that he didn't understand in any way. And he knew from bitter experience that things didn't ever fix themselves.

He was still disturbed by what he'd experienced on An-ren's doorstep. If that hadn't happened, then maybe he wouldn't have felt so concerned, could have laughed it all off. But, that name, whispered from God-knew-where, combined with the small jade shard that An-ren had quickly hidden away, made the decision for him.

He sent a quick message to Wang.

"We need to meet. Today if possible. Can I come to you?"

And then, his heart starting to beat faster, he opened his contacts, went to "A" and dialled.

CHAPTER FIVE

An-ren was woken by a noise from somewhere in the house. She wasn't usually a particularly light sleeper, but, for some reason, she'd still felt a little on edge when she'd returned home. Despite the distractions of William Reed and his 69 Mustang, she still hadn't been able to entirely dispel the sense of impending doom that had clouded her day.

She thought the noise had come from upstairs, on the second floor. There wasn't much up there, just two empty bedrooms and the unimaginatively named Mirror Room.

She listened hard, but the house was still and quiet. She desperately wanted to go back to sleep, to believe that it had simply been part of a dream. But she couldn't. She felt too uneasy.

So, very reluctantly, she pulled back the duvet and climbed out of bed, slipping her feet into her house slippers. Making sure all the buttons on her pyjamas were fastened, she made her way out of the bedroom and across the landing. She stopped at the foot of the stairs and listened.

The house was so quiet that she began to think that she'd imagined it, but it had sounded like the lightest sighing of a breeze, breathing a single word. An-ren.

That was crazy. Wasn't it? She wondered what that down to earth Englishman would have said if she'd told him she'd heard her name spoken so softly, so intangibly, in the dead of night. And it wasn't as if it had been the first time.

For the briefest moment, she thought about calling him, but she instantly parked that thought.

Firstly, he'd think she was completely mad, and she'd worked hard to project an entirely different image for his benefit. Secondly, he'd almost certainly be there before she'd even disconnected the call. Or maybe he wouldn't. Which would be even worse, in fact.

No, this was a ridiculous situation, her imagination running wild all because of that flaky stylist, Qi Mei. She had to face it alone. And, after all, what was it she was actually facing? An empty house and her overactive imagination.

She climbed the stairs, carefully, cautiously. She'd never noticed how much they creaked before. Every step seemed so loud in the still night air. If there really was anyone up there, they would clearly know by now that she was on her way.

She should have brought a weapon with her. Not that she had one. She'd never felt the need to have baseball bats, or even knives, hanging around in case of intruders. After all, as she'd noted earlier in the evening, this was Shanghai. This was China.

She reached the top of the stairs and paused. All was still and very quiet. Even the soft, sighing sound that she'd heard earlier had now gone.

She checked the empty bedrooms. They were just that. Empty. Almost empty, anyway. There was plenty of dust. She almost never visited this floor of the house, so, as a consequence, the rooms never got cleaned.

She opened the final door and went inside. Even in the dark the space was disorienting, surrounded, as she was, by full-length mirrors inset into the walls on all sides.

The house had come with the room like this. She'd asked what the purpose was, but there didn't seem to be an answer. She'd inherited the property when her *waipo* had passed away. Her own mother had been gone for many years by then, and her father was little more than a non-existent memory.

But, the property had been left to her, and she certainly wasn't going to look a gift horse in the mouth. She'd seen the look of surprise on Reed's face earlier, when she'd told him where she lived. He was right to wonder how a *MeiXiu* model could afford to live in Wukang Road in the French Concession, but at least he'd been sufficiently respectful and hadn't asked.

She looked around the room. Everything was just as it should be. She was relieved to find that she'd simply been dreaming, not that she'd ever believed otherwise, of course.

But then she heard something. The softest whispering, similar to the sound she'd heard downstairs, but now more insistent. One word, again.

'An-ren!'

She looked around, anxiety rapidly rising, trying to find the source of the sound. But there was no one there. She walked across the room, peering into the shadows, but they remained steadfastly empty.

She paused next to one of the larger sections of mirror, a long piece that covered an entire wall. Each mirror was framed in jade, and marked, for some reason she'd never understood, with a small and very stylised image of a wheel.

An icy blue hand suddenly sprang out from the glass and grabbed her around the wrist. She screamed in terror, and pulled hard against the grip, but it was too strong, and she found herself being dragged towards the mirror.

She screamed again as she was pulled closer, expecting to feel the impact of the hard, unforgiving surface, but was shocked to find that she simply passed through it, as if it were no more substantial than a light mist.

She was more than scared now, and her heart was beating so fast that she thought it was going to burst. She looked around fearfully. No one was holding her.

She was in a clearing, mountains on all sides, storm clouds overhead and lightning flashing in the distance. She looked for a way back to the Mirror Room, but all she could see was a long line of trees that flanked the nearby meadow.

'An-ren!'

She whirled around, gasping in horror and shock at the sight that met her eyes. She'd been completely alone, but now a figure stood in front of her. A figure that, in some ways, resembled a woman.

Her skin, smooth as polished glass and as fine as porcelain, was an impossibly luminous blue. Her eyes were a glassy cerulean, hollow with reflected memory, and as piercing as the most jagged shard of jade.

Long black hair cascaded down her back and over her shoulders, absorbing light rather than reflecting it, flowing with an unnatural grace, as if she were underwater.

She was dressed in a long and tight-fitting purple and red gown, a shallow circlet of radiating spires of glass and crystal jutting upwards, like frozen splinters, on her head. Shards of glass radiated outward from her dress, hovering and rotating in the air, catching and refracting the light that embraced her.

A chill raced down An-ren's spine; the air around her had turned thin and cold.

'Who are you?'

'Don't you know me?' the glass woman replied, disappointment in her voice. 'I walk in your shadow. When the wind stirs, I whisper your name. Haven't you heard me?'

'How did I get here? How do I get back to my house?'

The creature laughed, a cruel, mocking sound. 'An-ren, this is your house. The yin to your yang. It has always been here. My master and I have waited a very long time. And now the waiting is over.'

'Your master? Who is he?'

'He is your master, too. Or have you forgotten?'

'I don't know what you're talking about,' An-ren responded, confused. 'Please, just help me get home.'

The woman's expression twisted.

'Home. You really don't remember, do you? You betrayed me. And then you betrayed him. You led us both to damnation. Do you know what it is to have life but no hope? For eternity?'

'No,' An-ren whispered.

'Of course you don't. But you will.'

She stepped closer. An-ren backed away, terror prickling her skin. The creature radiated pure malice.

'Go back to your world,' the glass woman hissed. 'Enjoy what little time you have left.'

She raised her glassy hand. Crimson light erupted from her fingertip, slamming into An-ren's chest and swallowing her whole. Dizziness washed over her as she fell backwards into a dark, endless void.

She felt herself falling, surrounded by little more than a dull red glow that faded into the darkness surrounding her as she continued her descent. As the last of the creature's icy miasma faded away she realised she was lying on her back.

She sat bolt upright and opened her eyes. Her heart was beating frantically and she was in a cold sweat, her pyjamas clinging to her damp skin.

She looked around, feeling tears welling up as she recognised all the familiar things surrounding her.

She was in her bed.

CHAPTER SIX

The room was dimly lit, thick with the cloying sweetness of incense. Xu Bo shifted impatiently, glancing around. This place always unsettled him. The darkness, the strange replicas of ancient paintings. Xilin, Bone Silk Wyrms, creatures he couldn't name. All of it felt wrong.

Several portraits hung on the walls: a scarred, cruel-looking man in archaic clothing, and two of Lin Ye. One showed her as he knew her. Seductive, sensual, narcissistic. The other was stranger: Ye in an ancient military uniform, sword raised mid-battle, eyes blazing with cold fury.

But the most disturbing image was the full-length portrait of a blue-skinned creature shaped like Ye, carved from glass. Its pale, translucent eyes seemed to follow him wherever he moved.

'I've always thought that captured my natural charm,' a velvet voice murmured.

Xu spun around. Ye stood directly behind him. She hadn't been there moments ago, and her stiletto heels should have echoed across the hard floor.

'That's you?' he asked, glancing between her and the portrait.

'Is it not a good likeness?' she asked, striking a coquettish pose beside it.

Xu had no idea how to respond. Ye was the strangest person he'd ever met, and he rarely understood a word she said. Fortunately, she didn't waste many on him, and she paid exceptionally well. Far too well for the trivial errands she assigned him. But he wasn't about to complain. His *MeiXiu* salary barely covered his rent. Working for her meant he didn't need a second job.

'You work with all those self-obsessed models,' she pouted, 'and yet you can't recognise a goddess when she's standing right in front of you.'

He stayed silent. He never knew when she was joking. Her beauty was undeniable, but something about her felt wrong. Somehow inhuman. Her eyes were blue, which was strange enough. Models wore coloured lenses all the time, but underneath they were always brown. Ye's weren't.

'You really are a tedious man,' she sighed, stepping up close. 'Has anyone ever told you that?'

'What do you want me to do?' he asked, eager to finish and leave.

Her unpredictability unnerved him. Standing this close, he couldn't tell whether she might kiss him or hit him.

'Is that what we've come to?' she demanded. 'I click my fingers and you scurry in and out? Don't you want to talk? Buy me dinner? See where the night leads?'

She leaned in, her breath warm on his cheek. Her perfume was surprisingly subtle, sensual without being overpowering.

Seeing his confusion, she sighed and handed him a slip of paper and an envelope.

'When Xiang An-ren and Zhu Wei come to you, tell them exactly what I've written. Then give them the envelope. Nothing more. Understood?'

Xu glanced at the note. It made no sense, but she paid him well enough not to care.

'Do you understand?' she repeated, as if addressing a child.

'Yes, I understand,' he muttered.

'Good.'

She crossed the room again, stopping before the glass-skinned portrait.

'The money's already in your account.'

That was the only part he cared about. He turned toward the door, but her voice stopped him.

'Don't forget our little soirée tonight,' she said, eyes still on the portrait. 'I expect punctuality. And the outfit I specified.'

'Yes, Miss Lin.'

'Then go.'

CHAPTER SEVEN

She hadn't recognised the number when it had flashed up on the screen, but when she'd heard his voice, a great wave of relief had flooded through her. The dream had upset her in ways she couldn't really understand. It wasn't as if she hadn't had strange and weird dreams before, but this one had felt somehow personally menacing. Maybe it had just tapped into the sense of impending doom that had lain across her like a storm cloud the previous day. Either way, it had done nothing to ease her feelings of anxiety.

As a result, the voice on the other end of the line was surprisingly welcome. She'd only very reluctantly given him her number, but she was now pleased she had. There was something reassuring and comforting about Reed, although he sounded anything but calm right now.

'Hi, Miss An-ren,' the voice faltered. 'This is William Reed. You gave me your number last night.'

She smiled, amused by his obvious nervousness.

'I remember,' she responded. 'It wasn't as if you gave me much choice.'

There was a moment's silence at the other end, as Reed considered what she'd said.

'I'm sorry,' he apologised. 'I didn't mean it to seem that way.'

'I'm teasing you, Zhu Wei! I thought you British prided yourself on your humour?'

'I haven't lived there for a long time,' he told her, although she couldn't be sure whether his tone was one of disappointment or regret.

'And please drop the "Miss". Otherwise I'll have to keep calling you "Mr" Reed.'

'I'm not doing very well, am I?' he responded, offering a weak laugh in the process.

She was surprised. He didn't strike her as the sort of man who would feel the need to seek reassurance.

'I'm sure everyone's told you how demanding I am. And critical,' she told him, trying to make her tone sound light and self-deprecating. 'You should just ignore it. Everyone else does.'

'It's hard to ignore anything about you.'

Now she understood.

'I did phone for a reason,' he continued, before she could say anything, 'and it wasn't just to annoy you.'

'Did I say I was annoyed?' she interrupted, now feeling a little irritated.

'No, you didn't. Anyway, to get to the point. There've been some developments.'

'About what?'

'The situation at the hotel last night.'

'I've only just woken up. I make a point of not looking at my phone until I've showered and had breakfast.

What's happened? Has Mei sold her story about haunted mirrors to the gutter press?'

'Not as far as I'm aware. There are two things, really. The first is that I identified the provenance of the jade shard in the mirror you were holding last night.'

'And?'

'It had a small maker's mark on it. A friend of mine who does a little bit of dealing identified it as belonging to "Luo Ban". Does that mean anything to you?'

'Luo Ban?'

She considered the name, feeling something resonate deep inside her, almost like a hint of a hidden memory. She tried to focus on the words, or name, whatever they were. There was something, just at the edge of her consciousness, but, no matter, how she tried, it remained just out of reach.

'No,' she said. 'I've never heard of it before.'

'If you don't mind,' Reed continued. 'I'd like to take a look at the shard attached to your ribbon. Just to see if it might have the same mark on it.'

'That isn't very likely, surely?' she asked.

For reasons she couldn't explain, she felt unsettled by the thought of someone else handling the ribbon.

'Probably not, but it would be helpful to know. I understand how precious it is to you, but I won't do anything to it. I just want to see if there's a mark.'

'I'll think about it,' she said.

Every instinct in her body was screaming "no", but she really couldn't understand why she should feel so resistant.

He'd only said he wanted to look at it. He was right, it was precious to her, but it was, after all, just a jade shard.

'The other thing that's happened,' Reed continued, 'is that *MeiXiu* posted a set of photos of you holding that mirror. It seems one of your fans made them into a slideshow and plastered it all over social media. The thing's gone viral.'

'That's good,' she observed, although she knew it almost certainly wasn't.

After all, Reed was the fixer. It wasn't his job to tell her that she and *MeiXiu* had broken into new markets and sales had increased.

'In the clip, the second reflection, the one behind you, moves independently. Of you.'

She was silent, uncertain of what to think or say. She'd seen nothing, and both Xu and Liu had denied seeing anything. The photographer was probably focused on nothing more than finishing the shoot, but she would have thought that Xu might have noticed something like that. Only Mei claimed to have seen anything, and had nearly had a cardiac arrest as a result.

'What does that mean?' she finally asked.

'I don't know, but I plan to find out,' he said.

She was surprised by his determined tone. She couldn't help but wonder if that had more to do with her than the mystery itself.

'I'm meeting with a friend to try to find out more about the jade shard. Will you come with me and show him yours?'

She opened her mouth to respectfully decline, but stopped. She was suddenly reminded of her dream, which had, in fact, felt scarily real and the least dreamlike dream she'd experienced for a very long time. She wasn't much of a believer in the spiritual world, had never really set much store in portents or premonitions, but there was something about the events of the last twenty-four hours that left her feeling both anxious and worried.

And, of course, if Mr William Reed was taking a personal interest in her safety, then maybe she owed it to him to show willing, no matter how pointless it might all turn out to be. As long as he didn't play any more Blue Öyster Cult.

'I'd like to meet up with Bo and ask him about where he got that mirror,' Reed continued, bringing her back to the moment. 'Have you got his number?'

'Unfortunately, I have. But he'll never agree to meet. He's such a miserable worm.'

'Maybe if you ask him?'

She laughed at that. The thought of Xu paying her any more heed than Reed was, frankly, amusing. He, at least, seemed perfectly capable of resisting her charms.

'I'll try,' she offered, surprising herself.

'I'll come and pick you up when you're ready,' Reed said.

He was persistent, she had to give him that.

'I've only just got up,' she protested, although with little real conviction. She considered how long she might need to transform herself into the goddess that Reed obviously believed her to be.

‘Be here at 11.00 am,’ she finally declared.

CHAPTER EIGHT

She'd spent the longest time deciding what to wear. And she couldn't help but wonder why it had mattered so much. Of course, whenever she stepped out of the front door she wanted to look the best she possibly could, and especially if she was going to be seen by others in a professional capacity.

But, a large part of her suspected that her appearance was particularly troublesome today for a very different reason. A reason she didn't want to accept.

William Reed was a nice enough man, kind and respectful. And he was clearly in awe of her, but that was all there was to it. She hadn't wanted to give him her number, and she hadn't wanted to meet up with him. She was indulging him simply because he'd shown some old-fashioned concern for her wellbeing. That was all.

Eventually, she settled on a pale-blue long-sleeved top with a built-in scarf that fell like a quiet ribbon down her chest, and a white high-waisted knee length pencil skirt that hugged her hips as if it had been surgically attached.

Sometimes she felt like a slave to her clothes. She could, and often did, dress down, but her unrelenting high standards were never far away. She'd always had those, of course, but over the last few years they'd been powerfully reinforced by the requirements of being a *MeiXiu* top tier model. The fact was that she enjoyed dressing well, but it was often an exhausting experience, as today had demonstrated.

Once she was satisfied with her outfit, she spent some time cleansing and repainting her toenails a dark red, to match her lips, and completed her outfit with another pair of peep toe platforms, this time in white.

She had no issues with making herself so tall. Most of her adoring fans wouldn't accept anything less. She also enjoyed the fact that so many men were intimidated by a woman who towered over them. Reed, of course, was taller than she was, even in her highest shoes, but she'd caught the look in his eyes when he'd turned around and seen her at the Lumen House. He clearly had no issues with her height.

When she'd finished her hair and makeup, and applied some Ye Xiang, she'd finally made the call to Xu.

He answered after only one ring.

'Hi An-ren,' his weaselly voice greeted her.

She hadn't been expecting that. In fact, she hadn't expected him to answer at all. She knew that his antipathy towards her wasn't especially personal. He disliked all the models, saw them as a hindrance to whatever ridiculous career he really wanted to pursue. She had no idea what that might be, and, more significantly, she couldn't care less. If he wasn't prepared to treat her like something higher up the evolutionary chain than cattle, then why should she take any interest in him? It wasn't as if he was even particularly good at his job. So much so, that she thought most of the shoots he worked on would almost certainly run more smoothly and more efficiently without him being there.

Most of the assistants she worked with were better than Xu, which wasn't really saying much, but, more than anything she got the distinct feeling he was a woman hater. There was no question that he didn't see any of the models as the empowered women they were, asserting and expressing themselves in a world that desperately wanted to control them.

It didn't matter, anyway. What did matter was that he'd answered, and actually sounded reasonably friendly. That immediately made her suspicious.

'Bo, how are you?' she asked, realising just how cringeworthy that sounded.

When had she ever expressed any interest in his wellbeing, other than, on several occasions, wishing he were dead?

'I'm good. How about you? That was quite a scene last night. Have you seen the furore everywhere?'

"Quite a scene"? Xu never spoke like that. Had the Xu she knew and loathed been abducted by aliens and replaced with a far more human model?

'Yes,' she said. 'I don't know what to say about it. It's all a little crazy.'

'Very crazy. What was it about that mirror?'

'I don't know, but I wondered if you were free later to talk about it?'

'Yeah,' he said, his voice light and, she thought, almost pleased. 'I'm free this afternoon.'

'Oh, okay,' she responded, even more suspicious. 'I'll send you a text a little later, then.'

'Please do. It'll be good to catch up. Will Zhu Wei be with you?'

Somewhere in the back of her mind an alarm bell began to sound. Why was Xu so keen to meet with her, and what on earth made him think that Reed might be with her? He hadn't even been there when she'd been offered a lift home.

'Maybe,' she said, not wanting to tell him anything she didn't have to. 'I'll let you know when I'm free. Bye.'

She cut the call and put the phone down, looking at it as if it might just explode. Given Xu's normal attitude towards her, the conversation she'd just had was possibly the most unsettling thing that had happened over the past twenty-four hours. More so even than the dream. A dream was, after all, only a dream, no matter how disturbing. But Xu being on a charm offensive was highly concerning.

Her phone pinged. She ignored it for a moment, concerned that Xu might have sent her some message of support and undying love. But, then she realised what time it was. She stood up and glanced out of the window.

There it was, the crimson 69 Mustang. Even though it was idling, the Ford's gas-guzzling engine was so loud that she could hear it through the fully closed and locked triple-glazed windows.

She grabbed her phone, threw it into her clutch bag and ran to the front door, not out of any great concern for her neighbours, but more out of a desire to avoid bringing any unwanted attention onto herself.

Next time, she thought, if there was a next time, which she strongly doubted, she'd get him to wait in the next road.

To her surprise, when she opened the door and went outside, she was met with complete silence. Reed was leaning against the car, his eyes apparently checking out the neighbourhood. She wasn't fooled, though. She knew he'd have been eyeing the front door, and probably turned away the moment he saw it open.

She was pleased that he'd been considerate enough to turn the engine off, although maybe he'd just been expecting her to take her time.

'You look very nice,' he smiled at her, as she approached.

'Just "very nice"?' she demanded, stopping in front of the passenger side door and giving him her most disapproving frown.

'You look very beautiful, obviously,' he admitted, opening the door for her. 'I just didn't want you to think I'm a typical alpha male.'

She glanced at him quizzically as he shut the door and went back to the driver's side. If there was one thing she didn't think about him, it was that he was a typical alpha male. He'd already made it very clear that he felt intimidated by her, or, at least, a little overwhelmed. That definitely wasn't predatory alpha male territory. And, if she'd really thought that then she wouldn't be getting into his muscle car again.

'Nice perfume,' he said, fastening his seat belt and turning the engine on.

As the car roared into life, he jammed it into Drive and pulled away from the kerb.

'Thank you,' she said. 'Your cologne is nice, too. What is it?'

'It's called Vetiver Smoke. Do you know it?'

'I've seen it, but I've never known anyone who wears it. It suits you.'

'Thank you,' he nodded.

It occurred to him that this might just have been the first vaguely complimentary thing she'd said to him.

'No music today?' she asked.

He glanced at her, noting the mischievous glint in her eye that she tried very hard to hide.

'I've ripped out the music system,' he told her. 'Just in case you decide to torture me again.'

'Are you criticising my artistic and cultural heritage?'

'In this instance, yes. I had nightmares about that voice.'

He'd expected her to laugh at this, or to suggest that it served him right, but he was surprised to see a dark cloud pass across her face.

'William,' she began, pronouncing his very western name in a sharply nuanced way. He liked it, there was a very sweet charm in the way she didn't quite get it right. It was, he thought, far more endearing than if she'd uttered it exactly as it was written. 'What do you think about dreams?'

He glanced at her again. He hadn't expected quite such a leftfield question.

'What do I think about them? I think they're mostly an indication of just how disturbing our subconscious minds are. Well, mine, anyway.'

'What makes you say that?'

'I don't remember many of my dreams, but those I do are usually the upsetting or traumatic ones. It's obvious to me that they're usually the merging of something that I've seen or done the day before, and things that are bothering me, or making me worry.'

'You don't think there can be other causes?'

'Like what?' he asked.

'I don't know. Like other people, or creatures?'

He glanced at her for a brief moment. She now seemed very pensive, as if weighed down by something.

'Someone, or something, else intruding into your sleeping mind?' he suggested.

'Yes.'

'I don't see how that could be possible.'

'That's your western scientific perspective, I presume,' she said, and he could sense the irritation in her tone.

'Well, I am a product of my background and upbringing, so, yes, I suppose it is.'

'But this is China. Everything's different here. The magical and the supernatural are a part of everything.'

He glanced at her once more, wondering just what was driving this conversation. He hadn't known her long, but she hadn't given any indication of having anything other than the most practical beliefs about life and the universe around her. After all, she'd been completely underwhelmed about the mirror situation last night.

'Has something happened?'

'I'm just interested in what you think, that's all.'

He said nothing. He knew she wasn't telling the truth, but he wasn't about to pursue it. She was a bad liar, and he liked that. He'd known too many people who lied more easily than they told the truth.

'I heard you were a stunt driver,' she said, dramatically changing the conversation. 'In Hollywood. Is that true?'

'Yes,' he nodded. 'It's true. I worked there for about three years, just before I came to Shanghai.'

'What was that like? I can't imagine doing anything like that.'

'To be honest, it wasn't anything like as exciting as it sounds. Most of the work goes into arranging the stunt. Everything's mapped out to the nth degree. The actual driving takes up less than one per cent of the job.'

'Oh, I see,' she said, and he could tell she was disappointed.

Another illusion shattered.

'I never got hurt, never broke anything.'

'How did you get into it? Did you study to be a stunt driver?'

He laughed at the thought of that.

'No. It's a long story, and not a very interesting one. The opportunity came up at the right time and I went for it.'

'Do you miss it?'

'No way! I wouldn't swap the Golden Lantern for anything.'

That wasn't quite true, of course. There was one thing he'd swap it for, but that wasn't even a remote possibility. For the briefest of moments, he allowed his thoughts to turn inwards. However, he shrugged them off, forcing them back into the darkness they'd come from. Now wasn't the time to be wrestling with his inner demons.

'We're here,' he said, pulling the car into the kerb.

As he got out of the car, she realised she'd been right. He might be happy living in Shanghai, but he hadn't come here out of any great desire to embrace China. He'd come here to escape whatever it was that driven him away from England.

CHAPTER NINE

Wang Wei was at work. He owned an antiques emporium in Taikang Road, in Tianzifang. It was possibly flattering his business to refer to it as selling "antiques", though. Reed had only been there once before, to deliver something that Wang had left at The Golden Lantern after a night of heavy drinking, but what he'd seen hadn't exactly put him in mind of the many high-class sellers and dealers in the city.

Wang's goods were aimed at the tourist market, things that looked old and potentially valuable, but which had actually been mass produced in a factory somewhere in Shenzhen. That wasn't to say that there weren't real antiques there, but they were so well hidden, and so obscure, that most of the casual buyers who passed through wouldn't have looked twice at them. Everybody wanted a jade Buddha, but there really weren't too many of those in circulation. Not real ones, anyway.

Wang was a regular at The Golden Lantern, drank himself senseless at least once a week, sometimes twice, very occasionally three times. And, of course, any barman, even an English one, was like a priest taking confession. Reed knew all about Wang's failed marriage, his wife's apparent preference for men who sold double glazing, and his general disappointment with his son, who, at the mature age of 31, still hadn't settled on any sort of career or family.

Reed never sought these things out, they always found him. It was an occupational hazard of the job, it seemed. Yet, none of patrons knew any more about him now than they did on the day he first took ownership of the bar. He was an intensely private man, but with a compassionate and occasionally wise listening ear.

Wang spotted him as he entered the shop. Reed didn't think he seemed particularly pleased to see him, but he was amused by the dramatic change in the man's expression when he saw An-ren beside him.

As both men greeted and bowed to each other, Wang's eyes never once left An-ren. Reed wondered whether he should just carry on, and not introduce her, but he knew that Wang would be unable to function unless he'd been given official permission to talk to her.

'This is my friend, An-ren,' Reed said, as Wang bowed so low to her that his head almost touched the floor.

In contrast, she only gave him the most perfunctory nod of the head, appearing completely disdainful of the man's undisguised interest in her.

Reed reached into his jacket pocket and pulled out the small shard of jade.

'This is what I sent you last night,' he said, handing it to Wang.

Reluctantly tearing his eyes away from An-ren, Wang took the shard. He held it up to the light, turning it over and studying it from every possible angle.

'It's Luo Ban,' he said. 'As I told you. But it's modern.'

'What is Luo Ban?' Reed asked.

Wang looked at him in surprise, shaking his head, as if disappointed.

'How long have you lived here?'

Reed glanced at An-ren. Her face was a mask of disdain.

'So what is it?' Reed persisted.

'It's tied up with the shard economy,' Wang said.

'The what?'

'I don't get involved in it, you understand. It's secretive and, frankly, dangerous.'

'But what is it?' Reed demanded.

'It's complicated.'

Reed turned to An-ren.

'Can we show him your piece of jade?' he asked.

She looked at him for a long moment, a look of indecision on her face, before taking the wishing thread out of her bag.

She held it up for Wang to look at, but, when he reached out to take it, she pulled it away. As if that wasn't enough of a clue, the adversarial look that appeared on her face made it very clear that he wasn't invited to touch it.

He moved closer, and angled his head to get the best possible view of the attached shard.

'It's small,' he said, scuttling over to the shop counter, and returning with a magnifying glass.

He leaned forward again, and began to study the shard.

'Oh my!' he finally exclaimed, stepping back, a look on his face that Reed couldn't understand. 'It's Luo Ban, but it's ancient!'

He looked, if anything, a little fearful, almost as if he'd just seen a ghost.

'Is that good?' Reed asked.

'Please put it back in your bag,' Wang said to An-ren, his face almost beseeching.

She didn't need a second invitation.

'Why?' Reed asked, wishing that Wang would say something useful. 'Is it different from the other shard?'

'I'm busy!' Wang declared, stepping forward to usher them to the door. 'I'd completely forgotten, but I've got some important customers due now! I'll show you out.'

'We'll only take a few more minutes of your time,' Reed protested.

'You need to go now!' Wang insisted, opening the door and indicating, unequivocably, that they should leave.

'Come on,' An-ren said, grabbing Reed's arm, much to his surprise, and leading him back out onto the street.

'What was wrong with him?' Reed asked.

'He's scared.'

'What of, though? We only showed him some jade!'

'Let's get in the car,' she suggested.

Reed nodded agreement, and unlocked the Mustang.

Once she was seated inside, she pulled her phone out and started typing "shard economy".

She studied the results for a moment, before turning the screen to face Reed.

'Read this,' she said.

He did, although he found it a little hard to believe what he was reading.

'Did you know about this?' he asked, glancing at her as he read.

'No,' she replied. 'It seems crazy.'

There was something in the way she spoke that suggested that, deep down, she was concerned that it might not actually be crazy at all. But he didn't understand why that would be. She was a very down-to-earth woman, clearly not bound by superstitious beliefs of any sort.

'But,' he countered, 'the fact that there's a market doesn't make any of it true. There are many societies and belief systems on this planet that attribute divine or special powers to inanimate objects.'

She knew that he was one hundred per cent right, of course, and ordinarily she would have considered what she'd just read to be the ramblings of lunatics and profiteers, but she couldn't shake the strange events of the past day. Her sense of unease, the bizarre double reflection, the unspoken whispering of her name, and her horrible dream. And, now, the bizarre coincidence of the jade shard wedged into the hand-held mirror bearing the same maker's mark as the small piece she'd carried around with her for most of her life.

She couldn't look at Reed. He was a no-nonsense man, she knew that, someone who would remain steadfastly sceptical of almost anything that deviated from the norm, or suggested an otherworldly influence. And she was no different, yet here she was, doubting her own sanity and wondering whether the world she lived in had suddenly changed out of all recognition.

'What about Luo Ban?' he asked.

She nodded, and typed into her phone again. She frowned in confusion as she studied the search results.

'Nothing of any help,' she said, showing him the screen.

There were tens of thousands of sites listed, all focused on compasses.

'Try "Luo Ban shard" or "Luo Ban jade shard",' he suggested.

She typed into the phone, and her frown of confusion turned to one of bemusement.

'Nothing mentions Luo Ban,' she told him, 'and most of the results seem to focus on jade shards in computer games.'

'I don't understand that,' Reed pondered. 'Wang knew about it, or him. Surely there must be something online?'

'Apparently not,' An-ren muttered.

She agreed that it seemed a little odd, but, at the same time, she couldn't really argue with the search results.

'Let's go and see Xu,' she said, suddenly remembering the unsettling conversation she'd had with the man earlier.

'You got hold of him, then?' Reed asked, handing her phone back.

'It was very disturbing, Willam,' she confessed. 'He talked to me like I was his oldest friend.'

'I'm guessing he isn't.'

The look in her eyes made it very clear to Reed that he absolutely wasn't.

Her fingers danced over the keys, sending a message to Xu. She put her phone back in her bag, but, no sooner had she done so, than it pinged. She pulled it back out.

'That's him,' she said, reading the reply.

In her experience, he almost never answered messages or calls, and certainly not within 30 seconds. She had no idea what was going on, but she felt very uncomfortable about the whole situation.

As she read Xu's message, she began to pull a sour face.

'What is it?' Reed asked.

'He wants to meet somewhere called Tangshui Dian. In Jing'an.'

Reed almost laughed. An-ren was a sophisticated woman forced to live in a sometimes very unsophisticated world.

Tangshui Dian, the Sweet Soup Shop, really didn't sound like the sort of place she'd be seen dead. But, of course, he had no doubt that most of the people who frequented the places she favoured would almost certainly look down their noses at her if they knew she was a *MeiXiu* model.

'Thank you for coming with me today,' he said, as the Mustang pulled away from the kerb.

She glanced at him, surprised. She hoped he wasn't about to tell her that he'd "just wanted to see her again". She felt certain he was better than that, even if it was true.

'It wasn't as if I had anything else to do,' she said, staring out of the windshield, avoiding his eyes.

'You asked me about my stunt driving,' he said, taking a right as he did so. 'Do you mind if I ask how you got into the *MeiXiu* scene. You're a star now, but it can't have been easy.'

How very diplomatic, she thought. She might have thought he was mocking her, or being ironic, but she understood his tone. He was undoubtedly curious as to how she had found herself trapped in what appeared to the outside world to be a perverse and abusive profession. Maybe some part of him wanted to save her. That, of course, suggested she either wanted, or needed, to be saved.

His last point was the most relevant one. She was a star, one of *MeiXiu's* top draws. She'd gone to school, studied hard, but she couldn't afford university, found herself working lots of soul destroying and menial jobs, barely making ends meet. *MeiXiu* had brought her an income that, while hardly making her a millionaire, had, at least, allowed her to maintain her independence, and to have a certain degree of control over her life. A control that, if she were a simple wage slave like most of the people all around her, she simply wouldn't have.

Of course, she was very well aware that she was feeding into the sexual desires of insecure and inadequate males all over the world, but she was doing so on her own terms, and without actually having to humiliate and degrade herself.

Not that it had always been that way, of course.

'I was just lucky,' she responded, continuing to avoid his disbelieving stare.

It was a pathetic answer, she knew that, but it really wasn't any of his business. It wasn't as if he knew her well enough to be asking personal questions like that, anyway. And there was no doubt that they would never reach that level of intimacy.

She wondered if this was how westerners behaved. Perhaps they had no issues asking about the most personal details of someone else's life when they'd only just met. Well, this wasn't England, This was China.

They drove in silence the rest of the way. Reed had got the message loud and clear. He was disappointed, though. Aside from how distracting she was, sitting so close to him, her sensual perfume filling the Mustang, he found her fascinating.

She tried so hard to remain distant and disconnected, but he sensed that, not too far below the surface she craved something very different. Certainly, he'd picked up on moments of leaked vulnerability. He was sure she would have hated him for detecting it, but it was there.

He was a tough nut to crack, too, he knew that. He had built a wall around himself over the past decade, but he still hoped that someone might be able to knock the barrier down and drag him away from the misery of his lonely and very dismal dungeon.

It occurred to him that maybe the two of them weren't so very different after all.

Reed parked the Mustang in downtown Jing'an, just opposite the Tangshui Dian. As they got out of the car, he had to agree with An-ren's pessimistic evaluation. The neighbourhood was fairly down at heel, and the Sweet Soup Shop gave an aura of being cheap and not very cheerful.

He hung back as they approached the entrance. After all, Xu was her contact, not his, and she was the one who'd spoken to him. Reed could see just how resistant she was to him, so he didn't need to give her any extra ammunition.

Xu Bo was there, sitting in a tacky little booth, with a brown table and brown cushioned seats on either side. He was looking around, clearly expectant, and when he saw An-ren he jumped up and gestured excitedly to her.

She glanced at Reed, frowning, as she made her way to where Xu was waiting. That was a fairly clear communication, Reed thought. Something along the lines of "beware of weasels bearing gifts".

'It's so good you could make it!' Xu was enthusing.

An-ren hung back slightly, obviously concerned that he might try to do something execrable like hug her, or, even worse, force a bise kiss on her. She, for her part, simply bowed very slightly.

'And you brought Zhu Wei with you! That's excellent!' Xu continued to babble. 'Good to see you again, Zhu Wei!'

'It's been quite some time,' Reed muttered, taking note of the look on An-ren's face and squeezing himself into the booth first, opposite Xu.

Xu held up his arm in an extremely grandiose way, and a waiter scuttled over.

'What would you like to drink?' he asked.

'White coffee's fine,' Reed said.

'Nothing for me,' An-ren answered, pursing her lips in disgust as she took in the general ambience of the café.

'White coffee please,' Xu said to the waiter, who bowed obsequiously and hurried off.

'We want to know where you got the jade shard from,' An-ren told Xu.

No beating about the bush, Reed thought, impressed. Even though Xu had laid out the red carpet and was putting on his best, and most nauseating, charm offensive, she still went straight for the jugular.

'Which jade shard?' Xu asked, his face a picture of innocence.

'The one embedded in the mirror,' Reed clarified.

'Oh, that shard. That mirror,' Xu exclaimed, as if only just making the connection. 'I got it at a private auction.'

'You went to a private auction?' An-ren asked, unable to hide her disbelief.

'I go to them occasionally. I'm always on the lookout for something interesting to make the shoots that bit more unique.'

'I've never seen you with a prop before last night,' she told him.

'I don't take them to all the shoots. Ask your friends.'

'Don't worry. I will,' she said.

'What sort of auction?' Reed demanded.

'I go to all sorts. But I got the mirror at one that specialises in ritual mirrors. It's aimed at discerning collectors who value objects that hold a face.'

'Don't all mirrors hold a face?' Reed asked.

'Of the living,' Xu smirked.

'What are you saying?'

'I'm saying that there's a very big market out there for objects, and specifically mirrors, that have a connection to the past. To previous owners, in fact.'

'The shard economy,' An-ren whispered to Reed.

'Exactly that,' Xu nodded sagely.

'Why didn't you mention this when I came to the hotel last night? You saw how upset Mei was,' Reed demanded.

'I was irritated. I was wrong not to say anything, I know that, which is why I'm here now.'

Reed studied him. He realised that he completely agreed with An-ren's character analysis. Xu seemed more loathsome with every word that left his lying mouth. But, nevertheless, it was clear that he knew far more than he was saying.

'What do you know about Luo Ban?' Reed asked.

'Who?' Xu asked, his face impassive.

'The maker's mark on the shard that was embedded in the mirror was Luo Ban.'

'Never heard of him. Or them.'

'You're not really much use, are you?' An-ren scowled.

'Well, I can tell you something very useful, if you're interested. The same auction is taking place tonight.'

'Where?'

'It's at the Meridian Court Hotel, in the Bund.'

'Do you know it?' Reed asked An-ren.

'She knows every hotel in Shanghai!' Xu laughed.

An-ren suddenly felt an overwhelming urge to pick up the chopsticks in front of her and ram them into his eyes.

'I know it,' was all she said, staring at Reed so that she didn't have to look at the disgusting worm sitting opposite.

'How do we get in?'

Xu reached into his jacket and pulled out a slightly crumpled envelope.

'Just hand these in at reception.'

CHAPTER TEN

Reed's blandly insipid coffee had arrived soon after, and the conversation rapidly became awkward. Not that it hadn't been before, but it felt very strongly to both Reed and An-ren that Xu had said everything he had to say, and that the meeting was now over.

Reed desperately wanted to ask who'd really given him the mirror and who'd paid him to talk to them today, but he held himself back. He knew that even someone as untrustworthy as Xu was unlikely to give up his backer, at least not without some forceful persuasion. And, even if that sort of abuse could be inflicted in the public arena of a coffee shop, nothing that came out of Xu's mouth could be believed, anyway.

Reed strongly suspected that Xu's overzealous warmth towards An-ren, and him, had more to do with the fear of what might happen if he failed, than financial gain, although he also had no doubt that money was the carrot being dangled in front of the weasel's nose.

He opened the envelope and glanced at the tickets. He was thankful that they didn't have both of their names on them. That would have been the biggest red flag imaginable. There was very little information, beyond the date, time and venue. It appeared to be invitation only, which wasn't very surprising. He wasn't quite sure how someone like Xu would ever be given an invite to what was clearly a closed and relatively prestigious event, at least in collector's circles.

There was a heading, but that simply posed more questions than answers. 'Wheel Piece Auction". That told them nothing, although there was a small image of a highly stylised wheel in the bottom right corner.

However, when he showed the invitation to An-ren, he was completely taken aback by her response. Something changed in her eyes, but far more telling was the way her hand instantly moved to grasp his arm. That had shocked him.

She said nothing, though, simply continuing to stare at the small image of a wheel.

He knew she wouldn't want to discuss whatever it was in front of Xu, so he kept quiet as well. She was shocked, that was for sure. He couldn't imagine her grabbing his arm voluntarily.

He couldn't drink any more of the vapid coffee, so he got to his feet, and thanked Xu for his help and for the coffee. He knew he was right about everything when he saw the look on Xu's face. It was the one from the night before. An expression that mixed outrage with indignation. He'd delivered the message, and now he'd reverted to type. And he clearly didn't appreciate having to buy Reed a cup of coffee, horrible or not.

An-ren had almost run out of the Sweet Soup Shop, and thrown herself into the Mustang, without saying a word.

'Are you alright?' he asked, as he sat down next to her.

'I don't know,' she admitted.

He studied her dark brown eyes, wondering exactly what was lurking behind them. He could see worry, confusion and, more specifically, fear.

'Tell me about the wheel.'

'It's nothing,' she declared, turning her eyes away from his and staring blankly through the windshield.

'Nothing?' he questioned. 'It was enough to make you grab my arm. Or did you just want to touch me?'

'Alright,' she relented, her face still staring straight ahead. 'It was something. But I don't want to talk about it.'

'I thought we were a team,' he said, making no effort to hide his disappointment. 'I'm trying to help you.'

'Help me?' she said, finally turning to face him.

He was surprised to see anger in her eyes. He wasn't quite sure where that had come from, although he suspected she was using indignation to cover whatever it was that she was really feeling.

'I never asked you to help me. And what do I need help with, anyway? Some stupid image that someone's photoshopped into some pictures? I thought I was helping you.'

'Me? This has nothing to do with me.'

'No, it doesn't. But I saw how you looked at me in the hotel and in the car. I felt sorry for you, so I let you spend some time with me.'

Her eyes were still filled with anger, although he really had no idea why. He now felt anger rising, too, but he fought it back down. She'd wanted to hurt him, had picked her words carefully. What could be worse than being pitied by someone like An-ren? Being rejected outright would be far less humiliating

'I'll drive you home, then,' he said, his voice flat and emotionless.

'At last,' she muttered, slumping back into her seat.

He put the car into drive, and set off into the traffic. The only blessing was that it was a short journey. However, he decided that he owed it to himself, as well as her, to make one final attempt.

'You know,' he began, after they'd been driving for a minute or so, 'you're right. I was awed by you at the Lumen House. You're one of those rare people who people just want to be around. I'd be lying if I didn't say that I think you're very beautiful, but I saw so much more to you than just that.'

'Really,' she muttered, continuing to stare straight ahead.

'Really,' he agreed. 'And I'll admit I was pleased to have a mystery to investigate with you. But I just thought it would be something stupid that would simply fizzle out into nothing. But this is something else now.'

'What do you mean?' she demanded.

'Wang didn't want to talk about the jade or the shard economy. Why not? And what about Xu? Someone sent him to give us that information. Why? Something's going on here, and it's focused on you.'

'Me?' she exclaimed, finally turning to face him. 'What makes you say that?'

He glanced at her for as long as he dared take his eyes off the road, studying her face and eyes as intently as he could.

He'd been right. He'd known all along that he was. But the look on her face, and her earlier faux stormfront of anger, proved it beyond any doubt.

'I can't make any sense of it yet, but think about it. A jade shard jammed into a mirror given to you as a prop by Xu. A mirror that seems haunted in some way. The shard has the same maker's mark as your family heirloom. A maker's mark that doesn't seem to exist. That weasel Xu suddenly goes on a charm offensive and actually feeds us information, despite denying any knowledge of anything last night.'

'But that's all just a coincidence,' she protested, although he could see she was anything but convinced.

'I heard a voice last night, as you went indoors,' he told her. 'I thought it was the breeze, but it said your name.'

'My name?' she exclaimed, a look of horror appearing on her face.

He'd thought she'd mock him for being ridiculous, or fanciful, but he'd never expected his words would produce such a powerful response.

'Ren-ren, there's something going on. And if we don't take control, then I'm scared you'll get hurt.'

'But who could possibly want to hurt me?' she asked, although the memory of her dream, if it really had been one, came flooding back into her mind with full force.

The creature who'd resembled a woman had very clearly threatened her. An-ren hung her head and bit her lip. She didn't know what to do. She was scared, and she didn't want to accept that any of what had happened had any basis in reality. How could it? She was a rational woman living in a rational world. But she knew only too well that old China, the one of myth and superstition, hadn't gone anywhere. Who was she to be able to say there was no truth in any of it, just because she didn't want to believe it?

'I'm scared, William,' she finally admitted.

'Talk to me,' he said, making his voice as soft and reassuring as he could. 'Tell me everything.'

'You talked about hearing my name on the breeze. I heard the same thing when I arrived at the Lumen House. It's ridiculous, though.'

'If we've both heard it, then it's less ridiculous.'

'Is it? I'd had some sort of premonition of doom all day yesterday, maybe I just imagined it.'

'But that's not all, is it?' he asked.

She stared at him for a moment, fighting against her natural instinct to simply shut him, and all of this absurd stuff, out. She wondered if it might all go away if she simply ignored it. An image of Xu's horribly obsequious face greeting them at the Sweet Soup Shop swam into view and she realised that she really had little choice.

'When we get to my house, I need to show you something,' she said, before something else suddenly occurred to her. 'Did you just call me Ren-ren?'

He glanced at her and smiled, a warm, gentle gesture.

'I wanted to call you An-an, but I thought you'd probably slap me!'

'Am I really that bad?' she asked, a whole slew of emotions flowing through her. For some ridiculous reason, she thought she might actually start crying.

Reed was a genuinely thoughtful man, she realised. Ren-ren. It was actually a little old-fashioned, gently protective and formal. An-an was far more presumptuous, a diminutive that really implied a certain degree of intimacy, either lovers or close friends. But, it was also suggestive of teasing and affection. And now that he'd said it, and she hadn't actually slapped him, he'd received tacit approval to use it.

Right now, feeling so alone and miserable, the thought of someone wanting to call her An-an was actually very welcome. She decided that if he was bold enough to use it again, provided he wasn't crossing any boundaries, she wouldn't slap him.

'What's the diminutive for William?' she asked.

She realised she had no idea. It was an English name, after all, and a long and cumbersome one, at that.

'Will, Willy, Bill, Billy. You can call me Wei, if it's easier.'

'No,' she said. 'I won't do that. You're a William, not a Wei.'

'There are times when I've wanted to be anything but,' he admitted.

'Why?' she asked, looking at him in surprise, not really understanding.

'It's a long story,' he smiled weakly.

'I've got time. And I'm a good listener.'

'I'll tell you, but not now. It's a hard story to tell.'

Now it was his turn to stare straight ahead. But she sensed the terrible sadness that had just descended on him. She wondered just what this story was, what on earth could possibly have happened that might have made him not want to be here.

There were tragedies in every life, she knew that only too well herself, and she'd realised earlier on that he hadn't come to Shanghai because of China, but to escape whatever it was that haunted him.

Despite her own fears and her unwillingness to trust others, she was glad that she'd softened towards him. She hadn't wanted to, had wanted to send him on his way without even so much as a goodbye, but she was only too well aware that she had a habit of biting off her nose to spite her face, as the saying went. He was a genuinely kind and gentle man, and he hadn't even risen to her goading of him earlier.

She suddenly realised the car had stopped. She looked out of the window and saw her house facing her. She sighed, and pushed open the car door.

'You'd better come in,' she said, opening the gate and striding towards the front door.

CHAPTER ELEVEN

After taking his shoes off, Reed had waited patiently, watching as An-ren had gracefully raised each leg and slowly unfastened the straps around her ankles. He'd enjoyed it, in fact. As with everything she did, there was an element of performance, and her movements were both languid and sensual. Eventually, she stepped down out of the platform heels and into her house slippers.

An-ren led him through the hallway and towards the stairs. He glanced through the doors they passed, trying to absorb as much information as he could. The front room and kitchen looked bright and comfortable, although there was a sense of emptiness about it all. The walls were bare, and there were few ornaments and no books.

She led him up the stairs, and he tried hard not to stare at her legs as he followed. The task wasn't made easier by the lack of decoration all around them. The stairs were softly carpeted, as had been the hallway, and what he could see of the front room, and the walls were painted a bland magnolia, but there were no embellishments of any nature. Not even photos, family or otherwise.

They reached the top of the stairs, and she led him across the corridor to another flight, pausing for a moment, before heading up to the second floor.

The corridor that Reed found himself in was almost identical to the one on the floor below. An-ren stopped, turning to face him. He could see indecision on her face, coupled with a combination of worry and uncertainty.

'I didn't want to talk about this,' she told him, her head tilted slightly upwards, her eyes locked onto his, 'but I think I need to. I need to be honest with you.'

He nodded, not quite sure what to say. He didn't think she'd been dishonest. He suspected there were things she hadn't told him, but, then again, if that was a crime, then he was as guilty as she was.

'I'm going to tell you this, because for some reason I feel I can trust you. I've never told another soul.'

'Thank you,' he said, 'You can trust me, Ren-ren. Always.'

She broke into a weak smile. He had a comforting manner, and, so far as she could tell, seemed genuinely concerned for her. She took a deep breath and decided that maybe it was finally time to unburden herself.

'My mother disappeared when I was very young. I have no idea what happened to her. No one ever told me, and there are no police records worthy of the name. All she left was a lacquered box and a jade pendant.'

'I'm sorry,' he told her.

The pain and sadness that appeared in her eyes made his heart ache for her. He desperately wanted to reach out and pull her into his arms, but he knew that this wasn't what she wanted, or needed.

'Just let me finish,' she said, lightly brushing her right eye, as if nonchalantly wiping away a tear.

'I was brought up by my *waipo* in a one-room apartment in Xuhui. But, when she died, I received a letter from a solicitor I'd never heard of, requesting I come here. So, I came, although I had no idea what was going on. I was only 18 at the time, just a child, really.

'The house was much as it is now. Old, but well-preserved. The deed had been signed decades ago by a woman called Zhou Lianhua. I'd never heard of her, but she had my family name. It seemed that I'd inherited the house. The deeds were transferred to me and that was the end of it.'

'There weren't any letters or documents explaining anything?' Reed asked, genuinely surprised.

'Nothing. But I did find a journal written by someone whose writing was just like my mother's, as well as a photo of someone who looked just like her, dated 1936. They were in an old chest in the roof space.'

'What was in the journal?'

'I'll show you. But, first, you need to see this.'

She led him across the hallway, and opened the door that now faced them. She stood back, as if she wanted him to enter first.

As he stepped inside, his image leaped out at him from every side. Every gesture, no matter how small, was exactly copied by the many William Reeds surrounding him. It was unsettling, to say the least.

They were mirrors. Every wall was covered in full-length mirrors, stretching from the ceiling to the floor. He glanced up and realised that even the ceiling was a large mirror.

'This is weird,' he muttered.

He turned to face An-ren, who was still standing hesitantly on the other side of the threshold. She looked nervous, he realised.

'Did something happen in here?' he asked.

'Look at the mirrors,' she urged him. 'Look closely. What do you see?'

He stepped closer to the one nearest him and studied it. They were all bordered with jade, he realised, and he felt a chill run down his spine as he noticed the maker's mark. Unlike the two small shards, these were complete, and the branding was, in fact, a wheel.

He reached into his jacket pocket and pulled out the envelope that Xu had given him. Taking out one of the invitations, he held it up next to the nearest jade mirror and its surround. The stylised image of the wheel was exactly the same.

'Oh my God!' he muttered.

'What else do you see?'

Wasn't that significant enough, he thought? But he looked further, studied the mirrors themselves. And then he saw it. He walked down the length of the wall, looking closely at each pane of reflective glass. The same mark was there on each one.

He carried on walking the length and breadth of the room. Each and every jade border and mirror bore the same etched image. He had no doubt that the ones on the ceiling would be just the same, but he couldn't be bothered to look. He'd seen enough.

'There's something about this room,' he said, as he shut the door behind him.

'Did you feel it?' An-ren asked, her tone anxious.

'It's cold in there. Colder than out here. But there's nowhere for any draft to come in.'

'You're going to think I'm crazy,' she said, lowering her eyes, 'but sometimes, in the dead of night, I think I can hear my name being whispered from in there. I've always told myself it's just a dream, but now, talking to you about it, I don't think it is.'

'I don't think you're crazy,' he told her.

It was crazy, though, stone cold insane, but, as she'd told him, this was China. The old beliefs and superstitions steadfastly refused to go away. The country was as rooted in its spiritual past as it was in its bright and shiny new future.

'My *waipo* always told me never to look into mirrors at night,' she said. 'I used to think she was eccentric, but I'm not so sure now.'

He looked at the now closed door of the Mirror Room. He suspected her *waipo* knew far more than she'd let on.

'I want to go downstairs now,' she declared, leading the way back down the gloomy stairways.

He followed close behind, his mind whirling with thoughts and confusion. What on earth did it all mean?

'I had a dream last night,' she told him, as she led him into the front room and lowered herself onto the settee.

'Go on,' he urged her, sitting down on a chair opposite.

'I heard my name being called from that room. When I went in, a hand pulled me through the mirrors and into some horrible other world.'

'What happened?'

'There was someone else there. Some creature that looked like a woman, sort of, but wasn't. She was wearing a dress made of glass. She seemed to be mostly glass herself, as well.'

'Did she speak to you?'

'She threatened me. Told me that her master was coming, and that he was going to repay me for what I'd done to him in the past.'

'But that was just a dream? Surely that was all it was? Xu's mirror was probably playing on your mind.'

'I told myself that was it. But, the truth is I wasn't even slightly bothered about the mirror. Mei was the hysterical one. I really didn't care about it at all. But now, I'm not so sure.'

'We can just take the mirrors out,' Reed suggested.

'There was a covenant in the title transfer that stipulated that the room has to remain untouched.'

'But how would they know if we took them out?'

'I just worry that I'll lose my home.'

Reed said nothing. It struck him that this was only really half a home, at best. It was a nice property, in one of the most desirable and historic parts of Shanghai, but everything she'd just told him explained why it didn't feel like a home. He imagined she'd choose more vibrant décor, would be surrounded by elegance and sophistication. The truth was that she seemed more like a tenant.

'I don't want you to lose it, but I also want you to be safe.'

An-ren suddenly stood up and crossed to a cupboard that stood next to the front window. She pulled out a book and offered to Reed.

'This is my mother's journal,' she murmured. 'I've never shown this to anyone.'

He could see she was conflicted, desperately wanted to avoid having to open up old wounds that were still struggling to heal. However, he also suspected that she was secretly grateful for the opportunity to share her pain and suffering. He hoped he could do something to ease the pain.

He took it from her. It was a small notebook, the cover faded and blank. Inside, the pages were lined, and mostly empty. But some had been written on.

He turned to the last entry.

"The city above does not know the city below. There are wheels that turn where no sun reaches. I have walked among them, and they remember more than people do."

"The courtesan sings, though her voice is glass. The maker's hand is never gone, even when the man is dust."

"A daughter must learn absence, for absence is a kind of inheritance. What is given is not always meant to be kept."

"I write so that forgetting will not be complete."

'You're sure that this is your mother's handwriting?' Reed asked, handing the small book back.

'I'd recognise it anywhere,' she told him, replacing the notebook in the cupboard and returning to the settee.

'Do you have any idea what any of it means?'

'No. It all seems disjointed and random.'

'She writes about a daughter. Do you think that's you?'

'I've learned absence,' she said. 'But why would it be some sort of inheritance?'

'I really don't know. I'm sorry.'

'What do you think we should do?' An-ren asked, and he couldn't be sure whether she was referring to their current situation or her mother's journal.

'I think our first step is to go to the auction. There has to be some sort of connection. The image on the mirrors is identical to the one on the invitation. We can take it from there.'

'That's not much of a plan,' she muttered.

'It's the beginning of one,' he soothed. 'The more we know, the better we can plan.'

'I feel like I've burdened you, now,' she said, and Reed could hear the sadness in her voice. 'Everything I've just said sounds ridiculous.'

'It's not ridiculous,' he told her. 'I don't understand it, but if things happen then they're real, whether they seem rational or not.'

'Have you ever experienced anything like this before?' she asked. 'Ghosts, demons, spirits?'

'Not that I know of, but even back in England there are plenty of people who claim they have. And China is a far more spiritually aware country.'

She sighed deeply, shutting her eyes for a moment and shaking her head slowly, as if in complete disbelief.

'I'm the most rational person I know, but I'm starting to feel completely detached from reality,' she said.

'Then maybe we just need to broaden our definition of reality.'

'Is it that simple?'

'It is, if you let it.'

'I don't want to let it, though. I quite liked reality the way it was.'

Reed laughed gently. He completely understood.

'Think of it as an add-on,' he told her. 'The reality you want is still there, but something else is going on around it.'

'Is that meant to be a comfort?'

'It's just how it is.'

He could see that his attempt to lighten the mood had failed miserably. The truth was, he didn't know what he could say that would make any of it feel better.

He smiled at her, deciding that the best way to lift her spirits, even a little, was to change the conversation.

'There is one big question that needs to be answered.'

'Which is what?'

'The question of what we're going to wear tonight.'

'Tonight?' she'd temporarily forgotten about the auction. 'Shouldn't we go in disguise? If I'm being set up, then do we really want to walk in advertising our presence?'

'But, then again, if we go in boldly, then whoever's behind this won't suspect that we're onto them.'

'That's very flawed logic,' she told him.

'I don't think it is. I'm six feet two inches tall. Even if you go in flat shoes, everyone's going to notice me. I think we should go in making a powerful statement. Well, you should anyway.'

She sighed, and glared balefully at him.

'So you just want to see me dressed me up in some sexy dress. Is that what you're saying?'

'Yes, Ren-ren, always. But, in this instance, you just need to be yourself. I can't believe you'd go to any sort of function not looking your best.'

It was the truth, she realised. And, at least he was being honest. She couldn't blame him for that.

'Alright,' she finally, and slightly reluctantly, agreed. 'But on one condition.'

'Which is?'

'You have to wear a dinner suit.'

CHAPTER TWELVE

He'd tried hard to persuade An-ren to collect what she needed and go back to the Golden Lantern to shower and get ready. But she'd steadfastly refused, insisting that she was perfectly safe. Her rationale was that no one was likely to harm her when they'd already gone to such trouble to direct her to the auction.

He agreed, but he felt uncomfortable leaving her, even if only for a couple of hours. Nevertheless, he had to go and find his dinner suit, make sure it was still serviceable, and then find a clean shirt and tie to go with it. Not to mention a suitable pair of shoes.

So, having prised from her a reluctantly agreed promise to phone him if anything out of the ordinary happened, no matter how inconsequential, he got back into the Mustang and drove the short distance to the Golden Lantern.

The bar was, open, but it wasn't very busy yet. Things usually picked up in a big way as the evening wore on, although there were times, such as holidays and state events, when the place was packed during the afternoon. He hung around for a while, chatting to the few patrons and making sure his staff were okay, before retiring upstairs to his apartment and going searching for clothes.

He found his three-piece dinner suit hanging in a wardrobe, protected by a suit carrier. Fortunately, he'd put it away with a reasonable amount of care, and it was uncreased.

He tried to remember when he'd last worn the thing. It had certainly been a long time ago. He had a vague recollection of a reception that he'd been invited to at the local chamber of commerce two or three years previously, but the details, and what he'd worn, had long since faded away.

He went rummaging through the wardrobe again, finally finding a clean white dress shirt, although it also needed some remedial work from the iron.

The bow tie, however, proved more elusive. He rummaged around, emptying drawers, before eventually finding it in a small wooden box, hidden on top of the same wardrobe. His cufflinks were also inside, which was serendipitous, given that he hadn't even thought about the fact that his shirt didn't have buttons on the cuffs.

Now that he'd found his suit and everything else he needed, his thoughts turned to An-ren. He was tempted to think that she was the single most unpredictable person in his life, but he realised that she was, in fact, highly predictable. She was stubborn and resistant to any sort of help or support. Even now, after the day they'd had, she was still keeping him at arm's length, although he'd seen very clearly how much she actually craved a little bit of compassion and empathy.

He picked up his phone and called her. He had been uncomfortable leaving her, and he didn't really believe she was comfortable with it, either. But her pride and her determination to remain in complete control had meant she wouldn't consider any option other than staying put. She had agreed, without any argument, not to go anywhere near the top floor of her house. And, of course, her logical assumption about the auction was almost certainly spot on. But, he worried, nonetheless.

'I'm quite safe,' her disdainful voice answered after the third ring.

'That's good. Has anything happened?'

'Apart from not being able to decide what to wear, and spending ages trying to find a lipstick that was in the first place I'd looked, no.'

He laughed, unable to help himself. She had a very dry sense of humour, and enjoyed hiding it behind walls of irony and sarcasm.

'I'm glad you're amused,' she mocked. 'I hope you've found your suit.'

'Incredibly, I have. It took me a while to track down the tie, but it's all here now, looking almost as good as the day I bought it.'

'I'll be the judge of that,' she declared.

He was about to respond, but realised that she'd already cut the call. She worked very hard to hide her true feelings, he thought, so hard that they were mostly invisible. But he knew they were there. And, in some very perverse way, he couldn't help but feel she was warming to him.

Maybe that was simply delusional, he mused, nothing more than the triumph of hope over expectation. Time, he realised, would tell.

As he thought about the future, a dark cloud began to gather round him. It always did when he allowed himself the luxury of considering, no matter how vaguely, what might still be to come in his life. His heart suddenly hung heavy, all thoughts of An-ren temporarily banished.

He crossed to the small coffee table that stood next to his navy-blue velvet settee and picked up his wallet. He opened it and reached into the rear pocket, taking out the well-thumbed passport photo that had sat there for longer than he could remember.

He studied the young face that stared back at him. It would be twelve years soon. He'd believed in God back then. The Christian God. Not in the way that zealots did, but in a way that was gentle and kind to himself and others. He had always repented of his sins, not that there had ever been too many. Not until that day, anyway.

He'd come to learn that there were some events in life that challenged faith beyond the point of no return. No one had ever been able explain to him in any way that made sense why bad things happened. "It's all part of God's plan" was all he ever heard. If that really was true, then God's plan seemed cruel and uncaring.

He'd spent some time searching for answers, but eventually he'd given up. No answers were forthcoming, certainly not from Christians. He'd developed an interest in reincarnation, although more the principle than any specific belief. The thought of someone he'd loved and lost returning to this world to start over did provide him with some small shred of comfort, but it did nothing to expiate the tidal wave of guilt that still rose up to drown him, all these long years later.

He felt the usual arrival of tears, welling up in his eyes as they always did when he opened the door to the past that he was still trying to run away from. He tried to keep it shut, to keep those life-destroying memories locked away, but even the most secure of doors had a habit of opening when you least expected them to.

He put the photo away and wiped his eyes dry.

Maybe now was the time to move on. Properly. Not just going from one different world to another. Actually creating a new life where he was. The problem, though, was that it simply seemed so wrong. So completely disrespectful. Why should he move on, when she couldn't? If, at any time, he'd been given the opportunity to swap places, then he would have done, without a second thought. But, as with all these things, he'd never been given the option.

He forced the memories back inside, doing his level best to slam the door shut again.

As he did so, his thoughts turned back to An-ren, and he wondered when she'd last eaten. It had been a long day, and she hadn't even had a drink when they'd met up with Xu. Thinking about food made him realise that he was actually hungry himself.

He picked up his phone and sent a text message.

"I'm bringing some food. What would you like?"

He stared at the screen, hoping for an instant answer, but, realistically, not expecting any. After all, she was probably busy getting herself ready, distanced from her phone, and almost certainly not particularly interested in anything he might have to say.

He stared at the phone for a little longer, before putting it down. He'd forgotten what it was like to have feelings for someone. When An-ren had grabbed his arm at Wang's, it had felt almost as if an electric shock had passed through him. The warmth of another human being's hand and fingers on his body, even if only a clothed arm, had been revelatory. He'd suddenly felt anxious, his heart-rate increasing quite dramatically.

He couldn't help but wonder how it might feel to have her silken hair brush his face, her soft, yet firm, curves press against him. More guilt and sadness rose up as he struggled to push these thoughts out of his mind. He wondered why he insisted on tormenting himself in this way.

There was a pinging sound from the table, next to his wallet. He almost dropped the phone on the floor in his eagerness to pick it up. He clumsily swiped it, struggling to get his fingers to enter the correct PIN.

"Soup dumplings. Please. And don't forget ginger. Plenty of it."

He put the phone down and suddenly realised he was smiling. She texted just the way she talked. Imperiously.

He picked up his jacket and tie, and put on his chore coat. He certainly wasn't about to go picking up a takeaway in his finery. He hated wearing a tie at the best of times, so he'd put the hateful thing on and try to remember how to fasten it at the house on Wukang Road.

He hung around for a few minutes, chatting to his staff and patrons, before driving to the French Concession. He stopped, en route, at a bijou establishment he occasionally frequented, "The Worker's Break", where he picked up the Soup dumplings, with an extra side order of ginger, just in case the amount they supplied wasn't enough for An-ren's very demanding palate.

In another ten minutes, he was parked outside her house, and walking towards the front door, his jacket and tie in one hand, and a plain white carrier bag in the other.

As he opened the gate and strode up the short path, the door opened. He went straight inside, shutting it behind him and slipping his shoes off. He noticed that there were a pair of house slippers there. He knew that An-ren would almost certainly be wearing some, so he presumed that these were meant for him.

He put them on, working hard to suppress the little smile that had risen unbidden to his lips.

'I've got food!' he called out.

'I'm in the kitchen,' she responded.

He hadn't been to the kitchen before, but it was easy to locate, thanks to the sound of plates being dragged out of a cupboard.

He followed the noise and found himself in a bright, open space, with a central island, the room edged by continuous marbled surfaces concealing a variety of white goods. There were cupboards on two of the walls, and a glass-panelled door looked out on to a decent sized garden.

He couldn't help but be impressed, but not by the kitchen. An-ren looked, as he'd anticipated, stunning. He doubted that anyone at the auction would stand out more, especially if she chose to wear platform heels, as he expected she would.

She was wearing a fitted, long-sleeved sheath dress with a clean, modern silhouette. A centred front zip ran from her neck to the hem, which fell just above the knee. It was minimalist, almost architectural in its simplicity, but all the more stylish and chic because of that.

But, that wasn't all. She had a necklace on, made, apparently, of freshwater pearls, linked by an oxidised silver chain. It arced downwards, disappearing inside her dress. As she moved to the kitchen island, depositing the plates, he noticed something else. A ring of gleaming tiny pearls encircled the top of both thighs, protruding slightly from under the hem of the dress, each one ending in a small silver chain that dangled down, finished with yet more small pearls.

He put the carrier bag down on the table and tried to pretend he was more interested in the food than what she looked like and what she was wearing. He found himself considering the chains of pearls that circled her thighs. It occurred to him that they had to be connected to the necklace, otherwise they would surely fall down.

That led him to contemplate exactly what she might look like under the dress.

The room suddenly seemed very hot.

'Are you alright?' she asked, and he realised she was staring at him, a quizzical frown on her face.

He wondered if it would ever be possible to get used to a woman like this. He'd met many beautiful and powerful women in his life, especially during his stint in Hollywood, but he'd met very few who had the effect that she had on him. She was intimidating and overwhelming, in equal measures, but, at the same time, simply being in her presence was a remarkable and uplifting experience.

She knew the effect she had on him, that was obvious, but she thought nothing of it. It was an irony of life, perhaps, that the people with most natural power were the ones who least recognised it.

'You should have warned me,' he told her, focusing his attention on taking the small bamboo baskets out of the bag.

'About what?' she asked.

'My heart can only take so much,' he added, putting the two bottles of iced lemon tea on the island.

'You were the one who told me to make an effort,' she reminded him, now realising what he meant.

'I'm not complaining, and I'm sure it wasn't an effort,' he said, still avoiding her eyes. 'You look amazing, Ren-ren. You'll certainly be noticed.'

'Let's eat,' she suggested, ignoring his praise. 'I'm' starving. I hope you got extra ginger.'

'Of course. Your every wish is my command.'

'If only that were really true,' she muttered, opening the basket nearest her, and liberally applying the ginger, before unwrapping the chopsticks and starting to eat.

They were very satisfying, Reed thought, as he put a piece of dumpling into his mouth. He hadn't realised quite how ravenously hungry he was. He hadn't eaten since breakfast. All he'd had was that lousy cup of coffee in the Sweet Soup Shop.

'I heard something earlier,' An-ren told him, not looking up, her eyes focused on her food.

'From the Mirror Room?' he asked, looking up at her in alarm.

'I think so. I didn't go up there.'

'You should have called me.'

'I did think about it, but it stopped after a few minutes.'

'Was it your name?'

'No,' she said, lifting her head and locking her eyes onto his. 'It was laughter.'

CHAPTER THIRTEEN

It was a relatively short drive to the Meridian Court Hotel, which was nestled in the heart of the Bund, Shanghai's historic waterfront promenade, next to the Huangpu River. It was one of the city's most popular tourist destinations, famous for its colonial-era buildings and a stunning view of the modern Pudong skyline across the river.

Reed had come to China to escape from everything he knew, everything that tied him to his old world. He hadn't known much about the country before he'd arrived, but he'd rapidly fallen in love with it. The China he'd found jarred bizarrely with the image that had been fed to him in the west.

He'd soon realised that the world he'd come from had been firmly rooted in the past, whereas China was most definitely living in the future. The architecture, the engineering, everything he saw and experienced on a daily basis shocked and overwhelmed him for a very long time. Now, though, like everyone else, he took it for granted, and, of course, he struggled to apply the lesson being taught all around him to his own life. Despite uprooting himself, he'd found that some roots were harder to cast off than others.

His eyes had been opened to new wonders after he'd found himself signed up as a "fixer" for *MeiXiu*, and none were more wonderful than the one sitting in the passenger seat of his Mustang. Most of the models he'd met had been respectful and polite, although some were clearly complete divas, but none were in any way like An-ren.

He felt so distracted every time she got in the Mustang that he wondered how he managed to avoid crashing. Her subtly sensual perfume was quite intoxicating, but it was as nothing compared to her physical presence. And tonight, just to make the situation even more challenging, the silver chains that circled her thighs were completely visible now that she'd sat down and her short dress had risen up.

He wondered whether she simply wanted to torment him. Maybe she was simply testing the state of his heart. Thankfully, it seemed to be up to the challenge.

They'd driven in silence mostly, each alone with their own thoughts. Both wondered exactly what they were getting themselves into, whether there was even a point to what they were doing. But, even the highly sceptical An-ren had little choice other than to accept that something out of the ordinary was taking place around her. The deep, mocking laughter that she'd heard coming from the Mirror Room when she'd been getting herself ready had been the most chilling reminder imaginable.

She felt strangely nervous. She was used to crowds and attention, had long ago come to enjoy it and understand exactly how to get what she needed from the people around her, whilst at the same time giving them what they wanted. But this was different. She'd been to a few auctions in her time, none of which had been very stimulating. However, she'd never been to one where at least some of the focus seemed to be on her.

She was loathe to admit it to herself, but she felt comforted and soothed by the presence of the man next to her. She'd been both surprised and impressed when she'd seen him in his dinner suit. She'd had to help him with his bow tie, which he clearly had no idea how to fasten, but, once she'd done it for him, he looked really very handsome. Maybe, she thought, she could find ways to encourage him to dress more stylishly and to ditch his chore jacket and jeans.

He drove into the hotel's car park, parking as close as he could to the entrance, before hurrying round to open her door.

'And they say that chivalry's dead,' she purred, as she got out, graciously accepting his proffered hand, arching an eyebrow at him in mock deference.

'It's because I'm a gentleman,' he told her, shutting the door after her, 'not because you're a lady.'

She shot him a sharp, stinging glance. He laughed.

'I'm only joking, Ren-ren. I've never met anyone more ladylike than you.'

She pursed her lips momentarily, wondering exactly how to take that. But she let it go. They were both nervous, she knew that. There were more important things to consider right now than lame British humour.

As they approached the entrance, passing a steady stream of people either entering or leaving the hotel, she felt all eyes turning to gaze at her, either overtly or covertly.

'How do I look?' she asked, suddenly feeling a little self-conscious.

Maybe, she thought, she'd overdone it.

'You look stunningly beautiful,' he told her. 'Although, in my limited experience, it's the only look you have.'

'Thank you,' she murmured, both amused and pleased, despite his clear lack of objectivity.

The hotel lobby was blindingly bright after the darkness outside. Glass and mirrors were everywhere, large chandeliers suspended from the ceiling at regular intervals.

'More mirrors,' Reed muttered, wondering whether the choice of hotel was a coincidence.

'What did you say?' An-ren asked.

'What is it about mirrors?'

She was reminded of her *waipo's* frequent advice not to look into mirrors at night. Well, it was now dark and there were so many mirrors all around that it would be impossible to avoid them.

They arrived at reception and Reed handed over the invitations Xu had given them. The receptionist glanced briefly at the invites, before looking back up. He handed them back, smiling obsequiously at them both.

'The Presidential Suite is on the 41st floor. Show these again when you get there.'

'Thank you,' Reed bowed, leading An-ren towards the lifts.

He noticed her looking up as they walked. He'd already noticed the hotel's floors flowed around a large central shaft. That meant that you could see all the way to the top floor, the 43rd, from the ground, and vice versa. The very thought made him feel sick. He was no lover of heights at the best of times, but the thought of standing at the top of the hotel and staring down made his legs tingle and a tight knot form in his stomach.

The lift doors opened as they arrived, and they hurried inside. He pressed the button marked "41", and the cabin rapidly began to ascend.

In no time at all, the doors were open again, and they found themselves on the 41st floor. An-ren wandered over to the safety rail and looked down.

'Please,' he said. 'Don't stand so close to the edge.'

'It's quite safe,' she told him. 'Unless you decide to throw me over.'

'That's not funny,' he responded, staying as close to the inner wall as he could.

For a moment she felt confused, and then realisation dawned on her.

'You don't like heights,' she declared.

'I don't! And this sort of place terrifies me.'

'You picked the worst place to come and live, then,' she laughed. 'China has more skyscrapers than any other country in the world.'

'I know,' he muttered, heading away from the central torus and following the signs for the Presidential Suite, which led them down a side corridor.

They found themselves standing outside a set of double doors. Two men stood outside, both in dark suits and shades. They weren't especially tall, but they were thickset and muscular. Reed couldn't help but wonder what sort of auction needed a couple of heavies like these keeping guard.

'You can't go in without an invite,' one of them announced.

Reed reached into his jacket pocket and retrieved the envelope once more. He handed it to the man who'd spoken. He pulled it open and studied the contents for a moment, before handing them back and opening the doors.

'I just need to pat you down before you go in,' the other man said.

Reed sighed, and held his arms out while the guard gave him the once over. He nodded and let him through. An-ren followed close behind. He wondered what she'd have said if they'd asked to pat her down. There was no need, anyway. It was obvious that there wasn't room to hide anything under her dress, other than her body jewellery and what god had gifted her.

The Presidential Suite was grandly luxurious, or at least as luxurious as a mid-range hotel like the Meridian could manage. The main space was large, the walls an interesting shade of crimson, with oil paintings of various districts of the city and its famous architecture arrayed at regular intervals. The floor was covered with a not particularly thick carpet, decorated with traditional swirls and motifs. There was a door at the far end, which Reed presumed led deeper into the suite of rooms, with a long and relatively wide table placed along the wall next to it. There were more tables lined up along two of the other three walls, some of which held drinks, the remainder being given over to items that were almost certainly part of the auction.

Seats were lined up in the centre of the room, in neat rows, ready, Reed assumed, for when the auction finally began.

The room itself was full, packed with people, mostly, but not all, well dressed, some chatting feverishly, others apparently just waiting, mostly impatiently it seemed, for the proceedings to get underway.

'You look like someone who might speak the same language,' declared a voice from next to Reed's right elbow.

He turned to find himself facing a short, red-headed pale-skinned woman, in a short-sleeved black dress that ended just below her knees. Her eyes were blue, he noticed, her hair tied back in a ponytail. He hadn't heard an accent like hers for a long time, but it wasn't hard to work out that she was Irish.

'I'm Fiona Murphy,' she told him, before he had a chance to ask who she was. 'Paranormal detective.'

'Pleased to meet you,' Reed responded. 'A paranormal detective?'

'There's not too many of us about,' she told him. 'And who might you be?'

'I'm William Reed,' he said, bowing slightly, out of habit. 'This is my friend, Xiang An-ren.'

An-ren also bowed, although not as low as Reed had, but said nothing.

'Pleased to meet you both,' Murphy acknowledged.

'What brings you here?' Reed asked.

'Same as you, I imagine. The shard economy.'

'The shard economy?' Reed echoed, glancing at An-ren. 'I don't know much about it, I'm afraid.'

Murphy frowned quizzically.

'Why else are you here, then?'

'We were given invites. We're not really sure what's actually going on. Perhaps you could enlighten us?'

'I'm not sure it's my place to,' Murphy mused. 'Although, if you're here, it's not like you're not going to find out.'

She paused for a moment, clearly pondering the situation, before coming to a decision.

'It's really very straightforward,' she began. 'The shard economy is the social, cultural and commercial system that arises around the buying, selling, testing and attention-capitalisation of enchanted mirror fragments and related relics. These shards aren't simply objects, they're units of value whose potency grows, or fades, depending on how people look at them, talk about them and trade them.'

It sounded to Reed as if she'd just recited a well-worn speech. He glanced at An-ren, who wasn't even attempting to hide the disdain she was obviously feeling.

'We know that,' she told Murphy, speaking English, the first time Reed had actually heard her do so. 'Did you learn that from Baidu, or Google?'

'Is your girlfriend always so rude?' Murphy demanded, glaring at An-ren.

'My girlfriend?' Reed responded, glancing covertly at An-ren, who was glaring back at the Irishwoman. 'She's just being honest. I read almost that exact statement earlier today. On a phone.'

'But it's true,' Murphy argued. 'I couldn't put it better myself. Listen,' she continued, leaning in towards them both, and lowering her voice, conspiratorially. 'I've discovered that the shard economy is really a cover for a covert network that trades cursed artifacts.'

She stood back, a smug look on her face, which slowly turned to irritation when she saw the way Reed and An-ren were staring at her.

'Don't you get it?' she demanded.

'Not really,' An-ren replied. 'Do you?' she asked, turning to Reed.

'Each fragment contains a sliver of a larger metaphysical entity. If I can trace the shards, then I'll be able to fully uncover the greatest occult conspiracy the world has ever seen!'

Reed gave An-ren a look that said, "Please don't provoke her any more".

'Have you taken your medication recently?' An-ren asked, in Mandarin.

'What did she say?' Murphy asked Reed.

'She said she hopes you're successful.'

'Is that really what she said?' Murphy persisted.

It seemed to her that the disdainful look on An-ren's face didn't quite match such a positive statement.

'It's close enough,' Reed smiled.

'Look!' Murphy squealed in delight, noticing someone on the other side of the room. 'It's Victor Lam!'

'Who's he?' Reed asked.

'You don't know who Victor Lam is?'

Murphy seemed shocked at this revelation.

'I don't know who anyone is.'

'He's a local realtor,' An-ren whispered to Reed.

'He's a real mover and shaker,' Murphy explained. 'He's financed a lot of excavations in the old French Concession. A lot of the items here today have been sourced by him. And look who's with him!' Murphy exulted. 'Li Tong! I'm sure you don't know who he is, either, do you?'

'No,' Reed agreed.

'He knows all about fancy Tang-era symbols, the sort that bind spirits to flesh.'

'You should go and talk to them,' An-ren urged, speaking in English once again.

'I will. Thanks,' Murphy smiled, 'I'll catch up with you later,' she added, disappearing into the throng.

'Thank god she's gone,' An-ren muttered.

'You could have been a little bit kinder,' Reed suggested.

'Why? She's crazy.'

'For that very reason,' Reed said.

'Well, well, well,' a sultry voice purred behind them. 'Look who we have here. Mr William Reed. Zhu Wei himself, master of The Golden Lantern. And the delightful Miss Xiang An-ren, *MeiXiu's* shining star. What an honour.'

An-ren and Reed turned together.

The woman facing them was dressed almost as strikingly as An-ren, but in a very different way. Reed registered beauty first, then wrongness. Her hair flowed down her back in a shimmering cascade, glistening like finest silk in the bright light. She was tall, her height exaggerated by crimson platform heels.

Her dress matched the heels. Long, crimson, with a plunging neckline and a slit that revealed most of her legs as she walked. Pagoda shoulders, long sleeves, gloves that hid her hands, and a diamond-encrusted necklace glittering across her bare chest.

Her lips were vivid red, her eyes a deep, icy blue. Too blue, Reed thought. He wondered if they were contacts. Statistically, someone in China was more likely to be born with six fingers than with eyes like that.

Something about her was profoundly unsettling. Her manner was over-familiar, her gaze contemptuous, and even her dress seemed to pulse under the lights, as if made of glass.

An-ren's fingers clamped around Reed's arm. Hard. That alone told him everything he needed to know.

'We haven't been introduced,' the woman said. 'I am Ye. Lin Ye.'

She dipped her head in a gesture that looked like a bow, but felt like mockery.

'You have us at a disadvantage,' Reed replied.

'I'm a facilitator of sorts.'

'This is your auction?'

'Oh no. I merely facilitate.'

'And what do you facilitate?'

An-ren's grip tightened painfully.

'Things,' Ye said lightly. Then she stepped closer, smiling at Reed. 'But William, tell me about yourself. I've so looked forward to meeting you.'

'I do things. Sometimes I fix things.'

Her smile sharpened. Reed felt hostility rising beneath the surface of her sensual exterior.

'You're far too modest, dear William.'

She lifted a hand toward his face. Reed caught her wrist before she could touch him. Her skin felt cool, even through the glove.

'That hurts,' she chided, still playful. 'I thought you'd be a gentler lover.'

'Who are you?' Reed demanded, trying to push her hand down, and failing. Her strength was impressive.

Her voice dropped to a conspiratorial whisper.

'Why don't you ask your girlfriend? The wheel is still turning.'

She tore her wrist free and stepped back, turning her attention to An-ren.

'Enjoy your evening, An-ren. Make the most of it. While you can.'

Reed stepped between them.

'Are you threatening her?'

Ye laughed, a cold, mocking sound.

'Why would I threaten her? Consider it a friendly warning.'

She turned on her heel and strode toward the head table.

As she vanished into the crowd, Reed noticed a tall European man nearby. He'd been speaking with a group of collectors, but now he'd fallen silent, watching Ye's retreating figure with an expression of quiet longing.

Reed sensed the tension drain out of An-ren as she loosened her grip on his arm. He turned to face her, taking her hands in his.

'Are you okay?' he asked.

'No,' she said.

'Do you know that woman?'

'Are you sure she's a woman?'

'What do you mean?'

'I mean I'm scared, William. I'm sure she's the creature I saw in my dream. Everything about her is the same. How else would she know who I was?'

Reed was confused. An-ren had told him the creature in her dream was forged from glass. Ye was unlike any other woman he'd ever met, but she definitely seemed to be human. And it wasn't as if An-ren hid her face from the world.

'It's alright,' Reed soothed, not knowing what else to say.

'It isn't alright! Nothing's alright! I hate this place!' An-ren told him.

Reed noticed her eyes were glistening slightly in the harsh light. He squeezed her hands gently and tried to look reassuring, although the truth was Ye had left him feeling distinctly unsettled.

'My mother's journal,' An-ren said.

'What about it?'

'She wrote "The wheel turns, though no hand guides it".'

'And Ye said that "The wheel is still turning".'

An-ren was silent, but Reed could see the powerful emotions moving inside her, and he could imagine the dark thoughts that she was in danger of being overwhelmed by.

'I agree that it's a strange coincidence, at the very least. Listen, Ren-ren, we don't have to stay. Do you want to go?'

She stared into his eyes, trying to decide whether he was serious. She felt like she was standing on the edge of some bottomless abyss, and that maybe only Reed could save her from falling in.

'Would you really go if I said yes?'

'Of course I would. I want to know what's going on as much as you do, but I don't want you to feel unsafe or threatened.'

She thought about the Mirror Room. She could possibly ignore everything else that had happened, even Ye's words and her mother's journal entry, but she could hardly walk away from the house where she lived, the place that had been her home for so long. She felt a tight knot forming in the pit of her stomach, but it seemed there really was no choice.

'Thank you,' she told him. 'That makes me feel a little better. I don't think we really have any choice, though.'

'If you're sure. You know that there's nothing I'd like more than to be back on the ground floor.'

'We'll stay,' she said, appreciating his kindness, even if not his humour.

CHAPTER FOURTEEN

As they'd made their way to the drinks table, they'd finally met someone that one of them knew.

A young woman who seemed remarkably familiar to Reed suddenly arrived beside them, greeting An-ren like a long-lost friend. And, it turned out, that was exactly what she was.

'This is Ying Yue,' An-ren said. 'And this is William Reed.'

Reed bowed gently, amused that he'd been given the most neutral introduction imaginable.

He now realised why the woman had seemed familiar. Ying Yue was another model, albeit for a different online publication, *RongXiu*. Her career had mirrored An-ren's in many ways, starting off in almost total obscurity, but, thanks to her indisputable beauty, height and slender S-figure, had rapidly taken off, and she had become a minor superstar.

She was slightly shorter than An-ren, and her figure could best be described as willowy, rather than moderately curvaceous, like An-ren, but there were strong similarities between the two women, as, indeed, there were with so many of the models.

However, despite her rise to fame, she'd suddenly disappeared two years earlier, and he'd never heard any explanation why. It was possible that she might have married, or even launched herself into a different career. He simply didn't know, although he felt certain that An-ren would be able to enlighten him.

'It must be nearly two years!' Yue exclaimed, hugging An-ren tightly.

'At least!' An-ren agreed, her warm smile fading to sadness as she stepped back from the embrace. 'How are you? I heard what happened. I'm so sorry.'

Yue's smile hardened into impassivity at these words.

'I'm fine,' she said. 'Life goes on. What can you do?'

'That doesn't make it any easier, though.'

'I appreciate your thoughts,' Yue told An-ren, somewhat dismissively, Reed thought, 'but I've moved on. I can't live in the past.'

'Are you going to return to modelling?' An-ren asked.

'What brings you here, anyway?' Yue inquired, ignoring An-ren's question and glancing at Reed. 'Is this your boyfriend? Husband, perhaps?'

There was something in the way she spoke that suggested to Reed she knew he wasn't either. He couldn't help but wonder why she hadn't wanted to answer An-ren's question.

An-ren turned to Reed, and then back to Yue, looking a little flustered. Reed noticed her cheeks seemed unnaturally flushed.

'No, it's nothing like that. We're friends.'

'William Reed,' Yue mused. 'You're Zhu Wei, aren't you?' she asked, as if she'd suddenly had a revelation.

'That's me,' Reed nodded.

'So, you work together.'

'Not as such, no,' Reed responded.

'Yes, we do,' An-ren interrupted, elbowing him, not very subtly, in the ribs.

'Well, yes, I suppose we do,' Reed corrected himself.

Clearly, An-ren didn't want to have to explain their relationship, whatever she believed it to be, in any detail. Perhaps she didn't think she could.

'Why are you here, anyway?' An-ren asked Yue.

'I organised the auction.'

'You did?' An-ren responded, her brow furrowed in confusion. 'When did you get into relics and antiques?'

'I've had a lot of time to think since..., well, over the last couple of years. Victor Lam made me an offer I couldn't refuse, and here I am.'

'Were you at the last auction?' Reed asked.

'I'm at them all,' she told him.

'Do you remember selling a dull looking wooden hand mirror?'

'Mr Reed. William. I oversee a vast number of sales. So many that I can only remember the most outstanding ones. A dull hand mirror doesn't sound very memorable.'

'Do you have records of your sales?' he persisted.

'We do, but they're private.'

'How convenient,' Reed muttered.

He got another elbow in his ribs.

'I have to go now,' Yue declared, glancing over at the far side of the room, 'we're about to start, but it's great to see you A-An. We must catch up sometime.'

'That would be good. I'll message you.'

'Do that.'

As Yue walked off, gracefully sashaying away, An-ren turned an irritated face towards Reed.

'Did you have to be so rude to her?'

'Was I rude?'

'You weren't very polite.'

'She lied. To you, her friend.'

'What did she lie about?'

'Everything about her was off.'

'She was a little odd, I agree. But that's hardly surprising. Didn't you know that her fiancé died?'

'No. I didn't even know she was engaged.'

'It's not the sort of thing you advertise when you're a model. She was broken by it.'

'I can imagine. That's a terrible loss. What happened?'

An-ren was silent for a moment, and Reed wondered if she simply didn't want to say. It was private, after all. Maybe he shouldn't have asked.

'Nobody's quite sure,' she finally answered, her voice little more than a whisper. 'He was found dead in her apartment. It seems that a full-length mirror hadn't been properly secured to the wall. It shattered and some of the shards pierced his heart.'

Reed just stared at her.

'A mirror?' he asked, unable to believe what he'd just heard.

She simply nodded and looked away.

He didn't think there was much point in asking if the mirror had the mark of a wheel on it.

'I'm going to have a look at the items up for sale,' he told her.

'How very interesting,' An-ren muttered, although, despite the disdain in her tone, she proceeded to follow him over to the tables.

It wasn't like she knew anyone else, though, he thought. Apart from Yue. And she obviously had far more important things to do than socialise with an old friend. What was An-ren going to do, other than stick with him? Of course, there were plenty of men there who would probably be more than willing to offer her temporary sanctuary, but he knew she'd almost certainly prefer that even less than she would his company.

The tables were big, about ten feet in length, and there were two of them, both filled with a large number of mirrors and shards. It was very obvious this was going to be a long auction.

Most of the mirrors were hand-held ones. There were two that were larger, but there were certainly none that were in any way similar to the ones in the Mirror Room on Wukang Road.

The mirrors were mostly beautifully ornate, and, although he was no expert, they all appeared old, which, of course, was what he would have expected, given the nature of the event.

'It doesn't make sense,' he said.

'What doesn't?' An-ren asked.

'There isn't a single wooden mirror here. Xu said he got his at the last auction, but I don't believe it. If what Fiona Murphy told us is true, a mirror like that would be of no interest to anyone.'

'Maybe it was here because of the shard.'

'That is possible, I suppose,' Reed agreed, although he remained unconvinced.

'So, how are you enjoying it?' asked a familiar voice from behind them.

'Hi Fiona,' Reed smiled wanly, turning to face her. 'It's interesting.'

'It isn't really,' she laughed. 'But it'll liven up once the bidding starts. Some of these guys are deadly serious. And I mean deadly.'

'Do you know anything about Luo Ban, Fiona? Or the wheel symbol on the invitation?'

'I know a little, but this isn't the time to talk about it all. I'll give you my number and we can meet up and have a chat about it sometime.'

That was annoying, Reed thought. Why couldn't she just tell him what she knew. Maybe she didn't actually know anything, maybe she really was crazy, as An-ren had unkindly suggested.

He pulled out his phone, unlocked it, went to his contacts and handed it to her. She smiled, as if she'd won some great victory, and typed in her number, handing it back when she'd finished. He glanced at it, saw she'd entered "Detective Fiona Murphy".

'Thank you,' An-ren said, smirking wickedly at Reed.

Reed looked away, his attention drawn to something a little further up the table. A figure, seemingly male, stood there, features hidden by a black hoodie. There was something about the posture that seemed familiar, although Reed couldn't place it.

As he watched, the figure's hand reached out, furtively, palming a decent sized jade shard and quickly slipping it into a pocket.

'Did you see that?' Reed asked An-ren.

'It's just a shard,' she responded, shrugging her shoulders disinterestedly.

The figure glanced about, as if checking to see whether the theft had been spotted, before heading towards the far door.

Reed began to follow him.

'William!' An-ren protested. 'This isn't our battle!'

'It might be part of it,' he said, not looking back.

'Nobody thieves at an auction,' Murphy declared, a firm look on her face as she followed after Reed.

The figure glanced back, its face still hidden in the darkness of the hood. It saw Reed and Murphy following and broke into a run, pushing people out the way before kicking open a door and disappearing inside

Reed broke into a run, chasing after the thief, ignoring the protests of those forced to get out of his way.

The room the figure had escaped into was a bedroom, and a very luxurious one, at that, as befitted a Presidential Suite, but it was currently crammed full of boxes and crates, presumably the method of arrival for the auction items.

It stumbled over a box, fell to the floor, but clambered back up just as Reed arrived, before hurling itself through the door on the other side of the room.

Reed glanced back briefly. Murphy was behind him, but An-ren was ambling slowly in the background, looking highly irritated.

She did have her platform heels on, Reed thought. She was skilled at walking in them, but he doubted running would be that easy, even if she chose to. Unless, of course, she had to.

He ran through the door the figure had just exited, and found himself in a back corridor. There was a door on his right, a few yards on, that was wide open. He couldn't see the hoodie anywhere else, so that seemed the best option, and he went running through it.

Stairs led upwards, and he took them two at a time. He reached a mid-landing and continued his ascent. A door ahead had the number "42" painted on it in large numbers. Reed paused briefly, uncertain of what to do, but then he heard a noise from above, so he kept on running, carrying on after the mid-landing and rapidly coming to another door, with the number "43" emblazoned on it.

This, he knew, was the top floor. But the door was shut. He stopped again, pondering his best move. The noise of a heavy door being pushed open from somewhere in the darkness above made the decision for him.

He plunged forwards, running up the uncarpeted stairs that, he knew, led to the roof. He began to feel a tight knot forming in his stomach as he ran. Maybe he should stop and wait. Or even go back and tell An-ren's friend Yue about it. After all, as An-ren had very clearly pointed out, it wasn't his, or their, problem.

But he couldn't help feeling that it was. It was too much of a coincidence the theft had occurred while he was watching, and that anyone would steal anything at an auction, especially such a small piece. It also seemed a little odd that security weren't guarding all the doors. In fact, the more he thought about it, the more odd it seemed.

He heard some footsteps on the stairs from somewhere behind him, guessed that Fiona Murphy was still in the chase.

As he'd guessed, the heavy door leading to the roof was open. He stepped out into the chill and dark night air. Shanghai was a vibrant and brightly lit city at night, but the roof of the Meridian Court Hotel was in pitch blackness.

As his eyes slowly grew accustomed to the darkness all around him, Murphy arrived at his side.

'Where is the little bastard?' she demanded.

'Shh!' Reed urged her.

It was dark. If they couldn't see the thief, then the thief, presumably, couldn't see them. It was, therefore, highly stupid to start shouting and give their position away.

Reed slowly moved along the roof, keeping well away from the sides, and skirting the enormous HVAC units that covered much of the space.

'Stop walking, or take your shoes off!' Reed whispered to her, irritated by the loud clicking of her heels on the concrete beneath their feet.

'I bet you wouldn't talk to your girlfriend like that,' Murphy shot back at him, but, out of the corner of his eye, Reed saw her reaching down and taking her shoes off.

He glanced around in all directions, screwing his eyes together to try to see better. It would be a disaster if there was another way down, which, when he thought about it, there almost certainly would be. It was extremely unlikely that the hotel would only have one point of access to the roof space.

Cursing himself for not having thought of that, Reed continued to creep forward. And then he saw the figure. A dark shadow standing next to one of the HVAC units.

'There!' he whispered to Fiona. 'You carry on straight, I'll go around the back and grab him.'

She nodded, and carried on walking towards the vast silver unit while he scurried, as quickly and quietly as he could, around the other side.

He crouched slightly, and moved stealthily towards where the figure had been standing. He hoped that, whoever it was, didn't just run at Murphy. He doubted she'd put up much of a fight, despite her outward show of indignant bravado.

A dark shape suddenly emerged out of the darkness, running towards him. Reed was so shocked that he simply stood still, and the figure collided with him, knocking them both to the ground.

Reed was back on his feet first, and grabbed the figure, pulling him to his feet by the hood on his sweat top.

A fist suddenly came his way, and Reed ducked, whirling around and driving his right hand hard into the man's stomach. A gasp of pain filled the air, and the figure doubled over. Reed followed up by lifting a knee into the thief's face.

He let go of the hoodie, as the figure slumped to the ground. Reed was almost disappointed. He didn't like fighting, never had, but he would have thought a thief at a prestigious event like the one downstairs might have put up more of a fight.

'Have you got him?' Murphy shouted, arriving from around the corner of the HVAC.

'Let's see who he is,' Reed said, grabbing the man by the shoulders and hauling him to his feet.

He threw back the hoodie.

'You!' he exclaimed, shocked to find the all-too-familiar face of Xu Bo facing him.

'Get off me, you fucking idiot!' Xu blustered.

He looked a bit of a mess. His nose and mouth were bleeding profusely from their encounter with Reed's knee.

'Go fuck yourself!' Reed responded. 'You've got some serious questions to answer!'

'I'm not saying anything!'

'We'll see,' Reed muttered, forcing Xu's right arm up behind his back and marching him forwards.

Xu struggled and protested, but Reed was too powerful for him, and he was unable to shift his grip by even an inch.

As Reed began to shove Xu back towards the stairs, Murphy began to put her shoes back on.

'My feet hurt now!' she muttered.

'I'm sure Miss Ying will let you soak them downstairs,' Reed told her, pleased that she couldn't see the sardonic smile that crossed his face.

'What was that?' Murphy suddenly asked.

Reed stopped for a moment. There was some sort of almost fluorescent blue light coming from somewhere up ahead.

'Probably some sort of emergency lighting,' Reed suggested.

The light was getting brighter, and there was now noise. A sort of low growling, the sort of noise that a very angry tiger on steroids might make.

'I wish I'd brought my EMF Reader!' Murphy declared, and she started to run ahead.

In the rapidly increasing blue light, Reed could see that she looked excited. Clearly, she believed that something paranormal, or maybe supernatural, was about to occur.

'What's she talking about?' Xu asked.

'Electro-Magnetic Fields,' Reed clarified, although he could see that his answer meant nothing to Xu.

Murphy disappeared around the side of the HVAC, and then Reed heard two things, simultaneously. First, the low, remarkably sonorous growling transformed into a savagely unnatural roaring sound. Secondly, Murphy screamed and Reed could hear the clatter of her heels scurrying across the concrete.

He dragged Xu round the corner just in time to see Murphy disappearing. She paused for a moment.

'Save yourselves!' she screamed.

And then she was gone, running down the stairs faster than Reed thought she'd probably ever run in her life.

Reed could now see the source of the blue light and the feral roaring. His heart sank lower than it had sunk for many long years.

Standing about thirty feet ahead of him and Xu, and, most significantly, blocking their route to the stairs, was a creature that looked like it had been summoned straight from hell.

It was about ten feet long and five feet high, with four legs, and a very savage and vastly powerful body shape that most closely resembled a cross between a tiger and a lion, but with a face that seemed only able to express anger and loathing. Two long horns grew out of the top of its head, and a long tail thrashed about behind it. However, what really scared Reed was the fact that it was glowing a very vibrant and deep blue, sparks arcing outwards from every part of its body.

It looked completely unreal, seemingly made of electrical particles rather than having corporeal form.

It turned to face Reed and Xu, its translucent blue eyes burning with a merciless hatred, and roared. Then, eyeing them both savagely, it began to move forward.

CHAPTER FIFTEEN

'Oh my God, it's the Xilin!' Xu whimpered. 'She's sent the fucking Xilin!'

'What's a Xilin?' Reed demanded.

He knew nothing about the creature standing in front of them, slowly advancing, but he couldn't believe that it had any good intentions towards them.

'That's a fucking Xilin!' Xu blabbered, clearly terrified. 'It's come straight from hell! I knew she'd kill me! I never should have listened to her!'

'Who? Who's going to kill you!'

'It's all because of you!' Xu screamed, tearing himself out of Reed's grip. Xu looked at him accusingly, so terrified that he appeared almost deranged. 'You had to interfere! What's so fucking special about her anyway?'

'About who?' Reed demanded, now backing away.

'Your beloved An-ren, of course! I've seen the way you look at her. If you'd just left her alone, none of this would have happened!'

'Nothing's happened yet, you moron!' Reed shouted at him.

He didn't understand what Xu was saying, but this wasn't the time for questions, or answers, it was a time for survival.

The Xilin suddenly sprang at them. Reed jumped back, pushing Xu out of the way as he did so. The shard thief hit the HVAC full on in the face and the force knocked him to the floor, dazed by another blow to his nose.

The Xilin slithered to a halt, roaring loudly as it turned. Reed was now close enough to hear the electricity sparking and humming all over its body.

'Run!' he shouted.

Xu got to his feet, still stunned. The Xilin was only five feet away from him. It charged, opening its large mouth and roaring once again, the sound unnatural and terrifying.

Xu turned to run, but slipped. As he did so, the Xilin threw itself on top of him. Xu screamed as electricity surged through his body. He tensed, then started to shake uncontrollably, while, at the same time, his body started to glow the same colour as the unearthly creature.

The Xilin dug its long teeth into Xu's neck, ripping out chunks of charred flesh, before beginning to chew them. Xu was still twitching, but Reed hoped he was dead. The man was a worm, but even a worm didn't deserve that fate.

Distracted by its impromptu meal, the creature no longer blocked the stairs. Reed's plan was simple. Run to the stairwell, and bolt the door shut. It wasn't much of a plan, but it did at least promise the relative safety of him being inside the hotel and the Xilin being stuck on the roof.

He wondered what would happen after that. He seriously doubted that even the most effective and efficient pest control experts in Shanghai would be able to deal with a creature that seemed to have come straight from hell.

One step at a time, he thought. The first, and only worthwhile, step, at this stage, was staying alive.

He began to move forward in a crouch, edging past the creature that was still feasting on Xu Bo. But, just as he thought he'd safely circumnavigated it, the creature looked up, as if remembering that Xu wasn't the only human on the roof. It turned, baring its unholy teeth and growling at Reed.

He turned and ran, but the Xilin wasn't about to let him go. Foregoing the rest of its meal, it bounded towards him. As it closed the gap on him, Reed realised he was never going to get to the stairs, and instead, ran left, almost throwing himself around and behind the nearest HVAC.

The creature was big and far less manoeuvrable than Reed, and it slid past him, desperately trying to stop and turn. It was a small comfort to realise that it struggled to maintain a grip on the concrete of the roof.

He ran back along the curve of the HVAC, desperately glancing around to see what he could come up with as a Plan B. He thought about the edge of the building, wondered if he could lure the creature there and, somehow, trick it into jumping over the edge. He doubted that even an electrically super-charged creature from hell could survive a fall from the 44th floor of a hotel.

But that would involve him being at the edge, and he seriously doubted he could function in any meaningful way when he was so close to such an enormous drop. Adrenaline was flooding through his veins now. If he went to the edge, it might actually drown him.

One advantage he did have was the fact that the Xilin was generating a lot of bright blue light, whereas he was in a black suit, albeit with a white shirt. Of course, for all he knew, those translucent eyes of the creature might be designed for night vision, but he had to hope that wasn't the case. However, it did occur to him that if it was any way like other, more natural, animals, it would probably be able to smell his cologne.

He edged his way around the HVAC, deciding that his best bet was to continue to try to get to the stairs. Now that he thought about it, he wasn't even sure that the doors could be locked. What would he do then? If a creature that size threw itself at them while he was trying to hold them shut, he had no doubts it would simply smash him out of the way.

He was scared. He accepted that. It was a healthy emotion, given the situation. He hadn't felt scared many times in his life, not even as a stunt driver, and, when he had felt genuine terror, it hadn't been because of an external threat, but simply because of his complete powerlessness to be able to make any significant difference. But this creature, this Xilin, whatever it might be, was truly terrifying. The image of it chewing Xu's charred flesh swam into his mind. He felt bile rising from the pit of his stomach for a moment, but he forced it back down. This was no time for being sick.

He moved forward slightly, but, as he did so, a bright blue flash came streaking towards him. He reacted without thinking, throwing himself to the floor and rolling to his right. That saved him, as the Xilin flew through the air, sailing straight through the space he'd just been occupying.

The creature landed and skidded several feet across the roof, snarling angrily in obvious frustration as it glared at him.

That was a salutary lesson, Reed thought. The thing wasn't stupid. It had worked out what he was doing and correctly guessed where he was going.

He knew that he needed to be less predictable, but that was far easier said than done.

He half-crawled, half-dragged himself around the HVAC unit on his right, but the Xilin was merciless, galloping back towards him as soon as it had stopped. Reed clambered to his feet, and sprinted around the large device, before quickly turning to his left and running towards the other side of the roof.

He failed to notice the dark puddle that lay in front of him, and, as his feet hit the spilled oil, he slipped, and went flying through the air. For a terrifying moment, he thought he might actually sail over the edge of the roof and into the empty space directly above the car park, but he didn't. He hit the external wall, and bounced back.

As he lay there, winded, aching, his right shoulder burning with the pain of contact with the thankfully unforgiving brickwork, he wondered just how sane he was. What difference did it make whether he was fried to death and eaten by a creature from hell, or broke every single bone in his body crashing into the brutally harsh concrete of the car park.

He rolled over, and was about to force himself back to his feet, when he realised there was a bright, wildly flickering, fluorescent blue light hovering almost directly above him. He forced himself to look up.

The Xilin was three feet away from him, poised to strike, its razor-sharp teeth ready to sink into his soft flesh. It stared at him, its unseeing eyes hateful and malevolent, a low guttural growl issuing from its throat.

And then it lunged.

CHAPTER SIXTEEN

An-ren had been irritated by Reed's vigilante moment. After all, they were there to try to get to the bottom of the mysterious events that were threatening to take over her life, not to apprehend itinerant thieves. She'd watched, extremely irritated, as both Reed and that annoying woman, Murphy, or whatever her name was, had started to chase after the hooded figure.

She'd followed, but slowly, at her own pace. She wasn't about to compromise her dignity by lowering herself to running, And especially not in the shoes she was wearing. Her platform heels were designed for walking in, but running was a very different matter.

She'd been concerned that Reed might have bitten off more than he could chew. He acted tough, but she already knew him well enough to know that he really wasn't. He was easygoing and quite clearly not a man for a confrontation, at least, if he could avoid it. She had no doubt he could throw a punch and do a reasonable job in a fight, but she couldn't believe he was really much of a fighter. It suddenly occurred to her to wonder how she'd already worked out so much about him in so short a time. After all, it was less than twenty-four hours since they'd first met. It wasn't as if she liked him, or cared about him in any significant way. He was helping her, which showed what a kind and caring man he was, but that was all. And, besides, the reasons for his interest in her were fairly clear.

But, nevertheless, despite all of that, she couldn't help but feel some strange sense of duty, some sort of responsibility for him. After all, he was putting himself out for her, and, even if his motives might have been selfish and self-serving, he could have taken the easy path and elected to stay in his bar, serving his paying customers.

Even more significantly, she was suddenly swamped by an unsettling sense of unease. She was reminded of the feeling she'd had the day before. It had gone, but now it was back, and with reinforcements, it seemed. She'd never set much store by intuition or premonitions, but she had a powerful feeling that something bad was about to happen on the roof.

She wasn't sure what she could do to help, whatever the situation was, but she knew she needed to do something.

She knew she was right to worry when Murphy ran past her down the stairs, screaming for all she was worth. An-ren tried to stop her, to find out what she was running away from, but the woman simply ripped her hand off her arm and carried on running, taking the stairs two at a time.

An-ren had started to move more quickly at that point, her sense of unease rapidly transforming into something more closely resembling naked fear, fuelled by the terrible sounds she could now hear from above.

Some sort of low guttural growling had appeared first, but then a savage, unnatural roaring had filled the air. She suddenly felt very scared. A large part of her simply wanted to turn and sprint back down the stairs. But, she told herself, she wasn't Fiona Murphy. She was Xiang An-ren, she'd risen above every misfortune and tragedy that life had thrown at her, had conquered her inauspicious and miserable beginnings to conquer the world she lived in. She wasn't a quitter, and she wasn't about to let anyone down, especially someone who, for whatever reasons, was clearly in danger because of her.

She emerged onto the roof half-expecting something terrible and savage to instantly launch itself at her. But she was alone, only the deafening sound of her racing heart for company.

It was dark, but she could see a bright blue, almost fluorescent, light shining on the other side of the roof. That was where the growling and roaring was coming from. She moved forward, ignoring the cold that hit her. She'd forgotten how little she was wearing. But that was hardly important right now.

As she walked past one of the vast HVAC units she stumbled across a bloodied heap of flesh. She forced her hand across her mouth to stop herself from screaming. She didn't want to look, but she did, anyway. She gasped in shock, and fought down the nausea that rose from deep within, as she realised that the mangled, half-eaten body at her feet was that of the great worm himself, Xu

Bo. He was still wearing a black hoodie, so she presumed that he must have been the thief Reed had chased.

Xu appeared to have learned the hard way that if you sowed the wind, you were very likely to reap the whirlwind.

She increased her pace, trying not to make too much noise as she walked, but not wanting to take too long. She was terrified, but she knew there wasn't much point arriving when Reed was already dead.

She went past the lift machinery, and another two HVACs, and then she saw it. Saw them, in fact. Reed was lying on the concrete of the roof, next to the low wall that marked the edge of the building. He looked in pain, as if he'd hit the ground or the wall hard. But, what she wasn't prepared for was the creature, the thing, that was poised just a few feet away from him.

She'd never seen anything like it before. It certainly wasn't natural. Even if a creature built like that could have existed, which she was certain it couldn't, nothing from this world, the rational world that she'd lived in until last night, flickered and flashed with the spark of electricity, its fur arcing into the dark night air.

She knew she didn't have long, had to think quickly if she was going to be able to do anything to save Reed. She looked around, and something immediately struck her. It was crazy really. After all, she was a grounded woman, wasn't even a Buddhist or a Christian, believed strongly in what she could see and what meant sense, and disbelieved anything else. But she couldn't argue with the evidence of her eyes. And, even if she'd wanted to, this was hardly the right time for that sort of inner discourse.

She thought hard about what had just occurred to her. The more she considered it, the more she knew she was right. She wasn't a traditionalist, but the principles of yin and yang were as relevant to the materialist modern world as the old, spiritual, one.

Then another, almost revelatory, thought struck her, and her right hand moved down to her right thigh, and she briefly ran a finger along the pearls and silver chain that circled it.

She ran back to the lift as quickly as she could. There were a number of fire extinguishers lodged there, in case of disasters during maintenance work. She'd done some health and safety training many years ago when she'd attempted to hold down an office job, and one of the few things she could still remember were the different types of fire extinguishers.

She grabbed the Type C and, yanking it out of the wall, she hurried back to where the showdown between Reed and the creature was coming to a conclusion.

She put down the extinguisher and reached up to her neck, undoing the clasp at her nape. Ignoring the cold that ate at her bones, she unzipped her dress and pulled it down, unravelling the small chains that travelled around her naked breasts, her waist and down to her thighs. She pulled the whole piece down, stepping out of it, before quickly zipping the dress back up.

Taking the extinguisher in her left hand, she ran forward, stopping at the HVAC a few feet from where the creature was eyeing Reed, giving him a death stare preparatory to a final lunge.

She took the long body chain and quickly clipped the neck fastening onto the small grill at the bottom of the HVAC unit. Taking a deep breath, she then stepped forward and hurled the chain towards the creature.

She watched as it flew through the air towards the bright blue arcing nightmare. She was suddenly worried that it might not be long enough, that it would fall short and that the creature would simply pounce on Reed and kill him. She thought of the mess that had been Xu and prayed as earnestly as she could to every god she could think of.

The chain hit the creature and there was a tremendous explosion, blowing part of the HVAC unit apart. An-ren ducked down as savage metal fragments went flying past her. The creature howled in agony, a jarring, unnatural sound, as its vast power was suddenly earthed.

Straightening up, An-ren grabbed the fire extinguisher, stepped forward, and pulled the pin. A white cloud shot out engulfing the creature. She moved it up and down the long body, covering every piece of unreal flesh that she could, holding still until the cannister was finally empty.

She put it down and studied the thing. It was no longer glowing, covered in white foam, and very still.

Turning her back on the huge corpse, she rushed over to where Reed was collapsed on his back.

'Xiao Wei!' she cried out, dropping to her knees. She threw her arms around him, then gently lifted his head up, delicately cradling it next to her chest. 'Are you alright? Xiao Wei!'

CHAPTER SEVENTEEN

He opened his eyes and gazed up at her. Given that the last thing he'd seen was a creature straight from hell, a creature he was certain was about to slaughter him mercilessly, An-ren was the most incredibly beautiful sight imaginable.

'Am I dead?' he asked. 'Is this heaven?'

'You're alright,' she smiled, suddenly realising she'd been holding her breath. 'Thank god!'

'You killed it!' Reed exclaimed, noticing the still smoking corpse next to him. 'How?'

'It wasn't that hard,' she told him. 'It was a yin-yang thing.'

He pulled himself up into a sitting position.

'You saved my life,' he murmured.

'I did,' she agreed. 'You owe me.'

'I thought I was going to die,' he told her, staring hard into her deep brown eyes.

She put her arms around him and pulled him close again.

'You're safe now,' she assured him.

He leaned into her, wondering just how his whole world had managed to turn itself upside down in the space of little more than five minutes.

'I'm sorry I took so long, Xiao Wei,' she said softly. 'It was only when the Irish woman went running past me, screaming, that I realised something bad was happening.'

'You put yourself at risk for me, Ren-ren. You shouldn't have done that.'

'If I hadn't, you'd be dead by now. I couldn't just stand by and do nothing.'

'How did you kill it?'

'Do you remember my jewellery?'

'I could hardly forget that,' he told her.

'Well, it was one long continuous piece, from my neck down to my thighs. The creature seemed to be electrical, so I hoped that using the chain to earth it would kill it. And I used a CO2 fire extinguisher afterwards just to be sure.'

'That's incredible!' Reed frowned, staring at her in disbelief, before relaxing into a relieved smile. 'You are definitely a good woman to have around in a crisis.'

'Not really,' she said. 'I didn't have time to think, I just had to act. You would have died, otherwise.'

'We make a good team,' he told her.

'Yes, we do,' she agreed. 'You get into trouble and I save you. Great teamwork.'

'Xu seemed to recognise it,' Reed said, ignoring her irony. 'He called it a Xilin.'

'Whatever it was, it certainly seems to have liked him,' she observed, thinking of the half-eaten corpse she'd passed on her way. 'We should get away from here,' she added. 'I don't want to have to answer questions about any of this. Can you walk?'

'I'm okay,' he said, forcing himself up to his feet.

He groaned as he straightened up, flexing the shoulder that had hit the wall.

'You're hurt!' she exclaimed, concern returning to her face.

Reed liked that. He wondered if it was actually worth getting battered and nearly fried by a creature from hell in order to finally breach the walls around An-ren's kingdom.

'I slipped and fell. It's embarrassing,' he admitted. 'But I'll be okay.'

She nodded understanding, but reached out and grasped his arm, as if to steady him.

'Zhu Wei! An-ren!' a familiar voice boomed from the darkness ahead. 'I hope you're safe?'

Ye stepped out of the gloom, Ying Yue and two security guards behind her. She crouched beside the dead Xilin. For a heartbeat, something raw crossed her face, anger, grief, loss, before she smoothed it away.

She rose and walked straight to Reed.

'Remarkably resourceful, An-ren,' she said, though her eyes never left Reed. 'Who knew glamour modelling came with such transferable skills?'

An-ren's body tightened beside Reed.

'But you're unharmed, Weiwei?' Ye murmured, stepping closer until Reed felt her cold breath on his chin. 'I'd hate for anything to happen to you. You look like a man who knows how to please a woman. Wouldn't you say, Yue?'

Her laugh was light, almost musical, and utterly wrong in the presence of the corpse at their feet.

Yue looked away, unable to meet An-ren's furious stare.

An-ren's hands clamped around Reed's arm, pulling him close.

'What do you want?' she demanded.

'Want?' Ye echoed. 'What does any woman want from a man like this?'

She finally turned to An-ren. A cold fire flickered behind her eyes as she studied the woman holding Reed so tightly.

'I see,' she said softly, mockery dripping from every syllable. 'Your talents only work in front of a camera.'

She rose onto her toes, bringing her lips close to Reed's.

'If you ever need a real woman,' she purred, 'I'm always available.'

An-ren's fury surged. Still holding Reed's arm tightly, she pushed past Ye, avoiding her amused eyes. Yue stepped aside, shame flickering across her face.

Reed brought his right hand around and placed it on An-ren's. As they entered the hotel and began to make their way downstairs, he glanced at her. He was shocked to see there were tears in her eyes.

He wanted to say something, do something to ease her pain, to make her feel better, but he had no idea what that might be. It seemed to him that the best, and the kindest, thing he could do was simply to be with her in the moment.

'I hate that woman!' An-ren hissed, as they reached the 43rd floor and continued downwards.

'Nothing she said was true,' Reed soothed, although he knew it sounded weak. He didn't know what else to say, though.

'I hate her, but she scares me.'

'Do you still think she's the woman from your dream?'

'I know she is.'

'Who is she then?' Reed asked.

'I have no idea,' An-ren conceded, and some of the tension drained out of her as the words left her mouth. She suddenly felt very drained, the enormity of what had just happened only now beginning to fully sink in.

'She seemed very upset about the Xilin,' Reed observed.

'What the hell was it?' An-ren asked.

'No idea,' Reed shrugged. 'Xu knew what it was, though.'

'What about the police?' An-ren said, wondering just how they might react to finding a ten foot long creature from hell dead on the hotel roof.

'Something tells me they won't be involved,' Reed responded.

'What about Xu, though? He was an absolute worm, but he didn't deserve that.'

'He didn't,' Reed agreed, as they reached the 42nd floor. 'We can call the police. Anonymously.'

'I don't think they'll find anything.'

'You're probably right. I think we should just get away from here, and then decide what to do next.'

As they reached the 41st floor, An-ren began to make her way to the door that led back onto the corridor behind the Presidential Suite. However, Reed stood firm. She turned back to face him.

'Let's carry on down, and get the lift on a lower floor,' he suggested.

She considered this for a moment, before nodding agreement, holding tightly onto his arm as he led the way down towards the 40th floor. A thought had just occurred to her, one that scared her almost as much as the Xilin and Ye.

Everything had happened so quickly that, at the time, it hadn't occurred to her to wonder just why Xu had pocketed the shard. He was the one who'd set them up, so why had he done something so stupid? He was, of course, monumentally idiotic, but he'd clearly been following orders when he'd told them about the auction and provided the invitations. It made no sense, unless his role had been to lead Reed up onto the roof.

Anyone who knew anything about him would understand that he would almost certainly chase a thief. He was a man of honour and integrity. He wouldn't be able to stand by and allow a blatant crime like that to happen.

The fact Murphy had managed to escape reinforced for An-ren the terrible realisation that Reed had been targeted. Xu, too. His death had been expedient, she could see that. He undoubtedly knew too much and was, in essence, a liability. There was no question that when his paymasters had tired of him, he would sell everything he knew to the next highest bidder, no matter how scared he might be of whoever had been controlling him. She had some strong convictions about who it might be, too.

As they continued to make their way down the stairs, she grasped his arms even tighter, fighting back the tears of anger and desperation that continued to rise.

There was no question. Reed had been targeted. He'd been lured up to the roof, and the Xilin had been waiting for him. And, if she hadn't arrived and used her yin-yang instinct, he'd now be dead, fried and eaten by some creature from hell.

She wondered why anyone might want him dead. What threat did he pose to whoever was in charge of this disturbed and depraved game? And then she realised, and the knot in her stomach tightened even further.

'Let's get the lift,' Reed declared, breaking into her grimly spiralling thoughts.

She looked up, saw they'd now reached the 37th floor. He pushed the door open, peered out, and then led the way to the lifts.

In little more than ten minutes, they were back in the relative safety of his Mustang, speeding away from the Meridian Court, and on their way to the sanctuary of The Golden Lantern.

CHAPTER EIGHTEEN

As Reed walked through the door of The Golden Lantern, his staff and some of the patrons rushed to his side, concerned about his battered and bruised state. However, when An-ren followed him in, looking the very definition of flawless glamour, wearing a tight-fitting dress that barely reached lower than her thighs, any concerns about Reed's plight disappeared.

All eyes instantly turned to her. An-ren had no doubt some of the staff and patrons recognised her, but, regardless, she felt embarrassed that just the fact of her presence had relegated their initial alarm over Reed's injuries to the back-burner.

She smiled wanly at them all, politely declining selfies, and hurriedly followed Reed through the building, and up the stairs to his apartment.

'You're a star wherever you go,' he laughed, as he opened the door and let her in.

'They should be worried about you, not focusing on me,' she complained, reaching down to unstrap her shoes.

'I'm just their boss and barman. You're An-ren! They can see me every day, but a woman as beautiful as you is a real rarity.'

'Is that so?' she asked, stepping down out of her platforms.

Reed was amused by her dismissive tone. She didn't like praise. She knew she was beautiful, but she didn't like to hear others acknowledging the fact. He knew that it was all part of the defensive wall she'd constructed around herself, but it was still strange, given the nature of her career.

He undid his laces, slipped his shoes off, and crossed to where she was now standing barefoot, studying the contents of his living room. Shoeless, she barely came up to his chin.

She looked around, taking it all in. It was interesting, she thought. Standing there, seeing all the Chinese art and fabrics covering the wall, the framed photos of Reed with a variety of different people, the books, the CDs, the vinyl and the endless rows of blu rays and DVDs, made her realise just how functional the house on Wukang Road was.

It wasn't that this room was cluttered. Far from it. There was an order she found highly reassuring, no sense of chaos or disorder whatsoever. But, even more crucially, it felt like a home, a place that was lived in.

There was a large HD television mounted on the wall in front of the settee, a coffee table strategically positioned next to it, even a book in place, ready to be picked up and read.

'This is nice,' she muttered, wondering just what else the apartment held.

'It's not as big as your house,' he said, 'but it's home. Or what passes for home, anyway.'

She glanced at him. There was a sadness in those words. She was reminded of her realisation that he was running away from something. But who wasn't, she thought? Whose life was so perfect and blameless, so empty of tragedy, that they weren't running or hiding from something?

But he had uprooted himself and relocated at least twice. What, she wondered, could be so devastating that you would bury yourself in the world of stunt driving?

'It's nice,' she repeated, smiling wanly at him, her contemplation of his almost certainly tragic past threatening to drag her own to the surface. 'It feels like a home.'

'Thank you,' he smiled back, almost as weakly as she had. 'Can I get you a drink? Something to eat, perhaps?'

'Some water would be good.'

She realised she hadn't had a drink for quite some time, and she'd burned up a lot of nervous energy in the last couple of hours.

She followed him through a door on their left and into the kitchen. It was smaller than hers, but, again, filled with the trappings of life. A rice cooker, at least two woks, various saucepans, a knife block, microwave, washing machine, cooker, fridge freezer, and so much more. It wasn't that hers was lacking in equipment and utilities, it was simply that his looked like someone actually lived there.

She'd always felt a little like an impostor, living in Wukang Road in one of the most exclusive and expensive parts of the French Concession. She'd found it hard to really settle and claim the house as her own. Not a day passed that she didn't expect to hear a knock on the door and, when she answered it, to find someone telling her a terrible mistake had been made and she was now homeless.

That, though, was only half of the problem. The other half, the most disturbing part, was the Mirror Room.

'I can heat it up, or I've got some cold bottled water,' he told her.

'Cold is fine,' she replied.

In truth, she would have prepared hot lemon water, but she didn't want to waste his time, or hers. It was late, they'd been through a lot, and she didn't want him having to fuss over her, at least not any more than he needed to.

She was suddenly reminded of what had happened, and the pain he'd obviously been in when she'd held him close on the roof of the Meridian Court.

He handed her a glass filled with cold water and she thankfully took a long swig, enjoying the feeling of the refreshing liquid sliding down her dry throat.

She put the glass down and took his hand.

'Xiao Wei,' she said, 'Come with me.'

He frowned quizzically, but made no move to resist as she led him back into the living room, and to the settee.

'Sit down,' she told him. 'I need to check your injuries.'

'I'm fine,' he protested, wincing as he moved his right shoulder.

She helped him take his jacket and waistcoat off, removing his already half-undone tie, folding them and placing them carefully on the chair that sat next to the settee.

'Have you got a first-aid kit?' she asked.

'In the bathroom,' he said. 'But there's no need.'

'Which door?' she asked.

'That one,' he sighed, pointing at one of the two behind them.

She crossed and went inside. It was a decent sized room, with a wide corner bath, and a separate shower unit alongside. The bath, she observed, could easily accommodate two people. She stored that little piece of information away for future use.

She opened the cupboard above the sink and pulled out the green bag with a large red cross emblazoned on it.

She exited to the front room, put it down on the table, before briefly returning to the kitchen and filling a small bowl with hot tap water.

Satisfied she had everything she needed, she began to clean Reed up. She opened the first aid kit, and pulled out some cotton wool. Wetting it in the hot water, she gently began dabbing at the scratches and cuts on his face, carefully cleaning away the dried blood in the process.

She sat very close to him, so close he could feel her warm breath on his cheek. The gentle touch of her soft fingers on his face and the sensual aroma of her perfume made Reed feel a little intoxicated.

He had no doubts now that nearly dying had been well worth it.

She put down the cotton wool and sat back to inspect her handiwork. His face looked much better. The scratches were minor, and would probably heal in a couple of days. She was far more concerned about his shoulder, and whatever damage he'd suffered from hitting the wall. He'd been lucky, though. The brickwork wasn't very high. If he'd hit it with more force, he might have simply gone over the edge.

As she reached for the top button of his shirt, he studied her long, decorative fingernails. They were striking, but highly impractical, he thought. He couldn't see how she could do anything other than look glamorous with those on. But, much to his surprise, he realised the buttons were being unfastened.

'How can you do that with those nails?' he asked, genuinely impressed.

'You'd be surprised what I can do with these,' she murmured, arching an eyebrow at him, and continuing to unfasten his shirt.

As she undid the last button, she pulled the shirt out of his trousers and slipped it off his shoulders, again carefully folding it and putting it on the chair with his other clothes.

She sat back and studied his body, impressed, despite herself. He wasn't a muscle man, which was a definite plus. She'd always found strongly defined and overdeveloped muscles ugly, but Reed's body was simply well toned and nicely shaped. She didn't think he worked out, but he clearly took a pride in his appearance.

Reed, for his part, suddenly felt very exposed. It hadn't occurred to him that she might actually take his shirt off. She was studying him, he could see that. He hoped she wasn't completely dismayed by what she saw.

She reached out and touched his right shoulder. He winced slightly.

'Sorry,' she apologised, although she made no effort to withdraw her hand.

Instead, she moved it gently around his neck and down to the shoulder blade, as if feeling for something. Despite the aching he felt, the touch of her hand on his body was electrifying. He really hoped she wouldn't stop there.

'There's nothing broken,' she said, her voice now soft, almost a whisper. 'Just bruising.'

'You can tell that? Just from running your hands over my body?'

'I can tell a lot of things just from touching you, Xiao Wei,' she told him.

He couldn't be sure, but he thought that, just for the briefest of moments, a small, but satisfied, flitted across her lips. If it had been there, it was soon gone, and a different expression took its place.

She gently lowered her head and began to kiss him across his shoulder, her lips gently caressing his bruised flesh. As she slowly moved down his chest, her tongue delicately teasing his skin, her silken hair cascaded around his upper body, its soft touch combining with her sensual kissing to send a thrill of pleasure through his entire body.

She pulled back for a moment, brushing her hair out of her face, and enjoying the look of desire that now filled Reed's face, his eyes closed, before returning her lips and tongue to his chest. As she continued to kiss him, she began to move her hands gently across his shoulders and back, delicately caressing his battered and bruised body.

He said nothing, but she could sense his increased heart-rate, his breathing becoming increasingly shallow. As he sighed deeply, she lifted her head and gently pressed her lips against his. He met her with desire and longing, as she'd known he would, his arms instantly encircling her and pulling her closer.

They kissed long and hard, their tongues duelling as their passion and hunger for each other rapidly began to boil over. All the while, she continued to move her hands over his upper body, gently caressing his firm flesh.

She pulled back slightly, stood up and placed her right hand on the zip just below her chin. She slowly pulled it all the way down, and let the dress fall to the floor.

She was now naked, except for her briefs, and the pads that had kept her nipples from protruding through the thin material of her dress.

'You're beautiful,' was all he could say, and, although it sounded trite and cliched, he wasn't quite sure how else he could do justice to the goddess standing almost naked in front of him.

'Thank you,' she purred, for once accepting a compliment.

She took his hand and led him towards the one door she hadn't been through yet. She opened it, and, still holding his hand, took him inside.

As she'd known, this was the bedroom. It had to be, really, since she'd already visited the kitchen and the bathroom.

A large king-sized bed sat in the middle of the room, a couple of chairs and bedside cabinets on either side. She didn't notice anything else, though. Her attention was focused solely on Reed.

She pushed him down onto the bed, undressing him first with her eyes, then with her hands, hungrily, urgently, driven by a need that she could barely contain.

'Your turn now,' she breathed.

He sat up, hooked his hands inside the sides of her briefs, and slowly pulled them down, admiring the joyous curves of her body, and the small burst of hair between her legs. She stepped out of her underwear, pushed him back down and straddled his lap.

He reached up, carefully and gently removing the pads, before cupping her breast and starting to delicately caress her nipples. As she sat astride him, a warm glow starting to spread through her entire being, she returned her hands to his chest, enjoying the firmness of his warm flesh under her fingers..

She began to move her body against his, enjoying all the sensations that began to flow through her.

It really was crazy, she thought. Yesterday, and even earlier today, she'd been fighting to keep him at arm's length, but now she just wanted to make love to him, feel herself virtually as one with the man whose life she'd saved earlier in the evening.

She leaned forward, and almost cried out as she felt his tongue and lips on her nipples. She lowered her head and kissed him, completely surrendering to the passion that now engulfed them both.

CHAPTER NINETEEN

An-ren lay wrapped up in Reed's arms. She felt very pleasantly sated, her body and soul warm and joyful. It had been a long time since she had last allowed someone to be so intimate with her, and she hadn't been disappointed. Reed had been attentive and generous, concerned to fully meet her needs, almost at the expense of his own.

She had felt very safe and desired, and she had done all she could to reflect that back. Karma, she thought, was a completely unpredictable master. She'd only met Reed for the first time a little over twenty-four hours earlier, but, now, she felt like she'd known him for a lifetime.

They'd crammed a lot into their short time together, including her killing a creature almost certainly dragged straight from hell. And now she'd surrendered to Reed in the most intimate manner possible. But, in truth, it hadn't been a surrender in any way. More of a victory. For them both.

She'd surprised herself by how protective she'd felt of him earlier, especially when Ye had been covetously eyeing him. She'd chosen her words carefully in an attempt to both diminish and disrespect An-ren, but it hadn't worked. She was comfortable with herself, had been for a long time. It upset her, of course, but the words of a narcissist like Ye could never drag her down.

She leaned back into Reed's chest, enjoying the feeling of his warm, firm skin pressed against her back. His left arm was draped over her, gently cradling her breasts. She felt very secure, and began to feel the warm fuzziness of sleep starting to seep into her bones and her soul.

She shut down her thoughts and began to drift away.

A loud noise, like the sound of a mirror being shattered, suddenly rang out around the room. She opened her eyes with a start.

She looked around in complete shock and dismay. Where was Xiao Wei? And where was the bedroom? When she'd closed her eyes, she'd been lying in Reed's arms, in his bed, upstairs in The Golden Lantern. But now she was standing, alone in some sort of crumbling, decaying circular temple.

A large golden statue of Shangdi stood on the far side, surrounded by various creatures and demons she didn't recognise. That didn't surprise her. After all, she had no interest in the spiritual word. What did surprise her, however, was that she knew the statue was a representation of a god she couldn't recall having ever heard of before.

She studied the walls, noticed they were covered with a series of bas-reliefs, all of which depicted what appeared to be machines and mechanical processes of some description.

She felt a chill roll down her spine as she noticed images of stylised wheels that were an exact match for the ones in her Mirror Room and also on the auction invitation.

What was this place? It seemed empty and long abandoned, but, nevertheless, there was something about it that filled her with dread and fear.

She looked down, and froze. She was completely naked.

A dream, she told herself. It had to be. Some anxious fragment of her subconscious, dredging up fears instead of the far more pleasant memories she'd hoped for.

'Is it just a dream?' came the familiar voice behind her.

An-ren spun around. The glass-skinned creature from the previous night stood in the doorway that hadn't existed moments earlier. Darkly beautiful, terrifyingly inhuman.

'Who are you?' An-ren demanded, although she already knew.

'That isn't important. What matters is that my master grows stronger. Thanks to you.'

'What have I done?'

'Exactly what you were meant to. Every step you take feeds his resonance. The wheel turns, and he will have his revenge.'

An-ren glared. The creature was frightening, yes, but the melodramatic gloating, and the knowledge that she'd met her human counterpart, made her seem less overwhelming. What bothered An-ren more was her own nakedness, though she refused to cover herself. She would not give this thing the satisfaction.

'Is that all you do? Speak nonsense and threaten me?'

The creature stepped closer.

'You think this is only a dream,' she murmured. 'But I could end you here.'

A curved, gleaming knife appeared in her hand.

An-ren held her ground.

'You won't. You said your master needs me.'

The creature's movements blurred, and suddenly the cold edge of the blade rested against An-ren's throat.

'You're very sure of yourself,' she hissed.

'If he needs me, you can't kill me,' An-ren said, forcing her voice to hold steady.

'He needs you,' the creature said, laughter scraping like broken glass. 'But I need you, too.'

'I don't understand.'

'You don't need to. Your life is forfeit either way.'

'Why? What have I ever done to either of you?'

The creature's expression twisted.

'What have you done? You are the reason for everything!'

Her hand jerked, and the knife slid across An-ren's throat. She felt a sharp sting as the blade sliced a long line through her soft, pale skin. As An-ren gazed at the creature in shocked disbelief, blood began to seep from the gaping wound.

The creature stepped back, her eyes empty, indifferent.

An-ren dropped to her knees, hands pressed to her throat, trying desperately to stem the flow of blood now flowing down her chest, over her breasts, and onto the cracked floor tiles of the ancient temple.

She stared desperately at the creature, trying to speak. Tears began to spill out of her eyes and roll down her cheeks.

The world tilted, darkened, and swallowed her whole.

CHAPTER TWENTY

Reed lay still, spooning An-ren, her soft hair draped over his face and chest. His left arm lay around her body, his hand gently cradling her breasts. As they finally settled down to sleep, Reed felt soothed by the sound of her breathing, and the gentle rise and fall of her chest. He knew he was still in a heightened state of emotional arousal, but he found everything about her overwhelmingly beautiful.

In some ways, everything that had happened seemed like a dream. To go from nearly dying at the hands of the Xilin, to making love to An-ren, was more than a little surreal.

He thought back to the night before, when he'd turned around and seen her for the first time at the Lumen House. It had felt like some sort of karma. She exuded power and authority, but he'd also sensed an innate vulnerability, all of which was quite an intoxicating combination.

He knew there were women in this world, men, too, of course, who seemed different to the rank and file, who rose above the mundane and the mediocre, and who seemed somehow elevated above everyone else. It sounded crazy when he put words to it, but it was true. And An-ren was one of those people.

Really, the issue of the mirror had been something and nothing, just a way to try to keep her in his life, no matter how trivial it might have seemed. But somehow, and he had no idea how, they'd actually stumbled upon a real conspiracy, a supernatural one it seemed, which was either targeting An-ren, or was focused on her. He had no idea why, but that was less important than getting to the root of it all and keeping her safe.

In some ways he had to be thankful, since the events of the last twenty-four hours had drawn them together in a way that his simple charm probably never could have done, but, on the other hand, she was, it seemed, in real danger.

As he savoured the warm softness of her skin pressed so close against his, it occurred to him that he would happily lay down his life to protect hers, just as she had risked her own to save his.

That thought actually felt somehow healing. Given the pain that still pressed down so heavily on his heart, he couldn't help but wonder if the arrival of An-ren in his life represented the possibility of redemption.

He gently kissed the back of her neck, wishing this moment could last forever. He'd often wished it was possible to bottle or save the perfect moments in life. They'd been few and far between, and, when they had come, they'd been fleeting and desperately transitory, gone almost before he'd had the chance to really enjoy them.

This was one of those, and he wanted it to go on forever.

He felt her stirring slightly, murmuring in her sleep. He listened carefully, wondering if she was sleep-talking. But, there were no words, just vague sounds from somewhere deep inside her subconscious.

She started to move with more force, apparently agitated in her dream state. He shifted position and looked at her face in the semi-darkness. Her brow was furrowed and her mouth twisted with an expression that seemed almost fearful.

She suddenly began thrashing about, rocking from side to side, as if trying to escape from something.

And then she screamed.

Her eyes shot open, she sat up in bed, and she began to grab at her neck, her movements almost desperate, her breathing racing wildly.

She screamed again.

Reed reached out to put a reassuring hand on her shoulder, but she slapped his hand away, her eyes glaring at him with both anger and a terrible fear.

She continued to claw at her neck, as if she was attempting to hold the skin together.

'Ren-ren!' he cried out, 'it's me. William!'

Disoriented by her sudden waking, she stared at him as if seeing him for the first time.

'Is she still here?' she demanded, her eyes darting around, studying the gloom that surrounded them.

'Is who here?' he asked, trying to sound as calm and reassuring as he could. 'There's only you and me.'

'Where are we?' she asked, still looking fearful.

'We're in my apartment above The Golden Lantern. Don't you remember?'

She was silent, as if weighing up his words. He was pleased to see that the intense rise and fall of her chest was now slowing down, her breathing slowly returning to normal.

He reached out and tentatively put a hand on her left shoulder.

'It's alright,' he told her. 'You're safe. We're safe.'

She continued to stare at him wordlessly, before the fear finally started to leave her eyes. He moved closer and cautiously reached out, encircling her with his arms, and pulling her into his chest. To his relief, she made no effort to resist.

He held her close, realised that she was gently shaking.

'What happened?' he asked.

She remained silent, and he began to suspect that she wasn't going to answer, perhaps wasn't ready to talk about her nightmare.

'It was her,' she finally said, her voice so small and so soft he had to strain to hear.

'The woman in the mirror world?'

'If you can call her a woman.'

'What did she do?'

An-ren was silent for a long moment, before unconsciously raising a hand to her neck, touching it gently, almost fearfully.

'She cut my throat,' she whispered.

Now he understood why she'd grabbed so frantically at her neck. She'd been desperately trying to hold a non-existent wound together and staunch an equally unreal flow of blood.

'I'm sorry,' he murmured, holding her even tighter.

He didn't know what else to say.

'I know who she is.'

'You do?'

'She's Ye.'

'The Ye at the auction?'

'Do you know another one?'

There was an edge in An-ren's voice, as if he'd just asked the most stupid question imaginable. Maybe he had.

Ye and Ying Yue had been the first two on the roof after An-ren had killed the Xilin. He seriously doubted that was a coincidence. In fact, he couldn't see any coincidences in any of it. Xu stealing a shard, the Xilin appearing when the two of them were on the roof, Xu being killed, and him almost meeting the same fate.

'It's horrible, Rén-ren,' he told her, gently stroking her hair. 'But I think you're safe for now. It's me they want dead.'

She pulled away and stared at him. He saw a terrible sadness in her eyes.

She knew, had realised the moment she'd seen Xu dead and Ye arriving to gloat. But it upset her that Reed also knew. Maybe it was better he did, at least he could take steps to protect himself. Although she had no idea what steps anyone could possibly take against an enemy with creatures like the Xilin at its disposal.

There was one way she could save him. One very easy way.

She disentangled herself from his arms and got off the bed.

'What are you doing?' he demanded, jumping up and hurrying to get between her and the door.

'If you're not with me, then they won't want to kill you.'

'Ren-ren! If I'm not around, then who's going to save you?'

'I can take care of myself. I did for twenty-eight years before I met you. And, anyway, we don't know that anyone wants to harm me.'

'We know,' he said, locking his eyes onto hers.

She had to look away, unable to hold his gaze. The creature had made it clear both times she'd visited her dreams that she had a heavy price to pay. And cutting her throat was maybe a cruel forewarning of what was to come.

'Please don't do this,' he said. 'You and me, it just feels right. You have to admit that.'

'I don't have to admit anything,' she told him, although there was little conviction in her voice.

'You're so stubborn!' he exclaimed. 'Ren-ren. An-an! We beat the Xilin together. Whatever's going on, we can face it together and we can win!'

She was taken aback. She knew he desperately wanted to call her An-an, to be on such intimate terms with her, and, to be fair, they had just made love, which was about as intimate as anyone could get, but she was still a little surprised. She wasn't disappointed, though.

'I beat the Xilin,' she reminded him.

He laughed, despite the seriousness of the situation. That was so An-ren, he thought. So typically, so beautifully, her.

'But I set it up for you.'

'By nearly getting killed?'

'I knew you'd be there to finish it off. I got the timing just right.'

'Finish it off?'

'Allow me some small shred of dignity,' he said, smiling.

She wondered whether she could grapple him out of the way, but she seriously doubted it. In her bare feet he was seven inches taller than her, and, of course, reasonably muscular. The tension suddenly drained out of her.

Seeing the change, Reed stepped towards her and wrapped her up in his arms, pulling her in close. She resisted for a moment, before finally giving in and folding her arms around his back, allowing herself to nestle into the comfort of his embrace.

The absolute truth was that she didn't want to walk away. He'd awakened feelings in her she'd almost forgotten existed. She thought about how she'd felt on the rooftop, holding him in her arms, scared he was hurt, or, worse, dead. She couldn't deny it, couldn't deny the feelings that seemed to have developed almost overnight.

And, even more significantly, she'd saved him once already. She could, and would, do it again. Whatever it took. And, somewhere along the line, she felt certain he would do the same for her. He was right, she realised, they did work well together. He, she thought, was the yin to her yang. And who was she to deny the vicissitudes of karma and destiny?

'I'm scared of going back to sleep,' she murmured, from deep within his embrace.

'We don't have to sleep,' he responded, moving her hair out of the way and gently starting to kiss her soft and inviting neck.

CHAPTER TWENTY-ONE

They finally fell asleep, but this time An-ren was undisturbed, her dreams peaceful, devoid of any nightmarish visions from the world of mirrors.

Reed, once again, held her close. He didn't want her to feel suffocated, but he did want her to feel safe. And, selfishly, he wanted to feel her body next to his.

He eventually drifted off to sleep, and finally woke up, his head on An-ren's shoulder, an arm across her waist, the sun casting stripes across them both as it filtered through the blinds.

He carefully disentangled himself from An-ren and pulled himself over to the side of the bed, picking up his phone and checking for messages.

There were a few from the usual sources. Friends and acquaintances, suppliers, even the management of *MeiXiu* with a couple of tasks they needed help with. But, the vast bulk of messages, mostly written in capitals and with plenty of question and exclamation marks, and all in English, were from one person.

He'd completely forgotten about Fiona Murphy. In all the drama of nearly being killed by the Xilin and everything that had happened between An-ren and him, he'd never given Murphy a second thought. And yet she'd been there, had also seen the Xilin, before managing to escape. That, he thought, was further evidence, if any were actually needed, that he and Xu had been the sole targets.

The thrust of her messaging was very straightforward.

"Are you okay?"

He sent her a quick reply assuring her that both he and An-ren were safe, and suggesting they meet as soon as possible.

Reed had no idea what was happening all around them, other than the fact it was no game and the stakes were as high as they possibly could be. He'd never been much of a believer in the supernatural, although he'd always tried to maintain an open mind. He had friends who had stories of hauntings and spooky happenings, but he'd never experienced anything himself.

However, there was a distant childhood memory of the time he and his mother had stayed in a holiday cottage that had never left him. The cottage had been rented by his aunt, and was, purportedly, haunted. He could still clearly remember lying in bed in the middle of the night, hearing a horrible dragging, scratching sound, getting ever closer to him. And then a wet nose had touched his hand and he'd nearly had a heart attack. But it hadn't been a ghost. As far as he was aware, they didn't have cold, wet noses. It had been his aunt's ancient dog.

Murphy reminded him a little bit of a far younger version of that dog. Eager, keen, but essentially clueless.

However, despite all that, she undoubtedly knew more than he did, and, at this point, any information would be helpful.

Another name had occurred to him while he'd been holding An-ren as she slept. He wasn't sure why he hadn't thought of it earlier, in fact.

He sent another text, and then put his phone down, hoping to get some more time holding An-ren. But his phone instantly pinged, as he'd suspected it would. He sighed, unlocked it and read the message.

Murphy, it seemed, was desperate to meet. He knew why. Although she seemed genuinely concerned about his wellbeing, he was under no illusion the real reason for her multiple texts was the ten feet long corpse on the roof of the Meridian Court Hotel.

He'd initially wondered just how Ye might smuggle the bodies of the Xilin and Xu Bo out of the hotel, but he suspected that, getting rid of bodies, supernatural or human, would pose no great problems for someone, something, like her

He sent Murphy a message suggesting they meet at 10.00 am, downstairs in the bar. It seemed logical, really. The place wouldn't be open, and, if he sent the staff off on various errands, they wouldn't be disturbed.

He was about to put his phone down when it pinged again.

'It's like Piccadilly Circus!' he muttered, swiping it open again.

He read the message, thought for a moment, and then responded. Placing the phone on the bedside table, he turned back, to find An-ren perched on one elbow, studying him with amused interest.

She noted the look of disappointment on his face, but said nothing. She'd slept well the second time, but had been aware of his having held her all night. It had felt good for a whole host of reasons, and not all of them were to do with being secure and protected.

'Piccadilly Circus?' she asked. 'London?'

'One of the busier parts,' he told her, trying to keep his eyes on her face.

'Is that where you're from? London, I mean.'

He thought about that, realised he'd told her almost nothing about his past life. Not that he thought it was important. He was Zhu Wei now, a resident of Shanghai. That life in England felt like it belonged to someone else. In many ways he wished it did.

'Near there,' he told her.

'Do you miss it?'

'All that rain and bland food? What's there to miss.'

She studied his eyes carefully. She knew he'd run away, although she had no idea what from. But, however hard he tried to sound dismissive or disinterested in his past, his eyes told a different story. There was a tale he needed to tell, and she knew it was going to be a sad one. She also knew he'd unburden himself when he was good and ready. Just as she might eventually share her own story.

At the moment, after a night of passion and having only known each other for less than thirty-six hours, it wasn't important. What was important was staying alive and putting an end to the dangerous game being played out all around them.

'It's your home,' she said. 'It's where your roots are.'

'Shanghai's my home now,' he told her. 'Everything I need is here.'

She wanted to ask if that included her, but she could see from the look in his eyes that she didn't need to.

'I've never been to London, or England,' she ventured.

'You haven't missed anything, believe me,' he responded. 'I've never been to Chongqing,' he added, before she could respond.

'It's a beautiful city. Good food, too. You should definitely visit.'

'I wouldn't know where to start. I'd need a tour guide.'

'They're easy to come by,' she answered, holding his gaze all the while.

She hadn't lived in Chongqing since she was five years old. Her mother had moved there from Shanghai to live with An-ren's father, but had moved back when they'd separated. So, it wasn't like she'd be much use as a guide anyway, but she wasn't about to offer her services quite so easily. He'd need to work a little harder for that particular personal service.

'What were all those messages about?' she asked him, breaking the silence that had briefly fallen between them.

'Fiona Murphy sent me about a thousand SMS' overnight, worried about me, and interested in that thing. The Xilin.'

Murphy. An-ren had forgotten all about her. She'd been dismissive of her last night, but now, in hindsight, the woman seemed less flaky and delusional than she'd assumed. She'd come all the way to Shanghai from Ireland for a reason, and it almost certainly wasn't for the sightseeing and the food.

'I've asked her to come here at 10.00 am,' Reed added, glancing at An-ren cautiously.

'That makes sense,' she told him. 'I thought she was crazy last night, but now she may be the only sane person we know.'

'She clearly knows more than we do, however mad it seems,' Reed agreed.

'It's alright, Xiao Wei,' An-ren smiled, enjoying the appeasing look on his face. 'I'll behave.'

'I've also asked an acquaintance of mine to come over at the same time. He owes me a favour, and I think he might know more about this than all three of us.'

'An acquaintance?'

'When you run a bar you get to know everyone,' Reed told her, a knowing smile on his face. 'It can be useful, especially if you need a plumber, or an electrician. But I never thought I'd need Iron Palm Zhang.'

'Iron Palm?' she asked, incredulous. 'What sort of a name is that?'

'His name's Qiang, but everyone calls him Iron Palm.'

'Who is he? And what makes you think he might know anything?'

'He used to be a policeman, but after he retired he took up chi-boxing, supposedly to ward off poisonous spirits. That's why he's called Iron Palm.'

An-ren stared at Reed, unable to hide her disbelief.

'You're serious, aren't you?'

'Ren-ren, I think you know me well enough by now to realise I'm as grounded as you are. I've never believed in anything I can't see or touch. But I can't deny everything we've experienced over the past day or so. I always thought Zhang was crazy, in a nice way, but now I'm not so sure.'

She sighed, wondering just how her life had managed to reach this point. Less than two days ago, she'd been sitting in a taxi on her way to the Lumen House, with nothing more important to think about than having to contend with the idiocy of Xu Bo.

She paused that thought for a moment, remembering the sense of impending doom that had hung over her all day on Monday. And, of course, there had been the strange sounds and whisperings coming from the Mirror Room since she'd moved in.

Maybe everything had actually been moving inexorably towards this point. Was it possible that whatever was happening had been building to a crescendo ever since she'd moved into the house on Wukang Road? She'd just ignored all the signs, as any rational person would, and the forces that now seemed to be enveloping her had simply spread like an undiagnosed cancer.

'What time is it?' she asked.

'Ten to eight.'

'I need to go home and get changed.'

'Are you okay going back there?' he asked.

She saw that familiar protective look appear in his eyes.

'It's daytime. I've never heard anything during the day.'

She glanced down, as if studying her nails. She didn't want him to see the look in her eyes, the one that confirmed that she didn't really want to go back there. But what could she do? Everything she owned was there. Her clothes, shoes, makeup, perfume, everything that defined her as Xiang An-ren.

'I'll come with you,' he said. 'I can make us some coffee and breakfast while you get ready.'

She frowned at him, outwardly uncertain, but inwardly relieved.

'If you want to, you're welcome to pack whatever you need and bring it back here. Just until we get through this.'

He paused for a moment, and looked away, as if uncertain of his suggestion, before continuing.

'No, that's probably a bad idea. Forget I said it.'

She couldn't help but be impressed. He'd already worked out that if he actually suggested it, she'd almost certainly say no. It made her feel uncomfortable, not because of him, but because, after years of independence and making her own way, she suddenly felt she was in danger of losing it all.

She tried to rationalise the situation. Having sex twice in one night and sleeping in his bed definitely indicated a relationship of some sort was growing. He was a decent, kind, man who had clearly, and very quickly, developed some quite complex feelings for her. That was scary in itself. But, despite her natural tendency to live in isolation, she couldn't do this by herself. And, the truth was, if she allowed herself to be brave enough to admit she had feelings for him, she'd didn't want to.

'We'll see,' she said, getting off the bed and going in search of her clothes.

CHAPTER TWENTY-TWO

An-ren had reluctantly agreed Reed could have a shower at her house. If she hadn't, she would have had to wait around for him to get ready at The Golden Lantern, which would have seriously eaten into her preparation time, no matter how quick he was.

So, she arrived in Wukang Road in her white zip-up dress, and he, while not quite in his nightwear, hadn't fully prepared himself for the day.

While An-ren was showering, which, as he'd suspected, took an inordinate amount of time, he made some coffee and prepared a small breakfast. He had to be creative, too. He was shocked at how little food was in her refrigerator and cupboards. But, as a man who'd lived on his own for a good many years, he was able to improvise. He just hoped she'd like it.

He couldn't help but think about the room on the top floor. Taking his cup of piping hot coffee, he made his way all the way up to the top of the house. He paused at the door, wondering whether he should go in. They were only mirrors, he told himself, but, nonetheless, he simply stood in front of the door, suddenly feeling anxious.

He tried to get his head around what had happened. Removing the Xilin from the equation, there was some strange connection between the maker's mark of Luo Ban and jade mirrors. And wheels. Not just any wheels, though. These were very stylised, and certainly not designed for use on vehicles of any description, either ancient or modern.

He took a sip of the coffee and forced himself to push the door open. He peered inside. It didn't look any different to when he'd last entered with An-ren the day before, but he felt far less comfortable about it now.

The maker's mark and the wheel symbol were all still there, but there was nothing else. Just his reflection, cast infinitely, and very confusingly, around the room.

But then he heard something. Or, at least, he thought he did. What was it? Was it a voice? Like the one he'd heard uttering An-ren's name when he'd dropped her off after the shoot? No, it definitely wasn't a voice. It was so soft that he could barely make it out, but when he listened, when he really listened, forcing his ears to cut out everything else, even simply the sound of silence, he realised it was laughter.

Not the sound of happiness, or amusement, but a dark, ominous, mocking sound.

He couldn't be sure, since it was so quiet, but he thought it was a man. He remembered that An-ren had told him she'd heard cruel and taunting laughter yesterday.

'What are you doing in here?' a voice asked from behind him.

Reed nearly leaped out of his skin, having to work hard not to spill any of his coffee. He'd been listening so closely to what he thought he could hear, had shut out the rest of the world so completely, that he hadn't heard An-ren coming up the stairs and entering the Mirror Room behind him.

'Don't do that!' he exclaimed. 'I nearly had a heart attack!'

'Sorry,' she said. 'I didn't mean to scare you.'

'I'm not scared,' he scowled, unamused. 'I just didn't hear you.'

'What are you doing, anyway?'

Now that his heart had started to return to normal, and his adrenaline levels began to slowly reduce, he noticed she was wearing a short white dressing gown. From where he was standing, she appeared to be completely naked underneath. It was interesting, he thought, how in her presence he could move from virtual heart attack to overwhelming desire in a nanosecond.

'I don't know, really. I was intrigued, I suppose. I came up to have a look while you were showering.'

'Did you see anything?' she asked, a fearful look appearing in her eyes.

'No, but I did hear something. At least, I think I did. It was very faint. I was listening when you sneaked up on me.'

'What did you hear?' she asked, ignoring his mock rebuke.

'I can't be sure, but it sounded like laughter.'

He noticed the tautening of her body, the firm line of her lips.

'Was it a woman?'

'No, it sounded like a man.'

'A man,' she repeated, lost in thought for a moment. 'I thought it was a man's laughter I heard yesterday.'

'I can't even be certain I heard it,' he said. 'I'd better go and have a shower,' he added, changing the subject.

He felt unsettled, wanted to get as far away from the mirrors as possible.

'That's a good idea,' she agreed, eagerly leading the way out and shutting the door firmly after him.

'There's coffee and food in the kitchen,' he told her, as they went back down the stairs.

'Food?' she asked, looking surprised. 'Where did you get that?'

'It wasn't easy, believe me. What do you live on?'

'Takeaways.'

She showed him where the bathroom was, and indicated an empty room where he could get himself dressed, before disappearing into what he presumed was her bedroom.

He was interested in the bathroom. Unlike the kitchen, it was, if anything, overstocked. Every shelf was crammed with beauty products. Skin care, hair care, cosmetics, nail care, and much more. The list was almost encyclopaedic. But he wasn't surprised. Someone once told him that beauty came at a price. He'd never really understood until now, although he didn't think they'd been suggesting a financial cost.

An-ren earned a living being beautiful, glamorous and desirable. Reed realised there was no reward for being second best. From her earliest photoshoots, she'd set a very high standard, and he was under no illusions that if she ever let them slip, there was a long line of candidates queueing up to take her place.

Of course, An-ren had a natural beauty, inner and outer, combined with a real power, that elevated her well above the mediocrity surrounding her. But, of course, he realised his objectivity had disappeared the moment he'd turned around at The Lumen House.

He finished getting dressed, pulling on his dark jeans and a tailored royal blue collared shirt, before adding some cologne and deodorant, and heading back down to the kitchen.

He was more than shocked to find her already there, drinking coffee and making the best of the meagre rations provided.

He slowed down as he entered the room, giving himself time to study her carefully. Every time he saw her, she was dressed immaculately, powerfully, as if needing to make a statement. That was probably true, he thought. And he certainly wasn't complaining.

Today, she was a vision in brown and black. She wore a fitted dark brown long-sleeve crop top over a tight fitting ochre camisole, short enough to expose her pierced belly button. Below that she wore an above the knee, tight, black leather pencil skirt, sheer black stockings, or maybe *siwa*, and black strapped peep toe platform heels.

'What do you think?' she asked, enjoying the look on his face. 'Will this do? I can put on a jogging suit, if you prefer.'

'You're so cruel,' he said, melodramatically falling into one of the kitchen chairs, clutching at his heart in mock shock.

'I'll go and change,' she declared, putting her coffee down and heading for the kitchen door.

'No!' Reed exclaimed, leaping up and grabbing her arm.

They stood there for a long moment, staring into each other's eyes, unspoken words passing across the almost non-existent space between them. Reed finally broke into a smile, moving his hand down her arm. He pulled her hand up to his lips and kissed it.

'You're adorable, Ren-ren,' he told her, holding her hand in both of his, enjoying the softness of her skin.

'Weiwei, call me An-an,' she murmured, reaching across and kissing him gently on the lips.

Reed was shocked. Not only was An-an a very intimate form of her name, but her calling him Weiwei was as playful, soft and cute as she could possibly be.

He remembered Ye calling him by the same name the night before. She'd made it sound almost dirty and profane. From An-ren it sounded more than a little like heaven on earth.

CHAPTER TWENTY-THREE

They arrived back at The Golden Lantern shortly before 10.00 am. Fiona Murphy and Iron Palm Zhang were both already there, sitting in a booth drinking tea made by the morning staff, who'd already turned up to prepare for the bar's lunchtime opening.

The two invited guests looked awkward, sitting a slight distance apart, concentrating on their phones. Murphy didn't speak any Mandarin or Shanghainese, and Zhang spoke no English. And neither had met before.

Reed thanked his staff for taking care of Murphy and Zhang, and then suggested they go and grab a break at one of the local cafes. At first, they were resistant, determined to continue with their preparations, but Reed had eventually made them realise the four of them wanted some privacy.

It was Wednesday, typically a slow day, with business picking up later, so Reed reckoned they had a couple of hours to talk before customers started filing in for some liquid refreshment and good home-cooked food

An-ren was amused by Murphy. She was dressed in a long black leather trench coat, her red hair piled up messily on top of her head. She was also wearing trousers and flat shoes. Everything about her seemed to scream "I'm a detective!" A paranormal detective, of course, a point powerfully reinforced by the EMF Reader she was clutching to her chest.

Iron Palm Zhang, by comparison, was much less distinctive. She guessed he was probably in his early 60s, maybe slightly older. He was stocky, with large, weather hands, evidence of a life of hard work and graft. In his powerful grasp, the phone he was holding looked small, almost insignificant. His white hair was shaved short, and there was a faint scar, in the shape of a crescent, under his left eye.

The irony that "Detective" Murphy was unwittingly sitting alongside a real policeman, albeit retired, wasn't wasted on An-ren. In fact, she was very much looking forward to telling her.

'Thank god you're safe!' Murphy had gushed, as Reed and An-ren had arrived. Her eyes, however, had only focused on the Englishman. An-ren wasn't impressed.

'Let me make some introductions,' Reed smiled warmly, as he and An-ren towered over the two seated in the booth. 'This is Xiang An-ren, Fiona Murphy, Zhang Qiang, better known as Iron Palm.'

Reed was forced to repeat himself in English, for Murphy's benefit. It suddenly occurred to him that having someone who spoke no Mandarin in a meeting with someone who couldn't speak a word of English probably wasn't his best idea. There was little he could do about it, though. He'd have to make it work. Somehow.

Zhang glanced up from his phone, nodding curtly at Reed, before turning his attention to An-ren. His eyes expressed a brief surprise, a flicker of recognition briefly flashing across his face before he was able to force his expression back into its usual disinterested equanimity.

'This your girlfriend?' he asked.

Reed glanced at An-ren before answering. She gave him a sly sideways glance, providing neither encouragement nor discouragement. She was obviously interested to hear how he was going to answer.

'How's Mrs Zhang?' Reed asked, deciding discretion was the better part of valour.

'Six feet under, I hope,' Zhang scowled, but said no more, taking the hint.

Reed pulled a chair out for An-ren, before sitting down next to her.

'Thank you both for coming,' he said, repeating himself in English for Murphy's benefit.

This, he realised, was probably the best he could manage.

'What happened to that creature? The one chasing you on the roof?' Murphy demanded. 'And what was it?'

'Apparently, it was a Xilin. And it's dead.'

Zhang raised his eyebrows at the name.

'Dead? You mean "dead" as in "kicked the bucket"?' Murphy exclaimed, utterly shocked. 'How did you kill it?'

'An-ren killed it. If it wasn't for her, I'd be dead instead.'

Murphy looked at An-ren, awe and respect replacing her earlier coldness.

'I just did what I had to,' An-ren shrugged, although she shuddered inside at the thought of the beast, and what might have happened to Reed, and her, if she'd been wrong.

'You were amazing,' Reed corrected her. 'Some people just ran off.'

Murphy looked away and Reed felt instantly guilty. It was an unfair comment. After all, it wasn't every day you found yourself facing a beast dragged straight from the gates of hell. Most other people would have done exactly what Murphy did.

'What's this about a Xilin?" Zhang demanded.

'I was nearly killed by one on the roof of the Meridian Court Hotel,' Reed told him, switching to Mandarin. 'An-ren earthed it and then finished it off with CO2.'

Zhang looked at An-ren, a different look in his eyes now.

'Not many people can claim to have killed a Xilin,' he said.

'I'll put it on my CV,' she murmured, in English, just loud enough for Reed to hear.

'What were you doing at the Meridian Court?' Zhang asked. 'Was it a photoshoot?'

An-ren rolled her eyes dramatically. So the old man recognised her. At least he hadn't asked for a selfie yet.

'No. We'd gone to an auction linked to the shard economy.'

'Why would you do that? You're crazy! Those people are criminals! And dangerous!'

'Let me explain,' Reed said, irritated now, and concerned the whole conversation was going to wind up going nowhere. He'd asked Zhang there for a reason, and that reason wasn't simply to get him to pontificate about the dangers of secretive auctions.

'The story is this,' Reed began. 'An-ren did a photoshoot the night before last. She was given a wooden hand mirror to use as a prop. But the mirror had a jade shard wedged into it. Somehow, the shard seemed to create a second image on the mirror. One that moved independently of her.'

'A jade shard?' Zhang interrupted. 'Have you still got it?'

Reed reached into his jacket and pulled out the small piece of jade. He handed it to Zhang.

Iron Palm put his glasses on and stared at it, holding it up to the light to try to make out the maker's mark.

'This is Luo Ban!' he exclaimed, looking at Reed and An-ren as if they should be equally concerned.

'What is Luo Ban?' Reed demanded. 'No one seems to know anything, and the internet isn't any help, either.'

'Luo Ban is a who, not a what,' Zhang said, continuing to study the shard. 'From a long time ago.'

'Who is he?'

'He lived 2,200 years ago. His birth name was Meng Yao, but, not long after he became Imperial Preceptor, he cast it aside. He called himself Luo Ban. The Compass. And from that point on he no longer walked as a man, but as the axis of the Wheel.'

'I don't understand,' Reed admitted, glancing at An-ren, whose expression made it clear she had no idea either.

'What are you all talking about?' Murphy demanded, a petulant look on her face.

She clearly felt left out.

'I'll tell you when Zhang's finished,' Reed said. 'Sorry, but this is really important.'

'It's all about the Sepulchral Mandala,' Zhang stated.

'What's that?' Reed asked.

'You ever heard of the Tomb Wheel Dynasty?'

'No,' Reed replied, turning to An-ren. 'Have you?'

'No,' she said, but she began to feel the dark cloud of doom returning at Zhang's words.

She thought about the images etched into the mirrors in her house, and the identical one printed on the auction's invitations. And she remembered her *waipo's* admonishment not to look into mirrors after dark. "The Tomb Wheel watches through cracks."

'They were dark times,' Zhang said. 'The Tomb Wheel civilisation believed the universe was a great turning pattern, a wheel of shifting alignments. They built mirrors that stored memory, resonance engines that behaved like thinking machines, and an intelligence woven from cinnabar and spirit-breath to read the pattern for them. Their rituals weren't mystical; they were calculations. Meng Yao was the last of their scholars, and the most dangerous. He wasn't summoning demons. He was following the logic of a civilisation that thought life and death could be engineered, and corrected.'

Reed and An-ren exchanged a glance. They saw the same thing in each other's eyes. It was almost as if Zhang was speaking a different language. How could any of this be true? An-ren, in particular, knew her country's history. She'd been taught it ad nauseum in school, but she'd never heard any of this, had never read or seen anything anywhere that even hinted at the existence of a civilisation like the one Zhang had described. And yet, she'd seen and experienced enough in the last two days to know she had little choice other than to believe what Iron Palm was saying.

'What happened to him? And the Tomb Wheel Dynasty?' Reed asked.

'History doesn't remember them,' Zhang said. 'But stories do. Outside the cities, in some of the most remote villages, people still tell tales about what happened to the Tomb Wheel, although they don't realise that's what they're talking about. The most common one is about the "Earth-Swallowed Cities." I'm guessing you haven't heard it?'

An-ren frowned, unsure whether Zhang was joking or not.

'I've never sat around a campfire in my life,' she said.

'It goes something like this,' Zhang continued. '"They say the Wheel Lords grew too proud. Their cities shone brighter than the moon, and their voices carried farther than thunder.

'"But pride is heavy. The earth will not carry it forever. One night, the ground groaned like a beast, and the streets folded in on themselves. Towers sank, wheels turned downward, and the people were swallowed whole.

'"Some claim they still live below, turning their mirrors toward us, watching through cracks in the soil. Others swear the Wheel eats its own children, grinding them into glass.

'"So when the wind moans through the valleys, remember. It is the Tomb Wheel turning, and it has not forgotten."'

Zhang looked at An-ren and Reed, amused by the expressions on their faces. It was a dramatic, albeit short, tale. It was even better told outdoors at night, with only firelight and a low wind for company.

'There's another, less poetic, story,' he told them. 'It's said that the Celestial Registry sent their best Daoist masters to confront and defeat Luo Ban, as Meng Yao had become. They fought a long and desperate battle, apparently, before finally defeating him. They shattered his soul into a jade prison hidden somewhere beneath the old foundations of Shanghai. Ironically, the long centuries of urban development that built the city higher and higher kept him dormant.'

'So what's changed?' Reed asked. 'Why are his maker's mark and those wheels suddenly everywhere?'

A chill ran through him as he pictured An-ren's Mirror Room. If any of this was real, her house wasn't just decorated — it was a shrine. He couldn't begin to understand how that was possible. How someone like Luo Ban, an Imperial Preceptor from over two thousand years ago, a man who should have been nothing more than a footnote in a forgotten dynasty, could reach into the present and leave his mark on a room full of mirrors tied to the Tomb Wheel civilisation.

'Modern greed,' Zhang said. 'The shard economy.'

He held up the piece of jade bearing the seal of Luo Ban.

'This jade is charged. Everything bearing his seal is alive, in a way. And every piece that is used, every reflection in a mirror that's linked to these, gives him more power. Models like you,' he said, looking at An-ren, 'are being turned into vectors. He's drawing energy from every bit of attention he gets.'

Reed sat back, shocked. He'd never expected to hear anything quite like that. It made no sense, but, then again, it actually did. He turned back to Zhang.

'An-ren's house has a room full of jade mirrors. Each one has Luo Ban's mark, as well as a wheel etched into the glass.'

'The Sepulchral Mandala,' Zhang muttered, his eyes now fixed on An-ren, a look that merged concern with disbelief etched across his face. 'Where's your house?'

'Wukang Road, in the French Concession,' she responded, irritated that he wanted to know.

'Wukang Road?' Zhang repeated. 'Have you ever heard the joke taxi drivers make about Wukang Road sinking a little lower every year?'

'"The Wheel is pulling her back down",' she said. 'It's never made any sense to me.'

The Wheel. A tight knot began to form in her stomach.

'Who put the mirrors in your house?' Zhang asked.

'I have no idea,' she said. 'They were already there when I inherited the house.'

'Who did you inherit the house from?'

'What business is that of yours?' An-ren demanded.

'I'm trying to understand. I can't help you if I don't know,' he responded, reproachfully.

She sighed. She didn't want to share anything about herself, but, then again, she didn't want to have to face any more dreams with that hideous creature in them, either.

'I inherited it soon after my grandmother died,' she finally said.

'Was it her house?'

'No. I didn't know anything about it until after she passed away. The deeds had been signed in the 1940s by a woman called Zhou Lianhua, but I have no idea who she was. She had my family name, but that's all I know.'

Zhang stared at her, and then at Reed, as if weighing up what he should say next.

'Lianhua,' he repeated. 'Have you ever heard of a woman called Lin Ye?'

An-ren and Reed exchanged an ominous glance.

'I take it you have,' Zhang asked.

'We met her at the auction,' Reed replied. 'And An-ren thinks she may have met some not so human form of her in her dreams.'

An-ren sighed inwardly. She felt like every little bit of her life was being rolled out in public, for all and sundry to see and trample over. She didn't blame Reed, he wanted to help and protect her, but it all felt so intrusive.

'Lianhua is an old name for Lin Ye. She's also known as the Mirror Courtesan.'

'Which makes her what, exactly?' Reed pushed.

'It's complicated. She was many things, including being Meng Yao's most trusted general. But he betrayed her, reshaped her. He made her into a creature of mirrors, tethered to the Wheel's turning.

'What does that even mean?' An-ren demanded.

'It means she is unbound in terms of time and space. She can cross all boundaries, even those of dreams. Meng Yao was defeated and entombed, but she escaped and disappeared. However, sightings of her began to emerge a few years ago, and they've increased in intensity and frequency in recent months.'

'What does she want?'

'Ye serves Luo Ban,' Zhang explained. 'He wants to return and reclaim what he believes is rightfully his.'

'You mean Shanghai?'

'No. He wants to restore the Sepulchral Mandala.'

'But why are they so fixated on An-ren. What's she got to do with any of it?' Reed asked, glancing at her in concern.

'There is another story about the last battle with Luo Ban,' Zhang responded, his eyes moving from An-ren to Reed, and then back again.

As he focused his gaze on her, she felt the knot in her stomach getting tighter. She suddenly didn't want to hear any more. She knew it wasn't going to be good, and she didn't want to hear it, would give anything to wake up and find it was all a terrible nightmare.

'The Daoist masters fought hard,' Zhang said, 'but Luo Ban's forces were formidable, easily their equal. The story goes they were only defeated because his wife betrayed him.'

'What does that have to do with An-ren?' Reed asked, confused.

'The legend gives her name as An Lian,' Zhang answered.

Reed frowned, even more confused. He glanced at An-ren, who was looking impassive. However, he knew her well enough now to recognise some of what was going on below the surface. He could see she was feeling anxious, also confused, and increasingly fearful.

'I still don't get it,' Reed finally said.

'I can't say for sure,' Zhang told him, his eyes remaining on An-ren, 'but I don't think I'd be too far wide of the mark if I suggested Luo Ban believes An-ren is the reincarnation of An Lian.'

CHAPTER TWENTY-FOUR

Reed had noticed the look of intense frustration on Murphy's face. He understood how she felt. He still learned new words and phrases almost every day, despite having lived in China for so long. He was amazed she thought that undertaking paranormal investigations in a language she didn't understand could ever work

It seemed the conversation with Zhang had reached a natural break, so Reed began to explain, in English, everything that had just been discussed.

As Reed spoke, Zhang looked at An-ren. Her face remained impassive, but he knew that look only too well. He'd been a police officer for a long time, and had spent many an hour with victims, witnesses and perpetrators who were completely terrified, but hid behind a mask of assumed indifference.

'You have to stop feeding the mirrors,' he told her.

'I don't even go into that room anymore,' she replied, considering her next words carefully. 'But I've heard things.'

'What things?'

'My name, laughter. Sometimes a man, but mostly a woman.'

'Anything else?'

Isn't that enough, she thought?

'I've had dreams,' she sighed, resigned to having to tell Zhang everything. 'I've been pulled into the mirrors by this thing. I think it's Ye, but she looks like she's made of glass, with translucent eyes.'

'The Mirror Courtesan,' Zhang muttered. 'She must have entered your dreams through that shard.'

'I didn't take the shard home with me. Xiao Wei had it.'

Zhang's lips curled up slightly in amusement at her use of Reed's pet name.

'Unless you slept in the Mirror Room, there must have been a vessel near you. Something Ye could channel to access your dreams.'

'There wasn't anything,' she said, but then a terrible thought struck her. She opened her bag, and, after a moment's hesitation, brought out the ribbon that bore the shard given to her by her *waipo* all those long years ago.

She stared at the tiny green piece of jade attached to it and held it up.

'This was with me,' she said.

She felt sick at the thought of it. She'd carried it around with her for nearly twenty-five years, had believed in the good fortune it brought her. The ribbon was cinnabar coloured and her heart sank when she remembered what Zhang had said earlier.

Zhang reached out for it, but she found she couldn't let it go. It had been such an important, albeit small, part of her life for so long. To think that it might actually have had some sort of demonic impact on her life was devastating. As much for what it might mean about her grandmother, as anything else.

Finally, she let it go, watched as Zhang held it up to the light and studied it closely, moving it into every possible angle.

'It's Luo Ban. No doubt about it,' Zhang confirmed.

'I know,' she muttered.

'You know?'

'We found out yesterday. But it didn't mean anything then.'

'I'll destroy both shards,' he told her. 'It's for the best,' he added, seeing the look of sorrow on her face.

She felt Reed's hand grasp hers under the table. It was warm and reassuring. The room fell silent. An-ren realised the conversation had stopped and both Reed and Murphy were looking at her.

'She can't get to you now,' Reed said, softly, offering her a reassuring smile.

'I hope not,' An-ren murmured, looking away.

'Fiona was telling me about a salon in the French Concession,' Reed continued, his voice louder, looking at Zhang. 'Eternal Seal.'

'That's run by Madame Jiang,' Zhang ventured.

'You know her?' Reed asked.

'Only by reputation. She's quite a player in the shard economy.'

'There's a group there called the Whisper Knife Society,' Murphy chipped in.

She didn't understand what they were saying, but she could recognise the names and guessed what was being discussed.

Reed translated into Mandarin.

'They're called Whisperers,' Zhang said. 'They're dangerous,' he added.

'They can't be any more dangerous than a Xilin,' Reed suggested.

'I wouldn't be so sure of that,' Zhang retorted. 'Have you met that woman Ying Yue?'

'She's a friend of mine,' An-ren answered.

'Is she? Are you sure?' Zhang asked.

An-ren glared at him. Yue had, until two years ago, been her best friend, but had given up on her modelling career, and, it seemed, everything else she valued, in the face of her overwhelming grief. It had been quite a shock to see her standing at the shoulder of Ye, acting like some sort of lapdog.

Another thought suddenly struck her. Yue's fiancé had been killed by a falling mirror, his heart pierced by shards of glass.

She looked at Reed, trying to somehow communicate just how desperate she suddenly felt. Everything she knew and understood had been turned on its head. And the worst thing was she had no idea what could be done. She could deal with prima donna photographers and idiots like Xu Bo, she could even charm the management of *MeiXiu* into eating out of her hand. But this? This was different. She really didn't know how anybody could know what to do.

'There's another thing,' Fiona chirped up.

They all turned to look at her, even Zhang, who had no idea what she'd said.

'I saw this earlier.'

She opened her phone, moved her fingers over the screen, as if enlarging something, and then turned it around to show them all.

'What's that?' Reed asked.

'This is an enhanced enlargement that someone out there in cyberspace made of the image in the mirror from An-ren's photoshoot.'

The face staring out at them seemed the very epitome of cruelty and inhumanity. Two things stood out above all. The first were the deep-set eyes that cut like the sharpest blade, a look of the most callous and contemptuous hatred almost etched into them. The second was the sallow complexion, its skin waxed, almost metallic in the artificial light. Small, pale scars ran along the temple and around the eyes.

This was a face that spoke of malice and brutality.

CHAPTER TWENTY-FIVE

'Is that Luo Ban?' An-ren asked, voicing the question no one else had dared ask.

'His name is only spoken of in legends and myths,' Zhang responded. 'But, on the basis of everything's that happened, I'd say yes.'

An-ren turned away. She didn't want to see him anymore. This was the man, if a creature like that could be called a man, who believed she was the reincarnation of his treacherous wife and who was seeking revenge. She dreaded to think what that might involve.

'You are the nexus and the locus,' Zhang intoned. 'I believe Luo Ban is using you to draw himself back to this world.'

An-ren wanted to tell him to shut up. She didn't need to hear any more. He'd already said more than enough. She couldn't help but wonder if he was getting some sort of perverse pleasure out of her misery. For that was all there was in front of her right now. The misery of a force beyond the grave using her to return to this world, a force whose first action would presumably be to make her suffer. Badly.

Reed glanced at her, pursing his lips slightly. She realised she was squeezing his hand with all her strength. She stopped, let go, but he held on, not willing to let her fingers slip out of his. That, she thought, was some comfort, albeit a small one given what she'd just learned.

'I think we should go and visit Madame Jiang,' Reed suggested, glancing around the group, saying it again in English for Murphy's benefit.

'We?' Zhang queried. 'What's with the "we"? I've come here and told you everything I know.'

'You were a policeman,' Reed argued. 'Don't you want to vanquish evil and put the world to rights?'

'No. I gave all that up when I handed in my badge.'

'You're just like all the rest,' An-ren scowled at him.

'All mouth and no trousers,' Reed added, although he wasn't sure that such a uniquely British aphorism would make any sense in Mandarin. 'You owe me,' he continued, realising Zhang wasn't going to be persuaded by any tugging at his moral fibre.

'I've paid you back by interrupting my class and coming here to tell you what I know.'

'You owe me more than that. I saved your life. Or have you forgotten?'

Zhang stared at him, a resigned expression slowly moving across his face.

'Zhu Wei, you're a good man and, yes, you really put yourself out to help me. Don't think I'm not grateful. But I don't think any of you realise just what's going on here. It's not like Luo Ban's planning to rob a bank, or commit fraud. You don't have any idea just how dangerous he is. Or any of the people working for him.'

'Iron Palm,' Reed responded, hoping the use of his hard-won nickname might help soften the man up slightly, 'you seem to have overlooked one very significant fact.'

'Which is?'

Reed glanced at An-ren. He squeezed her hand slightly.

'We're stuck in the middle of this. We can't just walk away from it. You can. We can't.'

'What are you all talking about?' Murphy interrupted. 'I wish you'd speak in English!'

'Mr tough guy Iron Palm is trying to walk away,' An-ren told her, in English.

Murphy glared at Zhang, not that he cared. He'd barely even acknowledged her existence since his arrival, only looking in her direction when she'd pulled out her phone and shown them the enhanced image from the hand-held mirror.

'You can walk away,' Zhang responded, softly, as if he didn't want anyone else to hear.

Reed sensed a tautening in An-ren's body.

'No, I can't,' Reed told him, a steely look entering his eyes. 'I'll die trying to save An-ren if I have to.'

There was silence around the table. Even Murphy, who didn't understand a word, picked up on the power of what Reed had just said.

'Isn't that a little melodramatic?' Zhang asked, his tone mocking, but Reed recognised it for what it was.

'Maybe it is. Call it what you want. What matters is that it's the truth.'

Reed continued to stare hard at Zhang. He felt something resembling a maelstrom roaring around inside him. Emotions he hadn't felt for years were rising up, his adrenaline pumping hard. He felt guilt, shame even, but, in the midst of all that, he sensed something else, something that gave him some real hope for the future.

When he'd first arrived in Shanghai, hope had been the last thing on his agenda. He'd merely wanted to survive and eke out a bearable existence in a place where no one knew him, a place that had no tangible reminders of the life he'd left behind. The life that had left him behind.

But, as he savoured the warm softness of the fingers held firmly in his right hand, he realised that karma, destiny, whatever you wanted to call it, had returned hope to him. He'd lost it once, he wasn't about to let that happen again.

'You're a selfish man!' Murphy exclaimed, focusing her ire on Zhang. 'How can you not help them?'

Zhang turned to stare at her. He hadn't understood a single word, but he didn't need to, her expression was louder than her voice. What an infuriating woman. Sitting in a Shanghai bar, scolding him in a language he didn't even speak. The world had truly gone mad.

'If I'd known you were going to recruit me, I wouldn't have come here,' he said, turning back to face Reed.

He'd avoided looking at An-ren since Murphy had shown them all the photo. She knew he didn't have the guts to look her in the eyes.

'Iron Palm, we need your help and your expertise. It's that simple. Can you really look at An-ren and say you're not going to help her?'

Zhang stared at Reed, continuing to avoid glancing at An-ren, who was fixing him with a stare that would have withered almost anyone.

'You owe me now,' Zhang sighed, a look of resignation drifting across his face. 'Big time.'

'I was there for you before, I'll be there for you again,' he said.

'That's the sort of man he is,' An-ren interjected.

She wanted to add "unlike you", but reined herself in. He'd only just surrendered, so it probably wouldn't do to antagonise him while the wound was still raw.

'Did he agree?' Murphy demanded, expectantly.

'He did,' Reed told her.

'Reluctantly,' An-ren added.

'So what's next?' Murphy asked.

'We should go to Eternal Seal,' Reed suggested, repeating his words in Mandarin for Zhang, who rolled his eyes dramatically at this unsurprising revelation.

'What will that achieve?' he asked.

'If nothing else, we can gather information,' Reed responded, irritated by the man's negative attitude.

He'd been reluctant to help, Reed, thought, but now that he'd finally agreed, he could at least have been a bit more positive and supportive.

'And then?'

'And then we'll use what we've learned. You were a policeman. Surely you understand how an investigation works?'

'I never had to investigate Luo Ban or Ye.'

Reed shook his head and sighed.

'You should play him *Qing Ye Lament*,' he said to An-ren, in English.

'He looks like the sort of man who'd enjoy it,' she agreed.

'That's the *Silk Night*, isn't it?' Murphy interjected. 'I love that!'

An-ren and Reed shared a bemused glance. For his part, Reed couldn't understand how anybody could even consider listening to it. A shiver ran down his spine every time he thought about the unnatural voice that had filled the Mustang. Each to their own, though.

He looked at his watch.

'Let's meet outside Eternal Seal at 3.00 pm,' he suggested. 'That gives us all time to prepare ourselves.'

He glanced pointedly at Zhang.

'Perhaps we can give you a lift,' he said.

'I'll make my own way there,' Zhang responded, reluctantly adding 'I'll be there!' when he saw the look on Reed's face.

An-ren and Reed got to their feet, an unofficial announcement the meeting was finally over. Zhang and Murphy shuffled their way out of the booth, and Reed walked them to the front door, thanking them both, in their own languages, for coming.

'I'm hungry,' he told An-ren, 'Let's eat.'

CHAPTER TWENTY-SIX

Ye watched Madame Jiang speaking earnestly with Victor Lam and Li Tong. Their discussion meant nothing to her. The shard economy had its uses, a tool, nothing more, but most of it was an irritation she tolerated only because it served Luo Ban's return.

Her thoughts drifted back to the day, two millennia ago, when everything had collapsed. She and Luo Ban had stood with their army and their chiang shi constructs against the Celestial Registry's Daoist sects. They had known a reckoning was coming. They had prepared. The final battle had been long and brutal, and the Daoists should have fallen.

But they'd reckoned without An Lian.

Even now, the memory struck like a blade. Ye's naïve faith in Luo Ban's righteousness had led her into a fate she could never have imagined. He had become her master. Not by choice, but by coercion, by ritual, by the machinery of the Mandala.

An Lian had changed everything. Only now, after centuries of reflection, did Ye understand that Luo Ban had used them both. But An Lian had done something he had never believed she would dare to do.

He had been blind where she was concerned. Even after using her, as he used everyone, he had adored her. And An Lian, deceiver that she was, had let him believe it.

Until the day she shattered everything.

One woman had brought the Sepulchral Mandala to its knees. One woman had destroyed an empire's future. Luo Ban had been broken into his jade prison, and Ye had fled into the mirrors the Daoists used to bind him.

They had waited, patiently at first, then with growing fury as decades became centuries. Neither had expected the wait to last over two thousand years.

Luo Ban's love for An Lian had soured overnight into something monstrous, something no longer human. Hatred was too small a word for what he felt.

Shanghai's explosive growth, and the shard economy it birthed, had finally given Ye the tools she needed to free him.

Finding An Lian's reincarnation had been difficult. There was always uncertainty. But Xiang An-ren was unmistakable. The same face. The same resonance. The same fault line in the world.

The irony of her being a model, a conceptual muse, a vessel for images, was almost exquisite. Through cameras and screens, she had become the perfect vector for Luo Ban's return.

A sound at her side pulled Ye from her thoughts. Ying Yue stood holding an ancient military helmet of hammered bronze, lacquered wood, and faint gilt filigree. The Hollow Helm.

'Is everything ready?' Ye asked.

'Yes,' Yue replied.

There was a look on her face Ye recognised. Human hesitation, human doubt. She had always known this moment would come.

'Is there something you want to say?'

Yue stayed silent.

'Speak,' Ye snapped, her eyes flashing crimson.

'Do we have to do this?' Yue whispered, avoiding her gaze.

Ye's expression hardened.

'I'm disappointed. After everything I've done for you, everything my master has promised. This is your gratitude?'

'It's just... An-ren is my friend. She's a good person. Isn't there any way to do this without hurting her?'

'Let me be clear,' Ye said, her voice turning to ice. 'If you want my master to keep his promise, you will do as you're told. Have you lost your faith?'

'No! I'm committed. But she's always been kind to me.'

'Her kindness is irrelevant. If you fail, you may join Qishan. Is that understood?'

Yue bowed her head.

'I can't hear you,' Ye said, her voice icily sharp.

Yue didn't lift her head.

'Yes. It's clear,' she answered, barely above a whisper.

Ye's expression hardened.

'Good,' she said, making no effort to hide her contempt. 'Put it where I told you.'

She watched Yue disappear into the next room. A brief flare of crimson lit Ye's eyes before she turned back toward Madame Jiang and the two men. She smoothed her expression into a seductive smile, lifted the split of her dress to reveal a pale, flawless thigh, and strode toward them with purpose.

Chapter Twenty-Seven

It was only when An-ren started eating that she realised just how hungry she was. Up until the point she put the food in her mouth, she'd felt slightly nauseous, her stomach tied in knots. But, as usual, it seemed, Reed had the answer.

He'd led her through the alleyways around The Golden Lantern, until they'd arrived at the Lotus and Ledger. She'd heard of it, but had never eaten there before. It was an Asian-fusion restaurant, the sort of place her friends might have called "bijou".

It was bright, minimalist and reasonably empty. The waitress led them to a table by the window, and Reed had graciously allowed An-ren to sit facing outwards. They could have moved their chairs so they could both see out, she supposed, but he seemed far more concerned with food than the world outside.

She enjoyed people-watching, although she was only too well aware that, most of the time, she was the one being watched. But, for once, she could stare out and study everyone wandering past, lost in their own little worlds, unaware of the dark brown eyes scrutinising them.

Although she didn't feel like she could eat anything she ordered Citrus Soy Poached Prawns. After all, Reed had brought her to a restaurant, so it would have been disrespectful not to eat something. But, as soon as the first morsel entered her mouth, her nausea lifted and she became aware of the hunger that burned inside her. She'd used up a lot of nervous energy earlier, and she realised she was now running on fumes.

The food was wonderful. Chilled prawns, yuzu-soy dressing, cucumber ribbons and toasted sesame. She felt a warm glow spreading through her body as she ate, and she began to feel a little better, a little more positive.

Reed had chosen Tea-Smoked Chicken Bao. She hadn't doubted that he'd go for the carnivorous option on the menu. She'd already picked up on the fact that he was an unreconstructed meat eater.

When his food arrived, he ate it with his fingers, but he did so with assurance, carefully and delicately working his way through both buns, not dropping a single crumb.

It was very clear that he was also, as he'd suggested a little earlier, hungry.

An-ren washed her food down with some cold jasmine tea, while Reed indulged himself in the double hit of a single origin espresso and a ginger-citrus kombucha.

Afterwards, they agreed to share a plate of Matcha-Honey Yogurt Parfait. The layers of silken yogurt, matcha granola, honey drizzle and pickled plum presented a refreshing and satisfying counterpoint to the main course.

One plate, two spoons. She liked that. In some ways, she felt it represented the two of them, the separate destinies that karma had somehow woven into one.

When they finished, Reed paid the bill, and they made the short journey back to The Golden Lantern. The bar was now open, and a few early birds had turned up to lubricate their lunchtimes.

Reed chatted for a few minutes with the staff, before he and An-ren went upstairs. She realised that she now thought of it as "the" apartment, rather than simply "his". She wasn't quite sure how she felt about that.

'Did you mean what you said earlier?' she asked, as he turned the kettle on, preparing to make them coffee.

'I said a lot of things,' he smiled at her, 'which one do you mean?'

He was going to make her work for it, she thought. How was it possible their roles had suddenly reversed?

'You know what I'm talking about,' she insisted, not wanting to play that game.

'It was a little melodramatic, wasn't it?' he asked, a mischievous gleam in his eyes.

'Yes, it was,' she replied. 'Was it true, though?'

'Ren-ren,' he said, the gleam fading, replaced by something far more serious. 'Do you really need to ask?'

'An-an,' she reminded him. 'I don't need to ask, I just want to hear it.'

'You've cast your spell on me,' he joked, although she now knew him well enough to see beyond the façade, could see that, underneath the wall he'd built around himself, he meant it. 'It sounds cliched, but I'd do anything for you.'

'Is that about me, though, or what happened back in England?' she asked.

She suddenly felt nervous. She'd never been someone who pussyfooted around or beat about the bush, but this was a deeply personal question. Nonetheless, she needed to know. He'd raised feelings in her she'd kept under a lock and key for so long she'd almost forgotten they still existed. She'd made herself vulnerable and was, it seemed, in extreme danger. As was he. But, nevertheless, she needed to know.

Her heart started to beat faster. She could feel it banging so loudly in her chest that she felt certain Reed would be able to hear it, too.

She looked into his eyes and saw them fill with an overwhelming sadness. A sense of guilt washed over her as she saw the pain her question had caused.

'I'd lost hope,' he finally said. 'I had nothing. I had the bar, I had a life. But that was all I had. A non-existent existence. You've changed that.'

She felt his pain as if it were hers. She realised that, in fact, it reminded her of the pain she carried within her. She'd never really believed in karma, but this moment suddenly felt overpowering.

'Have I?' she asked, not knowing what else to say.

He crossed over to where she was standing and took her hands in his, gazing deep into her dark brown eyes.

'You are the hope I never dared believe could exist,' he told her.

'I'm sorry. I didn't mean to hurt you,' she said, pulling him closer and resting her head on his shoulder.

No one had ever said anything quite like that to her.

'It's okay. Well, it isn't, but I've carried this locked away inside me for so long. I've never told anyone about it, not since I left England.'

'You don't need to tell me anything,' she told him, although she desperately hoped he would, that she could be the one to help him unburden himself of whatever terrible guilt he carried deep within.

Was that selfish, she wondered? To want to be that one person that he could tell his tragic secret to? If it was, she didn't care.

'You're the one person I do need to tell.'

He pulled her in closer, enjoying the sensation of her silken hair brushing against his cheek. She was pressed so tightly against him he could feel how fast her heart was beating. She suddenly seemed very vulnerable, which, he thought, was highly ironic, given the fact that he was the one unlocking a door that he'd kept sealed for nearly a decade.

'A long time ago I was married. I had an average job, an average house, a wife and a daughter.'

He paused for a moment, before continuing.

'My daughter's name was Amara.'

He went silent, and she felt a change in his body. She realised he'd started crying, and she pulled back slightly, gently putting her hand on his cheek and lifting his face towards hers.

'It's alright, Weiwei,' she said, although she knew it wasn't.

How could it be when everything he'd said had been in the past tense?

'It isn't,' he said, tears slowly rolling down his cheeks. 'I'm sorry,' he apologised. 'I've never said any of this to anyone.'

'You don't have to say anything,' she repeated.

'Yes, I do. I need to face it. One day, when Amara was two, just after her birthday, I was getting her out of the car. I'd done some shopping before picking her up from nursery, and my hands were full of shopping bags.'

He paused again. An-ren said nothing, just holding him tight. She already had a terrible foreboding of what he was about to tell her. She felt a wave of powerful emotions beginning to rise up inside her, and she knew that her own tears weren't far away.

He sighed heavily, briefly removing a hand from her back to wipe his eyes.

'I unstrapped her from her car seat, put her on the pavement, and picked up the bags. But she just ran. She ran into the road. I shouted at her to stop. I screamed. But it was too late. There was a car coming. The driver tried to brake, but he was too close.'

'Weiwei,' she murmured, as a tear began to roll down her cheek.

'That was it,' he continued. 'That was my life gone in that moment. One second. That's all it took. She was there, and then she was gone.'

She pulled him tight, held him as close as she could, hiding her face in the curve of his neck so that he wouldn't see her tears. This was his moment, not hers.

'There was nothing you could have done,' she said. 'There can't be a parent who hasn't had a moment like that in their life.'

'But I'm the one whose daughter died. I'm the one who watched her run into the road while I was busy holding shopping bags! I lost her!'

'It wasn't your fault,' An-ren insisted. 'You're only human.'

'It was my fault. Everyone knew that. My wife blamed me completely. Every time she looked at me, all I saw in her eyes was disgust and hatred.'

'You're a good man. No one could believe you'd want that to happen.'

'It wasn't about wanting it to happen. I let it happen. One careless moment, one second when I wasn't watching Amara. And she was gone. She was my responsibility and I failed her.'

He sobbed deeply, as if letting out all the pain and the poison that had built up within him since that terrible day.

An-ren gently disengaged herself from his embrace, and led him by the hand into the living room, sitting down next to him on the settee and pulling him in close once more. It was more comfortable for him than standing in the middle of the kitchen, she thought, and she really didn't know what else to do.

'What happened afterwards?' she asked.

'My wife hated me, her family hated me. Even my own family wouldn't talk to me. I did the decent thing and left. I walked out and I've never been back.'

He learned forward, resting his head on her shoulders, and carried on sobbing. She leaned into him, gently stroking his back with her right hand. She tried to fight back her own tears, but they came anyway. She felt his pain, couldn't even imagine just how devastating it must have been for him. She thought about her mother. No matter how much she missed her, at least it had been the right way round. No parent should ever have to bury their child.

They sat like that for what felt like a lifetime. Her heart ached for him, her tears ran for him, but, at the same time, she felt perversely uplifted, honoured he would have shared something so soul crushing and so intensely personal with her.

The irony of it wasn't wasted on her, either.

After a while, she realised he'd stopped sobbing, and the rise and fall of his chest had settled into a more regular pattern. He sat back, wiping his wet, red eyes, while at the same time studying hers. She was surprised to see anxiety in his expression.

'So now you know,' he said. 'I killed my daughter.'

'You didn't kill her,' she gently reproached him. 'You mustn't think like that. No parent can watch their child every second of every day. You're only human. It was a terrible accident.'

'I would have thrown myself in front of the car if I could have. I'd have given my life for hers.'

'I know you would. But would she want you to suffer like this? Do you think she'd have wanted you to destroy your own life?'

'I don't deserve anything else.'

She gently placed a hand on his cheek, wiping away a single tear that still lingered.

'There are tragedies in all our lives. We owe it to the ones we've lost to move on and live the best life we can.'

He studied her as she spoke these words. He felt weak and despairing, but at the same time, he knew she was right. He'd never been able to accept it, had always found himself mired in self-pity and despair. He wondered if it was even possible he could forgive himself.

'She would forgive you,' An-ren said, as if reading his thoughts. 'You were her father. And she's still with you in your heart, and she still loves you. The real question is whether you can forgive yourself.'

It was a question he'd been avoiding for years. One that he really needed to face up to. Maybe his meeting An-ren had been God's way of giving him a chance to make amends. A way to fix his broken soul and save another.

'I'm sorry,' he said. 'I shouldn't have burdened you with all that.'

'Weiwei,' she admonished him. 'Why are you sorry? It breaks my heart that you carry so much guilt around with you. I understand it, but you are so much more than that.'

'It becomes a way of life.'

Strangely, despite everything, he realised he felt better. He'd never once spoken to anyone about how he felt since the day Amara had died. For years he'd kept everything bottled up, unable to speak to anyone about his feelings since the day Amara died.

'Don't let it be,' she whispered. 'I'm honoured you told me. Thank you.'

'Honoured?'

He looked at her, confused.

'Yes, honoured you felt you could share something so devastating and personal with me. I think you're a good man, probably the best one I know. What happened was awful and I understand how it's become a part of you, but I need you to be here with me now.'

'I am.'

'Then I can feel safe and reassured.'

'Really?' he asked, raising a wan smile. 'You're the one who saved my life.'

'I've got a feeling you'll be getting a chance to return the favour very soon.'

CHAPTER TWENTY-EIGHT

Eternal Seal was a large, sprawling, building, modelled on an ancient pagoda, situated only half a mile from An-ren's house on Wukang Road. Despite its proximity, it was located away from the main thoroughfares, and, until now, she'd never even known it existed.

The building was painted mostly dark green and red, with a few gold flourishes, here and there. The name "Eternal Seal", written in large Mandarin characters, was proudly emblazoned on the wall above the main entrance.

An-ren and Reed had arrived first, and were studying the building from a discreet distance, waiting for Zhang and Murphy to arrive. It was an impressive building, An-ren thought, but there was something ominous about it. She wouldn't have been surprised to find a sign somewhere near the entrance warning those entering to abandon all hope.

Coming here had seemed a logical step, when they'd all been back in The Golden Lantern, discussing the whole crazy situation, but, now that she was here, she wondered what they were actually going to do. She decided not to communicate her doubts to Reed. After all, it wasn't as if there were any significant alternatives.

A taxi pulled up next to them. Murphy clambered out, handing some cash to the driver.

'Hi!' she said to An-ren and Reed, smiling broadly, as she almost skipped over to them.

Murphy stopped in front of them, resplendent in her leather trench coat, clutching her EMF Reader to her chest as if it was her most valued possession, which it probably was, with an expression on her face that reminded An-ren of a child about to be let loose in a toy shop. She was excited, An-ren realised.

'Thanks for coming, Fiona,' Reed smiled.

Ever the diplomat, An-ren observed. She would have been less generous.

'I wouldn't have missed it for the world,' Murphy beamed.

'It's probably going to be dangerous,' An-ren told her, in English.

'I hope so!' Murphy laughed.

An-ren shook her head, bemused. She wasn't sure whether Murphy was a complete idiot, or if her naïve, almost innocent, attitude was just a carefully cultivated act.

She heard a cough behind her, and whirled round. Zhang was standing there, staring at the three of them as if he'd been waiting for days.

'Old Zhang! Glad you could make it!' Reed smiled, shaking his hand warmly.

'As if I had a choice,' Zhang muttered.

An-ren wondered how he'd got there without any of them noticing. The only car that had passed in the last ten minutes was Murphy's taxi. However, she decided not to think about it. Things were becoming so weird that she didn't believe it was worth trying to make sense of anything now.

'Let's go in,' Reed suggested.

'Before we do,' Zhang said, looking at each of them in turn, 'you need to be prepared for things that you won't be able to understand.'

'Like everything that's happened so far?' An-ren asked, unable to mask her irritation. She was beginning to feel anxious. It riled her when Zhang lectured them like some pretentious guru. After all, it wasn't his life on the line.

'No. What you're about to see in there will be strange, and very dangerous. You need to be prepared.'

How on earth could you be prepared for things that you couldn't prepare for, An-ren wondered.

Reed led them towards the vast building, and through the front entrance. The glass doors that fronted the salon simply slid apart as he approached, which took him by surprise. He hadn't been expecting automatic doors.

They entered a small, unremarkable foyer. It was plain with the exception of a single decoration above an inner door bearing the legend 'Eternal Seal, and a large picture of a middle-aged woman filling most of the wall to their left.

As Reed moved forward the doors ahead of him parted, welcoming him, and the others, into the heart of the salon.

They found themselves in a large rectangular room with a high ceiling. Three of the walls were painted red, covered in paintings and tapestries representing scenes from Chinese mythology. Reed recognised some of the fantastic beasts and creatures portrayed, but most he'd never seen before.

The fourth wall was painted a simple white and filled with what appeared to be either complete jade mirrors, or significantly sized shards of broken ones. A crowd of men stood around, some studying the mirrors, others simply talking in small groups.

'Good afternoon, ladies and gentlemen,' a gentle, slightly shrill, voice declared.

They turned to find themselves facing the woman whose photograph was on the wall of the entrance foyer. Reed guessed she was probably around fifty years old, although her shoulder-length hair was still completely black, and her face unlined. She wore a traditional green dress that reached from her neck to the floor, and held a slowly smouldering incense burner.

'I am Madame Jiang,' she continued. 'Welcome to Eternal Seal.'

'Thank you,' Reed responded, bowing towards her, clasping his hands in front of his chest in an old-fashioned gesture of humility.

An-ren stared at him in surprise, while Murphy and Zhang simply bowed.

Madame Jiang stared at each of them, in turn, almost expectantly.

'And you are?' she finally asked.

'We're collectors,' Reed told her. 'We're interested in jade relics from the Sepulchral Mandala.'

Madame Jiang gave him a quizzical look.

'I've never heard of the Sepulchral Mandala,' she said. 'What is it?'

She was lying, Reed could see that. She hid it well, but there had been a slight change in her expression, a brief hardening, before her facial muscles had relaxed into faux bemusement.

'We were hoping you might be able to tell us,' An-ren interjected.

'What are you talking about?' Murphy demanded, clearly irritated by the holdup.

'Don't you speak Mandarin, child?' Madame Jiang demanded, her tone disapproving, her English immaculate and unaccented.

'Well, no, actually.'

Madame Jiang tutted contemptuously, and turned back to face Reed.

'Please do feel free to look around. We always welcome serious collectors at Eternal Seal.' She paused for a moment, before adding, 'And we do need our serious collectors to have serious money.'

She laughed as she said this, but there seemed little humour in her words.

She waited for a moment, bowed, and then retreated, disappearing through a door on the other side of the room.

'Let's split up,' Reed suggested. 'An-ren and I'll check out what's going on over there,' he indicated the group of people milling about near the jade mirrors. 'You two can check out the other rooms.'

Zhang glanced at Murphy, his lips curled in disdain. She merely grabbed his arm and began to drag him away.

'Come on, Iron Palm, let's go and see what we can find!'

He started to protest, glancing at Reed for support, but he simply shrugged.

'Two wise heads are better than one,' he offered.

'But her head's empty!' Zhang protested.

Reed laughed, and watched as Murphy led Iron Palm towards the door Madame Jiang had just disappeared through.

'She was lying,' An-ren told him, as they walked towards the mirrored wall.

'Yes,' he agreed. 'She was. But I wonder why?'

'Perhaps she doesn't know who we are. If the Tomb Wheel shards are really as dangerous as Zhang says, then she might simply be protecting herself.'

Reed nodded, but he knew An-ren didn't really believe that. He seriously doubted that Madame Jiang could really be ignorant of who they were. Everything they'd faced so far seemed to have been carefully choreographed. Why should this be any different?

It soon became apparent that the group around the mirrors and the shards were split into several sub-groups, each engaged in different activities.

Reed and An-ren were both surprised to discover the first group seemed to be oiling some of the jade fragments. One of the men was holding a bottle labelled with the name "Yong Yin You", with the legend "cold-pressed camellia binding oil" printed underneath.

'Can you smell that?' An-ren asked.

'Sandalwood?' Reed responded.

'Cinnabar,' she said.

She had a remarkable palate, he thought. He never would have picked that up. But it was interesting, and possibly significant. For one thing, cinnabar was highly toxic. But, far more importantly, Zhang had told them that Luo Ban drew power from cinnabar infused mirrors.

As the first group continued to oil the mirrors and shards, the second group were standing next to the ones that had already been treated. They appeared to be whispering. Reed got as close as he could without being obtrusive and listened hard.

Each of the eleven men were repeating names over and over again. They all spoke in a dull monotone. He heard the names, but they meant nothing to him.

'Qiū Zhènzhú,'

'Lián Sùjūn.'

'Mò Xuánzhào.'

'Xiang Yèlán.'

'Táng Xuánxuán.'

There were others, but he was too far away to hear.

'Do you recognise any of the names?' he asked An-ren.

She shook her head, but said nothing. He noticed she was holding her left hand at an unusual angle, trying to conceal her phone as best she could while she covertly filmed proceedings.

He hoped no one noticed. That would raise questions they really wouldn't want to have to answer, as well as drawing attention they could well do without.

It was a good idea, though, Reed thought. He had absolutely zero idea of what was going on. If Zhang saw the video, it was possible he might be able to shed some light on what all the polishing and reciting was about.

Reed turned to face the third, and final, group of men gathered around the mirrors and fragments. They appeared to be simply watching.

'Look!' An-ren whispered in his ear, her voice shocked and disbelieving.

As the mirrors and shards were oiled and whispered to, the glass slowly started to move. It was almost as if they were breathing; pulsing and undulating with an inner life. And the third group were studying them, as if monitoring and recording the results.

Reed's phone suddenly pinged. All eyes turned to An-ren and him. She quickly slipped her phone back out of sight, while he pulled his out of his pocket, holding up a hand in mock apology and leading An-ren away from the now hostile looking group.

It was a message from Murphy.

"You need to come and see this. Now!"

He showed it to An-ren.

'She's so dramatic,' she muttered, but followed Reed as he made his way to the door on the far side of the room.

CHAPTER TWENTY-NINE

An-ren and Reed were faced with a scene so surreal it took them a moment to realise just what they were actually looking at.

'Come and have a look!' Murphy insisted, urging them to get closer.

The room was similar to the one they'd just left, albeit considerably smaller. A single, full-sized, jade mirror, disturbingly similar in design to the ones in An-ren's Mirror Room, hung from the plain wall facing them. A group of five men, all dressed completely in black, were ranged around, intently studying the bizarre scene taking place in front of them.

A young woman, dressed in black lingerie, black stockings, suspenders and silver high heels, was shimmying provocatively, apparently replicating a photoshoot, with the mirror replacing the lens.

She patrolled the space in front of the glass with a brash confidence, angling her jaw and fixing her eyes on the mirror with a strident sensuality. Her hips rotated and she gracefully lifted her right leg, bending it at the knee, and reaching down to seductively touch the heel of her shoe.

She straightened her leg and thrust her pelvis forward, at the same time reaching up to her shoulder, slowly pulling the strap on her bodystocking down and easing it over her arm until it hung loose at her side.

'Xiao Yu,' An-ren murmured, disbelief and surprise written all over her face.

'You know her?' Reed asked.

'Yes. She's a model for *XiuShi*. I don't really know her, though. We met once when a photoshoot was double-booked.'

'What's she doing here?'

'She's providing vectors,' Zhang answered, from behind them both. 'She's giving the mirror what it wants. It's using her to open a window into this world.'

Reed didn't know what to say. The implication was all too clear. This was a microcosm of what Luo Ban had been working towards with An-ren since that first tiny shard had found its way into her life.

'This is a dangerous place,' Zhang continued. 'The salon's hospitality masks hunger.'

'Hunger for what?'

Zhang never got the chance to answer. As he opened his mouth, a familiar voice sliced through the room.

'My dear An-ren, and sweet Weiwei! And you've brought friends. Wonderful. A proper party!'

Ye stepped into the light, only a few feet from Reed. Ying Yue hovered behind her like a shadow.

An-ren stiffened beside Reed, edging closer.

'I hope it's not like the last one,' Reed said. 'One of your guests was out of line.'

'You weren't very kind to him,' Ye pouted. 'Your girlfriend was especially rude.'

'What do you want? Why are you here?'

'I want you, Weiwei, of course!'

She laughed lightly and strode toward him.

She lifted a hand toward his face, but An-ren grabbed her wrist. For a heartbeat she held it, then recoiled violently, as if burned. Her expression twisted with shock. She seized Reed's arm and pulled him back.

Ye's eyes flared crimson.

'How dare you touch me!'

'She's not human,' An-ren whispered, voice trembling. 'Her wrist. It was cold. Hard. Like glass.'

Reed's mind flashed back to Meridian Court, the gloves, the chill he'd dismissed. Now her bare skin gleamed like polished ice.

Ye recovered her poise, amusement curling her lips.

'Enjoy your time here, Weiwei. Make the most of it. There isn't much left for either of you.'

She turned to Ying Yue.

'Do it.'

Then she pivoted, and froze when she saw Zhang. She stepped toward him, studying his face.

'You seem familiar,' she murmured. 'Have we met?'

'I've arrested a lot of people,' Zhang said flatly. 'I don't remember them all.'

Ye's expression chilled. She turned away and swept out of the room, Ying Yue following close behind.

'Are you okay?' Reed asked An-ren, taking her hands in his.

'She's not human!' An-ren repeated weakly.

She'd been angry, had intervened to protect Reed, a gesture that had come so naturally she hadn't even had to think about it. But she'd never expected the woman whose hand she'd intercepted would be made of glass. And she didn't even want to think about those crimson eyes.

She thought about her dreams, about the glass creature that had menaced and threatened her. She now knew with absolute certainty it was Ye. She felt sick, a tight knot forming in the pit of her stomach.

All the while, Xiao Yu continued to pose and slowly undress, carefully teasing the mirror, almost seducing it.

'What happened in the other room?' Zhang asked.

'You should show him,' Reed suggested.

'Show him?' An-ren asked, her thoughts still focused on Ye.

'The video.'

'Yes. Of course,' An-ren nodded, pulling out her phone.

They were all silent while the video played, Zhang bending down as close to the phone's speaker as he could to hear what was being said.

Reed wondered where Murphy had gone. He glanced around the room, saw that she was standing by the side of Xiao Yu and the mirror, brandishing her EMF Reader as if it was some sort of Geiger Counter. Which, of course, he realised, it sort of was. Except that it measured electromagnetic fields rather than radiation.

'The oil is marketed as a preserver,' Zhang announced, straightening up as the video ended and Anren put her phone away. 'But it isn't. Well, it is, but it actually has a much more sinister purpose. It's used to fix a shard's memory. I've heard that just a single smear can help a spirit identify the pattern to slip through.'

'What about the names?' Reed asked.

'They're spirits that are being exhorted for various reasons. Qiu Zhenzhu was a lighthouse keeper whose mirror once guided coffins. He's summoned to find buried paths and coastal tombs. Lian Sujun was a concubine who was famous for losing a jade pendant at sea. People call on her for help with memory, names, and vanished faces. Mo Xuanzhao was an obscure geomancer who stamped houses with a Tomb Wheel variant. He's sought out for rites that fix thresholds. Should I go on?'

'Please don't. How do you know all this stuff? We couldn't find anything about any of it anywhere,' Reed asked.

It had occurred to him that Zhang might just have made it all up. That would have been the ideal scenario. And, if it wasn't for the Xilin, he might just possibly have been able to believe it. But that ten-foot-long monster was too real, too lethal, and too hellish to be a figment of anyone's overactive imagination.

'Is that important? I know it, that's all that matters.'

Reed shook his head in frustration. At 10.00 am this morning, Zhang had simply been a retired policeman with some eccentric beliefs and pastimes. But now, Reed really had no idea who he was.

'Look at this!' Murphy squealed, scampering over to them.

She held up the EMF Reader for them all to see.

'Level 5?' Zhang queried, looking remarkably unimpressed.

'What does that mean?' An-ren demanded.

'And what's at level 5?' Reed added.

'The mirror!' Murphy exclaimed, so excited she could barely keep still. Reed got the distinct feeling that she was so excited she didn't know quite what to do with herself. 'A level 5 reading usually occurs when a level 2 or 3 event is a specific type of ghost interaction, with a 33 per cent chance of it being a level 5 emission instead!'

'That doesn't make any sense,' An-ren told her, looking highly sceptical.

'It's a ghost!' Murphy exclaimed, jumping up and down on the spot. 'It's a fecking ghost!'

'Keep your voice down!' Zhang hissed at her, although he hadn't understood a word she'd said. 'Those men are Whisper Knife.'

'I'm guessing that's bad?' Reed asked, surreptitiously glancing at them.

'I told you that earlier,' Zhang scowled.

The men still seemed focused on the mirror and Xiao Yu, who was now topless and performing what Reed understood was commonly called a "handbra". She was standing directly in front of the mirror, smouldering for all she was worth, while at the same time holding her right arm across her naked breasts, covering her nipples.

'Look!' An-ren cried out, grabbing Reed's arm again. 'Look at the mirror!'

Reed did look, although he couldn't quite believe what he was seeing. Just like the mirrors and shards they'd seen in the room next door, this one now seemed to be starting to pulsate and undulate, almost as if it was breathing in time with Xiao Yu's movements, reflecting back her sensual moves and her ever-increasing exposure of flesh.

As they watched, Xiao Yu kicked off her shoes and started to slowly unclip and peel off her stockings, one at a time. As she did so, the mirror continued to pulse in time with her. She seemed almost to be in a trance, oblivious to the warping distortions of the mirror.

Suddenly her reflection broke free of its jade confines. It moved independently now, lowering both hands to expose every inch of its naked body. Xiao Yu woke from her trance, the spell broken the minute the reflection was freed. She stared incredulously at her doppelgänger. It smiled coldly at her, parodying her movements, then touching itself and exposing everything she'd been working so hard to hide.

'No!' Zhang shouted, running towards the mirror.

He raised his hands, and blue streaks, like forks of lightning, began to arc out of his palms. He aimed them at the glass, moving his wrists about as if wrestling with something deep inside.

There were cries of outrage from the onlooking Whisperers. They threw themselves at Zhang, wrestling him to the ground. Iron Palm was strong, but the five men were stronger, and they held him down. He fought and struggled, but all to no avail.

Reed glanced briefly at An-ren and ran over to the melee, hauling one of the black-clad men to his feet and punching him. The man deflected the blow, and tried to kick Reed's legs out from under him. He side-stepped just in time, and managed to land a punch on the man's jaw.

As the Whisperer fell to the floor, crying out in pain, another one threw himself at Reed, hitting him in the midriff. Both men went tumbling to the ground.

Zhang was now faced with only three assailants, and he was able to wriggle free of their attentions. But, as he jumped back to his feet, turning to face the mirror, a deafening explosion ripped through the air.

The mirror shattered into a million fragments, all flying outwards with devastating force.

Everyone instinctively ducked, covering their heads and faces as best they could.

A scream filled the air. A blood-curdling sound that ended almost as soon as it started, followed by a dull thud as something heavy hit the floor.

Reed glanced up, brushing glass off his head and shoulders, checking that An-ren was alright. She was stirring, carefully flicking her hair to get rid of all the shards that had settled on her.

He saw that Murphy was safe, too, and Zhang, and even the Whisperers.

And then he saw Xiao Yu. She was lying on her back in a pool of blood, her body unmoving, her lifeless eyes staring straight ahead.

He rushed over and checked for a pulse. She was dead. That was very clear. She'd been hit by seven large shards from the mirror, all of which appeared to have pierced her heart. But as he noticed the pattern that the shards had formed, he felt a chill run down his spine.

The seven large pieces of glass, seemingly the only large shards thrown out by the mirror, had formed a pattern around her heart. A pattern in the shape of a tomb wheel.

CHAPTER THIRTY

An-ren ran to Reed's side, her eyes fixed on the lifeless body of Xiao Yu.

'No!' she cried, her voice filled with despair and disbelief. 'No!'

Tears began to glisten in her eyes.

Reed put his arms around her and held her close. He was shocked. It had been terrible to see Xu die, his corpse half eaten, but this felt far worse. Poor Xiao Yu, an unwitting and innocent pawn in Whisper Knife's diseased game now lay dead, killed by the very object she'd been employed to work with.

In an instant, the creative and artistic world of visual modelling had been transformed into something both sinister and degenerate.

A loud sound, like a bell being struck, rang out ominously from somewhere nearby.

'What was that?' Murphy asked, looking around fearfully.

'We need to go,' Zhang said.

The Whisperers had now lost interest in Zhang, and were simply milling around. They looked nervous, although Reed didn't understand why. They'd intervened to prevent Xiao Yu from being saved, so it seemed unlikely they'd all suddenly developed a conscience. Clearly her death had been anticipated, had been part of some sick plan.

The bell-like sound rang out again.

'What is it?' Reed asked.

'Your worst nightmare.'

Reed looked at An-ren. She was clearly still in shock, struggling to process what she'd just witnessed.

'Nothing could be worse than the Xilin,' Reed declared.

'You have no idea, Zhu Wei!' Zhang exclaimed, as the sound rang out once more, louder this time.

'What's going on?' Murphy asked.

She held up the EMF Reader. All five lights were flickering insistently, as if the machine were experiencing some sort of seizure.

'It's never done that before!' she cried.

'Look!' An-ren exclaimed, pointing at the door.

They turned just in time to see the wall above and around the doorway start to bulge inwards, accompanied by a loud, crashing sound.

'Shit!' Reed muttered, stepping backwards and grasping An-ren's hand.

'What is it?' she asked.

The room echoed with another terrible collision, and the door, as well as the brickwork around and above it, all collapsed inwards.

Reed heard the sound of running feet behind him, guessed the Whisperers were beating a hasty retreat. He didn't look around, though, he couldn't. His eyes were fixed on the creature that now stood where the bricks and the door had been.

'What the fuck is that?' Murphy demanded, her expression one of complete and utter disbelief.

Standing in front of them was a towering figure in fragmented armour, it's face hidden inside a blank, echoing, helmet. The only indication anything might be inside were the red eyes that glowed through small slits. It was tall, about eight feet in height, and as powerfully built as anyone Reed had ever seen before.

Power blazed through the cracks in the armour, glowing the same red as its eyes. It pulsed deeply, as if in step with its beating heart. The figure stood stock still, its head moving slowly from side to side, as if surveying the scene confronting it.

Reed squeezed An-ren's hand tightly, his eyes fixed on the object in the creature's right hand. It was holding a *guandao*, a heavy polearm with a vicious curved blade on top of the shaft. It was a massive weapon, and all the ones he'd seen before, usually in historical re-enactments, had required the warrior wielding them to use both hands. This creature, or whatever it was, held it in one hand, swinging it around, almost playfully, as if it were as light as a feather.

'The Moquai of the Hollow Helm!' Zhang gasped.

'The what?' Reed demanded, unable to take his eyes off the *guandao* that was still arcing through the air.

'It's the undead spirit of a disgraced Tomb Wheel general,' Zhang explained. 'The Moquai was buried alive for betraying the dynasty in a failed coup. His helmet was sealed in a Tomb Wheel chamber designed to spin endlessly, trapping his spirit in disorientation for eternity.'

'He's not trapped now,' Reed muttered.

'Obviously someone, or something, released him.'

The Moquai rested its eyes on An-ren, the red glow seeming to almost drill its way deep inside her skull.

'An Lian!' it spoke. Its voice most closely resembled a chorus of inhuman whispers, emanating from somewhere inside the helmet. 'My master will deal with you later.'

'I'm not An Lian!' An-ren retorted, but she was too scared to feel any anger.

She tightened her hold on Reed's hand.

The large helmet turned slightly, now focusing its attention on Reed.

'Zhu Wei!' it spoke. 'You will die!'

'No!' An-ren screamed.

The Moquai ignored her, its red eyes not moving from Reed. It began to march towards him.

'Don't look at it!' Zhang shouted.

Reed tried to turn away, but found he couldn't. His eyes were locked on the creature, and he couldn't shift them, no matter how hard he tried. As the Moquai approached, he felt a blurring all around him, a disorienting sensation, as if time and space had begun to loop and stutter.

He could hear screaming coming from somewhere nearby, realised through the fog in his head that it was

An-ren and Murphy, and that a hand was trying to drag him away. But he couldn't move, his feet and legs felt as if they were set in concrete, his muscles screaming with every step he tried to take.

The Moquai towered over Reed. It raised the blade ready to strike.

He stared up into the blazing red eyes shining out from the helmet, desperately trying to focus, to draw on every ounce of mental energy he could muster to clear his head, to find a way to move. But he simply couldn't think.

As the blade came arcing down, sweeping viciously through the air towards his head, he felt something crash into him, found himself falling through the air towards the ground, pushed sideways, away from the *guandao*.

'Zhu Wei!' a voice shouted into his ear. 'Zhu Wei! Snap out of it.'

It was Zhang, lying on the floor next to Reed, having thrown himself at him just as the blade came slicing down.

'It's got a Disorientation Field!' he explained. 'It can warp spatial perception. You mustn't look at its eyes!'

Reed looked at Zhang, forced himself to focus on what was being said. He realised that now he'd broken eye contact with the creature, his head was beginning to clear, although he still felt dulled and blurred.

He glanced over towards An-ren, who had been dragged away from the Moquai by Murphy. She was glancing between the creature and Reed, naked terror in her eyes.

'You need to get away!' Zhang screamed at Reed. 'An-ren's safe! It doesn't want her. It wants you! Go!'

Zhang was already back on his feet, hauling Reed back up.

The Moquai turned to face them, its movements jerky, almost as if it were being worked by invisible strings. It began to stride towards Reed, raising the blade again as it did so.

'I said go!' Zhang shouted, pushing Reed as hard as he could.

Reed glanced back at An-ren, paralysed with indecision. He knew he needed to run, but he also couldn't just leave her behind. He'd made her a solemn promise. He couldn't just go back on his word because he was about to die.

'Go!' she shouted. 'It's alright! You must keep yourself safe!'

'But what about you?' he demanded.

'You heard it! It doesn't want to harm me. You have to run, Xiao Wei! I'll find a way to stop it!'

Reed locked eyes with her for a moment, trying to tell her with that simple gaze that he loved her, that she was the most important thing in his world, and that he was sorry. Then he turned and ran towards the door on the other side of the room, the one the Whisperers had disappeared through.

The Moquai lumbered after him.

Zhang raised his hands and the blue energy that he'd summoned before once again sparked and crackled, filling the air with the smell of ozone as it built to an almost blinding intensity. He threw his hands forward, sending the energy smashing into the creature's midriff. It ground to a halt, jerking slightly as the energy beams hit it. It staggered backwards for a moment, transfixed by the beams, and Zhang moved his hands around, focusing his power as best he could.

'You have to find the helmet!' Zhang shouted at An-ren and Murphy.

'But it's wearing it!' An-ren called back.

'No! This is just a manifestation!'

An-ren was sceptical. It was possibly the most tangible manifestation of anything she'd ever seen. Even more so than the Xilin.

'Find the real helmet!' Zhang shouted, still shifting and repositioning his hands, trying to find the best angle to contain the creature. 'There's a small funerary mirror inside somewhere. It'll look like a bead, dark as mercury. That's the lodestone! It allows the Moquai to hold its form.'

'What do I do with it?'

'You have to say his name at the same time as you destroy it!'

'But I don't know his name!'

'Lu Shen!'

As Zhang uttered its true name, the Moquai raised its blade and sliced viciously downwards, cutting the sizzling energy beams in half. Zhang gasped and staggered backwards.

The creature strode past him, relentlessly following the direction Reed had taken.

CHAPTER THIRTY-ONE

Reed's head slowly cleared as he ran further into the interior of Eternal Seal. The door he'd gone through had led him into a smaller room, filled with yet more jade shards and mirrors, haphazardly piled against two of the walls. Without pausing, he threw the next door open and hurried through.

As he did so, he heard a tremendous crashing sound behind him as the Moquai broke through the doorway into the room behind him. He was scared, had no idea what he might do, but also felt a vast sense of relief that the creature was pursuing him, and not An-ren. That meant she was safe.

At least from the Moquai.

In the heat of the moment, he'd forgotten about Ye. His heart sank at the thought, but he comforted himself with the knowledge that Old Zhang and Murphy were with An-ren. Murphy might not be much use, but Zhang clearly had some powers and skills he'd kept quiet about. Reed couldn't help but wonder just how many retired Shanghai policeman could blast Xilin-like rays of electricity out of their hands.

Reed opened a door on his right and found himself facing a flight of descending stairs. Going further down didn't seem a great option, could only really end up with him becoming trapped. But, if he could somehow find his way outside, surely the creature wouldn't pursue him into the French Concession in broad daylight?

He knew, however, that this thought was little more than a self-indulgent conceit. A single-minded killing machine, as the Moquai obviously was, wouldn't care where it slaughtered him.

The wall behind him crashed down as the creature strode through the rubble towards him. It cut off the only other exit, and Reed was forced to take the stairs.

The small strips of emergency lighting in the ceiling cast a weak glow into the room. He saw a switch, but left it off, hoping the Moquai's night vision was no better than his own.

The light was no better down here and he had to squint to see in the semi-darkness. The space was a sort of storeroom. The walls were lined with cupboards and lockers and the floor littered with crates and boxes. With all the stuff scattered around, it resembled a crazy obstacle course

A loud noise from somewhere behind him told him that his pursuer had arrived on the stairs.

He ran into the room, aware that one wrong step could be the difference between escape or an unpleasant fate at the hands of the Moquai. He looked for a weapon, anything he could use to defend himself, not really believing anything could be an effective defence against a hellish creature like the Moquai.

He felt a draught of cool air from behind him, and threw himself to one side, just as the *guandao* came crashing down, missing his head by inches, and brutally slicing through a nearby crate. It shattered noisily, sending shards of wood and bits of its contents into the already treacherous mix of junk lying strewn around them.

Something glinted in the dim light, and Reed realised it was a sword. He darted forward, almost to the feet of the Moquai and grabbed the blade, quickly retreating and unsheathing it. He held it in his hand, gauging its power and weight. He recognised it as a *liuyedao*, a heavy sword. It was nowhere near as powerful as a *guandao*, but it was better than nothing.

The Moquai's blade came scything down again. Reed backed away, bringing up his own sword to parry the blow. The blades connected with a savage clash of metal on metal. Reed was knocked backwards with the force of the contact, almost dropping the *liuyedao* in the process.

He rolled to one side, narrowly avoiding the Moquai's blade as it came crashing down towards him. He jumped to his feet and scampered over to the other side of the room. His hands ached painfully from the force of the blow he'd parried, and he seriously doubted he'd be able to fend off many more attacks like that, even if his sword could.

He looked around desperately, searching for a door, but the wall was blank. He was trapped. His only hope was to coax the Moquai away from the door so he could escape back up the stairs.

The creature strode purposefully towards him, and the *guandao* once again sliced through the air, exploring an exaggerated arc as it targeted Reed. He brought up the *liuyedao* and parried the strike.

As the blades met, a cracking, shattering sound of metal filled his ears. He watched dismayed, as half of his blade flew off, hitting the wall behind him and bouncing away and out of sight.

In desperation, he threw the hilt at the Moquai, and it bounced off its helmet. The creature didn't even seem to notice.

He searched the room for something, anything, to help him getaway. Next to him a line of crates he hadn't seen before led to some ceiling ducting hanging invitingly near the left wall. He leapt onto the first crate and ran along them, launching himself as he neared the end.

As his fingertips fastened themselves around the pipes and he pulled his legs up, trying to wrap his feet around the ducting, he was suddenly very thankful for his height.

He felt a cold breeze sweep past his face, and realised the *guandao* had just missed him by inches. The creature slashed again, but the blade flew past him once more, missing by no more than four inches.

Reed breathed a sigh of relief. He was just high enough that the Moquai couldn't reach him. He knew it was only a brief respite, a moment of calm giving him a few precious seconds to think about how he could fight back. He moved a hand slowly, and tested the ceiling panels but nothing moved. He felt his grip begin to weaken.

He noticed vivid blue light sparking on the other side of the room, somewhere near the stairs. The arcing energy beams got closer, and Reed realised, with an enormous sense of relief, that it was Zhang.

He was under no illusions about his chances of survival. After all, Zhang hadn't been able to inflict any significant damage on it earlier. But at least he was no longer alone in his desperate fight.

'Are you okay?' Zhang shouted, as he angled his palms towards the Moquai, sending two huge balls of intense energy flashing from his hands to engulf the creature..

The Moquai staggered backwards, clearly unprepared for Zhang's counterattack.

'I've been better,' Reed responded.

The Moquai turned to Zhang and slashed wildly with its *guandao*, slicing through the arcing blue beams, knocking Iron Palm backwards. He collided with a crate and bounced off it onto the floor.

The creature picked up another crate, as if it were no heavier than a feather, and threw it at Reed. He had no way to defend himself, and he cried out in pain as the heavy wooden box hit him side on. He fell, landing hard on the unforgiving floor. The height of his fall added to the impact and pain coursed through every inch of his body. As he tried to move, his winded, bruised and aching body screamed in protest.

He looked up to see the Moquai towering over him.

'Zhu Wei will die,' it hissed in its ghostly voice, raising the *guandao* high above its head.

So this is how it ends, Reed thought.

He'd lived half a life for so long, hiding from the darkness that constantly threatened to consume him. And now, just when he'd found a reason to live, a reason that promised both redemption and resurrection, he seemed fated to die on a hard, unforgiving concrete floor in the basement of Madame Jiang's salon of the damned.

As he stared up at the large blade, glinting in the dim light, it occurred to him this was surely the final proof, if any were needed, that there was no god. Of any sort. Of course, when that blade eviscerated him, he'd find out first hand, although, by then, it would be far too late. He had no doubt that he'd crossed too many bridges to have any realistic hope of eternal life.

The blade suddenly scythed downwards. Reed stared at it, feeling strangely numb. He wasn't a coward. He didn't want to die, but he wasn't scared of death, either. There'd been times over the past decade when he'd actively craved it, but now, of course, things were different.

A blinding electric blue light suddenly arced across his face, and Reed felt his hair stand on end as the primal force narrowly missed him as it headed for the Moquai. Even more significantly, the *guandao* stopped short, deflected sideways by the energy field, bouncing onto the floor.

'Get up!' Zhang shouted.

As the blue rays rapidly faded, Reed forced his battered body to roll away, and he painfully clambered back to his feet.

Zhang was poised in front of the Moquai, his hands stretched out in front of him, beams of pure power now focused on the long-dead creature, filling the space between them. His face was a picture of concentration and effort.

'Thank you,' Reed said.

'Thank me when it's all over. If we're still alive! Now go!'

Reed didn't need a second invitation. He dragged his bruised body towards the stairs. But he was stopped in his tracks by a loud cry of pain. He turned to see Zhang being swatted out of the way by the Moquai, and then, far too late, he noticed the crate flying towards him. He tried to move, but there was no time.

It hit him full on, and the last thing he remembered before everything went black, was the sight of the Moquai striding purposefully towards him, *guandao* raised above its head, ready to strike.

CHAPTER THIRTY-TWO

An-ren watched in horror as the Moquai disappeared off in the direction Reed had taken, with Zhang in close pursuit. She was rooted to the spot, her every instinct telling her to go after them, to do what she could to help him.

It was clear this creature was far more formidable than the Xilin had been. That hideous beast had been as dangerous as anything she'd ever encountered or read about, but it had been just a beast. The Moquai had once been human, and therefore presented a far more sophisticated threat. Even Zhang's unbelievable powers had no significant effect on the thing.

Zhang's powers. He'd used them first on the jade mirror that had killed Xiao Yu. She'd been shocked at the sight of the vivid blue arcs of energy issuing from his hands. She couldn't help but be reminded of the Xilin. She had no idea how he was able to do that, or what they were, but none of that was important. Not right now, anyway. What was important was that he might be able to use his powers to save Reed.

She forced herself to breathe deeply, to bring the raging emotions inside her under control.

'What did Zhang say?' Murphy demanded, interrupting An-ren's thoughts.

'We have to find the creature's helmet.'

'But it's wearing it!'

'There's another one. It's got a funerary mirror inside, something that looks like a mercury-coloured bead. We need to find it.'

'Then let's do it!'

Murphy began to move, but An-ren grabbed her arm.

'Not that way. We came from there. It must be somewhere through here.'

An-ren led the way, Murphy following, still clutching her prized, and now very dormant, EMF Reader to her chest.

They entered the room Reed had run through earlier. An-ren paused by the open door that leading down into the basement. She could hear noises, sounds that sent a chill racing down her spine.

She felt an overpowering urge to race down the stairs, to do whatever she could to help. But she forced herself to focus, to stay in the moment. Zhang had been very clear. The best way she could help Reed was to do exactly as he'd suggested.

So, very reluctantly, her heart pounding in her chest, she hurried on, pushing open the door directly ahead of them.

It opened into a gallery space. Paintings of dragons and diabolical creatures lined the walls. Display cabinets filled the large room, most filled with reliquary items and demonic masks.

'It's all so creepy!' Murphy muttered, glancing around with disdain.

'That isn't the word I would have used,' An-ren said, looking around, desperately trying to see something that looked even vaguely like a helmet. But there was nothing.

She moved on, running now, Murphy close behind, wondering how someone could move so fast in such ridiculously high shoes.

An-ren opened the door facing them, and found herself in a wide foyer, with a glass front, and a door that led out onto the street. The room had a reception desk, which was unstaffed, and a set of chairs, as if it was some sort of waiting room. But there were no relics, no exhibits, nothing that even vaguely resembled a helmet.

An-ren turned back, unable to hold back the terrible sense of panic rising within her. She knew Reed wouldn't have long. No matter how bravely he fought, no matter how resourceful he was, she knew he wouldn't be able to keep a monster like that at bay for ever. She had to act now, she had to do what only she could do to save him.

She ran back into the room they'd just left and stared around, intensely scrutinising every item, cabinet, painting, anywhere that suggested a hiding place.

She paused in front of two paintings. They depicted either the Xilin or the Moquai, creatures that had invaded her life so recently. That, she thought was quite a coincidence. She turned back to face the rest of the room. The gap between the paintings was bigger than those between any others.

She looked back, and carefully ran her fingers over the wall.

'There's a door here!' she exclaimed.

When she focused, she could just make out the lines that formed its edge. But there was no handle, nothing that might open it.

She turned back to the room once more, looking around desperately for something that might help. But there was nothing. And then she had an idea.

She ran back to the foyer, picked up one of the very functional looking metal chairs and carried it back. She stood in front of the hidden door, poised.

'Are you ready?' she asked Murphy.

'I was born ready!'

An-ren rolled her eyes. Why did the woman have to be so consistently melodramatic?

She raised the chair and brought it crashing down, as hard as she could. The door splintered and fell inwards, revealing a flight of stairs leading upwards.

An-ren raced up them, Murphy close behind.

There was a small landing at the top, with a single door straight ahead of them. An-ren didn't hesitate. She grabbed the handle, turned it and pushed the door open.

The room was brightly lit, although there were no windows. It was empty, save for a single table rising up in the centre of the room. A table holding one item, a lacquered, hollow object with no eye slits, carved with weeping dragons. The Hollow Helm of the Moquai.

An-ren's heart sank as slow, mocking applause echoed behind them. She didn't need to turn to know who it was.

'Bravo,' Ye drawled, a cruel smile curving her lips.

Ying Yue stood at her side, Madame Jiang looming behind them.

'You didn't need to break the door,' Ye added lightly. 'Press down and it opens.'

'Why are you doing this?' An-ren demanded, fury flashing in her eyes.

'Your boyfriend is a fly in the ointment, An-an.'

'Then take me! You don't have to hurt him. He hasn't done anything.'

'He's done far too much. He put himself between you and us. Your time is coming. He's just an inconvenience.'

'I am not An Lian!' An-ren shouted.

'My master believes you are. That's all that matters. You'll resurrect him whether you're her or not.'

An-ren turned to Yue, who kept her gaze fixed on the floor.

'What did they promise you?'

'They are the light and the way,' Yue murmured.

'Did you see Xiao Yu's body?' An-ren pressed. 'Did you see what they did to her?'

'There are victims in every war,' Yue said, though her voice wavered.

'This isn't a war. Yu was just a woman with dreams, like you once had.'

'Sacrifices must be made.'

'She didn't sacrifice anything. She was murdered. Did you see her chest? Did that remind you of anything?'

Yue's eyes snapped up, fire burning behind them, but An-ren couldn't tell who it was meant for.

'Qishan will be reborn!' Yue cried. 'I'll have him back!'

'And will Xiao Yu come back too? Is Luo Ban resurrecting her?'

'You're wasting your breath,' Ye hissed. 'And you don't have much left.'

'She died like Qishan! Can't you see what's happening? They're using you. You're helping bring Luo Ban back, and they'll discard you the moment they're done.'

While the argument raged, Murphy edged behind Ye. She lifted her EMF reader and brought it down hard.

A sharp crack rang out. Ye collapsed to her knees with a cry. Madame Jiang lunged at Murphy, but Yue stepped between them, caught in the crossfire.

Ye touched her head, staring at the blood on her fingers. Her face drained of colour.

An-ren seized the moment. She grabbed the helmet and turned it over. It was empty. Panic surged. Zhang had been right about everything else. Reed's life depended on this.

She searched the interior, fingers probing every seam, and found a false lining. She dug her nails in and tore it free. Something small rolled into her hand. A bead, quicksilver-bright.

She set it on the table, unstrapped her shoe, and raised it to strike. She had just drawn breath to speak the Moquai's true name when a blow knocked her sideways.

The world spun.

Ye's voice cut through the haze.

'You can't save him,' she hissed. 'He's probably already dead. The Moquai doesn't stop.'

'Take me instead!' An-ren gasped. 'Just let him live!'

'You're tiresome,' Ye sighed. 'The star-crossed lovers! One destined to die in a basement, the other fated to restore the Sepulchral Mandala.'

'And what do you get out of it? You're not even human. Why would Luo Ban want you?'

Ye's expression twisted, contempt giving way to something darker.

'My master needs me, An-an. He is nothing without me. And his return is only the beginning.'

'Your promises mean nothing. Look at Yue! Qishan isn't coming back. Does she know you killed him?'

Ye sneered.

'Yue is pathetic. She clings to her grief like a trophy. But she's useful.'

An-ren lashed out with her legs. Ye stepped aside, straight into Yue's path.

Yue swung the Hollow Helm in a wide arc. It struck Ye's head with a shattering crack.

Ye staggered. Fine fractures spread across her face like spiderwebs, her perfect features splintering as the cracks deepened. Her eyes glazed, rolling upward for an instant, before she crumpled, falling to the floor, silent and unmoving.

Yue reached down and helped An-ren to her feet. They watched as Murphy wrestled with Madame Jiang, trying to get into a position where she could batter the older woman with the EMF Reader. The device really was far more useful than it had appeared, An-ren thought.

'You'd better do it, before it's too late,' Yue urged her.

'Thank you,' An-ren said.

There were tears on Yue's face. An-ren knew they were for Qishan, that she had finally thrown off the shackles of her denial and accepted the truth that had been staring her hard in the face for so long. And she knew there would be a heavy price

It was hard to imagine that there wouldn't be a heavy price to pay for such treachery.

An-ren raised her shoe above her head once more, and, as she brought the heel crashing down onto the quicksilver bead, she screamed the name, channelling all her frustration and fear into those two words.

'Lu Shen!'

The bead exploded into a thousand tiny fragments that flew out in every direction.

The room began to vibrate, the door suddenly started to open and shut of its own volition. An-ren felt a sudden dizzying light-headedness. The room began to swim around her. She fell to her knees, clutching her scalp as the most excruciating pain suddenly gripped her head.

The vibration increased, until it felt as if the entire building was going to shake apart. And, then, just as suddenly as it had started, it stopped. The room was still, filled with an almost oppressive silence.

As her head began to clear, An-ren looked around the room, just in time to see Murphy bring her beloved EMF Reader crashing down on Madame Jiang's head. The older woman collapsed onto the carpet, its red brocade hiding the blood that began leaking onto it. Despite herself, An-ren smiled as she took in the self-satisfied look on Murphy's face.

She frowned slightly at the dent the impact on the bead had left in the heel of her shoe, then quickly put it back on and got to her feet

Destroying the funerary mirror and saying the creature's name had done something, but the question was, had it been enough? And, even more significantly, if it had killed the Moquai, had it been in time to save Reed?

Without waiting for either Murphy or Yue, An-ren ran out of the room and down the stairs.

CHAPTER THIRTY-THREE

Reed opened his eyes to a vision of almost indescribable beauty staring down at him, concern and worry etched deep into her dark brown eyes.

'Have I died and gone to heaven again?' he asked An-ren, smiling weakly.

'You're alive!' she exclaimed, the tension easing out of her body, a small smile finding its way onto her lips.

'An-ren saved your life,' Murphy told him, standing to one side, next to Zhang.

Again, Reed thought. Never in his wildest dreams had he imagined, when he first saw her at the Lumen House Hotel, that she would be so proficient at killing creatures from hell.

'I couldn't have done it without Fiona,' An-ren conceded.

Reed glanced at her. That was some admission, he thought, given how she'd felt about Murphy up to now. He'd always suspected the Irish woman had something about her. He couldn't believe that anyone could be quite so naïve and reckless without having something secreted away to back it up.

'I found a new use for the Reader,' Murphy explained, holding up the device, which appeared a little the worse for wear, its uniform grey now mottled with patches of dark red.

Reed glanced around, saw the vast bulk of the prone Moquai out of the corner of his eye, and immediately sat bolt upright. He groaned with the effort, his body and muscles protesting painfully at every movement.

'Stop!' Zhang barked, as Reed tentatively reached out a hand. 'It might be dead, but its suit of armour is active. If you touch it, you'll start to lose fragments of your past.'

'We should go, Xiao Wei,' An-ren said. 'We need to get out of here while we can.'

He nodded and started getting to his feet. He winced as yet more pain coursed through his body.

An-ren leaned in, placing her hands on his torso to help. Murphy stepped closer, as if to add her strength, but when she saw the look An-ren threw at her, she backed away again.

Zhang marched off without waiting, taking the steps two at a time.

Murphy chased after him. An-ren was intrigued by the look on the other woman's face as she followed Iron Palm. She suspected that the brusque and irascible spirit warrior had won himself an admirer.

Reed winced as he walked. The crate had been heavy and he dreaded to think what might have been in it. Probably a consignment of Tomb Wheel jade. Either way, it had packed a punch.

Once again, he'd been lucky. He'd been at the mercy of another of Ye's demonic beasts. He glanced at An-ren, who seemed to be busy watching Zhang and Murphy. He was definitely lucky, there was no question about that.

As they started up the stairs, they heard the sound of shouting from up above. Reed hurried his pace, running the rest of the way to the floor above, ignoring the protests from his wounded body. He burst into the small room to find Zhang engaged in combat.

Five black-clad men, the Whisperers who'd watched so rapaciously as Xiao Yu had been killed by the jade mirror, were throwing punches and kicks. Standing just behind them, apparently orchestrating events, were Victor Lam and Li Tong, who he recognised from the auction at the Meridian Court.

Zhang, for his part, seemed unconcerned, returning their very basic attacks with some fancy moves of his own, landing kicks and punches as he danced around them.

Reed waded in, throwing a punch into the kidneys of the man nearest him. The Whisperer cried out, and whirled around, windmilling a punch towards him. Reed stepped to his left and drove his right fist hard into the man's stomach. As the Whisperer buckled over in pain, Reed brought his knee up into the man's face, as hard as he could. Blood burst from the man's nose as he reeled away.

Reed turned to where Zhang was still elegantly executing his mostly *quan fa* blows with precision and style. He couldn't help but be impressed that someone who appeared so large and thick-set could be so light on his feet and move with such apparent grace. As Zhang landed yet another blow, Reed noticed Murphy staring at Iron Palm with something approaching awe.

An-ren picked up one of the large jade mirrors resting against the wall nearest her, and brought it crashing down on the head of the Whisperer nearest to her. The glass shattered, showering the man with hundreds, if not thousands, of vicious shards, the blow to his head sending him reeling to the floor.

As Zhang and Reed finished off the two remaining Whisperers, Lam and Li glanced at each other, sharing a look of anger and frustration, then turned and fled back into the room where Xiao Yu had died.

An-ren briefly considered chasing after them, but she reined herself in, tried to think clearly through the adrenaline that was now flowing. It would have been a crazy thing to do, and would probably have played straight into their hands. She'd never been in a fight in her life before, not even as a child, and, whether they had any martial arts skills or not, they both looked powerful. And there were two of them.

She thought about Xiao Yu. She felt a wave of guilt sweep through at the thought of leaving her behind, but she didn't know what else they could do. If they went back for her body, they'd run the risk of running into Ye again. That thought terrified her.

The sight of Ye's face cracking into shards like one of her jade mirrors had been beyond horrifying. It was the final damning proof, as if any were really needed, that she wasn't human. An-ren shivered as she remembered the shattered face. She wondered how long an inhuman creature could take to recover from such a vicious attack, and whether she was merely comatose, or dead.

An-ren worried about her friend Yue. She'd heard Ye's words of mockery, and had responded in anger and desperation. But there would be a price to pay, there was no doubt about that. A very heavy one.

She wanted to find Yue, lead her to safety, but, at the same time, she knew that every moment they lingered in the salon left them more likely to be confronted by either Ye, or yet another of her creatures. And the next one might be truly unstoppable.

She turned back to the fight, which was now in its dying moments.

Zhang launched a vicious attack on his final opponent's midriff, raining punches in, and standing back to admire his handiwork as the man sank to the ground, beaten and unconscious.

Reed parried a punch, stepped to the side, and found a fist coming straight at his jaw. The contact hurt, but it just made him angry. He was tired of being chased and battered. He drew his fist back and threw it at his opponent as hard as he could.

The Whisperer had let his defence down when he'd attacked, and the blow careened into his cheek and nose. He reeled away, clutching at his bleeding face. Reed kicked him as hard as he could between the legs and delivered another haymaker to his jaw. The man collapsed in a bloody heap at his feet and lay still, his hands between his legs, moaning in agony.

'Let's go!' Zhang barked, heading towards the door that Lam and Li had escaped through.

'No!' Murphy retorted, heading the other way. 'This way's better!'

Zhang stopped and stared at her. He didn't understand a word, but he clearly picked up on her tone. He turned and followed her.

Reed and An-ren hurried after them. As Reed reached the next door, he realised that An-ren was no longer beside him. He turned back, saw her standing next to the smashed door that led to the room where the Moquai's helmet had been hidden. He hurried to her side.

'We need to go,' he told her.

She looked up the stairs, her expression mixing fear and worry.

'We need to take Yue with us.'

'Is she up there?'

'I don't know. That was where the helm was, where we fought Ye and Madame Jiang. But I have no idea what she did after we left. I just needed to find you.'

'You stay here,' Reed said. 'I'll go and have a look.'

'No!' An-ren exclaimed. 'If Ye's there, she'll kill you!'

'But we can't just leave Yue behind,' Reed responded, thinking about the lifeless body of Xiao Yu on the other side of the building.

'Let's go together,' An-ren sighed.

She didn't want to go back up there, but she knew that if she left without looking for Yue, then the guilt would be overwhelming. Her friend had made some bad decisions, had probably been implicit in everything that had happened, but she'd suffered, had made those bad decisions in the context of overwhelming grief. The bottom line was that she was An-ren's friend.

Reed grabbed her hand and led the way up the stairs, listening intently every step of the way. He had no idea what they'd do if they came face to face with Ye or Madame Jiang, but he'd deal with that if it happened. He prayed that it wouldn't.

He pushed the door open slowly. The room was empty.

'They're gone!' An-ren said.

Even the helmet had gone. She wondered why they'd bothered taking it, hoping it didn't mean the Moquai could be resurrected. She noticed something glinting on the carpet where Ye had fallen. She crossed and crouched down to take a closer look.

It was glass. Tiny fragments of glass. Pale, flesh-coloured glass.

She stood back up and hurried to the door.

'Let's go,' she said.

He followed her back down the stairs, and then into the foyer, relieved to see the sanctuary of the outside world through the large window that covered the far wall.

The entrance door slid open as they approached and they hurried outside.

An-ren felt a thrill of relief as her lungs filled with fresh air. The sun was shining down, and she shielded her eyes as she glanced around. She'd half-expected Lam, Li and more Whisperers to be waiting for them, maybe even Ye and Madame Jiang. But the street was empty, the building behind them quiet.

Reed took her hand and led her over to where Zhang and Murphy were impatiently waiting on the other side of the street.

Murphy, to be fair, looked more worried than impatient, but Zhang, as they'd all come to expect, looked grumpy and fed up.

'What took you so long?' Murphy demanded.

'We wanted to find Yue,' Reed explained.

'I'm guessing you didn't.'

'No. We didn't see anyone.'

'Let's go,' Zhang said. 'It feels very vulnerable standing here.'

'Where did you learn to fight like that?' Murphy asked him, following closely as he began to walk away from Eternal Seal.

'What's she talking about?' Zhang demanded, glancing at Reed.

'She says she likes your moves, Iron Palm!'

Zhang scowled, but Reed couldn't help but notice the admiring look in Murphy's eyes as she trotted after him.

'My car's in a side road,' Reed said. 'Do you want a lift?'

'No!' Zhang declared, not even having to think about it.

'I'll go with him,' Murphy answered, glancing impishly at Zhang.

'We need to decide what to do next,' Reed ventured, before Iron Palm could stride off into the sunset.

'Next? Are you serious?' Zhang demanded. 'I've repaid a lifetime of debts to you today!'

'Are you really just going to abandon us, Old Zhang?' Reed asked. 'They want us both dead!'

'That's not strictly true,' Zhang argued, 'but it isn't my problem, anyway.'

Reed glared at him.

'What's he saying?' Murphy asked.

'He's saying he wants to throw us under a bus,' Reed explained.

Murphy looked at Zhang in shock. She sidled up to him and grasped his arm tightly.

'Iron Palm!' she said. 'You can't back out now! They need us!'

Zhang glanced at her, moving his eyes to the hands gripping his arm.

'I don't know what you're saying,' he told her, 'but I wish you wouldn't stand so close.'

'What did he say?' Murphy asked Reed.

'He said that if he'd known he was going to meet you he'd have learned some Gaelic.'

'What did he really say?'

'He's a little in awe of you.'

'Really?'

Reed exchanged a quick glance with An-ren, who was wearing an expression that merged disbelief with disdain. He grinned at her.

'Pretty much,' he said.

Murphy squeezed Zhang's arm even tighter and smiled up at him.

'Okay,' Zhang conceded. 'I'll help, but only if you get her off me!'

'Come on, Old Zhang,' Reed said. 'No man is an island.'

'I am!'

Reed laughed. He didn't believe that for one moment. And even if he did want to remain an island, it was clear Murphy was going to do her level best to build a bridge, whether he liked it or not.

'We need to go on the offensive,' Reed ventured.

'How?' Zhang asked.

'Well, I think we should check out Victor Lam. What do you know about him?'

'Lam? He's a weasel. He passes himself off as a property developer and realtor, but he's just a criminal. He bankrolls shady excavations here in the French Concession, and he uses auctions to launder cursed items into his private collection.'

'What about Whisper Knife? How's he connected to them?'

'You saw them. They claim to be antiquarians, but they're just thugs. They draw the power from shards and ancient jade mirrors by orchestrating hauntings that are linked to Lam's real estate deals.'

'So he controls them?'

'It isn't that simple. There's no direct link between them. Lam works through that idiot Li Tong. He used to be a museum curator, but he discovered that smuggling was more lucrative. He sells Tang-era sigils and glyphs that can seal ghost-runes onto human skin.'

Reed pondered this sudden deluge of information. Murphy had said something very similar about Li at the auction, but the information about Lam was interesting.

'We need to check Lam out,' Reed declared. 'Where's his base of operations?'

'Meridian Estates operate out of The Meridian House on Fuxing Road. Not too far from here, in fact.'

'Meridian?' An-ren echoed. 'Does he have any connection to the Meridian Court Hotel?'

'He owns it,' Zhang told her.

'Shit!' Reed muttered, his mind racing as he tried to make sense of it all.

'It's a fancy place,' Zhang continued. 'It's a genuine art deco villa, built in the 1920s. There's a glossy sales office, gallery events are hosted in the old ballroom, and private viewings are held in the drawing room. And, underneath it all are their secret vaults and conservation labs.'

'We'll go tomorrow,' Reed said. 'Mid-afternoon.'

'I might not be free tomorrow,' Zhang responded, as off-handedly as he could manage.

'I'll either phone or message you in the morning to sort out the details,' Reed persisted.

He suddenly felt tired, shattered, in fact. His body ached and hurt in places he hadn't known existed. He couldn't be bothered to argue with Zhang anymore. However, he had a strong suspicion Murphy would be keeping a very close eye on him. She, undoubtedly, would ensure he'd be there.

'Let's go,' An-ren said, as they walked back towards where Reed had parked the Mustang.

She glanced at Reed, saw how tired and battered he looked.

'I'll drive,' she suggested.

'I didn't know you could drive,' Reed responded.

'I can't.'

CHAPTER THIRTY-FOUR

Ying Yue stared at the floor. She was held fast, her arms gripped so tightly by two of Victor Lam's Whisperers that she had lost almost all feeling in them. But that she knew, was the least of her problems.

Yue was in a dimly lit room, forced to stand, the lifeless body of Xiao Yu laid out behind Ye, as if to suggest the fate that awaited her.

Yue was resigned to it now. She'd finally accepted that Qishan wasn't coming back, that his death and everything that had followed had been little more than a ploy to suck her into the cult-like world of the Whisper Knife Society.

By the time she'd worked it out, it was far too late. She tried to bury the memory of that day deep in the recesses of her mind. To accept it would have meant that everything she'd said and done for the past two years had been based on lies and deceit. It wasn't as if Xiao Yu had been the first.

Qishan had been her life, her future. He'd blown into her world like a summer breeze, refreshing and revitalising. She'd been a model for the longest time, had never stopped enjoying and taking pride in her work, but she was no longer young. She still had her looks, her figure, and, most importantly, her devoted body of fans. But she was now 34. Despite his assurances that she still looked wonderful, her fear of her beauty fading kept her awake night after interminable night.

For how much longer would she rule the world of glamour modelling?

Qishan had changed all that. Safe in his protestations of love and devotion, she finally slept peacefully.

He'd proposed, down on one knee, in front of her friends, and the wedding had been planned. Everything was in place for a bright and happy future.

And then her world had suddenly gone dark. She'd been the one that had found Qishan, his body long cold, her jade mirror completely shattered, seven large shards embedded in his chest, encircling his heart. It was only later, much later, that she'd realised the significance of the pattern they'd formed. The Sepulchral Mandala.

Death by misadventure was the official outcome. She'd accepted that, just as she'd accepted the attentions of the kind and persuasive woman who began to worm her way into Yue's life.

At first, Ye had just offered comfort and sympathy, but, as time wore on, she hinted at secrets, dark secrets, that might just give Qishan the chance to return to this world. None of what Ye told her had made any sense, but that was less important than what she'd promised. Yue didn't need to understand the mechanics of mirror rebirth. She just needed to believe.

And believe she did. But, as with all such things, there was a price to pay. In order for Ye and her beloved master to be able to return Qishan to her, she needed to do something for them. She knew nothing about the shard economy or the dynamics of vectoring models. But she soon learned, and it fell to her to provide the raw materials for the Whisperers to rehearse their hauntings on.

She'd pulled in many models, especially the younger ones whose careers had never really taken off. for whatever reason. Some were too short, some were too big, some had habits or men in their lives that worked against them. As a result, with most glamour modelling doors shut to them, and few other skills or resources to fall back on, they were easy prey for Yue and Whisper Knife.

Yue glanced at Xiao Yu's cold, blood-stained body. She didn't see the staring, lifeless, eyes. She didn't see the awkward, unnatural angle of her arms and legs. She didn't even see the pale, almost blue, tinge to her skin. All she saw were the shards protruding from her chest, in the pattern of a Tomb Wheel.

She suddenly doubled up and vomited, everything she'd consumed during the day hitting the carpeted floor next to Ye's feet.

Ye moved, so fast that, for the briefest instant, she became little more than a blur. She didn't need that. She'd suffered enough indignities for one day.

Why, she wondered, did fate continue to conspire against her? Wasn't it enough that her soul had been crushed and her life destroyed, not once, but twice?

First by Meng Yao and then by the Celestial Registry, aided and abetted by the arch betrayer, An Lian. Ye had been dragged to the edge of the abyss, thrown in with only an empty promise of redemption for company, before her master was finally forced in after her.

Two thousand years of hiding. Two thousand years of interminable waiting, of plotting and counter-plotting. Two thousand years of the most crushing emptiness. And now this stupid waste of space had decided to vomit. If even one droplet had sullied her suede Jimmy Choo's she would probably have beaten her to death on the spot.

'Look at me,' Ye commanded.

Yue continued to stare at the floor.

'Look at me!' Ye barked.

Yue still didn't look up.

Ye reached out and grabbed Yue's chin. She felt every muscle in the woman's body tense as her cold, glass-like fingers dug into soft and delicate flesh.

'Don't touch me!' Yue begged, her voice shaking with fear.

Ye ignored her, instead forcing her chin up until their eyes were on a level. Seeing the tears welling up in Yue's eyes, the terror in her face, Ye felt cheered, her mood instantly lifting.

Yue had wanted to avoid staring at the face in front of her. It was a thing of nightmares. She was responsible, and she knew her fate was sealed.

Ye's face, normally strikingly and powerfully beautiful, was now fractured, fragmented into pieces like a mirror that had been viciously cracked. It was the same face, but it was now riven with lines and divisions, every sector shattered and broken.

It was possibly the most inhuman sight Yue had ever seen, and she'd seen many over the past two years. Ye was, to any casual observer, a graceful and sensually elegant woman, as beautiful as anyone she'd met, but this cracked face was the harsh reality of the creature that lay within. And her touch was as cold and unforgiving as ice.

'You can't even look at me,' Ye sneered. 'You're just a pathetic coward.'

She walked over to the corpse, carefully stepping over the puddle of vomit.

Her head still hurt and her face felt awkward and uncomfortable. It would heal, but the humiliation would remain.

She kicked Xiao Yu's body, taking care not to get any blood, dried or otherwise, on her expensive shoes. She gestured to the shards sticking out of the model's chest.

'Does that remind you of anything?' she asked.

Yue remained silent. Ye was like a cat, she thought, prowling around, toying with its prey, dragging out the moment when it would finally rip out its victim's throat out.

'Oh yes, of course,' Ye continued, slowly sashaying back to stand directly in front of Yue. 'Precious Qishan.'

'You're not worthy to say his name!' Yue hissed. 'You killed him!'

'It was such a tragic, unfortunate accident,' Ye continued, standing so close that Yue could see into the cracks that now marred the beautiful face. She felt a cold chill move down her spine and her hair stood on end as she realised there was something under the surface. Staring at Ye's broken face made Yue feel as if she were standing at the edge of the deepest cave, a shadowy chamber that held something vastly dark and incomprehensible.

Yue desperately wanted to lunge forward and smash her head into Ye's face, shatter her shattered features even more. But, she couldn't. The Whisperers holding her were far too strong for her to be able to move even an inch.

Ye slowly circled Yue. She stopped directly in front of her and brought her face so close to Yue's that they were almost touching.

'I think it's time for you to join him,' she whispered in Yue's ear, before driving her hard as glass fingers into the woman's chest, cutting through the flesh and piercing Yue's heart. Ye's face hardened as she twisted her hand viciously, scything effortlessly through the soft tissue.

Yue locked eyes with Ye, shock and pain swamping every atom of her body, before going limp, held up only by the efforts of the Whisperers behind her.

'Get rid of them both,' Ye commanded, withdrawing her hand from Yue's chest, and wiping her fingers on the dead woman's dress. She turned on her heel and marched away.

'My lady!' a voice called out, halting her in mid-stride.

She turned back, irritation written all over her fractured face. Two Whisperers had just entered through the far door, a tall brown-haired man held fast between them.

'What is it?' Ye demanded.

'We found this man examining the relics,' the Whisperer responded.

'Get rid of him,' she said, wondering why she was being bothered with such a trivial issue.

'He asked to see you, my Lady,' the Whisperer persisted, avoiding the eyes that were slowly turning from blue to crimson. 'By name.'

She turned her attention to the man held fast between the two Whisperers, and the fire instantly faded.

She felt both shocked and a little disconcerted by what she saw. Unlike An-ren and Ying Yue, who had looked at her cracked face with a mix of horror and revulsion, this man, who had asked for her by name, looked at her with a great sadness in his eyes.

She studied him more closely. He was a westerner of some description, tall, with tousled dark brown hair and a short, trimmed beard. His dark brown eyes stared at her with something resembling compassion.

Compassion? She struggled to remember what the word even meant.

'Who is he?' she asked.

'We found these on him,' the Whisperer who'd spoken before ventured, holding out some papers.

Ye took them and began to read. What she saw only increased her confusion.

"Aleksandr Nikolayevich Vorin," she read. "Archaeologist. On secondment to the School of Ancient History and Civilisation at the Shanghai Jiao Tong University from the Department of Archaeology at Saint Petersburg University."

She handed the papers back to him.

'What possible business could you have with me, Mr Vorin?' Ye asked, speaking Russian.

'I like your accent,' he responded, in Mandarin, 'but you don't need to put yourself out on my account.'

'I've seen you before,' she said, reverting to Chinese. 'You've been at the auctions. Are you a collector?'

'No. I'm more of a restorer.'

'And what do you restore?'

'Maybe redeem is a better word. Let's just way I believe that love can redeem even the most fractured soul.'

He held her powerful gaze, returning it with an intensity she hadn't expected when she'd first seen him. He'd seemed unimpressive, yet another outlier hoping to forge a connection with destiny, in the shape of a jade shard energised by Whisper Knife, but she now knew he had a very different agenda.

First he showed her compassion, now he talked about love. What exactly did he want from her? She suddenly felt almost destabilised, as if the values and beliefs she held about herself and the worlds she lived in were in danger of being torn apart.

'Goodbye, Mr Vorin. Don't come to any more auctions,' she said, turning to leave.

'I know who you are, I know what happened!' he called out as she opened the door. 'Yomei!'

She stopped, her blood running cold. She retraced her steps until she was standing so close to him she could almost hear the beating of his heart.

'That name is buried! Speak it again and I'll tear the tongue from your mouth!' she hissed.

She hadn't heard anyone speak that name for so long she'd almost forgotten it existed. A name that symbolised everything she'd lost, everything that had been stolen from her. A life crushed in the most callous and brutal way.

He broke free of the Whisperers and, moving so quickly she had no time to react, took her right hand in both of his and held it tight. She felt a shockwave ripple through her soul. She stared at their intertwined hands, confused and disconcerted. Only two hours earlier, Anren had held the same hand and thrown it away in horror and disgust. And yet Vorin was holding it with delicacy and care, as if it was the most precious human hand in the world.

The Whisperers moved to restrain him, but Ye shook her head. Her anger had been dispersed by her shock. She didn't understand what was happening, but she needed to find out. Vorin posed no physical threat, and, if he tried anything she could end his life in an instant, in any number of ways. But there was something else going on, something far more insidious and disconcerting.

'I understand how you've suffered,' he told her. 'I've seen Jinglun. I know about the Loom.'

Her eyes flashed crimson and she wrenched her hand out of his gentle grasp.

'How could you possibly understand? If you knew anything at all, you'd know that you could never understand!' she retorted, her anger rising again..

'I meant that I know you've suffered. I wouldn't presume to suggest I know what you've been through. How could I?'

'What do you know about suffering, Mr Vorin?' she mocked. 'It's all just an academic exercise to you, isn't it? If you really understood suffering, you'd never dare to utter either of those names!'

'I see things in you. Things that you believe you've lost.'

She realised she was now hyperventilating, her pulse racing. Was it simply because he'd spoken those names, and laid himself open to the curse, or had he managed to touch something that had been buried deep inside her for thousands of years? Something she thought she'd lost forever?

There was a look in his eyes that she hadn't seen for a very long time. A look that caused a desolate pain to rise up inside her, an agonising aching that was so powerful she thought she might scream. That scared her. The cruelty that she'd experienced so long ago had crushed almost every vestige of humanity that had ever existed inside her. This stupid man thought simply by voicing forbidden names and looking sorrowful, he could revive emotions and feelings that had died centuries before he'd even been born.

What can he possibly see, she asked herself.

'I haven't lost anything,' she said, her tone flat and cold. 'It was taken and crushed out of existence.'

He reached out again, but she stepped back, pulling her hands out of range. She suddenly felt vulnerable. She wondered how Vorin, out of the entirety of humanity, could make her feel this way.

'There's an old Russian proverb that says, "no one is too lost to be saved",' he told her.

'That isn't Russian, Mr Vorin,' she scowled, wondering if he was trying to lighten the moment with humour. 'It's a modern Christian adage.'

She paused for a moment, remembering the warm and gentle touch of his hands.

'As the modern Chinese say, "You walk your broad road, I'll cross my single-plank bridge."'

She bowed slightly, cupping her fists in front of her chest in a traditional *Bao Quan* gesture of respect.

'Take Mr Vorin home,' she said, glancing at the Whisperers. 'And make sure he arrives safely.'

As Vorin was led away, Ye turned on her heel and exited the room. She didn't want Vorin to see the tears that had started to trickle down her cracked cheeks.

CHAPTER THIRTY-FIVE

An-ren had passed her driving test eight years earlier, but at the time she hadn't been able to afford a car, and had since come to rely on public transport and taxis for getting around. She hadn't driven in Shanghai since passing her test, and, although she thought offering to do so was the decent thing, if Reed had actually agreed then it was highly probable her efforts to save his life would ultimately have been in vain.

The thought of driving his Mustang was also quite daunting. He loved that car, had feelings for it that, until two days earlier, had almost certainly been his only significant emotional attachment to anything on the planet, other than, perhaps, The Golden Lantern. Shanghai in the late afternoon was definitely not the place to start driving again after an eight-year gap, and especially not in someone's prized muscle car.

So, Reed drove. He was in pain, but the car was automatic and he was certain that driving would cause him less emotional, if not physical, pain than being a passenger.

The traffic was surprisingly light, given the time of day, and it only took them twenty minutes to get back to the bar. Reed parked the Mustang and hobbled inside, An-ren at his side.

The staff were shocked to see him in such a battered and bruised state, and, much to his irritation, and even more so An-ren's, they fussed around him until he finally told them, very sharply, to leave him alone and get on with serving their customers.

As he walked towards the stairs, he reprimanded himself, made a mental note to apologise to them all later, or maybe tomorrow. He was tired, in pain, and had experienced one of the most stressful days of his life. But that was no excuse, he knew that. They were concerned about him, and he was grateful for that. But all he really wanted was to get upstairs and lie down.

He stopped abruptly, An-ren almost bumping into him.

'What is it, Xiao Wei?' she asked.

He backed up slightly, turning to face the wall on his left.

'I don't remember that being there,' he said, indicating a jade mirror hanging there.

They both leaned in to study the object, their faces almost touching.

An-ren pointed at a small mark on the top left of the jade frame.

'Shit!' Reed muttered.

He scanned the glass, and there it was. First the Luo Ban mark on the frame, and then the Tomb Wheel on the glass.

'This definitely wasn't here earlier,' he said, turning away and returning to the bar.

'Gao Ming!' he called out.

'Yes, Zhu Wei?' the man asked, hurrying over.

'That mirror on the wall back there. Where did it come from?'

'A customer brought it in about half an hour ago,' Ming told him, glancing at the concerned look on Reed's and An-ren's faces, wondering whether he was now going to be in trouble. 'He said he was a friend of yours and that you'd mentioned you wanted an antique jade mirror. I thought it would be a nice surprise if I put it up on the wall.'

It was a surprise, all right, Reed thought, but not a nice one.

'This man. Who was he?'

'He said his name was Li Tong, that he was an old friend of yours. I'd never seen him before, but you have so many friends.'

'Okay,' Reed said, trying, not very successfully, to hide his anger. 'I need you to take it down, and go and throw it in the Huangpu River. Now!'

It sounded ridiculous, he knew that, but he couldn't think of a better place to dump the thing. It surely wouldn't be able to affect anyone or anything lying on the riverbed.

'Now?' Ming asked, no doubt thinking Reed must have picked up some sort of head injury, along with all his bruises and abrasions.

'Now! Please. I need it out of the bar and at the bottom of the river. The bar isn't busy. Take my car if you want to. Just get rid of the thing. And if Li ever comes back, he's banned. And, just to be clear, I don't want any jade mirrors of any description anywhere in the bar. Understood?'

'Yes, Zhu Wei,' Ming nodded, bowing as low as he could get.

Reed could see the man felt guilty, embarrassed and a little ashamed, although he had no reason to be any of those things.

'I could have handled that better,' he sighed, as he and An-ren walked back towards the stairs.

'You nearly died, and you're hurting and tired,' she said, putting her arm through his. 'Don't be hard on yourself.'

He smiled weakly at her, more thankful she was at his side than he could ever say.

They climbed the stairs and he let them into the apartment.

'You go and sit down,' she told him.

It was more of a command than a request, he thought, as she unstrapped her shoes and stepped down onto the carpet, before disappearing into the kitchen.

He thought about following her, but his body ached so much that he decided, for once, to do as he was told. He took off his shoes and socks, and headed into the living room, painfully lowering himself onto the settee and leaning back, letting the furniture take the strain.

As he sat there, An-ren hurried past, pausing to put a bowl of hot water down on the table, before disappearing into the bathroom.

He thought about what had happened, how, for the second day in succession, a creature from his worst nightmares had pursued him, hell-bent on killing him.

When the crate had hit him full on, he'd felt certain that death was only seconds away, just as he had the night before, as the Xilin had stalked towards him. He'd been angry, had cursed God bitterly for cheating him out of shot at redemption.

But, as had also happened last night, he'd been saved. And not by just anyone. Somehow, and he still didn't know how, An-ren had killed the Moquai, and saved his life in the process.

She came back into the living room at that moment, carrying a face cloth and a towel.

As she put them down on the table, next to the still steaming bowl of water, she noticed the look in his eyes as he stared at her.

'What is it?' she asked, concerned.

'An-an,' he murmured, looking away.

She sat down next to him and put her hand under his chin, lifting his eyes back to hers. There were tears there. Tears that mixed pain, shock and happiness.

'Weiwei,' she whispered into his ear, as she put her arms around him and pulled him close.

She rested her cheek against his, savouring the feeling of his warm skin next to hers. She suddenly realised she was about to cry, too.

She held him tight, wondering what she would have done if she'd been too late. She hadn't allowed herself to consider that possibility as she'd gone searching for the Hollow Helm. Being too late had never been an option. But she could see he'd fought hard, had held his own against a creature that was, quite simply, terrifying and almost indestructible.

The fact he'd still been alive showed he was a survivor. She felt selfish and guilty thinking it, but she hoped some of that desperation to survive was because of her.

She thought about poor Xiao Yu, whose body they'd had to leave behind. She'd barely known her, had only met her the once. They'd probably exchanged ten words in total. None of that made any difference, though. Nobody deserved to die like that.

She wondered what had happened to Yue. They'd been good friends until Qishan had died, and then Yue had all but disappeared. An-ren had heard stories about her getting involved in hiring young models for private functions, but she'd thought nothing of it and had never got around to contacting her. She felt a wave of guilt roll over her as she thought about that. Maybe, if she'd phoned her, or messaged her, she would have been able to walk away from Ye. It wasn't very likely, she knew that, understood only too well how grief could make even the most simple decision virtually impossible.

Her heart wept as she thought about Yue. Her friend had heard Ye mocking her, had learned the truth about Qishan from the lips of the monster who'd undoubtedly arranged his death. She knew Yue was probably dead, but found some small comfort in the fact she was finally free of Ye and her cruelty

At least Reed was safe. That, at least, made her feel better about herself. She'd saved his life. Again. Despite everything she couldn't help but feel amused by the thought. She'd never seen herself as a killer of demons and monsters, but she'd done it twice now. And she'd keep doing it if she had to, although she desperately hoped it wouldn't be necessary. Maybe Reed's plan to take the battle to the opposition would work.

She unwrapped her arms from around him and leaned back slightly. She'd fought her own tears back down, but his were still there.

'You were very brave,' she told him, gently wiping his eyes with her fingers. 'I don't know how you kept yourself safe. That thing was terrifying.'

'I don't know how I did it, either,' he said, a thin smile briefly moving across his lips.

She took the face cloth, dipped it in the hot water, and began to dab gently at his face, working to clear away the dried blood.

'You saved my life,' he said. 'Again.'

'You owe me. Again,' she responded, still carefully cleaning his cuts and scratches.

'I owe you so much,' he told her, lowering his eyes.

'That's true,' she agreed.

'An-an?'

He suddenly looked very serious.

'What is it, Weiwei?'

'Whatever happens, I won't let anyone hurt you.'

'I know you won't.'

'I mean it,' he insisted.

'I know you do,' she said, bending over to gently kiss his forehead.

She knew where these words came from, and exactly what they meant to him.

The image of Ye's shattered face suddenly flashed into her mind, and she put the face cloth down, turning away for a moment.

'What is it?' Reed asked, reaching out and taking her hand.

'Ye. When Yue hit her with the Moquai's helmet, she was standing right in front of me. Her face cracked into shards, just like a mirror.'

'Oh my god!' Reed exclaimed.

'I told you she was made of glass. When I grabbed her hand earlier it was horrible. It was cold and smooth like ice. Or glass.'

'I'm sorry.'

'I'd like to think she's dead, but I can't believe that.'

She picked up the face cloth, dipped it in the water once more, and carried on cleaning Reed's face.

'Thank you,' he said.

'I'm just cleaning you up.'

'Thank you for everything, An-an.'

She paused for a moment, staring deep into his blue eyes.

'You're very welcome,' she finally said, putting down the soggy, red-stained face cloth and gently drying his face with the towel.

'That's much better,' she smiled, admiring her handiwork.

It occurred to Reed that it was the first time she'd smiled since they'd entered Eternal Seal.

She put the towel down on the table, and turned back to face him.

'I'd better see where else it hurts,' she said, reaching out and starting to unbutton his shirt.

'It hurts everywhere,' he told her.

She paused momentarily, arching an eyebrow at him, before continuing with her task. Reed was still impressed she could be so dextrous with such impractical fingernails. But he realised he shouldn't be surprised at anything she did. If she could kill the Xilin and the Moquai of the Hollow Helm, then there was almost certainly very little she couldn't do.

She finished unbuttoning his shirt, pulled it out of his trousers, carefully easing it over his shoulders, down his arms and hands. She folded it, as she'd done the night before, and placed it next to the towel on the table.

She felt a terrible sadness wash over her as she studied his chest and torso. He was bruised and marked all over. He'd really taken quite a battering. She suddenly felt terribly guilty. He'd suffered all of this because of her.

But, despite her guilt and the aching in her heart at the sight of the beating he'd taken, she was thankful he was there, had put himself in harm's way. She didn't want him to suffer, but she was moved almost to tears that someone cared enough to risk their life in defence of hers.

She moved her right hand to his chest, gently moving her fingers across his warm, firm skin, touching the emerging bruises that covered so much of his body.

He winced slightly as she touched him, and she instantly pulled her hand away, not wanting to cause him any more pain.

'Don't stop,' he told her.

'But I don't want to hurt you.'

'I can live with pain. But I'm not sure I could live without your touch.'

She leaned over and gently kissed him on the lips, before lowering her head and delicately, very carefully, beginning to kiss his chest, moving slowly from right to left, her silken hair cascading across his face and down over his shoulders.

His heart started to race, his breathing suddenly shallower. The sensual touch of her lips and the gentle caressing of her fingers made him forget all about pain.

He moved his hands and lifted up her crop-top and the camisole beneath it, moving his fingers across the soft and delicate skin of her back.

She lifted her head and began to kiss him again.

In that moment, as they surrendered to their passion, he decided he should try to make sure she saved his life every single day.

CHAPTER THIRTY-SIX

'You come to me after failure?'

Ye struggled to control the anger that rose within her. Her eyes flashed crimson as she considered the face staring out from the ancient jade mirror secured to the wall in front of her.

It was a cruel face, made crueller by the scars that lined the forehead and eyes, the constant reminders of a battle that, it seemed, had never been theirs to win. His eyes had never changed, though, had always been intensely powerful and piercing.

She felt nauseated by the memory of how she'd once found herself flattered and seduced by those eyes, and the charm that had oozed from his mouth. She'd once thought him handsome and desirable. She remembered the touch of his flesh on her young body, and she almost wanted to vomit. Her naivety and her childlike desire to believe the empty, vacuous, platitudes Meng Yao had showered on her had taken her to the abyss that he and An Lian had callously cast her in to. She'd believed what she'd wanted to believe. That was the undeniable truth of her human life. She had been the unwitting architect of her own damnation.

She forced herself back from the brink, banishing the unbearably painful and crushing memories of her betrayal and enslavement back into the deep, dark place where she kept them locked safely away. There was no value in thinking about any of it now. Not ever, in fact. What was important wasn't the immutable, unchangeable past, but the fluid and highly flexible future.

She found herself thinking about Vorin. He'd talked, in a circuitous way, about hope, but his words had done little more than remind her of the misery and darkness that enveloped her. He'd made her feel more vulnerable than at any point in the last two thousand years. And she'd cried. How was that even possible?

She turned her thoughts back to the business at hand. She'd declined to venture back into the Resonance Plane, and Luo Ban clearly had no intention of manifesting himself, even though, within the confines of the Mirror Chamber, he could safely do so. It was all an unsubtle reminder of the power differential between them both, as master and servant.

She pushed the last of her fury back down inside, contenting herself with the knowledge that nothing was forever, and that change, dramatic change, was coming.

She had transformed back into her mirror form. She had long ago learned how to manage the complexity of being a creature of glass in the real world. It wasn't especially practical, at least in terms of interacting with the people around her, but she found being human, or, at least, as human as she could be, distressing. Her human form, after all, was, essentially, a fusion of flesh, blood and glass. It was a constant reminder of everything that had been so cruelly taken away from her.

Being in her mirror form had another advantage. It masked the damage that Ying Yue had done to her face. The blow from the Hollow Helm had caused her a great amount of pain and damage. If she had been truly human, the blow would almost certainly have killed her. The injuries would heal, and, although the cracks were already far less evident, she had no intention of letting Luo Ban see the ravages Yue had wrought.

'How exactly have I failed?' she asked.

'An Lian's safety is your responsibility,' Luo Ban replied. His voice remained calm. 'You allowed her to be endangered.'

'She will be delivered. Zhu Wei's presence changes nothing. He is irrelevant.'

'Irrelevant men have undone empires,' Luo Ban murmured. 'Are you certain you're not overreaching?'

'Why would I overreach? Your resurrection is my resurrection.'

A faint smile touched his lips. Humourless, cold.

'You speak, Ye, but your words have no weight.'

'Value is relative.'

'Are you still clinging to blame?' he asked softly. 'I preserved you. Without me, you would have died on that floor.'

Her jaw tightened. He always framed it that way, as if the ritual had been mercy, not violation. She felt the old fury rising again, and forced it back down. She needed him. For now.

'Your generosity is boundless, my Lord,' she said, bowing with a mocking flourish.

He watched her in silence. He was growing weary of her resentment, her unfounded and unspoken belief that she was the victim, and not him. There would come a time when he would take great pleasure sending her to join the man she'd loved.

'Tread carefully,' Luo Ban said at last. 'Your anger make you reckless.'

'I am yours to command.'

'Don't insult us both,' he replied. 'I know what you intend. When the Sepulchral Mandala rises and we walk the world again, you may find your righteousness inconvenient.'

She glared at him but held her tongue. She was tired of his rhetoric.

Then his expression shifted. Curiosity entered his eyes.

'Your face,' he said quietly. 'What happened to it?'

Ye froze.

'Nothing is wrong with my face.'

'I can see the fractures. Even when you're in this form.'

Her anger flared. How could he see what she'd hidden?

'It's nothing.'

'What happened, Ye?'

She stared defiantly at him, but remained silent.

'I asked you a question,' Luo Ban insisted.

Ye could see he was enjoying her embarrassment, was keen to humiliate her further. She fought to control her anger. She needed to be patient. The time for anger would come, but it wasn't now.

'Someone struck me with the Hollow Helm,' she conceded.

She lowered her eyes and focused on her shoes. She didn't want to see the gloating, mocking expression that she knew would be plastered across his face.

A sound emerged from the mirror, low, rasping, unfamiliar. It took her a moment to recognise it.

Luo Ban was laughing.

'Who?'

'It doesn't matter.'

'It does.'

His voice was soft, almost cajoling.

'Who was it?' he insisted.

'Ying Yue,' she muttered.

'I didn't hear you.'

'Ying Yue!' she cried, her voice cracking the air.

She raised her eyes, fixing him with the coldest, steeliest glare she was capable of.

She hated that he could still provoke her, hated that she shook with fury. If he'd been human, she would have ripped his heart out and crushed it into non-existence. But he wasn't. And she still needed him.

'How did such a fragile creature harm you?'

Ye tried to calm herself, taking slow breaths and forcing her thoughts onto the task ahead.

'She won't do it again,' she said. 'We need to move to the next phase.'

She felt the shift in him, could sense the anticipation, the hunger.

'It will be pleasant to see An Lian again,' he murmured.

The hatred in his voice was ancient, absolute.

He paused, scrutinising her closely.

'There's something you're not saying.'

'There were two others with An-ren and Reed. A man and a woman,' she said. 'I thought I recognised the man.'

'Impossible. Everyone we knew is long dead.'

'He seemed familiar,' she insisted.

'Who is he?'

'An associate of Zhu Wei. A former policeman who appears to a master of Mirror Sutra. And one of them knew how to destroy the Moquai.'

'Perhaps An Lian's memories are returning.'

Ye's eyes flashed.

'You're blinded by your hatred! She was never capable of anything but betrayal.'

'Then find out who they are,' Luo Ban said softly. 'And who among them knows our secrets. Nothing must obstruct us.'

Ye said nothing. Luo Ban had been locked away too long. He no longer understood the world he wished to conquer.

Luo Ban's voice dropped to a whisper.

'All who stand against us will be ground to dust beneath the Tomb Wheel.'

CHAPTER THIRTY-SEVEN

As they laid in bed, their passion sated, An-ren rested her head on Reed's shoulder. Her fingers gently explored his inviting chest, tracing idle circles on his naked skin. She stopped, partway through another circuit, as she remembered something. A very important something

She moved her head and whispered into Reed's ear.

'I've got a shoot tomorrow morning.'

'Do you have to go?' he murmured, tightening his arms around her.

'I do,' she said. 'If this ever ends, I'll still need a career.'

'I should come with you.'

'Should you? Haven't you had enough of watching me undress?'

He moved his head slightly, opening his eyes, a mischievous grin creeping onto his lips.

'Is that a serious question? If I live to be a thousand years old, I'll never have enough of that.'

'Even if I'm a thousand years old, too?'

'The chances are I'll be blind and senile by then. So, yes.'

A silence fell between them again, and she continued to move her fingers delicately across his skin, enjoying how firm and strong it felt to her touch.

An-ren had never considered asking Reed to go with her. She'd been modelling for so long it simply hadn't occurred to her. But the thought of him being there was surprisingly comforting.

'Maybe you could check for jade mirrors and shards,' she finally said.

'I could definitely do that,' he agreed.

'You wouldn't mind being there?' she asked.

He kissed her softly on the forehead. He understood the question, knew exactly what she was really asking.

'You're a star,' he told her. 'Who doesn't want to watch their favourite star getting undressed?'

She glanced across at his chest, identifying one of his bruises and poking it, before returning to her quiet exploration.

'Ouch! That hurt!' he complained, trying to hide the smile that crept back onto his face.

She moved slightly, hooking her right leg over his.

'I'm worried,' she confessed.

'It'll be fine. I'll be there. What can go wrong?'

'What can't go wrong with you around?' she laughed. 'But I didn't mean that. I meant now. What if I go to sleep and she's waiting for me again?'

'You heard Old Zhang. If there's no Luo Ban or Tomb Wheel shards or mirrors nearby, then she has no way to get at you.'

'But there could be something hidden in here. Li Tong was able to get that mirror on the wall downstairs.'

'No one's been up here,' he reassured her. 'And I'm sure Li only left that mirror in the bar to let us know they're in control.'

She moved her head slightly, angling it upwards so that their eyes met. He could see the anxiety and fear in her face, and it made his heart ache. He loathed all of them for what they were doing to her. He hoped they could find a way to bring everything to a rapid and happy conclusion, although he had absolutely no idea what that way might be.

Everything they knew, and everything they'd done, had been driven by Zhang, and Reed had no doubt that it would be Iron Palm who would be the one providing the conclusion, happy or otherwise.

The man was a complete enigma. He'd always claimed to be a retired policeman, but Reed genuinely doubted there was another policeman anywhere in the world, retired or not, who knew how to defeat the Moquai of the Hollow Helm. He seemed to know everything about Luo Ban, Ye and the Tomb Wheel civilisation, yet the wonderful internet, home of even the most speculative and spurious information, was clueless.

'What do you think about Old Zhang?' he asked.

'He's grumpy, rude, and bad-mannered.'

'Yes, he is, but I was thinking more in terms of his skillset. He doesn't strike me as your typical retired policeman.'

'He's your friend, Weiwei. If you don't know, then who does?'

'Well, An-an, the truth is, he's a patron. I call him a friend, but he's like most of my other friends. People I've served and talked to downstairs.'

'So you didn't know him before he started drinking here?'

'No. He's probably the only policeman who's ever been in here.'

'Right, so he's what? A reincarnated sorcerer with a badge?'

'I wouldn't go that far. He said he studied a martial art for dealing with demons and spirits — not creatures, exactly, but... disruptions. Places where the world goes out of alignment. I humoured him at the time. After what I saw today, maybe I shouldn't have. He once said you could "press the breath out of a bad spirit like kneading dough".'

An-ren laughed. Reed liked that. It was a warm and comforting sound, and it felt reassuring that in the midst of such craziness and terror she could still be touched by humour.

'Why did he owe you a favour?'

'One night he turned up in a total state. He told me his wife had kicked him out and he had nowhere to go, no money to even rent a cheap hotel room for the night.'

'Don't tell me you let him stay here?'

Reed glanced at her. She obviously already had the measure of him.

'Well, yes. I did. He was in a state, a real mess. I let him stay here a few nights.'

'Let me guess. "Until he got back on his feet again"! Did he snore?'

'I slept on the settee,' Reed told her, trying to banish the image of Zhang in his bed that had suddenly appeared in his mind.

'You let him have your bed? You're such a soft touch.'

'I know,' he agreed.

An-ren glanced at his chest once more, identified another bruise and jabbed her index finger into it, taking care, though, to avoid stabbing him with the nail.

'Ouch!' he cried out in mock agony. 'There was no need for that!'

'There was every need. My *waipo* always told me that a man needs to be kept in his place.'

'I know my place, believe me.'

'And I'm just reinforcing it. Think of it as a public service. How long did Old Zhang stay here?'

'Not long.'

'You were kind. Not many people would have done that.'

'But that isn't why he owes me.'

'It isn't? What did you do? Buy him a house?'

'Not quite.'

An-ren stared at him, stunned.

'You're not serious?'

'I paid the deposit on his apartment, paid the first six months' rent for him.'

'All this for someone you didn't even know?'

'I knew his favourite beer was Lucky Buddha.'

An-ren continued to stare at him, disbelief in her eyes, although, deep down, she was touched. Throwing money at people who were virtually strangers wasn't a great quality, but having that degree of compassion and care definitely was.

'He had nowhere to go. What could I do?'

'So you did all that just to get rid of him?'

'If I'd really wanted to do that, I could have just sent him to the Christian Youth Association. He was a nice guy, but he was down on his uppers.'

'What on earth does that mean?'

'It's a British phrase. It means he was penniless.'

'Well, he's lucky to have a friend like you. I can't believe he's so grumpy towards you. And we had to force him to help us!'

'That's just his natural charm. He was always going to help us.'

'Really? Was that why he said you owed him a big favour now?'

'Just banter. You know how it is.'

She moved her face towards his and kissed him.

'You're a sweet man, Weiwei.'

CHAPTER THIRTY-EIGHT

An-ren had slept peacefully, her dreams undisturbed by either Ye or the various nightmares of the Tomb Wheel Dynasty. They'd woken up relatively early, certainly earlier than Reed would normally have chosen to. He was definitely not a morning person, never had been.

He lay with his arms wrapped around her, and, as he slowly extricated himself, reluctantly allowing her to get out of bed, he winced with the aches and pains, primarily in his chest, that seemed to have doubled in intensity since the day before. It was always the way, he knew that, always worse the next day. But he hoped that once he was up and about it might all ease slightly.

He moved himself into a sitting position and watched as An-ren's naked form disappeared into the bathroom. Watching her didn't ease the pain, but it did stop him caring about it.

Later, after she'd showered and began to focus on her clothes, makeup and hair, Reed made use of the bathroom, before getting himself dressed and decamping to the kitchen to brew some coffee.

He knew that An-ren would normally make her way to a photoshoot dressed down. Apart from the fact it was more comfortable before the demands and rigours of a shoot, it also made it easier for her to travel incognito on public transport. She would dress herself in something far more striking and dynamic for when she left the venue, wherever and whatever that might be.

It was always likely someone would have leaked information on where she was, probably *MeiXiu* themselves, and, by the time she left, there would almost certainly be a small crowd gathered, ready to worship and adore. And grab selfies.

But today was different.

She was finally ready. As she emerged from the bedroom, he bowed down, professing his unworthiness. She frowned in mock disapproval, but he could see a little gleam in her eyes that said something quite different.

She'd chosen a black long sleeved top and a fitted black skirt reaching halfway down her thighs. She finished the look with sheer black stockings and black Christian Louboutin heels, their red soles designed to draw the eye all the way down her shapely legs.

Her hair hung loose, cascading around her shoulders and down her back, and she had accessorised minimally, with gold studs in her ears and a single narrow gold bangle.

Her outfit, and her look, was simple, but very powerful. On anyone else it might have looked mundane, but on her it looked like haute couture.

'How do I look?' she asked.

Reed wondered whether she was serious. Was it possible she actually doubted herself, at least in terms of her beauty? There was a vulnerability about her, it was true, but she kept it well hidden, secreted under many defensive layers.

He admired her poise, her ability to command a room, her self-confidence and self-assurance. He knew that most of those who followed her every photoshoot and eagerly waited for social media updates and fan selfies, were only interested in her glamour and her body. The real An-ren, with her remarkably sharp mind and almost limitless depth of emotion, was of no interest to them. All they wanted was their aloof ice queen.

He also knew she had changed her routine purely for his benefit.

'You look like Xiang An-ren,' he told her, crossing the short distance between them.

'What does that mean?'

'It means you look more than alright.'

He reached out to touch her, brought his face close to hers, as if to kiss her. But she stepped back.

'Sorry, Xiao Wei,' she said, a thin smile on her dark red lips. 'Hair, makeup, lipstick, clothes.'

'Really?' he asked, looking suddenly crestfallen.

'Really,' she laughed. 'You've been holding me and kissing me, on and off, all night. Haven't you had enough of me yet?'

'That's the most stupid question anyone's ever asked me,' Reed muttered, going back to his now cold cup of coffee.

As he picked up the cup, he realised he hadn't offered her any.

'Would you like some?' he asked. 'This is cold, but I can make some fresh.'

'Just some water.'

He went into the kitchen, pulled a cold bottle out of the fridge and took it back to her.

'Shall we go?' she said, opening the bottle and taking a small sip, being careful not to touch her lipstick.

She suddenly felt nervous. She hadn't been bothered by the mirror fiasco at the Lumen House. but so much had happened since then. She'd found it highly irritating, at least at the time, but now, after the Xilin, the Moquai, the death of Xiao Yu and the ongoing horrors of Ye, she felt worried. Not about anything specific, but the whole desperate business seemed to have started with a photoshoot. It was hard not to imagine that another one might lead to an escalation.

She had seriously considered cancelling, but she knew that, even with her level of popularity and the size of her fanbase, it wouldn't go down well with anyone. She had always delivered, and to the highest standard possible. She was, if nothing else, a professional, and she needed to try to rise above everything fate and karma were throwing at her.

As Reed had so rightly said, she was Xiang An-ren.

She walked over to where he was putting his shoes on, and placed a hand on his arm. He looked up at her in surprise.

'You might chip your nail varnish,' he told her.

'Thank you,' she said, ignoring his sarcasm.

'For what?' he asked.

She enjoyed the guilt that now filled his face.

'For giving me the opportunity to save your life,' she said, opening the door and making her way down the stairs before he could even think of a response.

Reed stared after her for a moment, nonplussed. And then he realised what she was saying. A small smile crept onto his lips, and he raced after her, shutting the door behind him as he went.

CHAPTER THIRTY-NINE

The Shanghai EDITION was an ultra-modern, minimalist luxury hotel, with dramatic lighting, rooftop terraces, and floor-to-ceiling windows. It was located near the Bund, close to East Nanjing Road and People's Square, a vibrant, high-traffic area very different to the tree-lined intimacy of the French Concession.

The hotel had been designed to be both international and aspirational. It was far more vertical, urban and cinematic than many of the hotels An-ren had worked in, all of which marked it out as a perfect venue for a *MeiXiu* photoshoot.

Despite the heavy morning traffic, Reed got them there early, and, as he parked the Mustang in the vast car park, they still had ten minutes to spare.

She'd had a message from the assistant, Zhao Na, informing her they would be using a suite on the fifteenth floor. As she and Reed got out of the car and made their way into the hotel, she wondered if anyone would ask her about Xu. Given that she'd spoken to him on the phone the day before yesterday, and that telephone conversations were hard evidence, she was a little surprised she hadn't heard from the police yet.

But then she thought about the Xilin and Ye. She realised that it was highly unlikely anyone would be stumbling over Xu's half-eaten body anytime soon. Ye could have taken his body anywhere in the universe, even into the Mirror World. No doubt the management of *MeiXiu*, as well as Xu's friends, assuming he had any, would eventually report him missing, but she doubted that would be happening in the near future.

The lift rushed Reed and An-ren up to the fifteenth floor, and she was soon knocking on the door of room 15-11.

She waited impatiently, tapping her fingernails noisily on her phone. She heard the security chain being removed and the door swung inwards.

'Good to see you,' Zhao Na said, standing back to let them both in, although she clearly hadn't been expecting anyone other than An-ren. She stared at Reed in surprise, taken aback by his presence and his height, as well as the cuts and bruising to his face.

'You too, Na,' An-ren smiled.

She was pleased that she'd been assigned someone reasonable, a softly-spoken woman around the same age as herself. Na was widely respected for her diplomatic skills, and specifically her ability to calm models who needed calming.

'This is Zhu Wei,' An-ren explained, indicating Reed.

'Pleased to meet you,' Na said, bowing reverentially. 'I'm Zhou Na.'

Na had heard of Zhu Wei, knew of his reputation as an efficient and methodical fixer for *MeiXiu*, although she'd never met him.

'I fell down the stairs,' Reed smiled sheepishly.

He'd considered suggesting that An-ren had beaten him up, but he doubted anyone, and especially not An-ren herself, would find it funny.

He bowed back, and followed An-ren inside.

The central room, which had a kitchenette and a bedroom with ensuite facilities leading off it, was large and spacious, replete with pale wood, stone textures and sculptural furniture. The overall colour palette was soft and neutral, ideal for a photoshoot.

The photographer turned out to be another Englishman, Oliver Beckett, an expatriate who'd lived in China for almost as long as Reed, but who'd only recently arrived in Shanghai from Guangzhou.

Renee Voss, a globe-trotting German, and the shoot's stylist, was the final member of the small team. She was renowned for her use of bold colours, sculptural silhouettes and theatrical accessories.

As An-ren disappeared to change, Reed found himself alone with Beckett and Na. He smiled briefly at them both, and then started to walk around the room, looking carefully for even the smallest shard of jade.

'What are you doing?' Na asked him.

'I'm just checking the room out. There were some strange goings on during An-ren's last shoot. Didn't you hear about them?'

'I did,' Beckett said, speaking English. 'Some sort of revenant.'

Reed glanced at him as he continued to prowl around the room. That was an interesting choice of word, he thought, especially as it seemed to be a fairly accurate description of Luo Ban.

'How long have you been here?' Beckett, starting to follow Reed.

'A long time now,' Reed answered.

The truth was he didn't like meeting the British. They almost always wanted to know about him, felt they had some sort of innate right to quiz him about his past, simply because they were born on the same island. It was one of the great joys of his bar that the patrons were almost exclusively Chinese.

'Where are you from?'

'Just down the road. I've got a bar not too far away.'

'No, I meant, where are you from in England.'

'It's not important,' Reed replied.

'I'm from Knaresborough.'

That explained the Yorkshire accent that had been carefully, but not completely, concealed, Reed thought. Not that he cared, of course. He also knew that Beckett would assume that because he'd shared personal information, Reed would now feel honour-bound to reciprocate.

'I've never been there.'

He carried on looking around the room, opening drawers and looking under tables and into corners. The room seemed clean.

'I can't quite place your accent,' Beckett persisted.

'That's because I don't have one,' Reed declared, turning around to face the photographer. 'Look, I know you just want to have a chat with a Brit, in a language you can speak, but I'm not interested, okay? It's nothing personal. It's not about you, it's all about me.'

He paused, amused by the shocked expression that had appeared on Beckett's face. He clearly hadn't been expecting such an assertively negative response.

'We've all got a job to do, so why don't we just focus on that?' Reed added.

Beckett nodded. He turned back to his camera and lights, his face turning sour.

Reed noticed Na staring at him. She probably hadn't understood much of what they'd said, but she'd clearly picked up on his tone.

He gave her a small smile, before crossing to the kitchenette and carrying on with his search. It didn't take long, and he didn't find anything. He felt an immeasurable sense of relief at that revelation. After discovering the jade mirror in the bar the night before, he'd begun to feel a little paranoid. Room 15-11 being a jade-free zone was both a blessing and a relief.

As he returned to the main space, the bedroom door opened and An-ren made her entrance, closely followed by Voss.

If Reed had been drinking anything at that precise moment, he would have undoubtedly choked to death. As it was, his heart started racing and he suddenly felt very hot. As she walked past him, giving him a knowing sideways glance, he couldn't take his eyes off her.

He hadn't actually thought about the details of the photoshoot at all, had simply focused on getting her to the hotel and doing his best to ensure the environment was safe. But, even if he had given it some thought, nothing could have prepared him for the sight that met his eyes.

An-ren was neither dressed, nor undressed, existing in some sensually seductive in-between stage Reed found highly arousing.

She was almost wearing a long, knee-length, lilac shirt, made out of a soft, translucent material. Her arms were in it, and it was draped over her shoulders, but that was as far as its coverage went. It was completely unbuttoned and fell loose, revealing the matching gold bra, briefs and suspender belt, with sheer white stockings, that she wore underneath.

Her shoes were similar to the black ones she'd worn to the shoot, but these were a pale, icy blue that shimmered in the light, with narrow ankle straps studded with small rhinestones.

Her outfit, or lack of it, was completed by a thin white lace choker.

He wanted to look away, but he couldn't. He was completely unprepared for this moment. Which was odd, really, he thought, given he knew exactly what constituted a *MeiXiu* photoshoot.

Reed watched as Voss fussed over her clothing, such as it was, while Beckett prepared his cameras. Na stood back, silently orchestrating, as if she was the glue holding it all together. That was her conceit, Reed thought. There was only one person in charge here, and it wasn't any of the four people this side of the lens.

He sat down on a chair by the dining table and settled down to watch. Over the course of the next hour, An-ren cast her spell over the room. Reed realised that simply calling her a model was the most egregious injustice imaginable. She was nothing less than an artist, and room 15-11 had been transformed into her blank canvas.

He was in awe of her, felt honoured to be able to witness such a unique and powerful performance.

When the shoot was finally over, the shirt was still hanging off her shoulders, but the only other item of clothing left on her body was the choker. And yet, despite all of that, her total control of her art ensured that, although she tantalised and teased, nothing had been visible that she hadn't wanted to be.

Reed felt emotionally drained, and he wondered just how it might feel for her. What must it be like, he thought, to perform for an audience that, when the shoot was released, would be sitting in their homes, or in an office, maybe even on a train or a bus, maximising every image and focusing on every little piece of her body, searching for whatever it was that drove their obsessive desire for her.

An-ren disappeared back into the bedroom and Beckett began to pack his equipment away. At the same time, Voss and Na began to chat away in pidgin-Mandarin as they tidied up.

Reed's phone pinged and he pulled it out of his jacket pocket.

It was a message from Murphy.

"How about we all meet at 3.00 pm? IP says there's a café on Huaihai Road near Meridian House where we can agree on what we should do. Is that okay?"

IP? It took him a moment to realise she meant Iron Palm. He read the message again and realised that not only were they together, but somehow Murphy and Zhang had worked out how to communicate.

"We'll see you there."

Reed sent the message and put his phone away.

The SMS had instantly brought his mood down. He'd been lost in a world that only contained An-ren and him up until the moment his phone had pinged. Now, reality had reared its ugly head once again and he had little choice other than to consider what would happen next.

As he sat there, lost in thought, he realised that a dark-clad figure had arrived next to him. He looked up. It was An-ren, dressed, once again, in the all-black outfit she'd worn earlier.

She looked lovely, he thought.

'How was it?' she demanded.

'You're seriously asking me?' he asked.

'Yes, of course. You were here, weren't you?'

'You were amazing,' he told her. 'I've never seen anything like it. You're an artist.'

'Thank you, Xiao Wei,' she purred. 'I don't believe you, but it's nice to hear.'

'You should believe me. It was incredible.'

'Let's go,' she said, turning towards the door.

Reed smiled to himself. She disliked praise and compliments, but he'd seen the satisfied look in her eyes at his words, the pleasure and pride of knowing she'd done a good job.

He waved a vague goodbye at Becket, Voss and Na, and then followed An-ren out of room 15-11 and down to the Mustang waiting patiently in the car park below.

CHAPTER FORTY

Reed explained the plan, limited as it was, to An-ren. He hoped Zhang might have some more revelatory insights and information to share that would help them form a more concrete strategy, one that didn't feel like they were just running from pillar to post.

An-ren said nothing, but she felt exactly the same way. They seemed to be at least one step behind Ye the whole time, which wasn't really very surprising, given that the game wasn't theirs, and that Luo Ban and Ye had both had over two thousand years to prepare it.

Reed suggested they get some food, and, although she felt a tight knot of anxiety in her stomach, she agreed. They had a couple of hours to while away, and eating seemed as good a way of passing the time as any.

He suggested an upmarket restaurant not too far from the hotel, in Dianchi Road, called Yun Lou, the Cloud Tower. It was perched high up on the 23rd floor of a restored Art Deco building near the Bund, offering sweeping, dynamic views of both the Huangpu River and the futuristic, towering skyline of the city.

Reed had never been before, had never had either the inclination or opportunity to eat in such a fine restaurant, but some of his patrons had, and they all spoke very highly of it. He couldn't think of a better place to take An-ren. Aside from the fact that its natural elegance and sophistication was a perfect match for hers, he hoped the setting and the views, not to mention the food, might help take her mind off what they were facing, even if only for a short time.

An-ren was impressed. She'd heard of Cloud Tower, but had never eaten there. It was certainly in a different league to the cheap and nasty place that Xu had dragged them both to. That, she thought, already felt like a lifetime ago. She found it hard to believe her photoshoot in the Lumen House, the start of this whole nightmare, had been only three nights earlier. So much had happened since then that it felt like time had slowed down almost to a crawl.

They took the lift up to the 23rd floor, instantly entering what felt like a parallel universe when the cabin doors opened. The dining room was wrapped in floor-to-ceiling windows, all filled with spectacular views of the city and the river. A central skylight cast a diffused glow over the lacquered tables and minimalist floral arrangements.

A waiter came across and asked them whether they had a reservation. Reed bowed respectfully, explaining that they didn't, but would appreciate a table for two, by the window, if that was at all possible.

The waiter stared at Reed's bruised and cut face, a look of disapproval creeping into place. But, then the man glanced at An-ren, who bowed and smiled sweetly at him. Reed saw the gleam of recognition in the man's eyes, and the face that was poised to say "no" suddenly lit up like a summer's day in winter and bowed obsequiously back to her, saying 'yes, of course' over and over again.

As the waiter led them to their table, with its dynamic view of Shanghai, An-ren glanced at Reed, saw the disgruntled look on his face and couldn't help but laugh.

'It's not what you know, or even who you know,' she told him. 'It's who knows you.'

'Clearly,' he muttered, struggling to hold on to his irritation in the face of her infectious laughter.

They both had a full meal. Neither had eaten breakfast, and both shared the unspoken uncertainty of when they might get to eat again.

Reed had a starter of snow pea shoots with sesame mist, while An-ren chose smoked tofu petals with chili vinegar.

For the main course, Reed chose wok-seared duck breast with tangerine peel crisp skin. He loved duck, and ate it whenever the opportunity arose, which, in Shanghai, it often did.

An-ren continued her fish theme by ordering steamed halibut with white tea broth.

They washed all of this fine food down with several glasses of sparkling plum water. Reed desperately wanted something stronger, but resisted the urge. For one thing, he still had to drive, but, more significantly, he had no doubt he'd be needing a very clear head later on.

By the time they'd both waded their way through the first two courses, they were starting to feel full, so they chose to share a dessert, ordering almond milk custard with burnt sugar.

When the waiter brought the single dish, he handed them each a spoon. A mirrored spoon. Reed noticed An-ren briefly transfixed by her own reflection. She hesitated for a long moment before picking it up and starting to eat. He said nothing, but he understood. Mirrors had been her constant companion since she'd started modelling, if not before. In some ways, they'd probably been amongst her best friends. And now, all of that had changed.

At least the spoon had a bone handle and not a jade one, he thought. That was a blessing.

They finished up with coffee, An-ren choosing an iced americano with a twist of orange, Reed opting for his usual strong brew with a dash of milk. It wasn't always easy getting a white coffee in Shanghai. He knew the majority of the world drank it black, but it was one old habit he was disinclined to part with.

He settled the bill, An-ren graciously gifted the waiter a selfie, and they made their way back down to the ground floor and the Mustang.

'Thank you,' she said, as Reed put the car into drive and made his way out of the car park.

'My pleasure,' he responded. 'It's always good to face a challenge with a good meal inside you.'

An-ren was silent, but Reed knew what she was thinking. It felt a little like they'd just shared the Last Supper.

As he drove up Huaihai Road, spotting the Octagon Lane Café on a corner, he guessed Zhang and Murphy would know they'd arrived. It was a quiet street, and if there was one thing the Mustang wasn't, it was quiet.

He turned into Octagon Lane, next to the little café, found a space and parked.

'Do you think Zhang and Murphy might have kindled some sort of flame?' Reed asked, as they walked the short distance back to Huaihai Road.

An-ren threw him a distasteful glance.

'I don't even want to think about that, let alone talk about it,' she said.

Reed laughed. It was a crazy thought, but, then again, they now seemed to be living in a crazy world.

Zhang and Murphy were already sitting at a table by the window when Reed and An-ren entered. Murphy threw her hand up in the air to attract their attention, somewhat unnecessarily, given they were the only two people in the place.

As Reed sat down, between Murphy and An-ren, and opposite Zhang, he glanced at the two of them. They didn't seem any different on the outside. Zhang still looked grumpy and Murphy appeared as eager and keen as always. But that didn't really mean anything.

'It's good to see you both,' Murphy said, smiling warmly at Reed and An-ren.

'You, too, Fiona,' Reed responded.

An-ren remained silent, her eyes on Zhang.

'We've already checked out Meridian House,' Murphy enthused, glancing at Zhang.

'It has a bad aura,' Iron Palm declared, in Mandarin.

Reed couldn't help but wonder how he'd known what Murphy had said, although he might have recognised the name of the building, mangled though it was by her Irish accent.

'There's an unnatural spiritual miasma shrouding it,' Zhang added.

Reed glanced at An-ren. He wondered just how many retired policeman were capable of detecting spiritual miasmas.

'Which means what?' he asked.

'It means that the place is dangerous.'

'You say that about every place we go to, Iron Palm.'

'And it's true. There is real danger here.'

'Then we need to be careful.'

'What exactly is the plan?' An-ren demanded, feeling the need to cut to the chase.

'We thought you should probably go to the sales office, see what you can find out there, and we'll sneak round to the back, see if we can get in through the service entrance, check out the vaults and the conservation lab,' Murphy declared.

'Fiona, you don't speak Mandarin, and he doesn't speak English. How exactly did the two of you come up with that plan?' Reed asked, looking from one to the other.

'Baidu Translate,' An-ren suggested.

Murphy squirmed in her seat, looking a little awkward, Reed thought.

'Yes,' she agreed.

Reed studied Murphy for a moment, as she continued to avoid his and An-ren's eyes, and then turned his attention to Zhang, who looked as fed up and recalcitrant as usual, maybe even a little more so.

Reed leaned back in his seat and glanced at An-ren, who pulled a face at him that made it very clear he should let the matter drop.

Baidu Translate explained how the two of them could communicate, but it didn't explain Murphy's awkwardness. There was only one explanation for that, and it involved a universal language, one that didn't really require much in the way of meaningful dialogue.

'What about Victor Lam?' An-ren asked. 'If he's there, he'll recognise us.'

'He's been called away on urgent business,' Zhang responded.

'How do you know that?'

'Because I'm the one who called him away.'

'And Li Tong?' Reed suggested.

'He's at an auction in Suzhou.'

Reed looked at An-ren. He could tell she was thinking the same thing that he was.

'Come on, then,' he said, getting to his feet. 'Let's get this over and done with.'

CHAPTER FORTY-ONE

Reed pressed the buzzer and stood back, wondering how long they'd have to wait for a response.

'Do you really think we can get away with this?' Anren asked.

She looked more than a little worried.

'Why not? If Lam and Li aren't here, then there shouldn't be anyone to recognise us.'

'What about Ye?'

'You said Yue smashed her face. She won't want to show that to anyone.'

'And what about you? You look like you've been in some sort of brawl.'

'I was in some sort of brawl.'

'Be serious, Xiao Wei! I'm worried.'

Reed took her hands in his and held her gaze.

'I know you are. We all are. But they won't be expecting us to come to them. We need to do something, find a way to take some control back.'

'I know that. But I'm scared! Why does Ye keep insisting that I'm An Lian?'

'Maybe you resemble her. I really don't know, An-an. I just know that we have to do something to stop them.'

An-ren was about to respond when a female voice burst out of the intercom next to the buzzer.

'Hello? Do you have an appointment?'

'Yes,' Reed responded, speaking into the microphone. 'My business partner and I are due to see Mr Lam at 3.00 pm.'

'I'm afraid Mr Lam isn't here right now,' the voice responded.

'Well, we definitely have an appointment. He was going to show us some exclusive jade shards.'

'Unfortunately, Mr Lam isn't due back today. Would you like me to leave a message for him to reschedule the appointment?'

'My partner and I have come all the way from Chongqing for this meeting. It isn't our problem that Mr Lam isn't here.'

'I'm afraid I can't help, sir,' the voice said, although Reed didn't think it sounded very sorry.

'Then I'll just have to tell Mr Lam how unhelpful you were. Can I please have your name?'

'My name?'

'Yes. It's a simple request. I presume you have a name? I'm sure Mr Lam will be pleased to hear how inflexible and unhelpful his staff are in his absence.'

There was a pause at the other end. Reed glanced at An-ren and grinned.

'If it's acceptable, I can arrange for someone to show you pieces that you might be interested in.'

'We'd prefer Mr Lam himself, but if he's not here, then that will have to do.'

The smoked glass doors slid open, and Reed led An-ren inside.

A young woman in a navy-blue business suit and white blouse greeted them, bowing low as they entered. She was wearing heels, but, when she straightened up she was still over six inches shorter than both of her guests.

'Feng Shanhu,' Reed said, ostentatiously leaning in to read her name badge. 'Thank you for seeing reason, Ms Feng.'

'At Meridian House, we always want our customers to feel welcome,' she retorted, her voice bland and anodyne, as if she were reading a script.

Her eyes, however, were far more animated, intently scrutinising the abrasions and bruises on Reed's face with unconcealed disapproval.

'Please excuse my colleague's face,' An-ren said, seeing the suspicion on Ms Feng's face. 'We were involved in a traffic accident yesterday. Our taxi was hit by another car on our way to the airport. If we'd taken the time to go to hospital, we would have missed our flight.'

'It hurts a lot,' Reed nodded, smiling wanly at Ms Feng. 'But it's bearable.'

She studied them both for a moment, and Reed could see she wasn't convinced.

'What did you say your names were?' she asked.

'We didn't,' Reed smiled. 'I'm Jack Burton and this is Yin Miao.'

Ms Feng continued to look sceptical, but eventually turned on her heel.

'Please follow me,' she said.

'Yin Miao?' An-ren whispered in Reed's ear as they followed her through the next set of doors, and into the palatial splendour of the main salesroom.

'It's a long story,' he grinned back.

They found themselves in a room that, although a gallery, was clearly designed to be more like a temple. It was polished, reverent, and quietly luminous, with light falling in soft pools from recessed fixtures and lantern pendants, catching the gloss of marble and the subtle sheen of lacquered wood.

A central wooden table anchored the space, clearly arranged for contemplative viewing, as well as close inspection. Glass display cases lined the walls, wide aisles led the eye from fine examples of porcelain, to equally impressive jade pieces and ornate scrollwork, and then outward to the bamboo garden that lay beyond.

Reed studied the room. There were blue and white porcelain vases, with tall, balanced necks and fine underglaze painting, alongside jade sculptures, displaying a variety of patinas from celadon to deep apple-green. Beyond these were a selection of calligraphy scrolls and paintings, both mounted, and rolled, on the central table.

'This is all very impressive,' An-ren announced from behind Reed, her voice expressing a mixture of disdain and disappointment, 'but we specifically requested that Mr Lam show us some of your best jade shards.'

Reed glanced at her out of the corner of his eye. She'd switched into performance mode, moving back into her modelling persona. Commanding, aloof and demanding. She was an artist, he realised, a highly skilled one.

'Of course,' Ms Feng conceded, clearly taken aback. 'I apologise for the oversight.'

She turned on her heel and hurried out of the room.

Reed turned to An-ren and was about to praise her performance, when he noticed a small, subtle gesture from her hand. He looked up, trying not to move his head as he did so.

There was a CCTV camera in the corner of the room, which was hardly surprising given the nature of the business.

He gave her an imperceptible nod.

'These people are pathetic!' he scowled. 'We've come all this way and they want to show us garbage!'

An-ren threw him a look that suggested he should try not to make it so obvious he was putting on an act.

He sighed. He clearly wasn't much use at this sort of thing. Certainly, she seemed to have more idea of what the situation demanded than he did.

Ms Feng came scuttling back in, closely followed by two young men, both also dressed in navy blue business suits, and carrying large trays filled with shards of jade.

Ms Feng carefully cleared a space on the central table, and the two men lowered the trays onto them.

'Thank you,' An-ren nodded, as she stepped forward to study the shards.

Reed followed her and began to scrutinise the jade, trying hard to make it look as if he knew what he was doing.

'None of these appear to be Luo Ban or Tomb Wheel,' he whispered to her, in English.

She didn't respond, but a frown suddenly appeared on her brow, her eyes expressing confusion and surprise.

'What is it?' he asked.

'Can't you feel it?'

'Feel what?'

'A pressure, in my chest, almost like the memory of a breath,' she murmured, her eyes suddenly fearful.

Reed didn't understand what she was talking about, couldn't feel anything. Then he heard something, an ephemeral whispering at the very edge of his hearing. He was taken back to the moment when he'd taken her home on the first night. The voice that was no voice.

Reed turned back to face the shards. He realised they'd changed. It was remarkably subtle, but there was a very faint mist forming around them, almost as if their surface temperature was changing.

There was something else, too. The light streaming through the windows from the direction of the bamboo gardens was reflecting differently off the shards, almost as if it was fractured. Small reflections ghosted across the jade, images of things he couldn't make out, but which he knew weren't actually there.

He stepped back, pulling her with him, gasping as his heart began to beat like a frenzied drum.

He had no idea what was happening, but he knew it wasn't good. These shards weren't even Luo Ban or Tomb Wheel artifacts, but they seemed to resonate to An-ren's presence as if possessed, much like the mirror at the photoshoot in the Lumen House.

And then he heard it, a deep, sonorous, male voice, no more tangible than the breeze ruffling the leaves on a tree.

'An-ren!'

CHAPTER FORTY-TWO

Zhang and Murphy had circled to the rear of the building, pausing and hiding behind a conveniently located shrub as an SUV drove out of the secured compound.

There was an entrance gate next to the vehicle access. Once the SUV passed, Murphy moved out of their hiding place. She stopped as Zhang grabbed her arm and pulled her back behind the bush.

'Look,' he said, pointing towards a CCTV camera above the gates.

Glancing towards where Zhang was pointing, she instinctively understood what he'd said. She sighed, looking around, hoping against hope that an unlocked door might suddenly appear out of nowhere.

Zhang merely raised his iron palms towards the camera. Blue light arced upwards, hitting the device, instantly destroying it.

Murphy ducked down and put her hands over her head as a large piece of the camera zoomed past, missing her by inches.

'We'll go this way, then,' she muttered, as Zhang strode past her and began to study the lock on the gate.

'Can't you just zap that?' she asked, as he reached into a pocket and pulled out a set of keys and small tools.

He glanced at her phone screen and scowled.

'Might isn't always right,' he responded, setting to work on the lock.

he had the gate open. Checking the area was clear, he hurried through and into the rear compound.

Murphy scampered after him, wondering, once more, just what sort of policeman could pick locks and blow out cameras with energy rays unleashed from his hands. She'd spent a whole night with him, had enjoyed some of the best sex of her recent life, but she still knew absolutely nothing about him.

He, on the other hand, was now the extremely reluctant possessor of her entire life story, from the backstreets of Sligo, in the very wet province of Connacht, to Shanghai, via a BSc (Hons) in Paranormal Studies and Associated Supernatural Elements from the University of Milburg. She'd also talked at length about the haunted forests of Hoia, in Romania, and Aokigahara, in Japan. He'd actually slept through most of it, but she was enough of a student of the mind to know that he'd received it all subliminally, although, of course, without Baidu Translate to help him, it was simply noise.

They reached the building's rear entrance, its corrugated rollup door wide open. Boxes and crates were piled everywhere, and a truck stood empty.

'Do you think this is a trap?' Murphy asked, glancing around, peering into every remote corner, expecting

Whisperers, or a Xilin, to come rushing towards them at any moment.

'Probably,' Zhang muttered.

He turned away from her phone and led the way into the darkened interior. He looked up, scanning for surveillance, but it seemed Victor Lam felt secure and comfortable inside his gated compound. Either that, or he didn't want even a private record of anything that happened there.

There were two simple doors in the large warehouse space, and Zhang assumed they led into the rest of the building. But, there was a third, far more interesting one, to their right, on an interior wall. Whereas the other two were straightforward wooden doors, the third one was significantly different.

In many ways it resembled the sort of door that secured bank vaults, although it was smaller and rectangular, rather than circular.

'I reckon there might be something important behind that,' Murphy said, as Zhang stood in front of it, apparently contemplating its operating mechanisms.

The centre of the door was dominated by a large hand wheel, acting as a handle. Next to the door a small black panel with a faintly glowing screen waited patiently for an access card and the correct code to be entered.

Murphy sighed. The sight of the door made her realise just what a bunch of amateurs they were. They'd simply turned up at the beating heart of Victor Lam's criminal empire, and expected the answers they were so desperately seeking would just fall into their laps. It wasn't just naivety, she thought, it was downright fucking stupidity.

It was embarrassing, and, of course, the whole sorry situation was made even worse by the knowledge that both An-ren's and Reed's lives were at risk.

She turned to Zhang, was about to blurt out her sense of hopelessness and futility, when she noticed he had gone very quiet and still, had his eyes closed and seemed to have disappeared somewhere deep inside. His breathing had changed, and he was now inhaling and exhaling very dramatically.

His chest rose and fall almost in waves, and she realised that she could sense something. A power,, unseen and intangible, but very real. And it was emanating from Zhang.

Her hair stood on end, and as the unknown power touched her she could feel her skin tingle, coaxed into tiny goosebumps along her arms. She rubbed them, trying to brush off the uncomfortable sensation.

Without opening his eyes, Zhang reached out and placed his hands on the control panel. His breathing intensified and Murphy could almost hear the power that transferred from Iron Palm's body into the small black unit.

There were sparks, flashes of electrical arcing, and then the panel exploded.

Murphy screamed and jumped back. Zhang opened his eyes and glowered at her.

'Be quiet!' he hissed.

'Sorry,' she apologised. 'I wasn't expecting that.'

Zhang grasped the hand-wheel and started to turn. Murphy frowned in disbelief. His hands had been over the panel when it had exploded, and she'd felt the force of the small explosion from where she'd been standing, yet his hands seemed completely unscathed.

He pulled the heavy door open and went inside. She followed, and he pulled it shut again.

'No need to advertise our presence,' he told her, noticing her anxious glance.

They stood on a small landing with a flight of stone steps leading down. Above them, motion activated strip lights flickered on, casting a dull light onto the scene. With no other option they began to descend the steps. Zhang took the lead, whilst Murphy followed in his stocky shadow. As they moved, the lights flicked on ahead of them, and went out behind, creating a feeling of dread in them both.

After about fifty feet, the steps abruptly ended, opening out into a large, echoing space. Above them, more lights flickered on, illuminating what Murphy presumed was Lam's conservation lab. Even with the strip lights on, the room looked dim. The walls were bare, just flaking plaster. It felt cold and sterile, a functional area, nothing more.

They wandered around, studying their surroundings. Ten glass cabinets filled the room, containing mostly jade shards, as well as mirror fragments suspended in resin.

Murphy noticed Zhang's attention had been drawn to something on the other side of the chamber. She crossed to where he was intently studying what appeared to be a pictogram.

It wasn't until she reached his side that she realised there was what looked like a sealed chamber embedded in the wall, and the glyphs Zhang was intently studying scrolled all the way around it.

'Is it a door?' she asked, showing him her phone screen.

'No,' he responded. 'It's a containment vault.'

'What's it containing?' she asked, instantly taking a step backwards.

'How would I know?' Zhang snorted, remaining focused on the images around the door

'What language is this?' she asked, indicating the pictograms. 'They're not Mandarin, are they?'

He snorted, giving her a disdainful scowl.

'They're at least a thousand years older than Mandarin. These are Tomb Wheel glyphs.'

'Tomb Wheel?' she repeated. 'You mean, Luo Ban and Ye?'

'Meng Yao and Ye are not the Sepulchral Mandala,' he sighed, giving her a look that matched the contempt in his voice. 'They are of it, but they don't define it.'

'Don't they?' she retorted, angered by his patronising attitude. 'The Tomb Wheel Dynasty ended with them, didn't it? They were responsible for its destruction. That seems pretty defining to me!'

'They define a shift into the darkness and the decline that followed, that's all,' Zhang responded.

'No one ever remembers what went before,' Murphy continued, warming to her theme. 'Civilisations are defined by their endings.'

Zhang was about to vehemently disagree, when a whisper of sound came from the wall on their right. He turned, senses on alert, searching for its source.

Murphy heard it, too. A sibilant sound, almost a sighing, as of the wind gently blowing through the last leaves of summer.

She noticed there was a mirror shard embedded in the wall, and, as she watched, horrified, a figure stepped out of it, decompressing and expanding into a fully grown woman as she arrived in this world.

Murphy felt a chill grasp her heart, and she sensed a tautening in Zhang.

Ye stood in front of them, wearing a sleeveless mid-thigh length purple dress, her skin glistening glassily in the dim light. The dress accentuated her slender curves, and her long black hair seemed to almost flow down her back and shoulders. She was sensual, seductive, and moved like a predator arrogantly stalking its prey.

But Murphy barely noticed, her attention drawn to Ye's still-cracked face, which resembled a mirror that had been shattered into large segments. There had been some healing since she'd last seen Ye at Eternal Seal. The fragments were now less clearly defined, the sharp edges no longer so savage.

Murphy wondered how that might work, how a creature that seemed to be a woman, but was made of glass, might actually be able to heal.

'I'm so glad you could make it,' Ye purred, a contemptuous smirk on her lips. 'It's curious how some things in life are so completely predictable.'

She walked towards them, stopping just in front of Zhang. She studied him, her face a mix of curiosity and frustration.

'I'm sure we've met before,' she said.

'We have. At Eternal Seal.'

'I don't mean yesterday. Who are you?'

Zhang simply stared at her. His expression was contemptuous, but there was something in his eyes that told a different story.

'You have real skills,' she smiled. 'It's such a shame to see you waste them on simple parlour tricks. I think you deserve a real challenge.'

She turned back to face the mirror shard she'd passed through. She said nothing and made no gesture, but the same whispering sound that had heralded her entrance suddenly filled the air.

Murphy looked on in horror as a shape began to emerge from the shard, disgorging itself onto the floor of the chamber. It almost poured itself out of the mirror, moving to a position behind Ye and settling into a tightly wound spiral.

Ye turned back to Zhang and Murphy, unable to stop herself from laughing as she saw the look on the Irish woman's face.

'This is *Gusi Jiao*,' Ye said.

'The Bone Silk Wyrm,' Zhang muttered, a hard, steely, expression appearing on his face.

It was long, serpentine like a snake, an eyeless creature woven from bone filaments and mirror thread. It was a pale white, the colour of ivory, quite unlike anything Murphy had ever seen or heard of before. Both the Xilin and the Moquai had been terrifying and unnatural, but this thing went way beyond either of them. It was utterly repulsive.

'What is it?' she said to Zhang, so terrified that she didn't think to hold her phone up for him.

'This is a creature born of failed bindings,' Zhang said, staring coldly at Ye.

'Even remnants have their uses,' Ye mocked.

She made a gesture, and the Wyrm uncoiled itself, following her as she crossed to the stairs and disappeared upwards, before stopping in front of Zhang and Murphy, effectively blocking their escape.

It turned its sightless face in their direction and hissed loudly, stretching out to its full length. It lifted its head high, and launched itself towards them.

CHAPTER FORTY-THREE

Zhang stepped sideways, shoving Murphy out of the way. The force of his action threw her all the way across the floor and she felt herself slam into the far wall.

'What the feck was that?' she muttered, shaking her head to clear the fuzziness from the impact.

The Bone Silk Wyrm turned its eyeless head and hissed loudly at Zhang, preparing to strike again. It was disgusting, he thought, utterly repulsive, in a way that neither the Xilin nor the Moquai had been. The creature was, essentially, little more than long discarded pieces of bone, all held together by infinitesimal glass filaments, its primitive lifeforce the essence of mirrors. To the naked eye, it seemed impossible that it didn't simply fall apart.

The worm lunged again. This time Zhang stood his ground, working desperately to control his breathing. As it opened its jaw to strike he held up his palms. Savage blue fire arced from his hands, raging upwards. It hit the creature full on, slamming it into the nearby wall.

In the fraction of a second between the attack and impact, Zhang chanted quietly. He focused deep inside, working to align the yin and yang that had divided his soul for so long. Spells and talismans that hadn't been heard outside of the Mirror World for over two thousand years spilled from his lips, creating faint, shimmering, patterns in the air around him.

The Wyrm turned back to face Zhang, pausing for a moment, as if re-evaluating its target.

Iron Palm studied it closely, keeping his breathing as shallow as possible, his body as still as the grave. He was only too well aware that the Wyrm didn't have ears, or eyes. A creature of the dead, it sensed breath and qi rather than sound and movement. Being as close to death as was humanly possible would make it harder for it to locate its prey.

As the Wyrm slowly moved closer to him, twisting its head from side to side as it sought him out, he felt a fragmenting in his mind. He'd forgotten the creature could distort memories, and fragments of past battles began to flicker through his mind, cutting into his thoughts. He saw Meng Yao and Lin Ye, as well as the armies of the Glass Phalanx and the Meridian Wheel.

A name he hadn't thought of for years rose up above the other memories. Zhang Zhenwu. He heard the words 'Master of the Mirror Sutra" echoing behind the name, as if a thousand voices spoke them in unison. He closed his eyes, tried to distract his thoughts from the world of the Tomb Wheel and focus on the creature that was now so close he could hear the rustle of bone against filament.

The Wyrm began to slither faster. Zhang turned, realised that by removing himself from its vision, it had focused on Murphy. She started to scream and pressed herself flat against the wall behind her.

He raised his hands, sending more streams of blue lightning into its body. Under the sting of Zhang's attack, the wyrm stopped abruptly. It swung its hideous head in the direction of Zhang's fire, turning its attention back towards him

Zhang let his breathing return to normal, feeling his *qi* return to normal, as if saying to the Wyrm "here I am, come and get me".

As the creature glided towards him, Zhang ran to the wall near the containment chamber and yanked out the jade shard Ye had appeared through.

The Wyrm gathered speed, giving Zhang only seconds to study the shard. But it was all he needed. He let out a sigh of relief as he saw what he'd been looking for.

He held the shard tightly in his right hand, and, as the Wyrm raced ever closer, he stepped slightly to his left, driving it as hard as he could into the creature's neck as it went past. There was a burst of red light, and the Wyrm reared up, hissing wildly, backing away from Zhang as if in agony.

Zhang moved quickly, getting as close to it as he could, all the while desperately scanning its neck. He sighed with relief as he spotted what he'd been looking for. Hairline cracks in the bone.

"Stay where you are!" he shouted at Murphy, hoping that even if she couldn't understand his words, she would pick up on his tone.

He turned back just as the Wyrm lunged at him again. He moved too late, and the creature hit him full in the chest. He tried to grab its head, but missed, and was thrown ten feet across the chamber, the shard flying out of his hand, landing heavily on the concrete floor. He was winded, his back sending out sharp waves of pain from where he'd landed, and he struggled desperately to get back to his feet.

The Wyrm had already spun around and was on its way back towards him. He gazed around the room frantically, trying to locate the jagged piece of jade, but couldn't see it anywhere.

And then he saw it, embedded in the Wyrm's body. He sighed, but stood firm as it slithered back towards him again. It put its head down, opened its mouth and lunged.

Zhang jumped diagonally, grabbing bone as he did so. As the creature bucked and twisted beneath him, he flattened himself along it's skeletal body and reached out for the shard. It was just beyond his grasp.

As he tried to drag himself closer, the Wyrm began to twist even more violently, desperate to shake him off.

But Zhang held firm, wrapping his arms and legs around the creature as it rocked from side. He hoped it didn't start to roll. If it did, he felt fairly certain he'd be completely crushed under its unnaturally heavy body.

He strained with every ounce of strength he had, inching his way up the writhing body, until he was finally close enough to touch the shard. He wrapped the fingers of his right hand around it and fired a red wave of arcing energy from his left hand through the jade and into the Wyrm.

It screamed, the first noise it had made since Ye had brought it through the mirror, a terrible, unholy and unnatural sound that made Zhang's ears ring.

He pulled with every ounce of strength left in his aching muscles, finally retrieving the shard. He leapt off the monstrous creature, scrambling to what he thought would be a safe distance. He looked up at the Wyrm.

A fine web of lines began to weave their way along the body of the creature, slowly growing into cracks and fissures before splintering into an increasing number of fragments. Remarkably, despite the damage, it still managed to hold itself together.

It suddenly moved its head, and he responded far too slowly. His mind focused on the damage, Zhang caught the full force of the creature's attack as it struck him. It threw him into the wall, winding him. Pain screamed though every inch of his body.

The Wyrm moved its head to face Zhang. It was relentless, he thought, and he wasn't sure how much longer he could continue to fight. As he lay on the ground, trying desperately to get his breath back and compose himself for yet another assault, he could sense the anger that existed within the creature. He knew, although he couldn't have said exactly how, that it wanted nothing more than to crush him into complete non-existence.

It slithered towards him again. He tightened the fingers on his right hand, but his heart sank as he realised his hand was empty. He'd lost the shard again.

He looked around, despair falling on him like a dark, dismal cloud. He couldn't see it anywhere. He turned back to face the Wyrm, saw that it was almost upon him, raising its head to strike.

He suddenly felt a terrible sense of failure and regret wash over him. In a previous life, he'd once managed, with some significant help, to overcome the forces that now drove the Wyrm. Even then, however, his masters had known that the forces of darkness would not be so easily defeated.

A rueful smile crossed his face. Now that he was about to die, he wondered what sort of welcome he would receive on the other side. He didn't think it would be a warm one.

'Take it!' a voice yelled at him.

Murphy was there beside him, her face filled with a terrible fear, but, also, a determination and a resolve that, even in his moment of death, Zhang found impressive.

And then he realised what she was doing. The shard was in her hand. He grabbed it from her, and drove it up as hard as he could into the creature that was now directly above them both. With his free hand he focused every ounce of energy his bruised body could muster, directing it into the shard. It radiated out and into the face and head of the Silk Bone Wyrm, setting off a deep, electrical hum in the air around them.

The creature's hybrid skull was only a few inches away from Zhang's when the arcing energy hit it, but the result was highly dramatic. The cracks Zhang had already opened finally shattered, rupturing its bones. The head exploded first, tiny fragments of bone and threads of mirror filament flying outwards, bouncing off the walls and floors. Its body hovered upright for a few seconds, as if still aware, before the rest of its splintered skeleton turned inwards, almost melting as it slowly disintegrated.

The creature's bones, already dead for over two thousand years, simply turned to dust and the Wyrm ceased to exist.

Zhang realised Murphy was at his side, her hands on his shoulders, a broad smile of relief and gratitude on her face. He realised what she wanted, and he pulled her in close and gave her a quick hug. It hurt, but he thought she deserved some sort of reward. She had, after all, saved his, and, by implication, her own.

He sat back and sighed, releasing the vast tension that had built up in his body. So much for Daoist teachings and the Mirror Sutra.

And then the realisation of what had happened and why swept over him.

'We need to go!' he barked at Murphy, pushing her off his shoulder. Scrambled painfully to his feet, he grabbed Murphy by the hand. Together they raced towards the stairs Ye had taken earlier

CHAPTER FORTY-FOUR

For a moment, Reed stood rooted to the spot, and then he turned to go, his hand still on An-ren's arm. The voice he'd first heard outside the house on Wukang road echoed in his ears as he hurried towards the doorway through which Feng Shanhu and her two colleagues had entered. He brushed roughly past them.

He'd wanted to take the attack to the enemy, but it seemed his plan had failed miserably. He was shocked that all the jade shards and mirrors in the room, none of which appeared to be either Luo Ban or Tomb Wheel, had begun to resonate and draw energy from An-ren.

And the deeply disturbing voice had sent a chill into the deepest reaches of his heart.

As they approached the door, it opened inwards, and a figure they both hoped they'd never see again strode imperiously into the room.

Ye, sensual and seductive, despite her face resembling a shattered mirror, stepped in to block their exit. She was followed by a group of black-clad men.

Whisper Knife, Reed presumed.

Ye's damaged face lit up as she saw An-ren and Reed.

'Did you really think you'd be able to stop me?' she asked, her mouth twisted into a contemptuous sneer.

'We've done it before, and we can do it again,' Reed retorted, glancing around anxiously.

There was a door behind them, on the far side of the room. He presumed it led further into the labyrinth of Meridian House, but, if it took them away from Ye, then it had to be good. They could worry about finding a way out when they'd escaped.

Reed tightened his grip on An-ren's arm, preparing to run past Ms Feng and her colleagues. However, he watched in dismay as the door opened and more black clad whisperers filed in.

They were trapped.

'Shit!' Reed muttered.

'You haven't done anything!' Ye exulted. 'An Lian has had to save your life twice! All you've done is survive!'

'I'm not An Lian!' An-ren insisted, anger and frustration briefly over-riding fear.

'You think that just because you have no memories you're not her? My master will help you remember.'

'I'm not her!' An-ren repeated.

'I'm bored with this,' Ye sighed. She turned to the men behind her. 'Get him!'

The five Whisperers flanking Ye rushed towards Reed. He pulled An-ren behind him, attempting to shield her.

'It's you they want to hurt, not me!' she said, peeling his hand off her arm and forcing her way back in front.

The men simply shoved her out of the way, sending her tumbling into one of the display cabinets Her momentum knocked it over, emptying ancient, priceless vases onto the floor. They shattered loudly, sending sharp porcelain fragments flying through the air in every direction.

'No!' Reed shouted, watching as An-ren steadied herself, somehow avoiding falling onto the shards of glass and shattered china.

He was so focused on An-ren's plight he never saw the fist that connected with his jaw. He staggered backwards, turning his attention to the five men who now surrounded him. The odds were already stacked against him, and he knew that even if he did somehow win this round, there were five more Whisperers waiting to take a piece of him.

He looked at the woman standing beside him and knew, in that moment, that nothing mattered more than her safety. He went on the offensive, throwing a punch and aiming a kick.

The punch missed, but his foot made contact, sending the Whisperer reeling back.

A fist connected with his back, and he gasped as the pain flooded through his body. He turned and threw himself at his attacker, hitting the man in the midriff, and wrestling him to the floor.

An-ren picked up the largest, sharpest piece of porcelain she could find and ran towards the fight. She rammed it as hard as she could into the back of the nearest Whisperer. He screamed in agony, instantly falling to his knees, glancing at her in surprise and shock. An-ren watched, horrified, as he flailed his arms in a futile attempt to stem the blood that was rapidly oozing out of the blow she'd inflicted.

'Stop!' Ye's voice boomed, echoing slightly as it bounced around the walls.

Her tone was commanding and so imperious that everyone, including An-ren and Reed did as she'd ordered.

'Hold him!' she ordered. 'I want him to see this.'

For the briefest moment, nobody moved, and then, as Reed threw another punch, the remaining Whisperers lunged forward and grabbed him. They pulled him roughly to the floor, pinning him face down, his arms held tightly behind his back.

As he struggled in vain to get free, he realised the other group of Whisperers were now standing over him. Ye didn't believe in a fair fight, he thought. First, the Xilin, then the Moquai, and now a group of neanderthal thugs. At that moment, Reed wanted nothing more than to grab her and smash her face into one of the other cabinets. He imagined that watching her shatter and fragment into a million shards of glass would be very satisfying.

An-ren lunged at Ye with the bloody porcelain shard, but the Mirror Courtesan merely held up her right hand and seized it. She ripped it out of An-ren's grasp and threw it across the room, contempt written across her face.

'You really are beginning to irritate me!' she hissed, her eyes burning a malevolent crimson. 'I'd forgotten just how much I hate you!'

'I haven't done anything to you!' An-ren screamed back, looking around for something else she could use, some way she could, at the very least, incapacitate Ye so that she and Reed could escape.

There was nothing to hand, nothing that might do any significant damage to a creature of darkness like Ye.

'Leave An-ren alone!' Reed shouted, every muscle in his body screaming as he fought against the hands restraining him. 'Take me instead!'

'You?' Ye laughed without even glancing his way, focused on the shapes her fingers were sketching in the air. 'You're pathetic. Not even worth killing. Your punishment is simpler. You get to watch the woman you claim to love slip beyond your reach.'

Only then did she turn, cerulean eyes fixing on him, a cruel smile tugging at her cracked lips.

'Poor William,' she murmured. 'You've already lived this tragedy once. And still you haven't learned how it ends.'

She laughed, and the sound startled him. It was disarmingly human, warm even, utterly at odds with the fractured, inhuman face before him. He'd expected something monstrous. Instead, the humanity of it made the moment feel far worse.

'Don't listen to her,' An-ren said, turning to face Reed.

She was scared, terrified, but she also knew just what Ye was doing. It was cruelty that went beyond any human understanding of cruelty.

'She's wrong,' she added, although she knew it sounded weak.

She saw the pain in Reed's eyes, the horror and self-loathing that Ye's words had triggered, and her heart wept for him.

In that moment, she knew she had to act, before it was too late, before both she and Reed were damned for all eternity.

She turned back to Ye, preparing to launch herself in a last-ditch desperate attack, but she was stopped in her tracks by what she saw.

Ye's fingers had been moving in precise patterns, and she had creating a two-dimensional sigil in three-dimensional space. The lines she traced had become almost tangible, a mirror glyph suspended in the air between the two women. It glowed red, as if some ephemeral fire burnt within.

Ye locked her eyes onto An-ren's. The intensity of the hatred An-ren saw there was so overwhelming that she tried to look away. But she found she couldn't.

'You were always meant to return,' Ye whispered, thrusting her hand at the mirror glyph, sending it flying through space.

As the sigil struck, An-ren felt her body go rigid, every muscle locked. She tried to move, but found she was completely powerless, her body totally unresponsive. A red glow flared around her briefly as the sigil embedded itself deep inside her. Then everything went black. As her consciousness slipped away, she collapsed towards the hard marble floor

But she never hit the ground. Ye acted with inhuman speed, every movement a blur, and scooped her up in her arms, with a delicacy and care belying everything that had gone before.

'Bring the mirror!' she commanded.

Two more Whisperers strode into the room carrying a large jade mirror. They moved around the still prone Reed and set it down in front of Ye, leaning it against the nearest display cabinet.

She turned towards Reed, her eyes, now returned to their usual cerulean blue. Her face was cold and impassive.

'Kill him!' she ordered, before stepping into the mirror with An-ren and disappearing.

CHAPTER FORTY-FIVE

Reed watched in absolute despair as Ye stepped into the mirror with An-ren. The glass seemed to shift and reshape itself as she passed through, almost as if it had transformed into some sort of liquid.

His despair turned to desolation when the same two Whisperers who'd carried the mirror, immediately poured what he presumed was some form of accelerant over it, pulled out a lighter, and set it on fire.

Reed was impressed by the stupidity of the two Whisperers, who continued to stand in front of the mirror as it began to bubble and hiss. It gave out a loud crack and they took a step backwards. The mirror exploded, charred shards of glass fracturing violently outwards, eviscerating the men in the process.

The two men holding Reed's legs were also hit, their bodies pierced as the jagged fragments flew through the air. Fortunately for Reed, they shielded him from the explosion, and as they collapsed in agony, releasing their hold, he summoned up all his strength to free his arms.

His battered and bruised body protested loudly, but he didn't care. His adrenaline was flowing and he channelled every available ounce of energy into throwing the Whisperers off his arms. With an immense surge, he ripped himself free, leaping to his feet in the process.

Fuelled by an overwhelming anger, Reed punched the Whisperer on his right as hard as he could. As the man reeled away, clutching his face, his jaw jutting out at an unnatural angle, Reed turned and savagely kicked the other Whisperer between the legs.

The thug gasped in agony, grasping his battered genitals and writhing in agony. Free at last, Reed turned to survey the room.

Ms Feng and her two colleagues were long gone, having escaped through the far door, no doubt trying to find some secure bolt hole deeper inside Lam's criminal empire.

The floor near the burning mirror was still covered in broken glass, fractured porcelain and shattered wood, both from the display cabinet that An-ren had been thrown into, and also the one the jade mirror had been propped against. The mirror itself was now little more than a frame, lying in pieces on the charred floor. Of the ten Whisperers that Ye had brought with her, only three were still standing.

A wave of unbridled despair threatened to overwhelm Reed as his mind filled with images that rose up to taunt and torment him.

He saw a child running into a road, laughing happily, as if it were nothing more than a game of tag. He saw the car that was too close to be able to do anything other than swerve wildly, slamming the child into the car she'd just happily leapt out of.

He saw An-ren, transfixed, incapacitated and abducted by a glass monster masquerading as a woman. He'd made her a solemn promise to keep her safe, and he'd failed her, just as he'd failed Amara.

He felt a hatred rise within him that he struggled to contain. He felt his hands shaking as he thought about Ye. She understood cruelty, knew exactly how to crush someone's soul under her heel as if it were no more substantial than the shell of a snail. He would make her pay. If it was the last thing he ever did, which it well might be, she would stare into his eyes and see what hatred really meant.

He raised his head and turned to face the remaining Whisperers, who, without Ye to tell them what to think, seemed uncertain of what to do next.

'Come on, then, you fucking morons!' he shouted, putting his fists up.

'That's so dramatic,' one of the thugs retorted. He reached into a pocket and pulled out a gun.

He cocked it and aimed at Reed.

'Do you believe in God?' the man asked. 'If you do, then you're just about to meet him.'

The other two smirked, no doubt relieved the situation was now under control. Reed was about to die and they could get on with more important things.

The Whisperer raised the gun slightly, targeting Reed's forehead and resting his finger on the trigger.

From behind Reed, a fierce blue arc of lightning shot through the air, hitting the gun and the hand holding it.

The thug cried out in pain, dropping the gun, and staring at his hand. Both were melted, twisted, as if some vast heat had seared them. A second burst hit him in the head. He slumped to the floor, his face little more than a charred wreck.

Another electric burst of energy shot across the room, hitting one of the other Whisperers directly in the chest. He collapsed, a large smoking hole where his heart had been.

Reed whirled around. Zhang and Murphy were standing in the doorway. Iron Palm had his hands raised and sent another blast out, hitting the final Whisperer, instantly incinerating his torso.

'Where's An-ren?' Zhang demanded.

Reed opened his mouth to speak, but didn't know what to say. He felt certain that if he uttered a single word, he'd break down.

Zhang followed Reed's eyes to the burnt, charred mirror frame.

'Ye?' he asked, his tone a little softer.

Reed nodded, still unable to speak.

'We should go,' Zhang declared.

'No!' Reed exclaimed. 'We can't just leave her!'

Zhang put a hand on Reed's shoulder, a gesture he obviously intended to be comforting, reassuring and supportive. It felt anything but, though, and Reed angrily shrugged it off.

'She's not here. If Ye took her through that mirror, then she's no longer anywhere near Meridian House,' Zhang told him.

'Then where is she? We need to go there. Now!'

'Let's get out of here first, Zhu Wei. Let's get to safety and then we can talk about it.'

Zhang turned on his heel and hurried out of the room. Murphy put her phone down and stared disconsolately at Reed.

'I'm sorry,' she said, before scampering after Zhang.

Reed didn't need sympathy, or words of kindness. What he needed was action, positive steps that would lead him to An-ren.

He thought about what Zhang had said. The irony wasn't wasted on him.

Safety.

He was about to scurry off out of the building, making himself safe, while An-ren was the prisoner of a bunch of psychopathic monsters. And Ye had already made her fate crystal clear.

Reed wanted to scream, wanted to rip Ye's head from her body. But he couldn't do the latter, and he wasn't about to indulge himself in the former. Instead, he simply ran after Zhang and Murphy, trying desperately to push the dark and dismal thoughts that taunted and mocked him out of his mind.

CHAPTER FORTY-SIX

They sat in Reed's Mustang. Zhang had wanted him to drive them to The Golden Lantern, but Reed had refused to budge an inch until they had a plan. He desperately needed something he could focus on to try to relieve the agonised and aching sense of loss and desolation in his heart.

Zhang was in the passenger seat, which Reed wasn't happy with. That was An-ren's seat, the place where she sat and tormented him with scarily disturbing Chinese opera while he admired her silky smooth legs. His resentment was completely unreasonable, Reed knew that. It wasn't as if Zhang had purposely sat there in order to make him feel even more miserable. It occurred to him that he might actually have preferred to sit in the cramped rear seats, up close and personal with Murphy.

'We met Ye in the vault,' Murphy was saying,. 'She was waiting for us.'

'She knew we were coming?' Reed asked. 'How is that possible?'

'It was very predictable,' Zhang said, reading the Mandarin translation on Murphy's phone.

She'd plugged it into the Mustang's USB to charge it, and was holding it up, moving it around as necessary. Her arm was starting to ache, though, and she really hoped this would be a quick debrief.

'If it was predictable, why didn't you warn us? Why did you even let us go there?' Reed demanded, unable to believe what he'd just heard.

'Zhu Wei,' Zhang sighed. 'This isn't about you.'

'No,' Reed agreed. 'It's about An-ren!'

'It isn't even about her, although, of course, she is important. To you.'

Reed really wanted to punch Zhang, but he held himself back. He was only too well aware that Zhang could kill him more easily than he could drink a cup of coffee. And, however irritating Iron Palm was, he knew he couldn't afford to piss him off. Zhang was the only one of them who actually had any idea about what was going on.

'She's more than important! What could be more important than keeping her safe?'

'You need to rein in your self-pity,' Zhang declared.

Reed glared viciously at him.

'You're not helping,' he said.

'If Meng Yao returns to this world, it's not only An-ren that'll be in danger.'

'What do you mean?'

'Don't be any more stupid than you have to be,' Zhang sighed, rolling his eyes in frustration. 'I know you're obsessed with An-ren, but she is just the beginning of Luo Ban's revenge.'

'The beginning?' Reed asked, wondering if Zhang was trying to provoke him, or whether he really was so detached and cold-hearted.

'Two thousand years ago, a force of Daoist monks sent by the Celestial Registry defeated the forces of Meng Yao and Ye. But they only carried the day because of an intervention from Meng Yao's wife, An Lian.'

'Who Luo Ban thinks has been reincarnated as An-ren.'

'But he doesn't just blame her for his defeat. Think about it, he's been locked up for over two millennia. He's had all that time to ponder his fate and ruminate over everything that happened. You can see the hatred that sits in Ye. They're both warped by their loathing of humanity and the world. They're no different from any other tyrant. They want the entire world to bow down and worship them as the gods they believe themselves to be. And they'll kill everyone who resists.'

He paused for a moment, glancing at Murphy, noticing the look on her face, and the way she was now holding her arm.

'Let me have that,' he said, taking the phone off her and raising it up for them all to see.

She smiled sweetly at him, and started to rub her aching shoulder.

'It was hard enough for the world to deal with people like Hitler and Hirohito. Imagine what it would be like if they'd had the powers Luo Ban has.'

Reed was silent, thinking about exactly that. He didn't understand the forces that Zhang or their enemies could command, but he could see just how potent they might be on a world stage.

'Imagine if Luo Ban was able to combine his powers with nuclear weapons,' Murphy ventured.

'But we don't even know where they are,' Reed complained, his heart sinking even lower than before.

'I know exactly where they are,' Zhang said, his tone irritatingly off-hand.

'How can you?' Reed demanded. 'Ye burned the mirror.'

'She's so dramatic,' Zhang sighed. 'They're in the same place they were 2,200 years ago, when they were defeated.'.

'What do you mean?' Murphy asked, looking confused as she read the translation.

'Jinglun. The capital city of the Sepulchral Mandala The Tomb Wheel Dynasty's hub,' Zhang explained.

'You said the civilisation was centred on Shanghai,' Reed said.

'Shanghai wasn't around then, but, yes. In essence, that's true.'

'So where is it, then?'

Zhang pointed downwards.

Reed was confused at first, but then he realised.

'Underground,' Murphy observed, nodding her head as if everything made sense.

'Are you seriously suggesting that the city of the Sepulchral Mandala still exists under Shanghai?' Reed asked.

Reed knew that modern cities and towns were mostly built on the ruins of earlier settlements. He didn't really understand how it worked, but there were layers and layers underneath any modern urban conurbation. However, the thought of an entire city under the ground seemed more than a little far-fetched, if not completely ridiculous.

'Have you never heard people say "When the ground hums, the Wheel is turning" whenever they feel the rumble of the metro?'

'Of course,' Reed said.

He'd heard it many times, but he'd never understood what it referred to.

'The knowledge of what went before is long gone, but the memories and legends persist. Where do you think all these Luo Ban and Tomb Wheel shards came from?' Zhang asked.

'You're saying the city is under our feet?'

'Yes, I am. Some of it is in ruins, but it's pretty much as it was when Meng Yao and Ye were defeated.'

'And that's where you think they'll be holding Anren?'

'Undoubtedly.'

'Then let's go!' Reed exclaimed, switching on the ignition. 'How do we get in?'

Zhang reached over and switched off the engine.

'There's no rush, Zhu Wei.'

'Of course there fucking is!' Reed almost shouted. 'In case you've forgotten, those psychopaths have taken Anren prisoner and they're planning to kill her!'

Murphy reached out and put her hand on Reed's arm. He wasn't sure whether it was meant to be calming or empathic, but it pissed him off.

'Get off!' he barked, and she instantly pulled her hand back, glowering at him.

'I'm sorry,' he said, seeing her hurt expression and instantly feeling guilty, 'but I'm worried and I really don't see how sitting doing nothing is going to save her.'

'Luo Ban isn't going to kill her yet. He needs her in order to re-enter this world. And then he'll want her to suffer,' Zhang said.

'Is that meant to make me feel better?' Reed exclaimed, starting to feel overwhelmed by anger and frustration.

'No, it's meant to make you realise that she isn't going to die just yet.'

'How can you be so fucking calm?'

'She's not my girlfriend,' Zhang replied.

Reed stared at him, wanting to ram his fist into Zhang's face, regardless of the consequences.

'You couldn't stop what happened from happening,' Murphy told him.

'How do you know, you weren't there.'

'I saw all those Whisper Knife goons. And that bitch is powerful. More powerful than you and me.'

'She drew some sort of shape in the air and threw it at An-ren,' Reed said, thinking back, trying to find ways he could have acted differently, things he could have done to save the day.

'A mirror glyph,' Zhang muttered.

'But you couldn't have done anything at the time,' Murphy persisted. 'What's important is what you do now. She knows you, Will. She knows you'll move heaven and earth to try and save her.'

Reed glanced at her. He had to accept that was true. He was frustrated right now because Zhang was being obstructive, standing in the way of immediate action. But he would do anything, even sacrifice his own life in order to save hers. He'd made a solemn promise, and he hoped, wherever she was, whatever those bastards were doing to her, she'd hold on to that small ray of hope.

The truth was, it was his small ray of hope, too. Saving her would save him, the both of them. He'd failed to save someone he loved with every fibre of his body once, he had to make sure history didn't repeat itself.

'There was nothing you could have done,' Zhang intoned.

'Why are we waiting?' Reed demanded, locking his eyes onto the steely gaze of Iron Palm. 'We need to go. Now!'

'We'll probably all die if we go now.'

'What are you talking about?'

'The entrance to the Tomb Wheel city is through a maintenance doorway just off the main tunnel at People's Square Station. We have to wait for the last train.'

Chapter Forty-Seven

An-ren felt disoriented as she swam back up towards consciousness. She remembered Ye drawing a complex, but seemingly abstract, shape in the air. She remembered that it somehow took on life, existing in the space between them. And she remembered it enveloping her and how her body instantly shut down. Everything after that was a blank.

The memory of the sigil brought back everything else that had happened, and as her heart started hammering and the adrenaline began to flow yet again, she was immediately fully awake.

'Xiao Wei,' she murmured, remembering everything.

It had been an unfair battle. Five of them against one of him. He was tall and strong, but even he couldn't fight off five thugs employed simply for their muscle. She felt overwhelmed by a desperate sadness as she recalled how Ye had taunted him, had mocked his inability to save his daughter's life.

She'd been scared of Ye before, had been repulsed by everything about her, and especially her hideously fractured face, but now, after her cruel and inhuman tormenting of Reed, she realised that fear had taken second place to loathing and hatred.

Reed had promised to protect An-ren, and she knew just how desperate he would be feeling right now, not even knowing whether she was alive or dead. More than anything, she simply wanted to take him in her arms and tell him she believed in him, that she knew he would be there for her.

She knew how Xiao Wei felt about her, saw it in his eyes every time he looked at her. Now she wished she'd said something, told him she felt the same way. He was a man of his word, too, she knew that. If he said he'd protect her, then he would. Whatever it took.

She tried to move, but found she couldn't. At least, not forwards. Her arms were fastened behind her back. She glanced over her shoulder and saw that her wrists were tied together, secured by tight leather straps bearing the mark of the Tomb Wheel attached to chains which, in turn, were fastened to the wall.

She pulled hard, but all that achieved was pain in her wrists and aching in her arms. It was very clear to her that she wasn't going anywhere very soon.

She looked around, studying her surroundings. She was in a large chamber, windowless, the walls lined with what she thought were probably ancient jade mirrors. They were either very old, or had been made to appear that way, since they contained no glass, and seemed to be mostly carved and polished jade.

The whole space looked ancient, she thought, even the chains that held her. She glanced down at the floor, guessed it was almost certainly made of fired brick.

There was something else about the chamber, too. It was hard to quantify, though, more of a sensation that reality had, in some way, been subverted. It felt almost as if she was standing on the threshold of something both ominous and overwhelming, trapped between two very different worlds.

'An Lian!' a voice suddenly boomed out from all around her.

She'd never heard the voice this loud, or this close, but she recognised it. She'd heard it enough times in her dreams, and late at night in Wukang Road.

She looked all around, trying to identify where it was coming from. And then she noticed the reflections. She'd presumed the shadowy shape she could see in the jade mirrors had been her own reflection, but now that she looked closely, she realised it couldn't be.

It was the silhouette of a man. A very familiar one, too. She'd first seen it when Reed had shown her the photos he'd found on the internet after the photoshoot at the Lumen House.

'An Lian!' the voice repeated.

'Who are you?' she demanded, trying to keep the fear she felt out of her voice.

Never feed the fire, she thought.

'Don't you recognise my voice? It's been a long time, but surely you haven't forgotten?'

'I know your voice. I've heard it late at night in my house.'

'You recognise my voice because you're my wife! The wife who betrayed me and the Sepulchral Mandala!'

'I'm not her!' An-ren insisted. 'I'm Xiang An-ren!'

'I'm not interested in what you call yourself now. You are the woman I loved with every fibre of my being, and who repaid me with treachery and betrayal!'

'How many times do I have to tell you that I'm not her?' An-ren exclaimed.

'I can give you your memories back, An Lian, and then you'll remember everything! You will know, my darling wife, if you don't already, exactly how you betrayed me!'

An-ren watched in horror as the mirrors began to pulse and throb, warping and distorting, almost as if they were breathing.

She gasped in horror as a figure began to emerge from the large, polished piece of reflective jade directly in front of her. The mirror flexed and bowed outwards, as if it were actively expelling something. The figure took shape, became a man, and stepped through the portal into the chamber. The mirrors immediately faded back into their previous inert state.

The man in front of her wasn't especially tall, probably five feet eight inches, she guessed, and certainly short her than she was in her heels.

He was draped in a very ornate deep blue and gold gown, with vastly deep sleeves. His hair was long, tied up on top of his head in a top-knot and flowing back down over his back and shoulders. An ornate jade headpiece sat on top of his head.

His face was clean shaven, and there was considerable scarring around his forehead and eyes, which served to further heighten the aura of cruelty that clung to him like an extra layer of skin.

He had an air of aloof and contemptuous arrogance about him, reminiscent, An-ren thought, of Ye. But what set him apart, and what really disturbed An-ren were his eyes. Ye's were unnatural and inhuman, but there was a fire and malevolence about them that seemed almost human. But his eyes were different. Completely different. Deep set, surrounded by scar tissue and almost obsidian, she felt certain that if she stared into them for too long, she'd be sucked in to the deepest, darkest abyss imaginable. They were so empty and devoid of feeling that she couldn't believe anything human lay behind them. This man, this creature, was a being that appeared human on the exterior, but, inside, was simply a hollow shell filled with nothing more than a desperate emptiness.

'I am Meng Yao!' he announced, portentously. 'Your husband!'

'You're not my husband!' An-ren shot back, glaring defiantly at him.

She didn't feel very defiant, though. Now that he was there, standing right in front of her, she simply felt scared.

'Let me demonstrate,' he said, smiling thinly as he raised both hands and placed them on her forehead.

She strained and struggled, desperately trying to squirm her way out of his grasp, but she was too well secured, and, once he'd grasped her head, she was powerless to stop him.

'Remember!' he hissed, pressing tightly.

She gasped and cried out in pain, as a thousand, apparently random, images shot through her brain, roaming, racing, circling, but refusing to settle. She felt violated, as if Luo Ban had actually forced his way physically into her head.

And then she saw her. A woman dressed in ancient robes, beautiful, elegant and tall. A woman who looked just like her. She saw her and this hideous creature, her husband, Luo Ban, entwined, their bodies as one, An Lian crying out in ecstasy, Meng Yao shamelessly triumphant.

She saw a young woman, first a warrior leading troops into battle, and then naked, astride Meng Yao, who was pawing at her soft, youthful body. She saw the woman who looked just like An-ren walk in and slash a knife across the young woman's throat, before driving it deep into her soft flesh, saw the life start to ebb away, bemused and confused by the look of amusement and triumph on Luo Ban's face.

And then she saw a battle. A group of warrior monks confronting the military might of the Tomb Wheel Dynasty, pitting their ancient skills against those of Luo Ban, Ye and their army of warriors and *chiang shi*.

And she saw something else, something that took her breath away. A face she knew. One of the Daoist monks. Zhang. Iron Palm. He was fighting valiantly, but the cause seemed to be a lost one. The monks fought hard and bravely, but the forces of the Tomb Wheel were too powerful, their dark arts overwhelming.

It couldn't be Zhang, though, she realised, any more than the woman she saw was her. The events she was being forced to relive had taken place over two thousand years earlier, two millennia before she and Zhang had been born.

The battle seemed lost, but then An Lian sought out the last remaining monk, the one who resembled Iron Palm, and she told him what he needed to know. She revealed the unspoken and arcane secrets of the Sepulchral Mandala, gave the monk the power to control and destroy Luo Ban and his forces of darkness.

She watched as the monk crushed the last resistance of the Tomb Wheel forces, and entombed Luo Ban in his containment chamber. The monk then turned his attention to Ye, but she'd already fled into the Resonance Plane, burying herself so deep into unreality that she became unrecognisable and well beyond the reach of even the Celestial Registry.

And, as suddenly as it had started, everything stopped, and it felt like her mind was her own again. She realised that Luo Ban had removed his hands from her forehead and had stepped back slightly.

'Now you remember,' he said, his tone, for once, soft.

'I saw what you just planted in my head,' An-ren responded, 'but I don't remember any of it. I wish I did. I'd be proud to have played some part in bringing about your downfall.'

Luo Ban struck her in the face, his entire body quivering with rage.

It hurt, and she could taste blood on her lips. It was interesting, she thought, that a man with so much power at his disposal, still chose to punch a defenceless woman. Human nature clearly hadn't changed much in two millennia.

'You are An Lian!' he spat at her. 'You were perfidious and treacherous then, and you're no different now.'

'What are you going to do with me?' she asked, although she already knew the answer.

A creature like Luo Ban needed others to suffer in order to massage his own inadequate ego. He was a classic psychopath, she thought, multiplied by at least two thousand. It occurred to her that, despite his words, he would never be able to kill her. What he wanted wasn't her death, but prolonged pain and suffering. For all of eternity, probably.

'When the time comes, you will suffer in a way that no human being has ever suffered before. But there is a task I need you for, first.'

'What task?'

'The task you've been performing for me ever since you received that jade shard when you were a child.'

She felt a stab to her heart. Her *waipo* had given her the shard. Why? And where had she got it from? Was her grandmother linked to the Tomb Wheel? It had been her, after all, who'd cautioned her not to look into mirrors after dark, had been the first person to raise the spectre of the Sepulchral Mandala in her life.

'I don't understand.'

'Of course you don't. The attention you receive every time you face a camera lens, or a mirror, is my greatest resource. Every memory of your movements is translated into vectors. Your craft and your so-called art has always been my greatest weapon and my greatest ally.'

An-ren still didn't understand, but that wasn't important. She didn't need to hear his narcissistic pontificating to know that he was openly delusional. But there was one thing that interested her.

'Why do you still need me? You're here, flesh and blood. Your hands are flesh and blood.'

'I exist in here, but not in your world. Not yet, but very soon. This is the Mirror Chamber. These,' he said, indicating all the jade objects strewn around, 'were where our jade mirrors were forged and consecrated. This chamber is the anchor point for the Resonance Plane. The Mirror World as you probably know it. You're standing in the liminal threshold between two completely separate worlds.'

She wondered how that could possibly be true, although it confirmed her earlier feeling about the room. As she stood there in front of Meng Yao, the great and dreaded Luo Ban, she cast her mind back four days. Sitting in the cab, on the way to the Lumen House, none of this had been possible, or even vaguely credible. If anyone had told her back then, as she'd made her way in to the hotel, she would have suggested they start taking their medication as a matter of extreme urgency.

But now, less than four full days later, she was in chains, the prisoner of an ancient lunatic, locked up in a chamber that sat between her world and the one of mirrors.

'There's no escape, An Lian,' Luo Ban told her, 'No one will be coming for you. You're alone, and you're going to suffer the most painful and horrible torment that any human being has ever endured.'

He turned, and stepped back into the ancient mirror he'd emerged from, his body rapidly dwindling in size and finally fading from view, until not even his reflection remained.

CHAPTER FORTY-EIGHT

Reed remained frustrated and highly anxious, but even he, in his current state of agitation, could see that walking into the tunnels of the metro during operational hours would be a remarkably stupid undertaking. It was disappointing, to say the least, and he found himself constantly praying to every god he could think of to keep An-ren safe until they could find a way to rescue her.

Rescuing wasn't enough, of course, because, even if he was able to save her, the twin hellhounds, Luo Ban and Ye, would still be coming after her. Somehow, the three of them needed to complete the task that had only been half-completed 2,200 years earlier. And only Zhang really had any idea of how that might happen.

That thought alone filled him with despair. He didn't understand anything about the nature of their adversaries, had never even vaguely believed in the possibility that supernatural forces were actually a thing, but now he had to find a way to kill two inhuman creatures who had survived, against the odds, for over two millennia.

Zhang had forced them all to go and eat something. He'd dragged them to some cheap and cheerful café nearby, and had ordered food and drinks. Reed had made himself eat, even though he hadn't felt hungry. Every mouthful had added to his already considerable burden of guilt and shame, but he did at least feel slightly better afterwards, less irritable and more able to hold back the negative emotions that had threatened to swamp him.

Afterwards, Zhang had insisted Reed drive them to An-ren's house in the French Concession. Reed wasn't sure why, but he was too distracted to ask. He was just waiting for the long hours of waiting to finally come to an end.

When they arrived, and Reed had parked, Zhang got out of the Mustang and ambled over to the front door. Just as he had done at Meridian House, he pulled out his little set of housebreaking tools, and forced An-ren's front door open.

Reed was shocked, unable to believe that Zhang had so casually violated An-ren's property. However, Iron Palm was inside before Reed could even open his mouth to protest.

Glancing angrily at Murphy, although it obviously had nothing to do with her, Reed stormed in, ready to launch into a broadside against Zhang.

But Iron Palm merely raised a hand, as if to tell Reed to keep quiet.

'Where's the Mirror Room?' he'd asked.

'Why do you need to know? And how dare you just barge into An-ren's house? Who do you think you are?' Reed barked.

'Zhu Wei,' Zhang retorted. 'You're letting your anxiety and fear rule your mouth. Please get yourself under control. You won't be helping Miss Xiang if you get hysterical. Just tell me where the mirrors are. Believe me, you'll both thank me for this.'

Reed glared at him angrily, his fists clenched again.

'He's trying to help you,' Murphy said, her phone still translating away. 'Can't you see that? You need to trust him. Without Iron Palm, we're dead in the water.'

Reed glared at her.

'You're only defending him because you're having sex with him,' he blurted, instantly regretting his words the moment they left his mouth.

'It's great sex, too,' she said, glaring balefully at him, 'but it's none of your business! No one here's talking about what you and An-ren have obviously been up to.'

'I'm sorry,' Reed muttered, looking away. 'I shouldn't have said that. It was out of order.'

'William,' she said, putting a gentle hand on his arm. 'I don't know what Iron Palm's up to, but we need to trust him. He's our only hope. I know you want to save An-ren more than anything in this world. We all do. You need to focus on what's important. Save all that emotion for when you've saved her.'

Reed stared at her, was moved almost to tears by the compassion and wisdom he saw in her eyes. She was right, absolutely right. He needed to pull himself together, get a grip and start to act like someone who was going to save her, not like the victim he'd let himself become all those long years ago.

'And think of just how great the sex will be afterwards,' she added, winking at him.

Reed just stared at her, perplexed. She really was quite something.

'Are they all like you in Sligo?' he asked.

'God, no,' she laughed. 'I'm one of the few normal ones.'

'The Mirror Room?' Zhang interrupted, impatience written in every line on his face.

'Second Floor,' Reed said.

Zhang disappeared up the stairs, leaving Reed and Murphy to trail behind.

By the time they caught up with him, he was already inside the room, looking around in alarm, staring at the infinite Iron Palm's reflected back.

'This is amazing!' Murphy exclaimed, her face filled with wonder and awe.

'Not so much amazing as infernal,' Zhang muttered.

As he stood there, unsettled by the sight of seeing himself everywhere he looked, Reed had a thought.

'Can we use these to reach An-ren?' he asked.

'No,' Zhang responded.

'Why not? They're Luo Ban.'

Zhang turned to Reed, a look on his face that suggested he was being forced to explain the blindingly obvious to a complete idiot.

'If you were driving that horrible car of yours, would you expect every road to take you to the same place?'

Reed was silent, feeling he'd been very firmly put in his place, although he didn't think it had been an unreasonable question. It was hardly his fault that he didn't understand the intricacies of cross-mirror travel.

'These were really already in the house when she inherited it?' Zhang asked.

'That's what she told me,' Reed replied. 'I suggested she remove them, but she said it was stipulated in the deeds that they had to remain or she'd lose the right to live here.'

'That would never stand up in court,' Zhang said.

Reed glanced at Murphy, and he suspected she was thinking the same thing as him.

'I'm trying to get my head around it,' he told Zhang, 'but it seems that she inherited a house, filled with Luo Ban and Tomb Wheel mirrors. A house which had been registered over eighty years ago by someone whose forename is linked to Lin Ye.'

'And she had that jade shard her grandmother gave her,' Zhang observed.

'What does it all mean?' Reed asked.

'I don't know for certain,' Zhang mused. 'But it would suggest this was a plan many years in the making. Maybe many centuries.'

'But she's only twenty-eight!'

'Ye exists outside of time and space, at least as far as you understand those concepts.'

Reed stared hard at Zhang.

'Who exactly are you, Old Zhang?' he asked. 'You're not really a retired policeman, are you?'

'I am!' Zhang retorted, looking deeply offended. 'I did my time on the force, and now, just when I was trying to enjoy my retirement, you dragged me into this shitstorm!'

'Do you really expect me to believe that?'

'You can believe what you want.'

Zhang pulled his phone out of his pocket, but, before he could use it, Reed grabbed his arm.

'Who are you?'

'It's a long story,' Zhang sighed. 'I'm many things, and maybe also none.'

'Spare me the bullshit,' Reed responded, rolling his eyes at Zhang's cryptic response.

'There's no time to explain now. Suffice to say, I was assigned a task a long time ago. And I'm trying to complete it.'

He pulled his arm back, dislodging Reed's hand, and began to dial.

When the call was answered, he spoke quickly and quietly, for no more than thirty seconds, before cutting the connection and putting the phone back in his pocket.

'Are there any tools anywhere in this house?' Zhang asked.

'I have no idea,' Reed told him.

'Go and look then. We're taking the mirrors down.'

'I'll go,' Murphy suggested.

'No,' Reed said. 'I'll do it. I know the house better than you.'

He hurried out and made his way back downstairs. He had no idea where An-ren might keep tools, and he also seriously doubted whether she'd have any. She'd never struck him as the sort of woman who'd even want to hammer a nail into a wall, let alone undertake any even vaguely serious programme of DIY.

He started in the kitchen, looking through every cupboard, but he barely found much food, let alone a screwdriver or a hammer. He searched through the rest of the ground floor, but found nothing. He was about to go and check the first floor, with little real hope of success, when he saw something that grabbed his attention through the kitchen window.

The house had a garden. Not a big one, but big enough to need a certain amount of maintenance and regular attention. He couldn't picture An-ren outside mowing the small lawn, but it was clear that someone did. More significantly, though, there was a shed.

He opened the backdoor and hurried over to it. It was secured with a padlock. He cursed, but realised he had little choice. He had no idea where the key might be, so he simply kicked the flimsy wooden door as hard as he could.

It splintered and fell inwards. He did feel a certain amount of guilt, but not very much. If he saved her life and helped make her house safe to live in again, he didn't think she'd blame him too much for having to get a new shed door. And, of course, he could buy her one as a "Happy Rescue" present.

He looked around inside. It was full of the sort of things people tended to shove into their garden sheds, with the intention of using at some point, but then forgetting all about them. Pots of paint, an old, rusty barbecue, various garden tools, and, much to his relief, a toolbox.

It looked ancient, undoubtedly unused in living memory. He forced it open, and rifled through the contents, pleased to find a generous selection of screwdrivers, chisels, and other tools, as well as two hammers. He secured the lid again, grabbed the handle, and went rushing back into the house.

When he reached the Mirror Room, Zhang held a hand up to stop him from entering.

'Put that down, and stand next to Fiona,' he said.

'What are you doing?'

'These things are toxic. We need to remove them safely. That means we have to neutralise them first.'

'How do we do that?'

'We don't. I do,' Zhang explained. 'Stand back.'

He went back inside the room, and Reed and Murphy peered through the doorway.

As Zhang stood in the centre of the room, looking all around, Reed sensed something. Intangible, inchoate, but definitely something. An aura, possibly. Menacing and malevolent. He began to feel uncomfortable, as if a thousand eyes were staring hatefully at him.

He glanced at Fiona, could see that she was also beginning to feel uncomfortable.

And then it began. Voices. First one. Then two, and then more and more. Increasing in volume, becoming cacophonous. A symphony of loathing and antipathy.

Zhang continued to study the mirrors, but there was a grim smile on his face now, and his lips began to move.

He was chanting, Reed realised. He couldn't hear it, the chorus of dissonance from the Tomb Wheel mirrors was so loud that he couldn't even hear what Murphy was shouting at him.

Zhang continued to chant, and, although Reed still couldn't hear it, he could sense that it was louder. Iron Palm raised his hands, and began to draw a shape in the air.

Reed was shocked. Zhang was doing exactly what Ye had done before abducting An-ren.

Iron Palm continued to move his fingers, the shapes becoming lines in the air that took on seemingly solid, three-dimensional form, glowing a vivid pale blue as he continued to trace the patterns.

They were sigils, Reed realised, although he didn't really understand exactly what they were. Some sort of ethereal talisman, he suspected.

As Zhang continued to weave the spell, the mirrors began to throb and pulse, the glass and the jade distorting and warping, moving as if with an inner pulse. The voices became more and more abusive and hateful, but Zhang simply carried on, chanting all the while.

He stopped for a moment, and then moved his fingers so quickly they became almost a blur. As he did so, the sigil multiplied, moving apart, but remaining hanging in the air around Zhang. He jabbed his hand at one, and it flew into the nearest mirror.

A grating, grinding sound filled the air, and Reed thought the mirror was about to explode. But, suddenly, it simply stopped pulsing and went inert.

Zhang then began to cast the sigils at the other mirrors, until every last one had gone quiet and had stopped its frenzied pulsating.

Everything felt different. The dreadful, doom-laden aura had now gone, in its place a sense of calm and peace. Reed didn't know quite what to think. Until three days earlier, mirrors had seemed remarkably boring and innocuous. Now, he wondered if he'd ever be able to look into one again.

A few minutes later, all three of them were busily removing the mirrors from the walls. Zhang had made it clear that, although he had rendered them inert and dormant, they shouldn't smash them, or do anything that might leave fragments of glass or jade lying about. He'd made it very clear that the mirrors needed to be removed intact, and then destroyed according to traditional Daoist methodology.

Less than an hour later, the walls had been stripped bare, revealing nothing more sinister than cracked and unpainted plasterwork. Laboriously, they began the process of carrying the mirrors downstairs, being careful not to cause even the tiniest shard to chip off.

Halfway through, there was a loud knock on the front door, which shocked Reed, who suddenly felt very guilty about being in An-ren's house. He wondered if maybe the neighbours had called the police.

But when he opened the door, he realised he was worrying for nothing. He was confronted by four shaven-headed men, all dressed in a variety of what he could only think of as "bohemian" outfits. Jeans, t-shirts, sandals, kaftans, ponchos, and the like. They were, he thought, the complete antithesis of the black-clad Whisper Knife. And that instantly put him at ease.

Zhang greeted them brusquely, barked a few instructions about ensuring the mirrors were undamaged in transit and that they needed to be destroyed according to "standard protocols".

The men nodded, bowing very deferentially to Iron Palm, before beginning to load the offending articles into the ancient and rusting white van parked outside.

'I'll go and check for any other pieces or shards,' Zhang said, as the front door finally shut and Reed heard the beaten-up old van roaring away down the road.

He nodded. He had a task he'd set himself, too, and so, while Zhang and Murphy began to check the downstairs, he hurried up to An-ren's bedroom.

He felt guilty going through her most personal belongings, but it had occurred to him that if she was being held in the ruins below Shanghai, then she wasn't really dressed for the terrain. It was probably an absurd thought on his part, but he wanted to take her some trainers and jeans, or jogging pants, that might make it easier for her when they escaped back up to the surface.

He rummaged around in her wardrobe in search of a rucksack.

The only one he could find was pink, which he wasn't too happy about, but he knew this wasn't a time to be fussy. He found some white Nike trainers, some pink ankle socks, and a pair of light-blue skinny jeans. He stuffed them into the bag.

Half an hour later, Zhang and Murphy had finished their sweep, and, thankfully, had come up empty. The house, it seemed, was finally a Luo Ban- and Tomb Wheel-free zone.

Gathering themselves together, they piled into the Mustang and Reed pulled the car away from the kerb, headed for the People's Square Station.

CHAPTER FORTY-NINE

They'd arrived at the station at around 10.25 pm, only five minutes before the line they had to use was scheduled to close. Reed had known the station platforms would be checked before the official shutdown. He'd felt anxious that they'd be thrown out, but when they were challenged by a security guard, Zhang had simply whipped out his old police ID, flashing it so quickly that the man only had time to register the word "Police".

Zhang had introduced Reed and Murphy as two Interpol agents helping out with an investigation into an international drugs cartel. It was obvious that the guard was sceptical, especially given Reed's pink rucksack and battered face, but Zhang was so bullish and dismissive that he allowed them past without asking any serious questions.

'Hurry,' Zhang whispered to them, as they made their way along the platform. 'He looks like the sort who'll go and check it out.'

As they reached the end, the lights began to flicker and dim. The low humming sound that had filled the air suddenly stopped. The power was now off for the night.

Reed took the pink bag off his back and produced three flashlights, handing one to Murphy as Zhang leaped down onto the track. Reed looked away as Iron Palm helped Murphy down. He really didn't want to see Zhang's hands lingering on her body. The man was a complete conundrum. It was hard to believe he was really nothing more than a retired policeman, but, then again, he wasn't acting much like a monk, either.

'Come on!' Zhang hissed up at him, offering a hand.

Reed ignored it and jumped down, although it was further than he thought and he almost fell over as he landed. That was stupid, he thought. He wouldn't be much to An-ren if he broke his ankle.

He handed the other flashlight to Zhang, and followed him into the darkness. He didn't even question whether the man knew where they were going. Zhang seemed to have all the answers all of the time.

With only the narrow flashlight beams to light up the darkness, Zhang led them further into the depths of the tunnel. It was an intimidating atmosphere, and Reed realised he was listening closely, waiting for the sound of a train rushing towards them. It was irrational, everything had closed for the night, but he couldn't help it. He felt remarkably vulnerable and exposed walking up the track.

They'd covered just over two hundred yards, when Zhang's flashlight lit up an alcove on their right.

'This way,' he said, leading them into the small space.

There was a door at the end, and he put his torch down for a moment, once more pulling out his housebreaking kit.

'Shine a light on the lock.'

As Murphy pointed her torch at the door, Zhang fiddled with the lock. He carefully moved the small tool around, listening carefully until he heard a small click. He stood back, turned the handle, and pushed the door open.

Murphy's flashlight revealed a set of stairs descending into darkness. The walls on either side appeared to be constructed from hand-laid brickwork. Although it looked old, and appeared to be some sort of long-disused service area, Reed noticed that the steps were mostly dust free.

This was the province of Victor Lam, Li Tong and the Whisper Knife Society, Reed realised, and was undoubtedly one of the main routes for smuggling ancient relics and artifacts out of the long-dead world that lay far below the streets of Shanghai.

Zhang started down the stairs, Reed and Murphy following close behind.

They descended for about thirty feet, before the stairs abruptly ended. They found themselves in a large hallway. It was ramshackle, completely rundown. Metal cabinets and lockers lay strewn around the floor, slowly subsiding into rust. Plaster had fallen off the walls. Rubble and masonry lay everywhere. The once polished floor tiles were now cracked and faded.

'This way,' Zhang said, leading them over to the one set of lockers that were still standing.

As Reed and Murphy zigzagged their way towards him, trying to avoid tripping over all the detritus covering the floor, Zhang effortlessly pushed the lockers to one side, revealing a dark hole in the wall behind.

Reed peered in, but it was too dark to see anything. He poked his flashlight through, but all he could see was more rubble.

'I can see you've never been down here before,' he muttered, as Zhang brusquely shoved past him, ignoring his irony, and squeezed his stocky frame through the small opening.

'After you,' Reed said, gesturing for Murphy to go next. She stepped through, passing through the gap without even touching the sides.

Reed bent down and went sideways through the hole.

They found themselves in yet another tunnel, but there was light at the end of it. An eerie, green tinged luminescence that was coming through a narrow gap in the far wall.

Zhang and Murphy had already disappeared through it, so Reed ran over and eased his large frame through the tight space.

As he straightened up and gazed at the sight that met his eyes, he felt a wave of shock and disbelief flood through him. He'd never seen anything like it before.

'Feck!' Murphy exclaimed.

'Behold Jinglun, the capital of the Sepulchral Mandala, the birthplace of the Tomb Wheel Dynasty,' Zhang declared, pausing for a moment as they all took in the vista that confronted them. 'The western suburbs, anyway,' he added.

Reed simply didn't know what to say or think. Spread out in front of him was a vast cavern. But the cavern itself was of no significance. It was just a space, but what filled it was like nothing he'd ever seen before. Ancient buildings and structures, ruined now, but quite evidently once part of a proud and highly technologically advanced civilisation, stretched in every direction, as far as the eye could see.

Jinglun, Zhang had said. It meant "Mirror Wheel".

A central dais, in the shape of a wheel, rose up from a river, deep blue water flowing eastwards, some fifty feet below where they were standing. A beautifully carved stone walkway stretched out in front of them, leading across the distant water below towards the roof of the island. At its centre was a raised structure. It was in a state of disrepair, looked as if it had been abandoned years, if not decades, earlier, although the inset door appeared almost new.

Six other walkways stretched outwards, like the spokes of a wheel, connecting to other parts of the cavern, each one leading to a series of pagoda-like structures that lined the walls of the vast chamber.

Reed glanced down, realised that there were floors extending far beneath them each one punctuated at regular intervals by windows. To his surprise, lights were glowing in some of them.

Stone lions, in varying stages of decay, lined the cavern walls, all staring outwards from the central wheel. They reminded Reed of the way that gargoyles stared outwards from medieval European churches and cathedrals.

On the other side of the cavern, linked by a walkway directly opposite the one in front of them, stood a domed temple. Like most of the buildings they could see, it was in ruins, its masonry crumbling and the walls riddled with gaping holes.

It suddenly occurred to him that they were in a fully enclosed subterranean cavern, yet they could see. The greenish-blue light was nowhere near as powerful as Shanghai daylight, but it was still far brighter than it should have been.

'Old Zhang, where's the light coming from?' he asked.

'It's a combination of bioluminescent organisms and luminescent ores,' Zhang explained.

'That's crazy,' Murphy laughed. 'There's so much light!'

'It was planned for,' Zhang added.

'By who?' Reed asked.

Zhang stared at him disdainfully for a moment, as if this was yet another idiotic question, and then started across the walkway.

Reed opened his mouth to say something to Murphy, but thought better of it. Iron Palm was a quite remarkable man, mysterious and immensely knowledgeable, but he could also be intensely irritating.

Murphy scampered after Zhang, and Reed followed behind. He took his time crossing the walkway. It had been built over two thousand years earlier, and it was a long way down to the water. If he fell through, he thought it was unlikely he'd survive the descent, but, even if he did, he had no doubt that the waters of the Tomb Wheel Dynasty's world would be full of creatures that were the aquatic equivalent of the Xilin.

The central wheel was constructed of concentric rings, four in total, with the raised structure at its centre. Reed suspected that the door that looked relatively new led down to the lower levels, to the rooms that appeared to be lit up.

He glanced at the other walkways, studying the buildings that they led to. He couldn't help but wonder what dark secrets might be hidden inside them.

'Is it me, or does this place feel bad?' he asked.

'There is something about it,' Murphy agreed. 'Some sort of presence.'

'There's a pall hanging over the city,' Zhang intoned. 'An ancient miasma.'

'A bit like Meridian House, then?' Reed asked, in feigned innocence, remembering Zhang's portentous and pretentious statement when they'd all been gathered in the Octagon Lane Café.

'Not at all like Meridian House,' Zhang scowled.

He turned and stepped onto the walkway leading to the large, circular temple. Murphy, as before, scampered after him, leaving Reed to bring up the rear.

As they were crossing, Reed realised that the two walkways on either side of them led to two buildings that were on the same level as the temple. He wondered if there was any significance in that. It certainly wasn't the same with any of the other bridges.

As Zhang waited impatiently for Reed to catch up, Murphy walked across to study the building on their left. It was more traditional than the temple, being rectangular in shape, with a traditional Chinese roof. The heavy and highly ornate bronze doors were firmly shut, sealed by a short piece of thick twine, with three small pieces of tattered red cloth draped across it. There had clearly been writing on them once, but it had faded long ago.

'Let's go,' Zhang called out to her. 'We're wasting time.'

But she ignored him, and continued walking.

'Fiona!' Reed called out, but she didn't respond.

She seemed somehow changed, he realised. There was something about the way she was walking, a change in her gait, that seemed odd, unnatural. He noticed that she was staring straight ahead, her eyes fixed, unseeing.

She reached out a hand to grasp the twine.

'No!' Zhang shouted, his voice booming around the cavern, echoing into the distance.

But Murphy continued to reach out, her fingers grasping the twine.

A blue bolt of lightning viciously arced into the ground next to her, and she let go, jumping back, and crying out in shock.

She looked at Zhang, but the anger in her face was soon replaced by confusion, as she realised where she was now standing.

'How did I get here?' she demanded.

'You seemed to be in some sort of trance,' Reed told her.

'A trance?'

'It looked that way,' Reed nodded.

'These buildings are dangerous,' Zhang informed them, arriving at Murphy's side. 'There are more things to be fearful of down here than just Luo Ban and Ye.'

'What do you mean?' Reed asked.

'I've said before that the Tomb Wheel wasn't just those two. There are some nightmares that you just wouldn't want to meet.'

Reed believed him. His whole world had been turned upside down over the past three days. He no longer doubted that the nightmares he'd always refused to believe in were almost certainly disturbingly real, and lurked in every shadow.

'Let's go,' Zhang repeated, reassured that Murphy was now back to herself.

As the three of them disappeared into the distance, the twine that Murphy had grasped slowly fell to the ground, and the talismans that had been attached fluttered away in the breeze that had suddenly sprung up from nowhere.

The doors slowly opened outwards, and light flooded in. Somewhere, deep inside, something began to stir.

Something that had been bound since the collapse of Jinglun in the Great Cataclysm 2,200 years earlier.

CHAPTER FIFTY

An-ren was jerked into wakefulness by a sudden pain in her scalp, as if someone had grabbed her hair and yanked her head back.

She realised that, somehow, she'd fallen asleep. Her shoulders and arms ached now, and she wondered how she could possibly have slept in such inhospitable surroundings.

She opened her eyes and winced as more pain shot through her head.

Ye was kneeling next to her, holding An-ren's hair very tightly in her right hand.

'You're awake,' Ye muttered.

She stood up, viciously pulling An-ren's hair after her. An-ren gasped in pain, clambering awkwardly upright, her hands still secured behind her back.

She wanted to back away, get as far from this living nightmare as she could, but Ye had a vicelike grip on her hair. All she could do was try to avoid giving Ye the satisfaction of seeing how scared she was.

Ye was in her mirror form. The faultlines and cracks that had so recently marred her human face had gone. It occurred to An-ren, crazy though the thought seemed, that Ye was far less scary like this than she was in human form, with her face cracked almost into fragments.

Ye let go of An-ren's hair and took her by the shoulders, guiding her around with a strength that was controlled rather than brutal. The movement unsettled An-ren. There was a fluid, unsettling grace to Ye, even in moments of force.

A sigil hung in the air behind Ye, and An-ren noticed a misty pall hung over the ancient jade mirrors that Luo Ban had emerged from.

'Some things are best unheard,' Ye whispered into An-ren's ear, her tone conspiratorial.

'What do you want?' An-ren demanded, recoiling in fear and revulsion at finding Ye's blue lips so close to her face. 'If you've just come to torment me, then don't bother. I've already had enough of that from your master!'

'My master?' Ye echoed, lips curling in a mocking pout. 'He may command this city. He does not command me.'

'Really? From where I'm standing, you're Luo Ban's slave.'

'You can't provoke me, An Lian,' Ye said, her eyes turning to ice.

'I'm not An Lian!' An-ren burst out. 'Your master showed me her memories, but they're not mine!'

'You are An Lian,' Ye replied softly, 'whether you choose to believe it or not, and you will restore him. The pattern remembers every debt.'

Terror churned in her, but hatred surged up to meet it. It lent her a dangerous boldness; even cornered, she longed for the sharp, forbidden pleasure of seeing Ye's flawless façade fracture.

'What is it you don't want your master to hear?' she asked.

'His obsession with you has made him weak.'

'You're going to betray him,' An-ren realised. 'Just like An Lian did.'

'Tell me,' Ye said, her voice turning cold. 'How do you betray someone who betrayed you first?'

'But you betrayed An Lian,' An-ren insisted. 'I saw you.'

'You saw what Luo Ban wanted you to see,' Ye replied. 'Are you truly that naïve?'

An-ren forced herself to look Ye in the face, reluctantly focusing on her translucent and completely cerulean eyes.

'You look at me with disgust. I repel you, but I was once like you,' Ye whispered, the contempt faltering into something desolate and self-hating.

An-ren was unprepared for this dramatic change, could never have believed that a creature like Ye had anything other than malevolence hidden inside her. She was surprised, but sceptical. She suspected this was just another example of the Ye's apparently limitless capacity for cruelty.

'You were never like me,' she said.

Ye smiled. A small, self-deprecating twist of the mouth, gone almost as soon as it appeared. For a heartbeat, something unguarded flickered through her.

'Is it so hard to believe I might once have been different? Do you think I came into the world like this? I was the greatest general of the Sepulchral Mandala. Grand Axis-Marshal. Blade of the Meridian Wheel. General of the Glass Phalanx.'

'Why should I care?' An-ren said, trying to sound dismissive.

'But you do,' Ye replied. 'I see it. You're trying to decide whether I'm lying. You hide behind that wall you've built. But I know what's inside it.'

An-ren watched in dismay as Ye's expression shifted, the brief flicker of vulnerability collapsing, replaced by a darkness that seemed to swallow the light around her.

'You know nothing about me,' An-ren murmured.

'I know you understand tragedy,' Ye said softly. 'We share that, at least.'

'We have nothing in common!' An-ren snapped, her mother's face flashing unbidden into her mind.

'There are no rewards for tragedy,' Ye said, smiling cruelly.

As An-ren tore her gaze away, sickened by the abyss she'd glimpsed, Ye reached out and laid an icy hand against her cheek.

An-ren tried to back away, scared of Ye's unpredictability, and fearful of the icy, glasslike fingers delicately caressing her face. She suddenly felt more alone and more vulnerable than she had at any point since Ye had abducted her.

Ye leaned closer.

'Some people were never meant to be saved,' she whispered.

She pulled her hand back, waved it dismissively towards the sigils, watching as they faded into nothingness, before turning on her heel and gracefully striding out of the chamber.

CHAPTER FIFTY-ONE

The vast cavern narrowed as Reed, Zhang and Murphy left the ruined temple behind. The walls on either side closed in and they began to descend slightly, the incline ending abruptly in a wall of rock.

Two large bronze doors sat in the centre. There were hints of ornately engraved decoration in places, but, for the most part, they had succumbed to the decay of verdigris over the centuries, and were now just a dirty shade of green.

They stopped in front of the doors and Reed rubbed at the corroded metal. A wheel slowly emerged. He carried on, revealing a Xilin, and part of what he thought was probably the Moqual.

'Give me a hand,' Zhang said, starting to push on the left hand door.

Reed pressed his right shoulder against the other door, ignoring the pain that suddenly appeared, and pushed. Murphy threw herself against it as well, and, with their combined strength, the door began to slowly, albeit reluctantly, creak open.

'That's enough,' Zhang suddenly declared.

The doors were now open far enough to allow them all to pass through. Zhang, as ever, led the way.

They stopped abruptly, unprepared for the majestic, ruined and decaying sight that greeted them.

They were inside what appeared to be an enormous building, hollowed out of the rock that lined the cavern. Two vast wheels were inset into the building's walls, one on each side, and situated thirty feet in the air. A large doorway was cut into the bottom of each circular structure, accessed by stone steps that led upwards from ground level.

As Reed gazed around, he realised that there were wheels everywhere. Some were inset into the side of the steps, others were simply lying, cracked and broken, all around them. They all bore the distinctive and stylised rendering of the Sepulchral Mandala.

More stone lions were scattered around the chamber, many on raised plinths. Some were relatively intact, but most appeared damaged, although it wasn't immediately clear whether this was down to the passage of time or human intervention.

A small stream of dirty water trickled slowly through the centre of what had once been the floor, meandering around the piles of rubble and fallen masonry. Reed presumed that the small waterway was fed by the vast river they'd passed earlier.

In the distance, past the large tomb wheels, and some fifty feet above ground level, a walkway connected both sides of the cavern, pagoda-style buildings located at each end.

'What's the deal with all the wheels?' Murphy asked, holding up her phone to Zhang.

'It's complex,' he responded. 'The people of the Sepulchral Mandala pictured death as a turning wheel of passage, and they created rites using rotating mirrors, drum-wheels and cyclical recitations to guide souls. They came to believe that a face seen once would return again and again in different mirrors, as if the dead kept turning back into the living.'

'That's amazing,' Murphy told him, a look of wide-eyed wonder in her eyes.

'That's why it came to be known as the "Tomb Wheel",' Zhang continued. 'Their practices and rituals bound memory into loops. Everything that left their courts returned as a ringed thing, a wound of lacquer and spiral, a way for the dead to keep turning back into the living.'

'How come there are no records of them?' Reed asked.

He found it impossible to believe that the physical remains of such a unique and remarkable civilisation could be located under Shanghai without anyone, aside from criminals like Victor Lam and Li Tong, knowing anything about it.

'All of this was built on darkness,' Zhang said. 'Initially, the people of the Tomb Wheel Dynasty sought to learn the truths of the universe, and to expand their knowledge of the world that they lived in. But a time came when that was no longer enough. They didn't just want to understand the universe, they wanted to shape it. They wanted to control it, in fact. And they turned away from the light towards the darkness. Their creativity and curiosity was replaced with negativity and cruelty. Meng Yao was the ultimate architect of their decadence. The battle that took place here was a little like a last stand. Light against dark.'

Zhang scrutinised Reed, expecting him to demand more, but he seemed satisfied. That was good, Zhang thought. What he'd said was the truth, but only a part of it. Maybe, he hoped, if their little foray was successful, none of the rest would ever need to be said. It was a forlorn hope, he knew that, but any hope was better than none.

'When we sat in The Golden Lantern yesterday, you didn't seem to know very much at all. But now you're the world's leading expert,' Reed said, frowning in consternation. 'I know we've asked this many times, but who are you? I mean, who are you really?'

Zhang stared at Reed for a long time, his eyes occasionally moving to Murphy, and then back again. He was silent for so long that Reed thought he wasn't going to answer.

'I'm Zhang Qiang, painfully divorced retired policeman,' he finally said, 'But there is something else. It's complicated, so let me say just that I've been here before, although I, personally, actually haven't.'

'Clear as fucking mud,' Reed sighed, wondering if Zhang could ever provide a simple answer to anything.

'I have a task,' Zhang added, ignoring Reed's sarcasm. 'One that only I can complete.'

'We're not children!' Murphy retorted. 'Don't treat us like we are!'

It seemed that even she was irritated by his continued and decidedly opaque obfuscations.

'If it's any comfort, Xiao Fei, I don't understand it all myself,' Zhang said, his tone softer now he was addressing her. 'It's a task I was born with.'

Murphy's eyes remained fixed on her phone long after Zhang had finished speaking.

'Did it get it wrong?' she asked, showing the translation to Reed.

'No,' Reed smiled at her. 'He really did just call you "Little Fi".'

'What does it mean?' she persisted.

'Haven't you noticed that An-ren calls me "Xiao Wei"? It's not because I'm small.'

Reed left her to mull over that, and turned back to Zhang, who hadn't understood a word. Thankfully, Reed thought.

He realised there was no point in pressing Iron Palm any further. And, in any case, they were wasting time. Standing around, discussing the relative merits of the Sepulchral Mandala and Zhang's role in it all was a little like fiddling while Rome burned. An-ren was still a prisoner, completely at the mercy of the combined malevolence of Luo Ban and Ye.

Without waiting for either Zhang or Murphy, he strode on, doing his best to avoid the filthy water, and skirting the larger pieces of rubble and masonry that lay in his path.

He walked past the steps, noticing a sealed bronze door on his left that appeared to lead into some sort of vault, secured with a number of heavy locks, all of which were covered with red talismans. He briefly considered asking Zhang what it was, but thought better of it. They'd already wasted enough time, and if An-ren wasn't behind it, then it simply wasn't important.

'Slow down,' Zhang said, his voice unusually quiet, as they passed under the high walkway. 'We're almost there.'

Reed began to feel anxious. His heart started to race. He prayed that An-ren was still safe, that she hadn't been hurt or made to suffer in any way. He realised that neither he nor Murphy had any clue as to what was going to happen next. They were, as ever, completely at the mercy of the irascible Zhang.

Ahead of them was a space that appeared smaller than the one they'd just left. Four more tomb wheels, like the large ones they'd just left behind, were set into the walls at regular intervals around the chamber. At the heart of everything was a raised circular platform, housing another domed building, accessed by steps cut into the dais.

Reed barely noticed, his attention drawn to the area directly in front of the circular platform. A large group of figures were standing around, dressed in dark robes, their faces covered and bamboo *douli* hats on their heads. At the centre of this group were three people. One was a man dressed in ancient Chinese robes. A strange looking creature stood next to him. She resembled a woman, and was wearing a long red and gold dress, but her skin was a pale blue colour, and her long black hair undulated and flowed all around her shoulders and back in a way that didn't seem natural.

His heart began to beat even faster and his thoughts started to race as he recognised the tall woman standing between them, dressed all in black, her hands secured in restraints.

An-ren.

CHAPTER FIFTY-TWO

The door opened, and Ye marched into the Mirror Chamber, closely followed by five dark-clad creatures, their faces and bodies completely covered, all wearing *douli*.

'Bring her!' Ye commanded.

An-ren backed away as the creatures advanced on her. She desperately wanted to be released from her restraints, to be able to stretch her arms and ease the aching pain in her muscles, but she sensed something completely unnatural and inhuman about the creatures about to lay their hands on her.

She'd expected Whisper Knife, but these were something entirely different, and far less pleasant. As they got closer, she noticed two things. The first was that they brought a distinctive odour with them. She'd never had any experience of the decay that came with death, but she felt certain that this was what it smelled like. The second thing was that they weren't breathing.

They grabbed her and held her tight. She struggled as best she could, but they were strong. The touch of their cold hands on her arms made her feel nauseous. Ye's hands were cold and glassy, but still felt like those of a living being, but these creatures, while icy, were also clammy and completely lifeless, lacking any of the muscle tone or flexibility she associated with living flesh.

She couldn't stop herself from screaming as they released the leather straps that secured her hands from the chains behind, and manhandling her towards the entrance. She tried to dig her heels in, but they were too strong, and all she succeeded in doing was losing her shoes.

'No!' she cried, noticing Ye smirking at her. 'Let me go!'

'There's no point in trying to fight them,' Ye laughed. 'They're *chiang shi*, reanimated corpses. And they answer only to me.'

'Then get them off me! I'll go wherever you want me to!'

'My dear An-ren,' Ye responded, following close behind. 'You've killed my Xilin and the Moquai of the Hollow Helm. Despite everything, you're actually quite resourceful. Do you really think I'd trust you?'

An-ren continued to struggle and scream as the undead creatures dragged her from the chamber. She felt violated, nauseated, desolate. These creatures, with their rotting hands roaming all over her, were like something out of her worst nightmare.

She knew about *chiang shi*, of course, had grown up both reading and learning about China's myths and legends, but she'd never expected to meet one, let alone five. The smell of decay had now become quite overwhelming, and she started to feel nauseous.

She was briefly distracted as she left her prison. She'd woken up inside the Mirror Chamber, and had no idea where she actually was. She glanced around as she continued to resist the creatures, realising that she was in a cavern, and that the room she'd been kept in wasn't a room at all, but a small, domed building, erected on top of a raised circular dais. She noticed four large, and very stylised, tomb wheels that formed part of the cavern's walls.

She was pulled down a short set of stairs and forced to stand in front of a large and very ornate jade mirror, inscribed with yet more Tomb Wheels, and bearing the mark of Luo Ban. A phalanx of large studio lights were mounted on metal stands, all directed at the position An-ren was being manhandled into, although none were switched on.

It occurred to An-ren to wonder where the electricity that was needed to power them might come from. There weren't any generators in evidence, and she seriously doubted that they could tap into Shanghai's electricity grid in such an obviously remote spot. She did notice, however, that the power cables were all connected to a large pile of jade mirror shards that lay on the ground nearby.

'It's time,' Ye declared, turning to the *chiang shi* at her side. 'Fetch the mirrors!'

The creature scuttled, off, taking a group of its fellow undead with it.

'Please make them let go,' An-ren pleaded, 'I promise I won't go anywhere or try anything!'

Ye studied An-ren for a moment, her translucent eyes narrowed in thought.

'Release her,' she finally ordered.

The *chiang shi* loosened their hold and shuffled back, much to An-ren's relief. She immediately fell to her knees and vomited, her stomach retching violently, as if trying to force out all the toxins she might have absorbed from her undead captors.

'Get up!' Ye commanded, her voice cutting through the air like a blade. 'I didn't bring you here to crawl.'

An-ren stared up at her, the convulsing in her stomach finally settling down. She could still smell the creatures, the stench of death all around, but she was thankful that she could no longer feel their rotting fingers and hands on her flesh. She was also thankful that they were completely covered from head to toe. She didn't even want to imagine what they might look like underneath.

'Get her up,' Ye said, and, to An-ren's horror, one of the *chiang shi* that had been holding her stepped forwards, grabbed her hands roughly, and yanked her back up to her feet.

She wanted to wipe her mouth, but her hands were still bound behind her back. The taste of bile clung to her lips.

'Please,' she managed, hating the word even as it left her mouth.

Ye stepped forward without a word. She crossed to the *chiang shi* that had hauled An-ren upright, tore a strip of cloth from its tattered clothing, exposing blackened, rotting flesh beneath, and pressed the filthy scrap into its hand.

'Clean her.'

'No! Please…' An-ren cried, but the *chiang shi* was already obeying, scraping the foul cloth across her mouth and chin.

'You're not built for this world,' Ye said, her voice as cold as her glass skin.

'I hate you,' An-ren muttered, swallowing hard against another wave of nausea.

She felt as wretched as she had ever felt in her life, and it took everything she had not to break down.

'You always carried your body like a charm, not a weapon. That's what made you dangerous,' Ye said. 'I despised your softness, the way people were drawn to you without ritual, without power.'

An-ren hesitated. Was Ye speaking to her, or to the woman whose memories haunted her?

'You never trained it,' Ye continued. 'But it worked all the same. A kind of ambient pull.'

'I've told you I'm not An Lian,' An-ren said.

Ye's gaze didn't shift.

'Did I say I was talking about her?'

Ye turned as the *chiang shi* returned with the mirrors.

'Set them in place,' she ordered.

The *chiang shi* went to work, forming a loose semi-circle on either side of the mirror that was already in place, and all directly in front of An-ren.

'Begin!' Ye commanded.

The lights suddenly burst into life, blinding An-ren. She put her hands up to cover her eyes.

'Turn them off!' she cried out.

The lights began to move, their blinding rays bouncing off her and onto the mirrors. She noticed that the *chiang shi* were operating them, and were starting to sweep them across her body. Two other lights were also angling her reflection off the other mirrors and onto the one that stood directly opposite, the one that had been there when she'd first been pulled out of the Mirror Chamber.

The mirrors began to pulse, almost as if they were breathing in and out, the solid glass seeming to be on the verge of reverting to a liquid state. An-ren saw her image warped and distorted, reflected from mirror to mirror, inverted, reverted, converted and finally transformed into her constituent elements, before being reformed and re-reflected from mirror to mirror.

As she gazed around, her eyes moving in disbelief and confusion as she tried to make sense of what she was witnessing, she realised that something was happening in the original mirror.

It was pulsing like the others, but something else was taking place. She saw herself reflected back, but it wasn't her. The other An-ren was wearing the same clothes, its legs and feet were sheer black and shoeless, but it was moving independently of her.

She didn't understand what she was seeing, but she was reminded of the horrible death of Xiao Yu at Eternal Seal. Just before she'd died, her reflection had seemed to take on a life of its own, had subverted the young model's attempt to create art into something sordid and degenerate.

An-ren's unchained reflection was also moving in ways that mocked her art, parodying her skills and artistry. It sneered at her while it began to rip its clothes off, showing itself in ways that made An-ren feel ashamed and denigrated.

But then she saw something else. As the other An-ren continued to gyrate salaciously, her naked body revealing all the things that the real An-ren had kept discreetly concealed for her entire career, she was no longer alone. Another figure slowly emerged, moving from the darkness that lay behind into the blinding white light.

It continued to approach the mirror-An-ren, before passing straight through her and finally coming to a halt at the threshold.

An-ren recognised him. She could hardly forget the face that had threatened and punched her only a few hours earlier. A face whose voice and spirit, she now knew, had haunted her life for so long.

And then, as she watched in horror and despair, Luo Ban crossed the threshold from the Mirror World and stepped into the world he'd been born into, over 2,200 years earlier.

'Stop!' Ye commanded, as Luo Ban looked down at his body, patting and touching himself, and breathing deeply, as if making sure that what he was experiencing wasn't simply an illusion.

The lights switched off, and the blinding brightness faded away.

It took a few moments for An-ren's eyes to readjust to the dimmer lighting of the chamber, but when she could see again, she realised that Luo Ban was staring at her with unconcealed loathing. Ye, on the other hand, was glancing between them both, her expression complex and unreadable.

'I have dreamed of this moment for so long,' Luo Ban exulted. 'There were times when I no longer believed it would happen.'

He turned to Ye, and bowed ever so slightly.

'You have served me well, Mirror Courtesan. I will see you rewarded for your devotion.'

A flicker of bitterness crossed Ye's face at the title. It vanished almost instantly.

'Your favour is reward enough, my Lord,' she said, bowing low. 'I deserve nothing more than to serve.'

As Ye straightened up, Luo Ban studied her face for a long moment. He had never been able to read her mirror face, couldn't be sure whether she was mocking him or not. He had no illusions about how she regarded him, though, but it seemed that her hostility was becoming increasingly less guarded.

He decided to let it go. What she said or thought wasn't important, at least not at this moment. This was his day, his grand return. Not hers. And he had vastly overdue business to attend to.

He stepped forward, closing the gap between himself and An-ren, stopping just three feet in front of her.

'An Lian,' he said, his mouth twisted in vitriolic anger. 'You betrayed me! Your treachery led to my being imprisoned for 2,206 years!'

His anger was now bubbling over into molten fury. An-ren stepped back. There was a look in his eyes that spoke of an almost insane fury, and she was scared that if he started hitting her, he would almost certainly beat her to death.

'I've spent a very long time thinking of exactly how I'm going to make you suffer!' he crowed, his fists balled so tightly that his knuckles had turned white. 'I'm going to enjoy this!'

He took a step towards her, but was stopped in his tracks by a noise from the other side of the cavern. He turned to Ye, a different sort of anger now etched onto his face.

'What is it?' he demanded. 'You're the Blade of the Meridian Wheel! Can't you even maintain order?'

Ye ignored his caustic tone, her eyes focused on whatever it was that was unfolding in the distance.

'I think we've got company,' she murmured.

CHAPTER FIFTY-THREE

Reed was about to ask Zhang what he thought their plan should be, when he heard a noise behind them. He whirled around to find a group of twelve figures moving menacingly towards them. They were dressed just like the creatures that he could see standing guard around An-ren, Ye and Luo Ban, completely covered from head to toe, their heads almost hidden by *doulis*. And each one was holding a brightly gleaming *jian*, a traditional double-bladed sword.

'*Chiang shi*,' Zhang muttered.

'Holy fecking shit!' Murphy exclaimed, her Irish brogue in control, a strange look in her eyes that merged fear with excitement.

It occurred to Reed that she was completely in her element.

'*Chiang shi*?' he asked.

'The undead,' Murphy explained. 'Corpses brought back to life.'

'Just what we need,' Reed sighed.

He hadn't thought they'd just be able to walk in, overpower Ye and Luo Ban, and snatch An-ren back, but he'd never expected they'd have to face an army of the raised dead.

Zhang held up his palms, and the familiar blue rays of super-charged energy arced out of his hands, smashing into the creatures. The two closest to them were blown backwards, their bodies disintegrating in mid-air.

'Get their swords!' Zhang shouted. 'You can kill them by decapitating them!'

For a moment Reed pondered just how you might be able to kill something that was already dead, but he shoved the pointless thought to one side and ran over to where the two had fallen, grabbing both swords.

As he turned, he found his path blocked by two more of the creatures.

'Fiona!' he shouted, throwing one of the swords over the heads of the two *chiang shi*.

Murphy stood back to let the *jian* hit the ground. It bounced noisily, coming to a stop by her feet. She picked it up and charged towards the *chiang shi* nearest to her, flailing the sword wildly as she rain.

Reed stepped back as one of the creatures lunged at him. He was reminded of his desperate battle with the Moquai, but at least this time the playing field appeared to be angled a little more in his favour.

He let the blade slip past his chest, before aiming a blow at the *chiang shi's* neck. The creature brought its sword back up just in time to parry the strike.

Reed jumped to his left, narrowly avoiding a wild swing from the second creature. He turned, arcing his sword upwards, and moved inside its failed strike. He slashed at its neck, his blade effortlessly slicing through the rotting flesh and bone, completely severing the creature's head with one blow.

To Reed's disgust, the skull fell to the ground and bounced slightly, before rolling towards him. He stopped it with his foot and kicked it away, scared it might start trying to bite him. As the headless corpse slumped to the ground, he was struck by the complete absence of blood.

Dead bodies don't bleed, he realised.

He moved to his right to avoid another attack, before summoning up all his strength and slashing wildly. His blow hit the creature's sword with such power that the blade was knocked sideways. Momentum carried Reed's *jian* on, and it jammed itself deep into the chiang shi's neck. The creature flailed about wildly, trying to get the blade out. Reed drove it in even harder and kicked the creature's legs out from under it.

Its misshapen body hit the ground with a dull thud. Reed pulled with all his strength, ripping the blade out of its body, and then brought it down as hard as he could, his blade clanging loudly as it severed the creature's head from its already dead body.

Reed bent down and picked up the *chiang shi's* sword. Having one in each hand seemed very reassuring.

He turned to see how Zhang and Murphy were getting on. Vivid blue strikes continued to crackle through the air, and Murphy was slashing wildly, screaming with what seemed to be a combination of joy and anger as she made mincemeat of the remaining *chiang shi.*

Reed could see that he was right. This was almost certainly what she'd come to China in search of. Sligo might be wild, but it certainly wasn't like this. He wondered if her business cards would now be amended to read "paranormal warrior".

He ran over to where she was battling the last two *chiang shi*. He swung his blade around in a wide arc, cutting through the neck of one of the creatures.

'That was my kill!' Murphy shouted, a wild look in her eyes.

'You can have the last one, then,' Reed told her, standing back as she slashed at the remaining creature, finishing it off with a flourish, almost pirouetting as she decapitated it.

As the creature's head and body hit the ground, Murphy punched the air with her sword, whooping with joy as she did so.

'Bualadh bos!' she shrieked.

Reed had no idea what that meant, but it was clear from her adrenaline-fuelled ecstasy that it was some sort of Gaelic war cry.

'There'll be more coming,' Zhang announced from behind them. 'We need to get to Luo Ban and Ye while we can.'

'Those things were easy!' Murphy exulted.

'They're just cannon fodder,' Zhang observed. 'If they sent these things first, it's because they can afford to lose them. The real threats don't get thrown away."

Without another word, Zhang broke into a run. Reed and Murphy chased after him, swords in hand. As they closed on the dome and An-ren, Reed realised that a whole army of *chiang shi* was moving to intercept them, spreading out in a long defensive line. Luo Ban and Ye hung back, An-ren held firmly between them.

Reed tried to make eye contact with her, to somehow let her know everything would be okay, but she was too far away still, the line of dead warriors blocking his line of sight.

Zhang threw his arms out, sending more bolts of pure blue energy screaming through the air. They crashed into the advancing line of *chiang shi*, frying an entire section of them. Reed raised both swords and began to slash with savage abandon. He briefly glanced to his right, saw Murphy, the same wild look in her eyes, slicing up *chiang shi* as if she'd been born to it. He noticed that she, too, now had a sword in each hand.

He looked to his left, saw Zhang blasting away at the creatures. They'd killed so many between them, but they kept coming.

Zhang suddenly began chanting. His breathing changed, and his chest began to rise and fall with a strange rhythm. He raised his hands higher and swept them across the air in front of him, in the direction of the massed ranks of *chiang shi* still confronting them.

A high-pitched keening sound filled the air, and a powerful wind sprang up from nowhere.

Reed struggled to stay on his feet in the face of the intense gusts, and the light that filled the chamber briefly flickered and faded.

Murphy shouted something, but Reed couldn't hear what she was saying.

Just as suddenly as it had started, the terrifying noise began to fade away and the wind simply died.

The *chiang shi* all ground to a halt. For a long moment, they stood still, unmoving, their hooded faces, mostly obscured by their large *doulis*, revealing nothing. And then, as one, they all turned. They raised their *jians* and started to march back towards Ye.

'William! Go!' Murphy shouted, chasing after the undead army. 'Rescue An-ren!'

Reed didn't need a second invitation. He sprinted over to where Luo Ban was still holding An-ren near the dome.

'Baobei!' she cried out as she saw him running towards her.

He couldn't be sure, but he thought there were tears in her eyes. She didn't look hurt, just haunted and pale. He noticed that her hands were secured behind her back.

When Ye had abducted An-ren from Meridian House, he'd been overwhelmed with a devastating sense of despair. His heart had ached so badly he'd thought it might break. He'd failed Amara, and now he'd failed An-ren. That was how it had felt.

He'd tried to think differently about himself. With An-ren at his side, that hadn't been too difficult. She was empowered and inspiring, someone whose presence in his life had helped hauled him up out of the dark hole he'd fallen into all those years ago.

And so, when Ye had taunted him so cruelly and then carried An-ren into the mirror and out of his world, it had been easy to believe that everything he'd always believed about himself had finally been proven to be true.

But, seeing An-ren standing in front of him, her red-rimmed eyes expressing so much hope, rekindled some of the positivity that Ye had so brutally ground under her heel.

'An-an!' Reed called out.

Luo Ban turned towards Reed, his face darkening in fury. He grabbed An-ren and pulled her away. She struggled against his grip, but he held her fast, dragging her back towards the circular chamber behind them.

A savage blue blast arced through the air past Luo Ban, hitting the still open door and reducing the external wall of the Mirror Chamber to little more than rubble.

'No!' Luo Ban exclaimed, turning to face Zhang, his eyes filled with an almost incandescent fury.

Still grasping An-ren with his right hand, he raised his left, as if to return fire, but paused.

He looked at Zhang in confusion.

'I know you,' he finally said.

Zhang was silent, simply returning Luo Ban's stare with a glare of steely contempt.

'You're Zhang Zhenwu!' Luo Ban suddenly exclaimed, realisation dawning on him.

'Not exactly,' Zhang responded.

'But that isn't possible!' Luo Ban cried out. 'That was over 2,200 years ago!'

'And yet you're here, alive and well, it seems. And freed from your prison.'

'I should have realised,' Luo Ban nodded, as if he now understood everything. 'These morons couldn't have got this far without help.'

'Did you really think the Celestial Registry wouldn't have considered that you might want to escape from your prison?'

'But you're not him.'

'I'm not Zhenwu. I carry what he left behind, as my family always has. That's all.'

'But you didn't defeat me, did you? Even with your Daoist warriors at your side. Even as Grand Master of the Mirror Sutra. You needed a woman's treachery to win.'

Luo Ban turned to Reed with a cruel smile, yanking An-ren in front of him. From his sleeve he drew a small knife, the metal catching the light.

'Your woman,' he mocked, lifting the blade so Reed could see it clearly before pressing it hard against An-ren's throat.

CHAPTER FIFTY-FOUR

Murphy raced after the advancing *chiang shi* as they marched towards Ye.

The Mirror Courtesan, however, simply stood her ground, showing not even the slightest hint of fear, apparently unfazed by their changed loyalty. Murphy had no idea exactly what Zhang had done, but presumed that he'd somehow reversed what she could only think of as the *chiang shi's* "programming", directing them against their own general.

She thought Zhang was remarkable, secretly admired the way he'd slowly revealed his arts and skills. She was a very open woman, but she was drawn to enigma, and she'd never met anyone who embodied the concept as effectively as Iron Palm.

Who would have thought a retired policeman from Shanghai would be some sort of master of the supernatural arts? He had skills in other areas, too, as he'd demonstrated the night before.

She had to admit that she was completely enamoured, and had even downloaded a "teach yourself Mandarin" app to her phone. He was what her mother would have called a "dark horse", but she had no doubts whatsoever that her feelings were reciprocated. He was, after all, a man of action rather than words, and his actions at Meridian House had spoken louder than any number of words could ever have done.

Up ahead, the *chiang shi* had come to a standstill again, halted in their tracks, for some reason, as they approached Ye. Murphy crouched down and cautiously edged her way around the back of the paused line of undead warriors.

Ye stood calmly, no more than five feet from the most advanced *chiang shi*. In front of her, hanging in the air, as if held by invisible threads, was a burning red sigil. Murphy had no idea what it was, but made the reasonable assumption that it was responsible for the *chiang shi* having been stopped in their tracks.

Murphy realised Ye hadn't noticed her yet. She was absorbed in whatever she was assembling, sketching out another sigil with brisk precision. Murphy didn't understand the system, but she didn't need to be an expert to recognise the pattern.

Murphy looked around. She had two swords, but she couldn't believe that they would do much harm to Ye, at least not in her mirror form. Glancing behind, she spotted some fallen masonry near where she was crouching. She inched her way towards it. Most of it was enormous and far too heavy for her to lift. Maybe if Zhang had been there, he might have been able to pick it up, but he wasn't.

She glanced back. Ye now had a satisfied smile on her face, and Murphy realised her window of opportunity was rapidly closing. She scrabbled about, and finally found what she was looking for. It was big, but not too heavy, and just about the right size for her to be able to aim and throw.

She put both swords down, being careful not to make any noise, and picked up the sandstone block. She looked back towards where Ye was still drawing lines in the air. Murphy knew she'd never be able to sneak up on her holding a lump of fallen masonry, so she needed to act quickly and rely on the element of surprise.

She leapt to her feet and raced forward. Ye instantly turned. Her face darkened menacingly, and she raised her hands as if to launch an attack. But, before she had time, Murphy launched the stone block, watching as it moved through the air towards Ye.

A look of horror instantly replaced dark menace as the lump of rock hit her in the chest. For a moment, time seemed to stop. Murphy watched, filled with a mixture of hopeful expectation and raw fear, as the block appeared to almost stop moving as it collided with Ye's body.

Then time started again, and the heavy rock crashed into and through Ye. Her body disintegrated into a thousand fragments, shattered as if it were simply a mirror and not a living, breathing creature. A scream of the most intense pain and agony escaped from the Mirror Courtesan before the shards fell to the ground, the heavy lump of masonry bouncing and coming to rest in front of the still stationary *chiang shi*.

'That was easier than I thought,' Murphy muttered, as she wiped the dust off her hands and slowly, cautiously, made her way to where the pile of fragments lay scattered across the ancient floor.

She glanced nervously at the *chiang shi*, half-expecting them to suddenly start lumbering towards her, ready to slice her up into a hundred pieces. But they didn't move.

For a moment, the briefest moment, she felt tempted to pull up the face mask of the one nearest to her, but she forced herself not to. She reminded herself that there were some things that you simply couldn't unsee.

She crossed to where the remains of Ye lay, spread out over an area about five feet wide. It was hard to believe, she thought, that this collection of tiny, jagged, fragments was all that remained of the creature that had terrorised them all so cruelly and so mercilessly.

She was about to turn away and go in search of Zhang and Reed, when she heard something. A scraping sound. She looked around, but couldn't see where it was coming from. The *chiang shi* hadn't moved an inch, and Ye had been annihilated.

But the sound continued. It was a horrible sound, one that put her completely on edge, and reminded her of fingernails being scraped over glass.

A chill ran down her spine, and she looked down. She couldn't prevent herself from crying out in shock as she saw the pieces of glass that had only recently been Ye starting to move, slowly drawing back together.

She bent down, grabbed a shard, swearing bitterly as it cut her hand. She tried to pull the fragment towards her, but she couldn't. In fact, it was pulling her hand towards the slowly coalescing mass. It was phenomenally powerful, and she had to let go, before it cut its way through her fingers.

She leaped up and backed away, horrified at what she was witnessing.

Faster, ever faster, the shards pulled back together, rising up from the ground to reconstruct the body that Murphy had only just shattered into fragments. It was the stuff of nightmares.

Murphy was rooted to the spot, unable to even move, let alone run away. She watched in shock and increasing fear as Ye flexed her shoulders and torso, as if easing aching muscles and groaning tendons.

She turned to face Murphy, and a cruel, mocking smile returned to her lips, as her cerulean eyes blazed with icy fury.

'Did you really think it would be that easy?'

CHAPTER FIFTY-FIVE

Reed's blood ran cold. He felt sick. All he wanted to do was get his hands on Luo Ban and smash his head into the nearest tomb wheel. But he couldn't. All he could do was stand and watch as the Imperial Preceptor held the blade against An-ren's throat.

'Throw down your swords!' Luo Ban shouted at Reed. 'Over there,' he added, indicating the direction they'd come from.

Reed did as he'd been asked. The weapons landed with a loud metallic clang, about ten feet behind him. He knew that Luo Ban wouldn't kill An-ren, that would be a monumentally stupid act, given that she was currently his only significant leverage, but he could still maim and mutilate her.

'She isn't An Lian,' Zhang said.

'This is karma,' Luo Ban mocked. 'She's here, you're here — it was always meant to be.'

'You were blinded by hatred then, and you're no different now,' Zhang replied. 'You've learned nothing.'

'I've learned that revenge doesn't fade.'

Zhang gave a short, incredulous laugh.

'Revenge? For what? You corrupted the Sepulchral Mandala. You broke Ye. Everything that followed came from your hunger for power and control.'

'My hunger?' Luo Ban snarled. 'Who made the Celestial Registry judge and jury of this world? Who gave them the right to destroy the Tomb Wheel Dynasty? They, and you, were jealous. I gave the Tomb Wheel life, and it gave me power. Your masters wanted what we created. They wanted to steal it.'

Reed barely heard them. His eyes stayed fixed on An-ren. The knife at her throat drowned out every word.

Then he realised Luo Ban was speaking to him.

'Ask your friend why the Celestial Registry moved against the Sepulchral Mandala. Go on, ask him.'

'You turned the Tomb Wheel against everyone,' Zhang shot back. 'Even your own people.'

'And you came to steal the Wei Qi.'

Luo Ban and Zhang had fallen into a stalemate, hurling accusations and invoking histories Reed couldn't begin to follow. He didn't understand how a Tomb Wheel could be "awoken", and *Wei Qi* was no clearer. He knew what it meant, Artificial Energy, but what that had to do with a civilisation that supposedly vanished 2,200 years ago was beyond him.

He glanced over to where the *chiang shi* were now standing immobile. He couldn't see either Murphy or Ye, and he wondered what was happening. He knew that if Ye joined the battle with Luo Ban, then all would be lost. He had no idea of the full extent of Zhang's powers, but Luo Ban had made it very clear that the only reason that he'd been defeated all those years ago was because he'd been betrayed by his wife.

Reed doubted that his Zhang was any more powerful than the original one, and he couldn't believe that he would be anywhere near strong enough to carry the day against both Luo Ban and Ye.

It struck him then. This was exactly what Luo Ban wanted. All the grandstanding, all the theatrics. He was buying time, waiting for his general to arrive. And why did he need her? Because he was human again. Mortal.

That, Reed thought, was almost certainly his biggest mistake.

He made a decision. He didn't know if it would work, but he didn't think they had a choice.

'An-an!' he shouted, holding her gaze and making a small backward gesture with his head.

He saw the acknowledgement in her eyes, the firm set of her mouth that told him she was prepared for what would follow, whatever that might be.

'Zhang!' Reed shouted, nodding at An-ren at the same moment.

He saw her take a deep breath, glance at him, and then throw her head back as hard as she could. Reed heard the sound of cracking bone even from where he was standing.

Luo Ban cried out in agony, letting go of An-ren and throwing his hands up to his damaged and bleeding nose.

An-ren turned around, kicked him hard, knocking him to the ground, and ran off.

Reed desperately wanted to run to her, to hold her in his arms and feel the reassuring warmth of her body next to his. But he didn't. He knew that he had a job to do, and he needed to do it. Not just for An-ren's sake, but also for his own.

He sprinted toward Luo Ban, who was dragging himself upright with stubborn, furious effort. Zhang raised his hands, lightning bursting from his palms toward the mirror behind the weakened figure.

As the powerful rays hit their target, the mirror exploded, shattering into a thousand fragments, knocking Luo Ban forwards and onto his face, as glass and jade shards flew outwards.

Reed saw Luo Ban's knife on the ground near him and ran towards it. But, as he tried to pick it up, two powerful hands latched onto his left leg and pulled him backwards. He fell to his knees and then onto his front, desperately reaching for the knife. He kicked out at the hand holding him, but it continued to haul him back, further away from the small blade.

He could hear An-ren somewhere behind him screaming at Zhang to do something, and he heard Zhang shouting back that he couldn't risk hitting Reed.

He heard the sound of feet running. He hoped it was either An-ren or Zhang, and not Ye.

He turned to face Luo Ban, saw him up close for the first time. He was repulsed by the degeneracy he saw in that face, the scars around his eyes and on his forehead, the blood pouring from his obviously broken nose. He pulled his foot back and kicked him as hard as he could.

Luo Ban cried out in agony, letting go of Reed's foot in the process. Reed scrambled to his feet and grabbed the knife.

Turning, he was hit full-on in the midriff as Luo Ban launched himself through the air. Both men tumbled to the ground, rolling over as they both struggled for control.

Luo Ban was strong, but Reed was bigger and hadn't spent the last two millennia years locked away in a mirror world. He was fit and in good shape, despite his recent encounters with the Xilin and the Moquai, and, even more importantly, he was in the mood for a fight.

He raised his fist and hit Luo Ban in his already bent nose, before grabbing his head and smashing it back down onto the ground.

Luo Ban was stunned, and in the instant it took for him to regain his senses, Reed took the small knife and rammed it into his neck, burying it up to the hilt.

'This is for An-ren!' he hissed. 'And An Lian!'

Luo Ban gazed up at him, his eyes wild with fear and pain. He opened his mouth to speak, but nothing came out. The blade had cut straight through his larynx.

Reed got to his feet and kicked Luo Ban as hard as he could.

Luo Ban gasped, and suddenly started to spasm violently, dark blood bursting out of his mouth. He forced himself up onto an elbow, and mouthed something that Reed couldn't understand, before he suddenly fell back, life starting to fade from his eyes.

Reed stood back, unable to believe what had just happened. He towered over the body at his feet, shocked, disbelieving. He'd just killed a man. And not just any man.

He didn't even notice the sound of feet running towards him.

An-ren pulled him around and threw her arms around his neck, burying her face in his chest. Reed still felt numb, and it took him a moment to realise what was happening, but then he wrapped his arms around her, pulling her in as close as he could.

He sensed Zhang walking up behind them, but he wasn't interested. All that mattered was the woman enveloped in his arms.

'Baobei,' she murmured. 'You came for me.'

'I love you,' he told her.

He felt shocked as soon as the words left his lips. He'd thought it so many times over the past day. Since her abduction, he'd wondered whether he'd ever get the chance to say it to her. He'd promised himself that when he rescued her, he'd tell her, without hesitation and without fear. The words had almost become a mantra in his mind over the past few hours, his personal spell to keep her safe, to bring her back to the light. But, despite all of that, he still couldn't quite believe that he'd said it. He'd opened his mouth and the words had just fallen out.

'I know you do,' she whispered, and then he heard her begin to sob, the tears that she'd held back for so long finally flowing.

Zhang moved away, understanding that he had no place in their reunion. He started to walk towards where the *chiang shi* were still immobile, concerned about Murphy.

Luo Ban's body lay beside the shattered remains of the jade mirror. His blood spread slowly across the floor, cooling as it crept outward. When it reached a large fragment of jade, the shard twitched.

Zhang was gone, and Reed held An-ren close, both of them focused entirely on each other, oblivious to the shard's faint pulse beneath the blood.

CHAPTER FIFTY-SIX

'Feck!' Murphy exclaimed.

As Ye began to march towards her, she turned, running in the direction of the fallen pile of masonry. She was acting purely on adrenaline-fueled instinct. Her swords were there, although she felt certain they'd have no effect on Ye. However, she had no idea what else to do, and if she had a sword in each, she could, at least, go down fighting..

She fully expected to be blasted in the back by some sort of laser bolt or flash of lightning, similar to Zhang's weaponry, but nothing happened. She picked up her swords, and turned back.

Ye hadn't been walking towards her. She'd been returning to her half-drawn sigil. She was now moving her hands in the air again, and the look of smug triumph on her face indicated to Murphy that she'd just about finished.

Murphy composed herself, took a deep breath, and charged at Ye.

'I'll fecking banjax you, you fucking glass-faced bitch!' Murphy screamed, sounding like a crazed banshee, swinging both swords dramatically.

Ye whirled around, moving so quickly that her movements appeared blurred. To Murphy's horror, she grabbed the blades of both *jians*, and ripped them out of her hands.

'You're becoming very tiresome,' she said, brushing her fingers along each blade. The metal buckled and folded in on itself with a dry, cracking sound.

The ruined blades clattered to the floor as Ye let them fall, her gaze settling on Murphy with a cold, unblinking disdain. Her left hand shot out and clamped around the Irishwoman's arm

'Get off!' Murphy shouted, as Ye pulled her closer.

She raised her right hand and her deep blue fingernails sliced through Murphy's jacket and shirt, her icy hand coming to rest directly over her heart.

Murphy stared down at the glassy blue hand in fear, struggling for all she was worth. But Ye grip's was like a vice.

'Your heart seems to be beating quite fast,' Ye observed. 'I can help you with that.'

Murphy screamed in terror as Ye's razor sharp fingernails began to drill into her flesh.

'No! Please! Get off!' she shrieked, tendrils of pain shooting outwards from her chest.

'Xiao Fei!'

Ye paused. She sighed in exasperation, rolling her eyes dramatically.

'I'll deal with you later,' she muttered, pulling her fingers out of Murphy's bleeding chest and almost throwing her towards the pile of rubble and broken masonry. She turned back to her nearly completed sigil and hurriedly began tracing more lines in the air.

Murphy hit the ground hard, her momentum broken by crashing into a large stone block. She cried out in pain. She forced herself to look down at her chest, scared of what she might see.

Blood was oozing out of a small hand-sized hole in her clothing. She tentatively reached inside, and was relieved to find that the wound wasn't very deep. Ye had been interrupted before she could do any serious damage.

Murphy had been terrified. She'd stared death in the face, and she really hadn't liked what she'd seen. Ye was monstrous, indestructible, it seemed. Yet, if Luo Ban was able to control a creature like her, how much more powerful must he be?

'Xiao Fei!'

She looked up, almost crying with joy as she saw Zhang approaching from behind Ye.

'What have you done?' Zhang hissed, staring at the bloody patch on Murphy's chest.

Murphy opened her mouth, but couldn't speak. Zhang knelt down next to her, peering at the gaping hole in her clothes. As she wiped her eyes, he put a reassuring hand on her shoulder.

He stood back up and approached Ye.

'Luo Ban's dead,' Zhang said.

Ye tilted her head slightly.

'You think so,' she said. 'How quaint.'

She turned back to her sigil, moved her right hand diagonally, and smiled in satisfaction.

'Despite all your interruptions, I've finished,' she said.

'Look!' Murphy screamed.

The *chiang shi* started to move, and it seemed they were no longer interested in Ye.

She laughed as she watched the undead creatures launching themselves towards Zhang and Murphy.

Zhang whirled into action, kicking the creature nearest to him and punching it hard in the chest. As it dropped to the floor, he wrenched the sword out of its hand.

'Xiao Fei!' he shouted, throwing it over the heads of the *chiang shi* that were moving towards her.

Murphy forced herself to her feet, wincing in pain. She picked up the sword, a resolute and determined look on her face, and began to advance on the *chiang shi*, slicing and slashing as she went.

CHAPTER FIFTY-SEVEN

An-ren and Reed both turned to face the far side of the chamber.

'They're moving!' An-ren exclaimed, as the distant *chiang shi* began to move.

Her heart sank. Safe in Reed's arms, and with Luo Ban dead, she'd forgotten all about Ye.

'Where's Zhang?' Reed asked, gazing around.

'He's otherwise occupied,' announced an all-too-familiar voice.

Ye was standing directly behind them. She smiled at Reed.

'Hello, Xiao Wei,' she purred. 'You're looking a little the worse for wear. And that pink bag really doesn't suit you.'

'What do you want?' Reed demanded. 'Your master's dead. There's nothing left for you now.'

Ye laughed — a thin, bitter sound.

'Is that what you've convinced yourself?'

She stepped closer, eyes glittering.

'Sweet William,' she simpered. 'If only things were ever that simple.'

Ye reached out a hand towards Reed's face, but An-ren grabbed her wrist before she could lay a finger on him.

'I've warned you before about touching me,' Ye hissed, her glare vicious enough to cut.

'It's not because I want to, believe me,' An-ren shot back, recoiling from the glassy chill of Ye's inhuman skin. 'You disgust me.'

Ye laughed, a brittle, humourless sound, and tore her arm free.

'The feeling's mutual. But, Weiwei,' she said, turning to Reed, pouting, fluttering her lashes with exaggerated sweetness. 'If you ever want to know what a real woman feels like, you only have to ask. My bed is always available.'

An-ren stepped between them, fury rising like a tide.

'You're not a real woman,' she said, voice shaking with the effort to stay in control. 'You're a monster.'

An-ren knew that Ye seemed to take great pleasure and satisfaction out of tormenting everyone, but she seemed to gain especial pleasure from trying to demean and humiliate her. She was tired of it, was sick of the sight of that hideously unnatural face and body.

Ye shimmered and blurred, her features warping as she shifted into the other version of herself, the one with smooth, inviting pale skin, cerulean eyes bright with seductive *wo can*, and long, silken black hair cascading over an S-curve figure framed by a tight purple dress and matching heels.

'Is this more pleasing?' she simpered. 'I'm more of a woman than you'll ever be, An-ren.'

'An-ren's right,' Reed snapped. 'You're a monster!'

Ye held his gaze for a beat, then her form rippled again, collapsing back into cold mirror-flesh.

Ye moved with a liquid, impossible speed. By the time Reed's mind caught up, she had already slipped behind An-ren and locked her arms in an unbreakable hold.

'It's time to go,' Ye whispered into An-ren's ear.

She turned to Reed and thrust her right hand towards him, unleashing a force that sent him flying backwards through the air.

He hit the ground painfully, bouncing and rolling past Luo Ban's corpse, and coming to a halt just in front of the now ruined Mirror Chamber.

He clambered to his feet. Ye was already disappearing into the distance, dragging a vainly struggling An-ren after her.

Reed felt almost numb with shock. He'd saved An-ren, had kept his promise, had actually been the one who'd killed Luo Ban. But now, An-ren was once again Ye's prisoner.

A terrible wave of despair swept across him. For the briefest of moments, he'd believed in himself, had dared to dream that maybe he could rise above what had happened. But Ye, it seemed, was determined to prove him wrong.

He heard the sound of running feet, and whirled around. He was relieved to see Zhang and Murphy hurrying towards him, a pile of shattered and mutilated *chiang shi* lying in their wake.

'What happened?' Zhang demanded.

'Ye happened. She's taken An-ren again,' Reed said, noticing the blood all over Murphy's jacket. 'Are you okay?' he asked her.

'I'll live,' she told him. 'But we need to go after that fecking crazy bitch!'

'I don't understand why she's taken her,' Reed said, turning to Zhang. 'Luo Ban was the one who wanted her.'

Zhang exhaled sharply.

'Ye needs him as much as he needed her. Meng Yao made her into what she is. She was a normal woman once, a decorated Tomb Wheel general, Grand-Axis Marshal of the Sepulchral Mandala. She swore herself to him, and the price was catastrophic. Her spirit was fractured, resurrected through lacquered mirrors and forgotten devotion. She's bound to him now, whether he's dead or alive. And she uses seduction as a way to reclaim what she lost.'

Reed scowled.

'Fascinating. But it doesn't explain why she needs An-ren.'

'An Lian is the vector,' Zhang said. 'The vessel of liberation.'

'An-ren isn't An Lian,' Reed snapped.

'Luo Ban and Ye seem to think she is.'

Murphy stepped forward.

'What do you mean, "vessel of liberation"? Are you saying Ye wants to take her body?' she asked.

'It doesn't matter right now,' Reed said, cutting her off. 'What matters is saving her.'

The idea horrified him, and yet, disturbingly, it made a kind of sense. He shoved the thought aside. He couldn't afford to dwell on it. Not now. He had something far more important to do. A promise to keep. Again.

Without waiting for either Zhang or Murphy, Reed collected his discarded swords, and began to run in the direction Ye had taken, back the way they'd come.

Zhang and Murphy soon caught him up, and they continued in silence, trying to keep up a good pace. Reed's body ached and hurt, and it was only as he tried to maintain a decent speed that he began to realise the battering he'd taken over the last two days. He wasn't particularly fit, either, which didn't help. But he pushed himself on, ignoring the pain that tore at his lungs and the screaming of the muscles in his legs. He knew only too well that if Ye were to reach the surface, they wouldn't stand a chance of tracking her down. Even with Zhang's inherited skills.

As they passed by the vast tomb wheels, Reed stole a glance at the sealed bronze door. It was now on his right. He thought he heard something, a ceramic click, immediately followed by a small, wet rasp that died. A sound like a throat being unmade. But he couldn't be sure.

Zhang and Murphy remained silent, and this certainly wasn't the time for going back to investigate, not that he even wanted to. His experiences with the Xilin and the Moquai of the Hollow Helm, not to mention Luo Ban and

Ye, had more than cured him of any vague interest he may once have had in the supernatural world. And he remembered Zhang's chilling words from earlier about what lay hidden in the city.

He told himself that he almost certainly hadn't heard anything anyway. He was on edge, desperately watching out for Ye and An-ren. The sound of six feet splashing through the dirty water that covered much of the ground blocked out almost everything else, anyway, so he told himself that whatever he thought he'd heard was almost certainly just a trick of his overwrought imagination.

The doors they'd opened earlier were still ajar, and they ran straight through. They immediately began to ascend the incline that led to the vast cavern that marked the furthest limits of the ancient city of Jinglun.

Reed knew that if Ye got past that point, then they almost certainly wouldn't catch her before she reached the city so far above their heads.

Reed's legs were screaming loudly now, his muscles begging for mercy as he forced them to run up the slope. But he forced himself on. Zhang was close behind, and Reed felt ashamed that a man in his 60's, reincarnated Daoist monk or not, seemed to be able to maintain the pace so effortlessly.

By the time Reed reached the top of the slope and saw the ruins of the domed temple just ahead, he felt certain that his lungs were about to explode. He desperately wanted to pause. His body was pleading with him to take a break, but he ran on. There was no choice, and that was the absolute truth. An-ren's life depended on it. He had to carry on, no matter what. He could indulge himself in all the relaxation he could endure afterwards, but not now, not yet.

As he ran through the centre of the crumbling temple, his heart, already fit to burst, suddenly ramped up a gear. Ahead of him was the central island that rose up out of the water that now surrounded them on all sides, linked to the rest of the cavern by the seven spoke-like walkways. And, straight ahead, on the nearest bridge, no more than twenty feet ahead of him, were An-ren and Ye.

CHAPTER FIFTY-EIGHT

An-ren fought Ye every step of the way, but the Mirror Courtesan was far too strong. Despite her best efforts, An-ren found herself dragged forcibly through the ruined remains of Ye's old world.

An-ren noticed very little of the ancient scenery that they passed, however. She was focused entirely on trying to either escape, or slow their progress down enough to enable Reed, Zhang and Murphy to catch up. She knew that Reed would be doing everything humanly possible to reach them.

'Why are you doing this?' An-ren demanded, digging her stockinged heels into the ground as she twisted against Ye's vice-like grip.

'I need you,' Ye said through clenched teeth, relentlessly dragging An-ren forward.

'Why? Luo Ban wanted me because he thought I was An Lian. What do you want?'

Ye stopped abruptly and spun An-ren to face her.

'Meng Yao betrayed me, just as An Lian betrayed him. He used me.'

'And you used him,' An-ren shot back. She didn't trust a word Ye said, especially anything that sounded like confession.

Ye's glare sharpened, and for a moment An-ren glimpsed something behind the inhuman eyes, pain, injustice, but she knew better than to believe it.

'When I met him, I was a soldier of the Sepulchral Mandala.'

'A soldier?'

'The Tomb Wheel state was enlightened. Some women escaped domestic slavery. I earned my rank. I fought for it. By twenty-five, I was a general.'

Ye's gaze drifted past An-ren, lost in a world that had collapsed around her 2,200 years earlier.

'Meng Yao noticed me. Not because I wanted him to, because he could. He took an interest. He made sure I was always near him. I didn't understand why at first.'

An-ren frowned.

'I thought he loved An Lian?'

'He did,' Ye said, her voice tightening. 'But he was a man with limitless power. He took what he wanted. And he wanted me close.'

A shadow crossed her face.

'An Lian found us. She thought I'd betrayed her. She attacked me. I was dying. Meng Yao told me the only way to survive was to cross into the Resonance Plane.'

'And you agreed?'

'I had no choice. I was bleeding out. I didn't choose this. I was pushed into it.'

'That still doesn't explain why you need me.'

Ye's eyes snapped back to An-ren, a bitter smile curling her lips.

'Meng Yao tethered me to a soul.'

'An Lian's?' An-ren whispered, dread rising.

'The only way I can return as a human is to become An Lian.'

'But I'm not An Lian! I'm sick of saying it!'

'But you are,' Ye insisted. 'Her reincarnation. Luo Ban promised you to me once he was done, but he lied. He wanted control.'

She glanced around suddenly, as if noticing the world again.

'Clever. But it won't save you.'

She spun An-ren back around and marched on, grip tightening.

'You're lying!' An-ren spat, struggling again. 'Everything you say is a lie!'

'Believe what you like,' Ye said. 'All that matters is that I have you, and Luo Ban doesn't.'

'He's dead!'

Ye didn't answer. She only dragged An-ren faster, forcing her through the ruins of a domed temple, and into a vast cavern. An-ren was shocked by the size of it. For the briefest of moments, she was distracted from her desperate situation.

Ahead of them and far below was a vast river, an artificial island, shaped a little like a wheel, rising up from its centre. She was surprised to see lights in some of the windows further down towards the waterline.

Seven walkways connected the island to the surrounding cavern walls, and there was one directly in front of them. Ye was almost effortlessly dragged An-ren towards it.

As they approached the island, An-ren realised that, with the bridges, the entire scene was a physical representation of the mark of the Tomb Wheel, so insidiously branded on all the jade mirrors that linked her and the outside world to Luo Ban.

The cavern seemed to end after the far walkway. An-ren knew that if she was going to escape, this was her last real chance. She had no doubt that Ye was heading for Shanghai, which she guessed was somewhere far above their heads. Once they were back above ground, Reed would have almost no chance of finding her.

Ye began to drag her onto the bridge. An-ren stopped resisting for a moment, allowing herself to be manhandled onto the walkway. She waited until they were nearly halfway across, and then, with every ounce of energy she had left, threw herself towards the edge, momentarily breaking free of Ye's grip and latching onto the stone wall that bordered the bridge.

'He won't save you!' Ye hissed, fastening her hands onto An-ren's arms once again.

An-ren didn't answer, instead focusing all her strength on holding on to the wall. It was no easy task. Ye was remarkably powerful, and it was all An-ren could do to keep her grip. She kicked out, twisting her body and trying to do everything she could to keep Ye at bay.

'Enough!' Ye snapped, yanking harder.

An-ren gritted her teeth and tried to tighten her grip. Ye was going to kill her, she'd made that very clear. Or, at least, she was going to somehow possess her body. Which was no different from being killed.

She continued to lash out with her legs, but Ye was relentless. An-ren's muscles were screaming at her, but she dug her fingers in to the masonry as hard as she could. Letting go simply wasn't an option.

And then, suddenly, Ye let go. An-ren barely had time to tighten and readjust her grip as a powerful punch crashed into the small of her back, sending a tidal wave of pain through her entire body.

She cried out in agony and collapsed to the floor of the walkway, clutching at her back. She looked up to see Ye towering over her, a smugly victorious look on her inhuman face.

She reached down to grab An-ren, but then suddenly looked up.

She heard a familiar and highly reassuring voice calling out from close by.

'Ye!'

There was a noise of running feet, followed by the sight of a body launching itself through the air.

An-ren looked on in horror and dismay as she saw Reed catapult himself towards Ye, hitting her in the midriff. His momentum carried them both forward, smashing through the small stone wall at the edge of the walkway, and disappearing over the side, towards the water below.

CHAPTER FIFTY-NINE

Reed watched in horror as Ye punched An-ren in the small of her back, forcing her to release her grip on the bridge wall and fall to the floor, agony etched all over her face.

He ran onto the walkway. Ye was distracted, and was no longer holding An-ren. He quickly glanced back, could see Zhang and Murphy, but they were trailing behind. Reed knew it was or never.

'Ye!' he shouted.

As she glanced up, a look of surprise on her face, he launched himself through the air. He knew she was strong, that he needed to use every ounce of force he could muster to overcome her.

He hit her full-on in the stomach, knocking her off balance. His momentum carried them both forward, and they crashed into the bridge wall that An-ren had been holding onto.

The ancient stonework crumbled and collapsed and they both went flying over the edge. Reed instinctively reached out with his right hand and grasped the edge of the bridge, abruptly stopping his fall.

As he latched onto the brickwork with his left hand, ready to pull himself up, he felt powerful fingers digging into his left ankle. At the same time he was almost dragged downwards, and he desperately tightened his grip on the bridge.

He glanced down to see Ye holding onto his foot. He looked up. The bridge was holding, but his fingers were starting to slip. The muscles in his arms and shoulders were already aching, and he wondered just how long he could hold on for.

He tried to shake her off, but all he managed to do was drag his fingers closer to the edge.

'Let go!' he shouted at her.

It was a stupid, pointless thing to say, but he was panicking. He'd launched himself at her without a second thought, but, now that he was dangling fifty feet above the water, Ye attached to one leg, his fingers slowly losing their grip, he knew that, unless she let go, he was almost certainly going to die.

He'd acted without thinking, and, now that he was seconds away from a certain death, he realised he should have waited for Zhang.

'The wheel is still turning,' she called up to him. 'Even now.'

'What the hell are you talking about? Just let go!'

'Weiwei,' she said, managing a mocking tone despite her parlous situation. 'You need to save me. You and your friends have stirred forces even I would hesitate to face. But I can help you. I will help you. You just have to save me first.'

'You're fucking insane!' Reed shouted. 'I can't hold on much longer!'

He felt his fingertips slip off the edge, felt time stand still for the merest instant, before gravity took over and he started to plunge to the water far below.

And then he suddenly stopped. He felt two strong hands gripping his wrists. He looked up to see Zhang staring down at him, every vein in his forehead bulging with the effort.

'I can't hold him for long!' Iron Palm shouted, briefly glancing over his shoulder.

Reed saw Murphy throw herself down and add her strength to Zhang's, but the strain was visible on both their faces He knew they'd only be able to hold them both for a few minutes, at the most.

He saw An-ren approaching the edge of the walkway.

'Hold on, Xiao Wei!' she shouted.

She was holding a piece of the bridge wall. Reed had seen much of it fall into the water below, but some of the stonework must have fallen sideways onto the bridge.

As he watched, An-ren lifted it high above her head and hurled it down past him, into the prone figure of Ye. She almost exploded as the rock hit her, shattering, once again, into a myriad of glass-like fragments.

Reed felt himself almost leap up in the air as her hand disintegrated, releasing his ankle. He watched as the fragments of her body fell towards the water, the air shimmering as gravity dragged them downwards. He saw them hit the water, and then rapidly sink below the surface.

He was pulled upwards, almost hurled onto the walkway. He rolled onto his back and just lay there for a moment, allowing his muscles the luxury of not having to even move. He ached all over. He didn't think there was probably a single muscle in his body he hadn't abused or strained over the last two days.

'Weiwei!' An-ren cried, throwing herself down onto her knees and pulling him up to a sitting position so she could wrap her arms around him.

His body cried out in agony as she held him close, but he ignored it. He put his arms around her, shutting his eyes and enjoying the reassuring sensations of her warm, soft skin and silken hair pressed against his cheek.

'You saved my life again,' he murmured in her ear.

'You really owe me now,' she whispered back.

'There are some debts you can never pay back.'

'I know,' she agreed, and he could hear the smile in her voice, knew that she wasn't talking about his debt, either.

'I'm sorry to have to break up the happy reunion,' Zhang announced. 'But we only have forty minutes until the station opens.'

'If we don't go now, we'll be trapped until tonight,' Murphy added, unnecessarily.

An-ren glared at Zhang, but said nothing as she helped Reed to his feet. He pulled the rucksack off his back and opened it.

'Why are you carrying that?' An-ren asked. 'That shade of pink really doesn't suit you.'

'It's your bag,' Reed told her, pulling out the jeans, ankle socks and trainers that he'd packed.

She looked at him in surprise.

'You packed these for me?'

'They're not my size,' Reed responded.

'He was worried about you,' Murphy added, winking at Zhang, who simply rolled his eyes and looked away.

'Thank you,' An-ren said, giving Reed an appreciative smile.

She moved her hands to her skirt, but stopped, frowning at them all.

'Sorry,' Reed said, as all three turned their backs.

She changed quickly, carefully folding her skirt and ruined pantyhose and putting them in the bag, which she then handed back to Reed, a mischievous gleam in her eye.

Reed flashed an indulgent smile, before putting the rucksack on his back. As he did so, he noticed Zhang glancing to their right. He followed his gaze, saw the doorway where Murphy had become transfixed. The door was now open, the securing twine, and the red talismans, lying on the ground in front of it.

'Is that something we should worry about?' Reed asked.

'Not now,' Zhang said, although his face told a different story.

'Ye said that the wheel was still turning. Is that what she meant?' Reed asked.

'No,' Zhang sighed. 'Come on, let's go, while we've still got time.'

They set off across the walkway, and onto the central wheel, hurrying across it and towards the entrance to the modern world far above their heads.

'What about Ye?' Murphy asked. 'Won't she simply re-form and come after us again?'

"Us?" It wasn't them that she was after, An-ren mused. They would simply be collateral damage.

'She will re-form,' Zhang said, 'but underwater it'll take her about a thousand years. Water is far more solid than air.'

Reed sighed with relief. Luo Ban was dead and Ye was in pieces until at least the year 3,000.

With a sense of lightness in his heart that he hadn't felt since before they'd visited Meridian House, he reached out and took An-ren's hand in his.

She smiled at him, letting their fingers intertwine.

'You're quite a hero,' she said.

'Me?' he protested. 'You've saved my life three times.'

'So we're both heroes. That's good.'

'You're a remarkable woman, An-an.'

'Am I? I just did what I had to. I can't help it if you can't keep yourself safe.'

He laughed, squeezing her hand tightly, and led her through the opening in the cavern wall that signalled the end of Jinglun and the beginning of Shanghai.

CHAPTER SIXTY

They arrived back on the tracks of the People's Square Station at 5.18 am, just twelve minutes before the station returned to full operational life for the day.

They hurried through the tunnel and into the blinding artificial light of the station. Zhang clambered up onto the platform and helped Murphy up, before Reed painfully climbed onto the polished tiling and did the same for An-ren.

The few station staff on duty watched in shocked surprise as these four dusty, bruised people made their way along the platform and up the escalator towards the exit.

It was still dark as they re-emerged into the city, but none of them cared. Reed breathed in deeply. He'd almost forgotten how good fresh air was. The air down below was stale and dank, which, he thought, was a pretty good metaphor for the world they'd found themselves in.

He looked up, thanking God for the city all around them. He'd lived in a lot of places over the years, but he'd come to love Shanghai, and now, after all this time, it suddenly felt like home.

He glanced at Zhang and Murphy. The seemed lost in conversation, her phone held up between them. Murphy was her usual excited self, but Zhang's expression reminded Reed of someone whose lottery numbers had come up, but realised he hadn't bought a ticket. He laughed to himself. How very Zhang!

Reed was surprised, though, to see how old Zhang suddenly looked, as if his body had been drained of energy. Maybe that was the case, he thought. All that power surging out of his palms had to come from somewhere.

He turned to An-ren, who was gazing up at the skyscrapers, a contented smile on her face. He took her hands in his and drew her close.

'I promised you I'd keep you safe,' he said. 'But I thought I'd failed.'

'Weiwei, you never failed. I knew you'd come. And you did. Twice. Thank you.'

Her smile had gone now, replaced by something far more serious. He held her gaze, studying her soulful deep brown eyes.

'I love you,' he told her, his heart beating so loudly that he felt certain that she, and everyone in the square, would hear it.

'I know you do,' she replied.

Again.

She smiled when she saw the disappointed look in his eyes.

'I love you, baobei,' she murmured, pulling him close and kissing him. She was pleased to feel how fast his heart was beating, knew that hers was doing exactly the same thing.

She kissed him long and hard, for once not caring that they were in a public place, not even bothered if anyone recognised her. The most important thing in her world was right in front of her, safe in her arms, his lips on hers. Nothing else mattered. And, what filled her with even more happiness and joy, was the knowledge that the dark hole in his heart, the void that had threatened to crush him out of existence, was finally beginning to heal.

She pulled back slightly, keeping his hands in hers.

'Let's go home.'

ACKNOWLEDGEMENTS

Writing is a solitary pastime, but, nevertheless, books are seldom written in isolation. My journey with this book has been greatly helped and eased by the support, friendship, and advice of the following people.

As ever, a massive thank you goes to Chris Hilmi, who spent a lot of time reading this book in its many drafts, and who, at times, pestered me for more! Her suggestions and thoughts were always on the money and remarkably insightful. Chris can't be blamed for any shortcomings within these pages, but she should be thanked for helping to ensure it's the best book it can be.

Chris is also responsible for inventing the genre that perfectly describes the books I now write: "Epic mythologies for the modern age". Thank you!

I'd also like to send an enormous thank you to Emilija Rakic of Emily's World of Design (https://www.emilysworldofdesign.com) for her superb cover design. Emili has designed the covers for every book I've published, and her work is never less than inspiring.

Big thanks are due to my son Mudiwa, who has put up with endless monologues about Shanghai and Chongqing in particular, and China in general. He's been a great inspiration, and I hope that, in time, he'll find some value and pleasure in reading this book.

To Anran and Jang: thank you!

AUTHOR BIOGRAPHY

Martin Dench keeps writing books and they keep being published. He is extraordinarily pleased about this.

Martin is a global citizen, with a particular interest in the history, arts, culture and food of China, South Korea, Lebanon and Uzbekistan. He is also a proud fan of the KZN Sharks, Die Bokke and the Proteas.

He currently lives with his family in the idyllic underground paradise that is Jinglun.

Printed in Dunstable, United Kingdom

79967217R00285